PENGUIN BOOKS
Missing Pieces

'I'm a self-confessed David Raker (ergo Tim Weaver) addict
and as such was concerned that this latest book was a standalone.
Would it be as pacy and as exciting as the previous ten Raker epics?
Of course it would! Absolutely stunning'

'Fans of Tim Weaver will know his previous novels
following David Raker, the missing persons investigator, but
this is a standalone novel which I consider equally as good as
any of his previous books. I would like to think other readers will
enjoy this consuming read as much as myself'

'I've read all of Tim Weaver's David Raker books and
hoped this novel would live up to them. I needn't have worried;
this book is among his best. Fast-paced, lots of twists and turns
and characters that draw you in, I didn't want to put it down'

'As the title suggests, this book starts with pieces
everywhere, which, as you read on, slowly begin to fit together
like a giant jigsaw puzzle. The plot is incredibly worked out and
keeps you guessing right to the end. One of the best and most
gripping books I have ever read'

'Wow! This was different, engaging and utterly thrilling.
I was on the edge of my seat, reading this, and my heart was
leaping out of my chest most of the time in fear. I thought it would
take me ages to read this with it being a bit of a beast at 512 pages
long. However, I literally devoured it. I just couldn't put it down; I
shirked all my responsibilities for a few days to get this read'

'I'm giving this 5 stars as it hit the mark in every area I can
think of. I hope you love it as much as I have'

Missing Pieces

TIM WEAVER

PENGUIN BOOKS

PENGUIN BOOKS

UK | USA | Canada | Ireland | Australia
India | New Zealand | South Africa

Penguin Books is part of the Penguin Random House group of companies
whose addresses can be found at global.penguinrandomhouse.com.

First published by Michael Joseph 2021
Published in Penguin Books 2021
001

Typeset by Jouve (UK), Milton Keynes
Printed and bound in Great Britain by Clays Ltd, Elcograf S.p.A.

The authorized representative in the EEA is Penguin Random House Ireland,
Morrison Chambers, 32 Nassau Street, Dublin D02 YH68

A CIP catalogue record for this book is available from the British Library

ISBN: 978–1–405–94376–5

www.greenpenguin.co.uk

For Camilla

BOOK ONE

I
Rebekah

I

She stumbled along the aisle.

It was so dark, she could barely put one foot in front of the other, her hands out – helping her feel her way forward – her hair soaked, skin slick, clothes matted to her body. When she got halfway down, she stopped and looked back. It was like she was adrift in some vast black ocean.

The window she'd crawled through hung in the shadows, like a picture frame, glass still ragged along one of its edges, the rest shattered on the floor beneath it. She could hear rain on the roof – a relentless, mechanized rhythm – and see lightning flaring in the sky: whenever that happened, her surroundings would briefly strobe into life, giving her the chance to try to make sense of what was around her. She needed food, a change of clothes. But more than either of those, she needed a mirror and a sewing kit because the blood wasn't just leaking into her eyes now, it was running all the way down her face.

Wind shook the bones of the building.

She was terrified. She was hurt. Worse, she was totally and utterly alone. *Just give up.* Something tremored in her throat.

Drop to the floor and give up.

She squeezed her eyes shut, pushing the voice away, waited until the next fork of lightning, then made a beeline for the back of the room. In the darkness, she fumbled around, knocking things over, but soon had her hand around what she'd been looking for.

A flashlight.

She switched it on.

A dazzling white glow skittered ahead of her and she saw how small the place was: it had seemed massive in the pitch blackness, but it was just thirty feet across.

She swiped a candy bar from the nearest shelf, ripped open the packaging and took a bite, ravenously hungry. Then, as more blood ran into her eye, she switched her attention to the other side of the room, where boxes of Band-Aids were lined up. It wasn't until she was right on top of them that she realized there was a first-aid kit too, half hidden at the back of the shelf. It had everything in it she'd need – scissors, antiseptic, sterile dressing, butterfly closures. But no needle and thread.

Her strength faded – and then something caught her attention close to the counter.

Fishing equipment.

Under the glass was a bait needle, on the counter a selection of fishing lines. She scooped up the thinnest thread she could find, plucked a Zippo from next to the cash register, then returned to the first-aid kit.

Nearby there was a mirror on a rotating stand of sunglasses. She shook off all of the glasses and adjusted the stand so that the mirror was at eye level. Unravelling the fishing line, she fastened it to the needle, then used the scissors from the kit to snip off about six inches of thread. She took a breath and leaned into her reflection, tilting her head, so she could see the wound next to her right eye. She'd glimpsed it in the windshield of her car a couple of hours ago – maybe three, maybe four: she had no idea what time it was now – but the dirt on the glass had helped conceal the severity of the injury.

Another wave of emotion hit her.

'Why is this happening to me?' she said softly, her voice barely audible above the rain. She sterilized the end of the needle with the Zippo, readying herself for what was coming, but then her eyes filled. Tears mixed with blood, pink trails casting off down her cheeks, like coloured roads on a map.

6

She could suture in her sleep, so it wasn't the idea of stitching her face together that was overwhelming her.

It was something much worse.

'Please let there be someone else here,' she sobbed, her words smudged. She raised the needle to her face, her hands shaking. 'I don't want to be alone in this place.'

Before

Even the dead can talk.

That was what Rebekah's father kept telling her at the end. She hadn't taken much notice at the time. Over those last few months, in her bedside vigil, she'd watched the gradual deterioration of body and mind, an old man, borderline hallucinating, talking about things that made no sense. Where once there had been strength and colour, now her father's skin was waxy and translucent, an atlas of pale blue veins. He'd become the ghostly inverse of the person who'd brought up the three of them.

In those moments, Rebekah would hold fast to the image of him before he got ill: their guardian and keeper, the glue that had held them together. He would sometimes allude to the impetuous kid he'd been when he'd shipped out to Vietnam, but it was always hard for Rebekah and her brothers to imagine him that way. Growing up, they rarely saw him lose his temper, and pretty much the only impulsive thing Henry Murphy had ever done had happened before any of them was even born: he'd married a woman he'd known for only four months.

At the time, he was stationed at RAF Lakenheath, at the US Air Base there, and it was in Cambridge, twenty-seven miles away, that he'd met Fiona Camberwell. She was twenty-four, a village girl who'd never been further west than Peterborough, so she was totally swept up by the idea of being with an American from New York City.

A year after they got married, Rebekah's brother Johnny was born. Less than two years later, Rebekah arrived, and soon after that, Henry – following an honourable discharge from the army – became a police officer in the Cambridgeshire Constabulary. He immediately fell in love with the work, even though he was only a bobby.

But at home things weren't as good.

Rebekah's father rarely elaborated on what had gone on in those final few years, but early on Boxing Day morning in 1985 – as the tinsel caught the glow of the tree, and fairy lights blinked in the windows – Fiona had walked out on them, just a blur of red hair and pale skin. At the time, Johnny was five, Rebekah was three, and their younger brother Mike only eighteen months.

They would never see their mother again.

Rebekah watched her father's coffin being lowered into the ground. The day was dark, almost monochrome, rain somewhere close, its charge in the air. A couple of times, she looked out across the East River, and saw sun breaking through in the distance – but it faded as quickly as it had arrived, a promise unfulfilled, and they were left there, abandoned, staring into the murk of the grave.

She looked around at the other mourners, at Johnny next to her, at the priest reading monotonously from a Bible. Finally, her eyes went to the parking lot. There was no sign of the Jeep. No sign of Gareth.

Where the hell was he?

Beside her, Johnny moved closer, and she felt him take her hand, grasping it in his. Momentarily, she was surprised, unused to such a show of affection from her older brother, but when she glanced at him, he winked at her reassuringly, as if he could see right into her head. 'He'll be here, Bek,' he whispered softly.

Rebekah gave Johnny's hand a squeeze in return, unsure if he believed what he was saying, or whether he was simply doing what he always did: insulating her, trying to make things better. He'd been doing it ever since their mother left, but it had become more frequent once they knew their father was terminal, as if Johnny had subconsciously moved into the space that Henry was relinquishing: the patriarch and bulwark.

Johnny gripped her hand a little tighter and, as the grey morning and last rites came back into focus, Rebekah saw why: a Jeep Cherokee was pulling into the lot next to them.

She looked at Gareth, seeking him out behind the windshield, and when their eyes met – anger coursing in her veins – she left him in no doubt as to what she thought of his late arrival.

Her husband looked away.

2

Rebekah woke with a start, uncertain for a moment where she was. But then it all pulled into focus: the shelves on either side of her, the debris scattered at her hands and feet. The first-aid kit. The bait needle.

The general store.

Getting to her feet, she looked at the smashed window: a rectangle of butter-coloured light was leaking in and across the room. Next to it was a clock on the wall. The last time she'd checked, it was 5 a.m. Now it was nearly ten.

She'd slept less than five hours.

The pain in her face had got worse during the night, throbbing in the space next to her eye, flaring in her ear, her cheek, her nose. The fishing line, as thin as it was, had been agony going in, the bait needle even worse. She had antiseptic but nothing to numb the pain of stitching herself back together.

Nothing to numb the pain of being in this place.

Alone.

She moved to the broken window. Using the edge of the counter, she hauled herself up and through, trying to avoid the glass still rooted to the frame. She heard something tear, felt the glass snag her pants, but she managed to wriggle through without puncturing her skin. The previous night, she'd used a dumpster to climb up to the window; this morning, it had rolled away from the wall, propelled by the ferocity of the wind, and her feet flailed as she tried to find a solid platform.

She dropped onto the dumpster's lid, then down into a bed of mulched leaves. When she looked around her, it was like the after-math of an explosion: branches had been torn from the trees, debris from the harbour was scattered everywhere – roof tiles, clapboards, huge lakes of seawater.

For a moment, as she stood gazing out at the Atlantic, she felt so small, so swamped by the enormity of her situation.

She was still alive. She was still breathing.

She'd survived.

But she was trapped a hundred and one miles of ocean from anywhere.

The thought dragged at her, made her stumble slightly. And then, as that hit home, something else took hold – more urgent and even more desperate.

Johnny.

That was when her eyes landed on the bicycle. It lay on its side outside the store, pretty much exactly where she'd left it the night before. If she was going to find Johnny, she had to go back to the forest: that was where she'd last seen him.

It was where her Jeep was too.

She picked up the bike and started pedalling, her stitched wound hurting as she gritted her teeth, pain streaking all the way down the right side of her head. Pretty soon, it became so bad that her vision blurred. She tried to ignore it, cycling hard out of the town, up onto the road that would take her along the southern flank of the island. The further she rode, the colder she got: it dulled the pain in her face, but it turned her fingers to ice, then any patch of exposed skin. A mile, then a second. By the third, with the cold cutting through her like a knife, she realized she was going to need more clothes, quickly.

Up ahead, a gas station appeared on the left.

She knew she must be close to the forest because she remem-bered the gas station being nearby the day before, and the houses opposite, boarded up, swamped by weeds and long grass. Her eyes switched back to the gas station: there was a huge pile of old tyres at its rear, hemmed in by a chain-link fence. She hadn't seen it the day before but in that pile there might be one that fitted the Jeep.

She'd come back later.

For now, all that mattered was Johnny.

She had to find her brother.

Before

After the funeral – after Rebekah had avoided Gareth at the wake so obviously that, eventually, he'd had no choice but to leave – she and Johnny decided to take their father's rust-eaten Plymouth Gran Fury for a drive across the Verrazzano Bridge. The plan had been to take it out to Staten Island and then loop back, a journey for old times' sake, a way to be close to their dad, to something he'd loved, because he'd always loved the Plymouth. But when they got to Staten Island, they decided to keep going.

They headed down the Parkway to an old motel near Union Beach called the J. It was special to them, a place their father had taken them every summer when they were kids, even though he could barely afford it. Except when Rebekah and Johnny finally got there, the motel was closed – and not just for the day.

In that moment, as they looked at the derelict building, then at each other, tears filled their eyes. They knew why: there was a strange resonance to the place, a symmetry to this ending, as if the life of the motel had ceased alongside their father's.

Back in the car, Rebekah said, 'Dad kept repeating something weird at the end.' Johnny glanced at her. ' "Even the dead can talk." '

This time, her brother looked at her like she was losing it.

'That's what he kept telling me. He said he learned it as a cop.'

'Okay,' Johnny replied, although it was clear that he remained unconvinced. 'I might use it in my next book.'

'I'm serious, Johnny.'

He nodded, as if realizing his comment hadn't landed. 'Dad was on his way out, Bek, you know that.'

'So?'

'So you know how he was. He was mumbling a lot.'

'You really think I misheard? Why would I mishear that?'

Johnny didn't say anything, just smiled reassuringly, but she could see the answer in his face. *Because we just lost our dad. Because we're grieving, and we're hurt, and we're tired.*

In that moment, on that day, what Johnny had said to her seemed to make sense. But, in the weeks afterwards, she started to think more about what her father had repeated, about what he'd believed, the rules he'd adhered to, and then memories of Rebekah's mother returned, as they always did eventually. In truth, Rebekah had never stopped thinking about her.

She was always there, their stranger and betrayer, a woman who'd not shown any interest in her kids, never put up any sort of fight for them, even after their father – when Johnny was thirteen, Rebekah eleven, and Mike nine – had made the decision to move them to New York. She'd never sought out Rebekah in the years after that either, even when Rebekah had made the tough decision not to go to the States with the others, but to stay behind in London and take up a fully paid athletics scholarship at a prestigious private school. In the weeks before he left her, Rebekah's father had sat at the kitchen table and cried his eyes out every night, even though he knew what an opportunity it was for her. He'd even promised to fly Rebekah out to the US at the end of every school term, even if he had no idea how he'd ever pay for it.

But Rebekah's mother just remained silent.

Until the year Henry Murphy had returned to New York with Johnny and Mike, and Rebekah had headed to halls of residence in north London, the four of them had lived in the same house Fiona had walked out of, so it wasn't like she didn't know where to find them. They had the same phone number. Henry worked at the same police station. If she'd come back at any point in those eight years, she would have found them easily.

'Has Mum called today, Dad?'

For a long time, Rebekah would ask Henry the same question. He'd always insist that the four of them eat together, so she'd most frequently ask it at the dinner table, and whenever she did, her brothers would stop, the same as her, forks paused above their plates, and await their father's answer.

But their father's answer would always be the same. 'No, honey. She hasn't.'

'Why?'

Henry would reach to Rebekah then, to whichever of his sons was on the other side of him, and put his hands on their arms, reassuring them, settling them down. 'I think if your mother was going to call, she would have done it by now. But it's not your fault. None of this is any of your fault. You're the best kids any parent could have asked for.'

'Is she dead?'

Mike.

It was always Mike who asked that, spoiling the tenderness of their father's words. He was the youngest, so he had a ready-made excuse for his tactlessness, but he remembered Fiona less too. He had been a baby when she left, his mother just a flicker in the dark.

'I don't know, Mikey,' their father would say.

'If she was alive,' Rebekah asked, 'she'd want to see us, wouldn't she?'

But their father would never respond to that.

After six years apart from her family, only seeing them in the holidays when Henry could afford to fly her out, Rebekah decided she'd been away from her dad and her brothers too long and applied to American universities. At eighteen, she completed her A levels and bought a one-way ticket for New York.

In that time, her mother still hadn't come up for air.

By then, Rebekah's resolve had hardened, and she'd convinced herself she didn't give a shit. When she arrived at JFK, the three of them were waiting for her, and she knew straight away that – as alien as America was to her – she'd made the right choice to leave the UK. Home wasn't a place.

It was wherever her family were.

And so, on that first day, as her father drove them back to their house in Brooklyn, as Mike made jokes about his sister's plummy accent and Johnny talked passionately about the novel he wanted to write, she told herself she was completely at peace.

But, like all lies, eventually it fell apart.

3

She bumped onto the mile-long track that left the main road and went down the slope to Simmons Gully. On the descent, every dip and crag seemed to spear at her through the saddle, the vibrations shuddering up her arms and into her face, but eventually the track flattened into a muddy, uneven parking area.

There was only one car: her Jeep.

It was coated with fallen leaves, sown by the storm, but otherwise it was exactly as she'd left it. The window was still shattered, the tyre still slashed.

She put the bike down carefully, suddenly afraid: what if someone was here? What if they were waiting for her to come back to look for Johnny?

'Johnny?' she said quietly, fearfully. She looked at the wall of trees that surrounded her. 'Johnny?' she said again, a little louder, then waited for any reaction from nearby: any noise, any sign of movement.

All that came back was silence.

She headed into the forest, following the path she and Johnny had taken less than twenty-four hours before. Somewhere, close by, there was a stream. Soon, though, the sound of it faded, the trees grew thicker, roots punching through the ground like fists, and the path became a clotted, unnavigable maze, swamped with leaves and fallen branches from the storm. Pretty soon, she realized she was no longer on the route she was meant to have taken and had unwittingly carved out a new one. She was lost.

Panic hit her.

As she retreated, trying to get back to the trail that she and Johnny had used the day before – the trail that had led to the dig site – she called out.

'Johnny!'

She was shouting, her desperation making her careless.

'Johnny, it's me. *Johnny!*'

If someone *was* still there, they'd have heard her. They'd be coming for her. *I shouldn't be shouting his name like this.*

I shouldn't be –

She didn't get to finish her thought.

Suddenly she was stumbling sideways into a tree trunk. It stopped her dead. Winded, her hands slimy with moss, she looked up at the branch that had come out of nowhere and swiped her in the throat.

Tears welled in her eyes.

She wiped them away, trying to gather herself, but instead she slumped to her knees, thinking of the last time she'd seen Johnny: the glimpse of him ahead of her in the trees as they'd run for their lives.

She let herself cry, let it consume her, then hauled herself to her feet again, going through her pockets automatically, searching for her cellphone. Except it wasn't there. All she could feel were the keys to the Jeep.

Her phone was long gone.

It had been taken for a reason: there were no utility poles on the island, no physical phone lines, and only one cell tower.

And a cell tower was no good if you didn't have a cellphone.

She continued her retreat, back in the direction she thought she'd come, mud caking her. Her hair was damp, her skin cold, and under the shade of the trees she'd begun to shiver. She called Johnny, then again once she'd found her way back to the trail.

And then she came to another stop.

What if her cellphone hadn't been taken away from this place completely, just dumped somewhere in the forest? If it was close enough, she could use the Bluetooth function in the Jeep to connect to it – and she could make a 911 call from the car.

A charge of adrenalin hit her.

She broke into a sprint.

4

She yanked the driver's-side door open and slid behind the wheel. The passenger seat was soaked with rain and strewn with glass from the smashed window; the dashboard was wet too, the instruments misted, and there were leaves everywhere.

She didn't worry about any of it.

Putting her keys on the centre console, she pushed the ignition button and listened to the Cherokee rumble into life. The touchscreen display blinked – the clock showing the time as 14:12 – and then the Jeep logo flashed up and disappeared, and two rows of icons filled in.

She leaned forward, tapping a finger to *Phone* in the bottom row, but she already knew something wasn't right. There was no Bluetooth logo on the *Phone* icon, as there should have been, and when she hit the next screen, she felt her whole body cave: no cellphone was connected. She tried searching for one, knowing hers would automatically have paired if it was close enough, and after ten seconds, a message appeared, confirming nothing was in range.

'Shit!'

She smashed the steering wheel with the flat of her palm, then again, and again, so frenzied, she accidentally hit the horn.

Its blare was shockingly loud in the quiet of the forest.

Slowly, she slumped forward, her head almost touching the wheel, and stared into the trees, forlorn.

'Why?' she muttered.

She was so cold she couldn't feel her fingers.

'Why is this happening to me?'

The wind gently stirred the leaves inside the Jeep.

She turned to the back seat, searching for something – *anything* – she might have discarded the day before that she could put on to warm herself.

There was nothing.

Just two empty child seats.

Before

Kyra wouldn't stop crying.

'Ky, *please.*'

The traffic hadn't moved in ten minutes. Rebekah had a headache behind her eyes that she just couldn't shake. And every time she thought of her father, she felt like she was going to burst into tears.

Worse, her and Gareth had barely talked since the funeral. In fact, now she thought about it, they'd hardly spoken in months – certainly not a conversation of any substance. They didn't sit down to dinner together. He had breakfast at work. They went to sleep at different times, because she was the one getting up during the night, and by early evening she was fried. Her entire focus was Kyra, and Gareth's focus was . . .

Rebekah paused.

She didn't actually know what Gareth's focus was.

The sound of her phone snapped her out of her thoughts. A second after it had started buzzing on the passenger seat, it switched to the Cherokee's speakers. As if on cue, the display in the centre console flashed GARETH. Seeing his name surprised her. He never called from work.

She hit Answer. 'Hello?'

'Hey, sweetheart.'

That immediately pissed her off. This was pretty much the first time he'd tried talking to her in two weeks, apart from his muted apology at her father's wake, and he was acting like nothing had happened.

When Rebekah didn't reply, Gareth said, 'Are you okay?'

She shook her head, incredulous, her eyes boring into the dash, as if it could relay her anger. 'Are you kidding me? What do you think, Gareth? Do you think I might be "okay"?'

'Look, Bek . . .' A pause. 'I told you I was sorry.'

'Oh, *that* was your apology, at the wake?'

'Yes. I mean, no. I mean . . .'

He faded out.

'You don't get it, do you, Gareth?'

'I told you at the wake, I got stuck in traffic –'

'I don't give a shit. Okay? I don't give a shit *why* it happened, it's *that* it happened. You didn't apologize properly, we've hardly talked in months, we haven't talked *at all* since Dad died – and now you're calling me "sweetheart", like you're husband of the year.'

'I'm sorry. That report had to be in –'

'A *report*? Are you serious?'

'It was a mistake to try to take it in that morning. I can see that now. There was no way I planned to miss the funeral. I wanted to be there.'

'But you weren't.'

'I know,' he said. 'I'm really sorry.'

He sounded so sincere, it knocked her off her stride. She felt confused, lightheaded. In the eleven years they'd been together, she'd never known him give in so easily. 'Why are you calling me in the middle of the day like this?'

'I'm really sorry, Bek,' he said again.

'What's going on, Gareth?'

'Nothing's going on,' he replied. 'You're upset. You buried your father two weeks ago, and I let you down. I'm sorry I haven't been around much. I'm starting to think I got screwed at work, that this promotion will never come. All these extra hours I'm putting in, it's so we can have a better life, but all I'm doing is driving you away. You deserve more than that.'

Rebekah didn't know what to say.

'I want to start sitting down and eating together,' Gareth said. 'I think that should be our new rule. After Kyra's down, we cook a meal, and we talk.'

Again, Rebekah felt thrown.

'Do you agree?' he asked her.

'Yes,' she said, still surprised. 'I do.'

Kyra was quietening now, her tears playing out as a few solitary sobs, and as Rebekah ended the call with Gareth and looked back at her daughter, she felt a familiar sensation of failure: she saw how Kyra's sobs still pulsed through her body, an echo even as she slept; she saw how the new toy her baby was holding, a pink giraffe, spilled further from her grip with every whimper; she remembered the awful sound of her own raised voice and her anger as she'd shouted Kyra down.

She didn't want Kyra to remember her like that.

She didn't want to be that mother.

5

Rebekah stared at the pink giraffe, discarded between the two empty car seats, its tail chewed, the rest of it dotted with bits of food.

She swallowed her emotion.

She didn't want to cry again.

But it was hard: as she looked at the seats, the giraffe, she realized it had been barely twenty-four hours since she'd seen her daughters yet it felt like days. Weeks. She thought of them being so far away from her, how confused and scared they must have been when she didn't come home. And the hardest bit was, she didn't know how to get to them. She didn't have a way to contact home. She had no phone, her car was useless unless she found a new tyre – and no one knew where she was, or what had happened to her.

And where the hell was Johnny?

Hauling herself out of the Jeep, Rebekah headed back into the forest. She needed to find the dig site. If she found the place they'd ended up in the day before, she'd be closer to where she'd last seen Johnny. But the more she called his name and was met with the absolute silence of the trees, the more the doubts kicked in again.

She tried to dismiss the possibility that he wasn't answering her calls because he couldn't – couldn't let the hopelessness of that thought derail her search. Instead, she forced herself onwards, upping her pace, trying to get warm through movement, through speed, through sheer effort and willpower. She'd spent thirty minutes inside the Jeep running the engine, sitting in front of the heaters as they pumped out full blast, but now she was cold again: it was the last day of October, and there was no frost on the ground yet, but it was in the air. Winter was coming, and it felt almost like a threat. *It'll be so much worse than this if you don't find a way off this island.*

And then her attention switched.

Ahead, she could see a clearing.

She broke into a run, weaving between the trees, trying not to trip – and, after a minute, she passed from the forest onto a sloped patch of earth.

The dig site.

She'd found it.

The ground dropped away twenty feet in a series of ridges, like a staircase. It was bereft of grass, trees, anything but earth, the ground cut into, carved out, brushed down, revealing shapes buried beneath the surface. A piece of thin red barrier tape encircled the site, flickering as the wind picked up and fell away again. Tools had been left scattered everywhere.

'Johnny!'

She looked from side to side. The dig site was surrounded entirely by trees, by the density of the forest. Calling Johnny's name again, she moved from the top to the bottom. 'Johnny. It's me, it's Bek. *Johnny!*'

Heading into the trees beyond, she continued along the same trail they'd taken only twenty-four hours ago and then, eventually, stopped at the edge of a nearby ravine. Below her, breaking out of the side of a bank, was a set of exposed tree roots.

She recognized them immediately.

Beneath those was a mound of freshly dug earth.

6

She continued on, thinking about the freshly dug earth. It wasn't Johnny down there, buried under that mud – but her thoughts still lingered on the image. She doubted she would ever forget it.

Or the memories of what had happened there.

After a couple of minutes, she came to a sudden stop: directly in front of her, under a thick swathe of canopy and protected by an old, gnarled oak, was a flawless boot print.

She instantly recognized the zigzag of the tread.

For a second, she allowed herself to believe it might be fresh. But then she saw more of Johnny's prints leading into and away from the one she'd stopped at, and some of her own alongside them, and she realized how absurd the hope had been. They were all from the day before.

She screamed into the trees – pained and furious – and, after it was over, as she stood there, heaving and breathless, she glanced at her watch.

Except that was missing too.

Gareth had bought her a Maurice Lacroix for their third anniversary. It had cost him a month's salary, but it had spent the last six months buried at the bottom of Rebekah's jewellery box. Since she'd stopped wearing it, her cell had become how she'd kept track of time, but every so often she'd still find herself pulling back her sleeve to look for the watch.

She had no clue how long she'd been out here. An hour? Two? All she knew was that she was cold again, the cut on her face was throbbing, and the light had given way. Above her, the sky remained clear, but it was mauve, not blue.

It's getting dark.

She headed back in the direction of the dig site – out of breath, unfit – and realized how stupid she'd been. She'd left the flashlight at the general store. If she didn't find her way out of the forest soon – if it got much darker – she'd lose the trail completely.

Fear hit her, hard as concrete.

She broke into a run, sliding on the mud, not wanting to be caught out here at night. She kept looking over her shoulder, the pounding in her ears sounding like footsteps, like a person trailing in her wake. When she reached the dig site, it felt like no victory at all because she knew she had so much further to go, and the paths beyond this were the ones that had vanished in the storm. She felt almost hysterical.

She tripped over, then scrambled to her feet, her palms slathered in earth. She'd hit the ground hard and now every part of her hurt. Branches slapped at her as she started again, ripping her hoodie, nicking her cheeks, her neck, the back of her hands. Sweat froze all the way down the ridge of her spine, and it was even worse on her face, cold as ice. After a while, the dressing she'd used on her wound began to peel away, slackened by the moisture. It flapped as she ran, the gauze obscuring her view.

She tore it off and tossed it into the forest.

I'm never going to find my way back.

I'm never going to find my way –

At last she emerged into the parking area.

She stopped, relief flooding her, and almost collapsed in on herself, her hands on her knees, her breath struggling up through her chest.

Next to her, in the wind, the Cherokee rocked gently on its suspension, making a slight wheeze. The sound brought her back: she was four miles from the store, from the only place she knew she could seek shelter when it got dark. She had no idea about the rest of the island, other than the little Johnny had told her the day before. There might have been better places to stay the night, or to find clothes or food, but there was no way she'd find anywhere quickly without her car.

The bicycle wasn't going to cut it any more.

She had to fix the tyre on the Jeep.

Before

Rebekah and Gareth's new routine lasted three months.

She'd been doing locum work – trying to fit it around Kyra, around the nights that Gareth was home, or her best friend, Noella, could babysit – but then orthopaedic departments had become short-staffed in two of the hospitals she'd been working in, and she gradually found herself doing more and more shifts. At the same time, Gareth had started working longer hours, chasing the promotion his boss had dangled in front of him. So, although for the first few weeks they sat down for dinner, watched movies together and went to bed at the same time, those routines soon became sporadic.

There were other, smaller, changes too.

After the routine started to fracture, Gareth seemed to become angrier. One night when a deal went south, he returned home and threw a tumbler at the wall. Another time he wanted to have sex, but Rebekah had come off a shift, then been up all night with Kyra, and was bone-tired, so said no.

'You're *unbelievable*,' he spat at her and stormed out of the room. The next time they had sex, he was weird and different: silent, aggressive, selfish.

Then, when the anger stopped, he became uncommunicative, incapable of saying so much as a word to her as he arrived home, before disappearing up to bed. Some nights she'd smell whisky on him, or cigarettes, even though he'd told her he'd given up smoking when they met. And then, a few nights later, she caught a whiff of perfume, indistinct and difficult to place, and that was when she thought of the call he'd made to her in the car when he'd first suggested the new dinner routine. She remembered that it had felt so out of character, how he'd apologized so easily – about the funeral, about being late. But had he *really* been feeling guilty about his late arrival – or was something different going on, some other ghost he'd been exorcizing? Hating herself for doing it, the following night she waited for him to go to sleep, then crept downstairs and went through his phone.

She couldn't find anything on it.

At the start of June – almost four months to the day after she'd buried her father – she began to feel nauseous.

She went out to the drugstore to pick up a test, even though she didn't need to. She knew what was up without having to pee on a stick. But she did the test anyway, and she got the blue cross, and that same morning – as she drove Kyra to a play date with one of the mothers Rebekah worked with at the hospital – she called her doctor from the Jeep and booked an appointment.

That was when she almost crashed the car.

As she was finishing the call, she took her eyes off the road for a split second and, as she did, an SUV seemed to come out of nowhere, whipping in front of her. She slammed on the brakes.

Something hit the back of her foot.

'*Asshole!*' she screamed, but the other car was already out of sight. The driver in the lane beside hers shook his head and rolled his eyes in sympathy. She shrugged at him, then reached down to find out what had struck her foot.

To her surprise, it was a cellphone.

She'd never seen it before.

7

Rebekah put the Jeep into Reverse and let it inch back. It did, but jerkily: every time the wheel went through a full rotation, the entire axis seemed to drop and reset. Not knowing what to do, or ever having driven a car with a flat, she kept dabbing at the brake, hoping that the slower she went, the more control she would retain. Eventually, she was facing the exit: the muddy, uneven trail that ascended out of Simmons Gully, to the main road.

She let the car drift forward. The first part worked fine: she hit the exit, the car kept going, she applied a little gas, and – although it lurched and the slashed tyre spun – she kept moving. It was fine even as the gradient steepened: she was moving back and forth between the brake and the gas pedal, trying not to hit either too hard, the slow pace helping to offset the irregular movement of the car.

Halfway up, she hit a pothole.

Suddenly, the car felt like it dropped about thirty feet, lurching awkwardly to the right, even though the depression could only have been a tiny fraction of that. She jammed on the brake, alarmed, unnerved. *It's okay. It's okay.* She tried to calm herself by looking into the mirror, seeing the distance she'd managed, then through the windshield to the main road. She could see the change up ahead between this trail and that, the switch between brown mud and grey asphalt.

It's okay. It's not far.

Gently, she pressed her foot to the gas.

The wheel spun in the pothole.

She stopped, hit the brake.

Come on.

She tried again and went nowhere.

Come on, please work.

She pressed on the gas a third time.

The wheel spun, the noise like a shriek. As she glanced to either side of her, she saw the drop-off, became aware of the way the trail canted sharply into the trees. If she lurched, if the Jeep came out of the hole at any sort of angle, she would careen into the forest and drop fifty feet.

Please. This has to work.

'This has to wor–'

Her cry was swallowed by the roar of the engine. Before she knew it, the Jeep was moving, thumping against the ruts of the track, but heading straight.

Thirty seconds later she reached the top.

As soon as she hit asphalt, she pumped the brake and stopped dead. Her heart was pounding against her ribs. Her head hurt. Her eyes went to the mirror, to the wound on her face, its rawness and ugliness, to the baby seats in the back, to the rear windshield: out the other way, the road unfurled, an arc of grey that followed the southern coastline before it bent left.

It was darker in that direction, the day fading from east to west, clouds gathering above the curve of the earth. She glanced down at the Jeep's clock.

Almost five.

She hit the accelerator and headed for the gas station.

8

She drove faster along the empty road, less concerned now by the lurch of the car, a series of long-abandoned buildings passing her on either side.

Johnny had told her the island had been in a state of neglect ever since Hurricane Gloria had ripped through it in 1985. Before, it had been touted as New York's version of Martha's Vineyard, an affluent summer escape for the city's rich and famous, but now all Rebekah saw was wreckage: fallen tiles, imploded windows, guttering cleaving away, like old, broken bones.

Gloria must have wrought an almost Biblical destruction.

When she got to the gas station, Rebekah pulled the Cherokee to the side, close to where she'd spotted the pile of tyres. The station was only small: a couple of pumps and a building with a single window – but all the pumps were off and the building looked dormant. She remembered something else her brother had told her: nowhere outside Main Street, and the harbour area, was on an electrical grid, so everything else was generator-powered.

She parked and walked over to the building.

Inside, she could see an empty cash register, some basic items for sale, like car oil, but nothing to eat or drink, and certainly nothing she could wear. She backed away from the window and did a circle of the building. At the rear, she found a locked door, as well as a generator, which was secured inside a padlocked cage.

Rebekah refocused on her immediate need and hurried back to the forecourt, dropping to her haunches next to the Jeep's puncture.

Some sort of serial number was printed on the side wall of the tyre. Now she just had to hope she could find a match.

Making a mental note of the number, she headed to the mountain of discarded black rings at the side of the gas station. She started going through them, dragging them out of the way once she'd checked them. Some tyres were so old and worn they didn't even have numbers on them, or they'd faded over time. Others had flattened and lost air pressure. Eventually, she found one with a similar set of numbers that looked the right size, and rolled it out and away from the others. It was almost dusk, the sun gone, her body aching. She was so tired, so sore.

And now the doubts were flickering again.

The hard part, changing the wheel, was still to come. She knew the theory, because her father had taught her, back when she'd passed her driving test, but he'd looked over her shoulder, making sure she was doing it right. In the years since, she'd stood at the edges of a repair shop and watched the mechanic do everything for her.

And then she thought of something her dad used to say.

He'd said it that first time he'd watched her change a tyre, and he'd said it over and over to the three of them as they were growing up.

'Take pride in the hard work,' she repeated quietly.

She rolled the tyre towards the Jeep.

Before

Take pride in the hard work.

Rebekah's father hadn't meant just physical labour, he'd meant things that were equally hard, like saying sorry, admitting you were wrong, honesty, kindness and loyalty.

The last was especially important to him.

After returning to the US, Henry had started working for the NYPD out of the 68th Precinct in north-west Brooklyn. His beat was only four square miles, but it was his part of town, full of his people, and he walked it with pride. Sometimes, when Rebekah and her brothers were much older and his shift was over, their father would meet them at their favourite diner on Macdonald Avenue, and Rebekah would ask him why he was still walking the beat in his sixties. He'd had the chance to move up many times – he'd even passed the detectives' exam – but his response to her was always the same.

'Take pride in the hard work, Bek.'

Hard work bred loyalty and respect, something he would often remind them of, given how little of either their mother had shown them. He would never criticize Fiona, never name her in conversations, and Rebekah admired him for that – but their mother's relevance was always implicit. Even when they were young, they understood that much. And Rebekah and Johnny understood it more keenly than ever when, thirteen months before their father passed, Mike lost control of his Tesla on Hutchinson River Parkway, his car leaving the road so hard and so fast it landed on its roof in a reservoir a hundred feet away.

He'd died before the first responders ever got close to the scene.

Mike's death hadn't gone unnoticed: he was the creator of a successful social-media app, always appearing in newspapers and on TV; he had a beautiful house in a picture-perfect White Plains suburb, and he was wealthy. People knew him. Their mother, wherever she was, couldn't have failed to hear about the death of her youngest son, not least because the accident happened on the night of his thirty-fifth birthday. But, still, the hard work Rebekah's father talked of didn't apply to Fiona: she hadn't shown them any loyalty, kindness or honesty, she hadn't ever said sorry, and when Mike died, she didn't even call.

She just sent a card.

'Did you tell her where we lived?' Rebekah said to her father, when the card turned up. 'Are you still in touch with her, Dad?'

'No,' her father said.

'Then how the hell did she know where to send the card?'

'I don't know, Bek,' Henry said, weary, broken.

'It would have been easy enough to figure out,' Johnny said to Bek, trying to defuse the situation, as he always did. 'There's a ton of details about Mike's death online. It says in the reports that his family lives in Dyker Heights.'

Their mother sent another card when Henry died – almost exactly the same: plain white with a pale pink rose – and both times Johnny, graciously, said the gestures were better than nothing. But Rebekah disagreed. Not coming to her ex-husband's funeral was one thing, but staying away from her son's was another.

'What kind of a mother doesn't bury her own child?' she kept saying.

Johnny had just shrugged. Of the three of them, he'd always been more forgiving, more of a believer in redemption.

Once, towards the end of high school, he'd dated a girl called Julisa, whom he adored, and who'd cheated on him after they'd been going out for six months. Rebekah and Mike had told him to dump her, that what she'd done to him was indefensible, but Johnny took her back without hesitation.

Rebekah always remembered the call she'd made to her brother from London a few nights after that. She'd just come back from a track meet, because she was two days out from running the 1500-metres in a national schools championship, and her times had been slower than they had been the week before. She returned to the halls, pissed off, exhausted, and in the call with Johnny had ended up angry with him, telling him he was giving Julisa free rein to do the same thing again.

But Johnny's response always stuck with her: 'I'm not, Bek. That's not what I'm doing at all. I'm giving her the chance to make something right.'

Rebekah could think of no comeback.

I'm giving her the chance to make something right.

It helped that Johnny remembered their mother the clearest of any of them, or at least a version of her. Sometimes, when the three were younger, alone and out of earshot of their dad, Johnny would talk to Rebekah and Mike about her, what she was like. In fact, the only things Rebekah really knew about her mother had come through Johnny.

'What did she look like?'

That was always Rebekah's favourite question, born from not being able to remember anything of Fiona except a streak of autumnal hair.

Johnny would always reply patiently. 'She was tall,' he'd tell them, 'about five nine or ten. Do you know how big that is?' Rebekah and Mike would shake their heads, and Johnny would get up and go to the wardrobe in Rebekah's room. 'It's about up to here,' he'd say, always on tiptoe until he finally became tall enough in his teens, his fingertips marking out a point at the edge with the flat of his hand. 'And she was slim.'

'Was she pretty?'

'Very. Dad used to call her "glamorous". She had very pale skin too, but not like she was sick. It was creamy, like Angela.'

Angela had been one of Rebekah's dolls.

Rebekah would say, 'She had red hair, didn't she?' even though she knew the answer was *yes*. It was the only thing she really knew about her mother.

'Yes,' Johnny would respond, 'like leaves in the fall.'

Ever the writer, Rebekah would think later, when they were all teenagers. By that stage, the conversations about their mother had stopped coming as often – and, when they did, the tone was very different.

'Fuck her,' Mike would say.

'Mike, don't say that.'

'Why not, John?'

They would only ever call him *John* if things were serious.

'She's your mom.'

'She's not *my* mom, Johnny. She's not *your* mom either. She stopped being our mom when she left us. She's got "hair like leaves in the fall", and she's "glamorous", and you say she "used to sit us in a circle around her and play games with us" – for what? Like, ten minutes before she dumped us?'

'We don't know why she left.'

'We don't *need* to know, Johnny,' Mike fired back. 'All we need to know is that she abandoned us. Nothing else matters.'

'That's not true.'

'She's not coming back, Johnny. Don't you get that?'

And then Johnny would look at Rebekah, and Rebekah would look back at her brother, and – for a while, at least – Fiona would be forgotten again.

But not completely.

Never completely.

9

Rebekah's hands slipped from the wrench. '*Shit.*'

She was on her knees, next to the wheel, under the roof of the gas station. The work was so hard, so monotonous, that she'd drifted back to the things that always comforted her in her lowest moments – her family, her memories.

Her girls.

I need to get home.

They'll think I've abandoned them.

Picking up the wrench again, she snapped it into place, on the last of the lug nuts, as random memories of her daughters flashed in front of her eyes. Like a videotape, she paused on the time she'd first put Kyra's hair into a ponytail, right in the centre of her head, a fountain erupting from its source. Ky had sensed something was new and different and had started pawing at it.

And then Rebekah was back in the gas station.

She saw how dark it had got, even with the Cherokee's head-lights on bright. Beyond the forecourt, she couldn't see anything.

She tried not to let the thought disturb her, but as – teeth grit-ted, muscles taut – she levered the wrench around in another rotation, she found her gaze drawn back to the darkness. She remembered that there were some old buildings directly across from the gas station. She knew the ocean was somewhere on the other side of them. She knew that the town lay to her right, and to her left the forest, but she couldn't see any of it.

I've never known a night as dark as this.

Goosebumps scattered up her back.

And then something moved.

Rebekah stopped instantly. Leaving the wrench where it was, she got slowly to her feet, her eyes fixed on where the movement had come from. For a moment the only sound was the wind, the ocean obscured somewhere behind it – but then, as that faded, something new filled the void.

Was it some kind of click?

What would be making a clicking sound out here?

She looked down at the wrecked tyre, at the replacement waiting on the ground, at the jack propping up the underside of the car. She couldn't move the Cherokee, swing it around so the headlights revealed what was out there. *And maybe I don't want to*, she thought, because now she could hear the clicking again. More regular, almost uniform.

'Hello?' she said. 'Hello? Is anyone there?'

The wind came again and, this time, a branch rolled out of the shadows, into the edge of the light. A second gust propelled it across the blacktop towards the gas pumps. Finally, it came to rest twenty feet from her, contorted and damaged where it had been ripped from a tree.

Everything settled again.

Was that really what she'd heard?

A branch?

She looked into the darkness, trying to see if anything else was out there, any other sign of movement, but now it was almost serene: the wall of night wrapped itself around the entire gas station – unbroken, impenetrable.

Just get the wheel done and get out of here.

She glanced down at the tyre.

And then what?

What was the point of any of this? What was going to happen even if she *did* get the wheel changed? It wasn't like she could simply drive off an island. She was a hundred and one miles away from the mainland, in the vastness of the Atlantic.

There were no people.

There were no boats.

And no one was coming back for five months.

IO

She woke on the second day to a leak. In the corner of the store, where all the candy bars had been left on the shelves, rain was coming through a patch on the ceiling.

During the night, she must have cried because tears had dried on her cheeks, like trails of frost. Hardly a minute passed without her thinking about her girls, even when she was almost asleep. Her absence would be making them frantic and confused. And even though they weren't old enough to process it all, part of them might think Rebekah had *deliberately* abandoned them.

'I haven't, I promise,' she muttered. 'I wouldn't.'

Never.

She'd spent the first part of the night in the Jeep, running the engine and the heaters, but then she'd started to worry about burning through the gas still in the tank. She had no idea if there was any left in the pumps at the station, and trying to find out would involve starting the generator, which probably meant breaking into the office on the forecourt. Until her first night here, when she'd sought shelter inside the store, she'd never broken into anywhere.

She was near-certain a rescue was coming, near-certain that Noella or Gareth had reported her missing by now and that it would be just a matter of time before the cops arrived on the island – and, yet, there was still a sliver of doubt in her, two nights on. She knew she might need a Plan B.

One way or another, she *had* to get home.

She had to get back to Kyra and Chloe.

In the here and now that meant fresh clothes. It meant food that wasn't just chocolate. It meant a water source because she'd already been through four of the eight remaining soda cans left in the store. To keep warm, she needed a heater, some blankets. From what she could remember, Johnny had said there weren't any hotels or bed-and-breakfasts or, at least, none that weren't boarded up or abandoned long ago. Anyone who stayed for any length of time used the hostels built for the fishermen. There, she might find a mattress and a blanket.

She needed to get a proper idea of the geography of the island too, so she could find her way around: there were no maps in the store, but if she could find one, it might help her get an idea of where Johnny had gone, and where she might find food. She could have used the GPS in the Jeep, but only roads were marked on that. She needed a bigger, more detailed overview.

She moved to the window, looking out at the sky: it was raining again. She could hear the ocean, though the window was too high for her to see it.

Stay calm, she told herself.

This hell will only be temporary.

Before

After Rebekah found the cellphone in the car, she held onto it and did nothing. It was number-locked, so there was no way for her to access it, and – when Gareth wasn't at home – she'd veer wildly between believing there must be a simple explanation for a stranger's phone to have fallen under the front seat of their car, and being certain that her husband was lying to her. But every day of the pregnancy, she became a little more tired, and after four months, she still hadn't done anything about it.

When her belly began to swell, she started telling herself it was better that, for now, she didn't know. The new baby would turn their lives upside down anyway. Rebekah just wanted things to be normal.

But unanswered questions were never normal.

Eventually, something had to break.

'I'd like to scale back the locum work for a year.'

They were standing across from one another in the kitchen, the table a mess of food and toys. It was after ten thirty at night and, on one of the countertops, Kyra's monitor crackled with a faint static.

Gareth's face coloured. 'Are you shitting me?'

She watched him, saying nothing, her hand on her belly. It was now only seven weeks until her due date, and everything hurt: her back, legs, feet.

'Absolutely not,' Gareth said. 'That's insane.'

'Why?'

'*Why?*'

He frowned and stepped back from her, as if Rebekah were some species he'd never seen before. His tie hung limp, like an inverted noose, and one of his shirt tails had escaped the belt at the back of his pants. It had been a few weeks since they'd stood so close to one another and, for the first time, Rebekah thought how old Gareth was looking. It was in his eyes, in the lines there, and in the colour of his skin: grey, anaemic.

'*Because,*' he said, slowly, patronizingly, 'we can't afford it, Bek. If you give up work, the pressure's all on me. You get that, right? I've already got a hundred million problems to deal with – I don't need money being another.'

'We can afford it,' she said calmly.

'You won't be *earning*, Bek.'

'We won't be paying for daycare. Plus I've saved some money.'

He frowned again. 'What?'

'From the locum work. I've set some money aside.'

'And you didn't bother telling me?'

'I told you,' she said, 'but you obviously weren't listening,' and then she started loading cutlery into the dishwasher. 'I've got the money to cover us for a year, so there won't be any pressure on you. And I didn't say I'd give up the locum work, just scale it back so I can spend some quality time with Kyra and the baby when she comes along. After a year, I'll start searching for something permanent.'

'As easy as that.'

'No, it won't be easy, Gareth – but life isn't easy, is it?' She looked up at him and saw that he was nodding. But he wasn't agreeing with her, he was seething. 'There are no permanent positions in orthopaedics anyway – not in New York – even if I wanted one. Which I don't. But I've seen jobs in Oklahoma City and Fort Worth. I even saw an orthopaedic role in North Dakota. Shall we all move up there, Gareth? Would that be better?'

'You're so clever, aren't you?'

She loaded the last mug into the dishwater, snapped the door shut, and straightened. 'No, I'm not clever,' she said. 'But I'd like to give this a chance. I'd like to be around for the girls as much as I can.'

His eyes were narrow, dark, resentful.

'It won't be easy.'

He laughed. 'You're damn right it won't. While I'm busy busting my ass trying to pay the bills, you'll be doing yoga, and shopping at Pottery Barn. This is great for you. You get to relax at home, while I'm out there d–'

'Yeah, because bringing up kids is so easy.'

'It's not as hard as going to wor–'

'Not as hard as going to work?' She felt every muscle in her body tense. 'Did those words seriously come out of your mouth? Okay, so why don't *I* start doing locum work full-time and you can bring up the kids? You can change their nappies –'

'Diapers.'

'Whatever.'

'You've been living here twenty years, Bek.'

'So? So what?'

'"Look at me, everyone. I'm British." *Please*.'

She stared at him. 'I *am* British, Gareth.'

'We don't call them "nappies" here, and you know it.'

'What the hell difference does it make?'

'It's fucking irritating. That's what difference it makes.'

She didn't respond. It was petty and he knew it, but he was angry and trying to hurt her in whichever way he could. When they'd first got together, he'd told her his dad was Italian, and when she'd joked that *Gareth* Russo was the most un-Italian name she'd ever heard, he'd said his mom was from Wales. He kept telling her he loved the English accent, adored how Rebekah spoke. Taking a breath, Rebekah looked at him. 'You support me – or you don't.'

They glared at each other, and then he stormed out of the room.

Rebekah realized that that was probably the moment when the façade finally, irreparably, cracked for good. In the weeks before the birth, he began returning home late at night, drifting through the house and up to bed without saying a word to her. Sometimes, after Chloe arrived, he'd look in on the girls on his way through, but often he'd pass their doorway, as if he didn't have an obligation to them – or he'd forgotten they were in the house at all.

Before long, he smelt of whisky again, of perfume, and when Chloe was a month old, Rebekah dug out the cellphone she'd found in the car: she'd hidden it inside an old jewellery box, knowing Gareth would never think to look inside. And as she held it, staring at the passcode screen, the memories came flooding back: she remembered his apology and how he'd folded so easily just as she'd been about to tear into him about her father's funeral; and she remembered how, deep down, she'd wondered if he wasn't apologizing for missing the start of the service but for something else.

That was when she understood there was only one way to know for sure.

She had to find a way to unlock the phone.

11

She climbed out of the store window onto the dumpster.

Her arms were so sore, it hurt to just lift them. Her palms still smelt of metal, ingrained from the wrench. She'd been squeezing so hard, had had to expend so much effort the previous night just to get the lug nuts off the wheel, that simply opening her hands this morning was agony. She hadn't slept well either – cold, scared – and kept thinking about the clicking sound she'd heard at the gas station. It hadn't been the branch rolling out of the shadows.

It had been something else.

She was relieved it was daytime. When she was in the store at night, at least she had a flashlight, its solitary glow bringing her some small measure of comfort. But at the gas station, the blackness had been absolute. It was why she wouldn't go out again at night without a light.

She looked down towards the harbour, the boats gone, the parking bays vacant, and then the other way, beyond the store, to Main Street. It marked the centre of the island's only town, although it was nowhere close to being a town, and Main Street was way too grand a title for a single sloping streak of asphalt lined with a collection of broken buildings. Her eyes went to a rust-speckled sign mounted at the bottom of the slope, the name of the town in faded black lettering.

Helena.

Whenever she saw it, a memory would spark at the back of Rebekah's head: she'd gone to school with a girl called Helena. The two of them had been best friends all the way through primary and

48

had spent hours at each other's houses. But then Helena's father had become ill, and she hadn't been at school for a week, then a month, and the next thing anyone heard, Helena and her family had moved to Yorkshire. A few nights later, Rebekah's father had found her crying in her room, and when he asked what the matter was, she'd said, 'It's my fault Helena left.'

'No, it isn't, honey,' he'd replied. 'Why would it be your fault?'

'Because the people I like always leave me.'

She tore her eyes away from the sign, jumped off the dumpster, and made her way up to Main Street. In its heyday, Johnny had said, there were ice-cream parlours and crab shacks and diners, but all that was left now was the store Rebekah had been sleeping in, and a small bait-and-tackle place. It was barely more than a wooden shack.

This whole island is just a memory.

It was the way it looked: after Hurricane Gloria had ripped through, nothing was ever fixed properly, just repaired enough, or the damage ignored entirely. It was its isolation: three hours south of Montauk on a ferry, on the wrong side of a hundred miles of ocean. Mostly, though, it was the way it had retreated so far from the minds of mainlanders that most people had forgotten it even existed. Once the fishing season was over, it closed every year from November to March, and even when it was open, it was only ever visited by trawlermen and a few hardy academics who came to study the marine life. *Why the hell would anyone come here?* Rebekah wondered, as she got to the Cherokee.

Why had she?

She slid in at the wheel and pulled the door shut. *I came here for Johnny*, she thought. *Because I loved him. Because he was my brother.*

Is my brother.

Is.

She started the ignition.

He's still alive, Bek.

In an effort to keep the rain out of the Jeep, she'd covered the broken passenger window with an old, torn tarp she'd found at the gas station, but in the store there was a roll of plastic wrap under the counter, which she was going to use instead: it was much less cumbersome, plus she could see through it.

She pulled away, heading out of Helena, and as she did, images of Kyra and Chloe formed behind her eyes – Kyra, two and a half, running after a beach ball in the backyard; Chloe, eight months, cheeks red, gumming Kyra's old giraffe – and whatever strength Rebekah had drawn from the idea that she was being searched for, by the plans she'd been making to survive just long enough to be saved, disappeared. In its place came a profound sense of loss.

For Chloe, it might not have registered as completely, but Rebekah couldn't bear to think of how her absence might be affecting Kyra. They hadn't spent a night apart for two and a half years.

Don't lose focus.

She looked out to sea, in the direction of the mainland. It was a vague grey line on the horizon, what little shape it had shrouded by a swirling mist.

Someone is coming back.

You're going to get home.

You're going to see your girls again.

12

The hostels that the trawlermen used during the fishing season were two double-storey buildings on the north coast. They were miles apart, as if they couldn't bear to be with one another, one facing out to the ocean, the other towards the centre of the island, where the highest point, Nuyáhshá, was.

'Highest point' made it sound grander than it was: for the most part, as far as Rebekah could tell, the island was virtually flat. There were a few solitary buildings scattered on the side of Nuyáhshá, but the highest point was more a mound than a peak, and almost all of the buildings were rubble.

She pulled the Cherokee alongside the first of the hostels and got out. The rain had turned to a fine drizzle, but it was still cold, and when she passed from the warmth of the car to the rawness of the morning, a thought hit her: *If it's already this cold and it's only November, how cold will it be in January?*

She pushed the idea away.

I'm not going to be here in January.

Even as the words came to her, she wasn't sure she believed them, doubt clinging on, flickering images of still being here as the snow fell, the winds roused and winter gripped. But, again, she suppressed them, concentrating on the hostel instead. As she walked from front to back, her breath clouding in front of her face, she could see there were doors on both sides: the one at the rear was padlocked, the one at the front secured with a key.

She returned to the front and stared at the simplicity of the keyhole. It looked like a simpler task than breaking open a padlock, but she knew it wouldn't be. She'd seen people kick doors down with ease in movies and on TV, but that had always been one of her dad's pet hates – whenever some actor cracked open a door with a single kick, he'd say, *You can't just walk up and kick open a locked door. If it's an exterior door, it might be reinforced, so all you're doing is busting your ankle. You've got to listen to the sound it makes when you kick. If you can hear wood crack, it's game on. If it's a dull thud, you've got a problem. If it's a dull thud and the door has a steel frame, or there's bolts on it, you've got an even bigger problem.* Rebekah looked at the door.

It didn't have bolts, but it had a steel frame.

That made it likely to be reinforced but she took a step back anyway, then focused her attention on the area just below the keyhole. *I always aimed for the deadbolt or the knob*, her father would tell them. *And I kept my foot flat to the door on impact. That's important, unless you want to be going to the ER.* Flat foot, deadbolt. She took a breath and kicked out.

Nothing happened.

You've got to kick the door in the direction it swings.

She looked at the door. No way did it swing out, not with the steel frame built around it. She readied herself and kicked again.

Pain speared up her leg.

'*Shit*,' she muttered, rubbing her calf.

She thought about shoulder-barging it.

But then she remembered, *Never shoulder-barge. Never try to breach a door with anything other than your foot. There was a cop I knew who tried to use the side of his body to bust open a door and he couldn't move his neck for four weeks. There's a reason we used a Stinger.* Her dad had told them that the Stinger was a thirty-five-pound, thirty-inch battering ram.

Rebekah returned to the car and got the jack.

She grabbed the wrench too.

It was time to switch her attention to the door at the back of the hostel. Neither the jack nor the wrench was ideal – she guessed a crowbar would have been the easiest way to lever off a padlock – but she'd have to make do.

There's no skill in this, she thought. *It's just brute force.*

She smashed the jack down as hard as she could against the padlock. It rattled for a moment, then came to rest, unimpressed.

She gripped the jack even tighter, fingers blanched with the effort, and crashed it down a second time. This time, the padlock *pinged*, swinging inside the ring of the metal plate to which it was secured, and then – like a metronome slowing – it was still again.

Rebekah looked at the metal plate. It was hinged: once the padlock had been removed, the half of the plate that was on the door just folded back against the wall. *As simple as that*, she thought bitterly.

Unless she could smash a window.

On the ground floor, there were three windows, then a set of rusting metal stairs that went up to a fire exit on the first floor, where there were three more. All of the windows had thin metal bars. Rebekah wondered why – they were miles from anywhere, and even when the hostel was open, hardly anyone was on the island – but then, from the ocean, came a huge boom. She glanced out at the water as a wave crashed onto the shore. It looked tormented already, and while the wind was only light, discarded junk was being whipped up and scattered: nets, fishing lines, plywood, styrofoam cups. In a bad storm, that would be replaced by masonry, roof tiles and chunks of rock, and the glass would be as effective as paper at shielding the hostel's interior. The bars were just damage control.

Again, Rebekah's thoughts spiralled back to what it might be like here in the winter. What if another hurricane hit?

What if she was still on the island when it did?

She clasped the jack with both hands, refocusing her attention on the padlock.

Come on, you can do it.

She crashed the jack against it. When it didn't break, she did it again, and again, and again. She paused, shoulders heaving like a piston, her heart stomping beneath her ribs, out of breath, hot. She started to forget why she was even trying to get inside the hostel. She wasn't going to sleep here because, when a rescue came, it would be from the mainland, and that meant she needed to be at the store, close to Helena. She needed to see the boats when they arrived at the harbour. So why *was* she here?

I need supplies. I need clothes. I need blankets. She tightened her grip on the jack again.

I need to get this door open.

She started again, the pain in her hands worse than ever. It was all along her arms too. Her jaw was clenched so tightly that her teeth throbbed. She kept going, even as she slowed and the blows became less forceful, even as the jack started to slip from her grasp, and her hair was blown across her face by the wind.

But, just as she was about to give up, her luck changed.

The padlock made another soft *ping*.

This time, it dropped to the ground.

Travis

'Hi, guys, I'm Louise Mason.'

Headphones on, and with the noise from the squad room reduced to a low, featureless hum, Frank Travis watched as the woman smiled at the camera. His cellphone screen was small but her smile didn't get lost: it was big, vivid, genuine, and as she introduced herself, she buttoned up her paint-spattered white overalls and tied her hair into a bun. Once she was done, she smiled into the camera again and said, 'This is my studio.'

She was thirty-five, had a small star tattoo at the nape of her neck, and bright pink hair. On the driver's licence Travis had pulled from the system, it had been black or dark brown but, in the time between the licence being issued and the video being shot, she'd dyed it. Somehow the hair colour suited her. He imagined, in life, most things had suited Louise.

She was standing in a vast loft space and, as she spoke, she gestured to a wall full of paintings. Mostly, they were hanging from wires that, in turn, were connected to the ceiling, but a few were still displayed on huge easels. It was the sort of art that Travis didn't get, or even pretend to, but he'd read up about Louise's work, her career, exhibitions and installations, and he knew plenty of people got it just fine: only three weeks before she disappeared, she'd sold a painting entitled 'A Broad View from the Carpet' for $458,000.

Travis watched as Louise discussed the work she had in her studio, and talked about a new installation she'd designed at MoMA PS1. The opening had been delayed for two months after she went missing, but in the end her family told the museum that Louise would have wanted it to go ahead, so Travis had taken a trip out to Long Island City to see it. It was absolutely packed, the reports about Louise's disappearance helping to massage the crowds, the whole thing like some coarse, ghoulish wake. Travis didn't enjoy the crowds, and he didn't much enjoy the art either, but it was a useful way to talk to her friends and extended family.

Not that it had got him anywhere.

He took off the headphones and the noise and hustle of the squad room snapped back in. Next to him, on the wall, were two photographs of Louise, one with pink hair, one – a little older, the image more faded, the corners creased – where her hair was something close to its natural colour. The pink had become part of her brand, but in between public appearances, or when she wasn't on YouTube, her family said she tended to dye it brown or black.

It had been that colour the night she'd vanished.

Alongside the photographs of her was another, this one on a Xeroxed Missing poster. He looked at the image, then at the information listed below it. 'Louise Mason. Description: female, white, 35 years of age, 5' 8, 130 pounds, slim build, black/dark brown hair, brown eyes. Last seen on 09/23/2021.' Under that was Travis's direct line at the Missing Persons Squad. He'd put the poster together two weeks after Louise had vanished, when the search had been kicked up the chain from the 9th Precinct. Until then, and despite her family's protestations, uniforms in the East Village had been wavering between believing she'd deliberately left town, or it being some kind of publicity stunt for her new show. It had taken one conversation with her family for Travis to know that neither of those things was true. She was an only child, she and her parents were close, and there was just no way she'd ever go quiet on them for such a long time without warning them first.

What was harder to say was why, of all the cases he'd had in the past six months, he found this one the hardest to shake. Maybe it was the total lack of decent leads. She'd gone to a fundraiser at a hotel in the East Village on 23 September at 6 p.m., and Travis had a single crappy image from later in the evening, taken from a surveillance camera in an adjacent room, of her talking to – or possibly talking to – an unidentified male in the hotel bar. At almost exactly the same time the camera recorded the image, her cellphone had pinged a tower a block from the hotel. That had been at 9 p.m.

At 9.10 p.m., her cell went completely dead.

He'd gone to the hotel and spoken to the people who worked there, had been down the list of fundraiser attendees and picked up the phone to every single one of them. No one remembered seeing Louise leave that night. He'd returned to the hotel and requisitioned more footage from its cameras, but coverage wasn't as comprehensive as he needed, and the cameras that were there failed to capture any images of Louise exiting the building. So all Travis really had was a rinsed-out image of her in the hotel bar that night, in the fifteen minutes before she'd vanished. And even then it was pretty far from a slam-dunk: he wasn't even one hundred per cent certain it was Louise. She'd had dark hair that night, not pink, which made it harder to be absolutely sure. Plus, all he could see of her was a forehead and browline.

The cell records he pulled for Louise showed no calls or texts from numbers she didn't have listed in her address book, and the only people she'd been in contact with in the hours prior to going missing were friends and relatives Travis had already visited, talked to and crossed off the list. For a while, the lead with the biggest potential seemed to be the guy Louise had started to date a few weeks before her disappearance, and who'd gone to the fundraiser with her that night — but even he'd long since proved worthless. He confirmed to Travis that he'd accompanied her to the fundraiser, but had had to leave when one of his close friends was rushed to the ER. Cell records and GPS data confirmed his story, as well as video from the cameras at the hospital, and a geo-located text he sent to Louise to apologize proved he was still there at 9.31 p.m. By then, twenty minutes had passed since Louise's phone had gone dead.

So maybe, when all of that was taken into consideration, it wasn't so surprising that Travis couldn't let go. This was a search he rarely conducted any more. Louise wasn't some teenage runaway. She didn't have dementia.

She was a genuine unanswered question.

He pushed out from his desk and, joints stiff, right knee creaking, wandered over to the kitchen. There was a machine in the corner that did passable coffee, and as he waited for it to pour, he checked his phone. He'd missed a call while he was watching the video. It was from his ex-wife, Naomi. She'd sent him a follow-up text, then left him a voicemail.

Travis didn't bother reading the text.

He didn't listen to the voicemail either.

Instead, he stared out of the nearest window. It was an oppressive day in mid-December, snow scattering against the glass as a wind rolled in off the East River. The cold played hell with his hips and knees, all screwed up after years of being taken down on the football field. Since his shoulder op, he'd also had to put up with constant pain along his collar bone.

'What's up, Trav?'

Travis looked up to see Amy Houser approaching. She was a smartly dressed cop in her late thirties, with whom Travis had been paired during her first couple of years in the Missing Persons Squad. She'd been a good partner: quiet, respectful, always asking questions, always wanting to learn. They had got drunk one night at a bar near the fish market, and she'd ended up telling Travis all about the father she'd never known. He'd sat quietly and listened. He and Naomi had brought up two kids, their son Mark and their daughter Gabrielle, and Travis had loved both of them with everything he had, so it didn't take a shrink to see through to the subtext: Houser had never had that and, in some small way, Travis had become a surrogate.

'How you doing, Ames?' he said.

'You still on that machine swill, even at the end?'

'It's not the end yet.' He raised the coffee cup to her. 'Salute.'

She laughed as he drank the coffee, the way he smacked his lips as if to tell her it was delicious, then said, 'How you feeling about the big day?'

'I haven't given it much thought,' he lied.

'Sure.' She didn't believe him. 'You celebrating big-style?'

'Is celebrating retirement a thing?'

'You know it is. Especially when you're only forty-five.'

He smiled. 'Your maths ain't up to shit, Houser.'

'What — you're not forty-five?'

'You're only about fifteen years out.'

'You don't look a day over sixty, Trav.' She winked at him.

'Until then,' he said, 'I still got work coming out my ass.'

'Anything in particular?'

'People keep going missing. What can I say?' But Houser knew he was talking about Louise Mason. They'd discussed her a couple of weeks after she first vanished, and again as they ran into each other in the corridors of One Police Plaza once Houser had got a promotion to Major Crimes. Travis barely had a week left on the force and Louise Mason was the only long-term case that was still unsolved.

'I saw you looking at one of her paintings the other day,' Houser said, gesturing towards his work station. 'Some abstract thing I didn't get.'

'It's all abstract things I don't get, Ames.'

'That one was different. It's why I didn't come over and talk to you. You were right in the zone there, Frank, like you'd seen something in it.'

He knew straight away which picture she was talking about. It was called 'Sole' and was the only one of Louise's he really, genuinely understood: a silhouette of a figure looking out from the top of a hill, with the rest of the world gathered in the valley below, apparently unaware of him.

Maybe that was the answer.

Maybe that was why he couldn't let her go.

Because she'd painted his retirement.

'That case is – what? – almost three months old now?' Houser asked, bringing him out of his thoughts. 'You getting rusty in your old age, Trav?'

He smiled at her because he knew she didn't mean it.

'You want to talk about it?' Houser prompted.

'It's fine,' Travis said, taking another mouthful of coffee. 'I'm sort of burned out thinking about it. Maybe I need to let go of her for a while.'

Houser eyed him.

He smiled. 'Something on your mind, Detective?'

'You're just gonna let go of her.'

She didn't need to say anything else.

Because, deep down, both of them knew the truth.

Travis never let go of anyone.

At the same time as Frank Travis was saying goodbye to Amy Houser and walking back to his desk carrying a lukewarm cup of machine coffee, a mile and a half away Nick Tillman was standing at the top of the stairs leading down to the 8th Street subway station, with a burner phone in his hand.

He was calling a number he knew by heart.

He listened to it ring, his eyes constantly moving, watching all the time for faces he recognized.

A click. 'Hello?'

'It's me,' Tillman said.

A pause on the line. Snow swirled and changed direction as the wind picked up. He took a step back, using a doorway as cover from the weather.

'Anything to report?' a woman's voice said.

'Same as before.'

'No change?'

'Nothing.'

Another long pause.

'This Travis guy, is he going to be a problem?'

Tillman shook his head. 'He's out in a week.' He checked up and down the street, then the people coming up the subway steps, ensuring no one could hear what he was going to say next: 'But, don't worry, just in case, I'm going to make absolutely sure he knows where to look.'

'Good,' the woman said simply.

She hung up.

Before

Rebekah took Gareth's phone to a place in Dyker Heights to get it unlocked, pretending she'd forgotten her code. They told her they could do it, but there was a good chance it would reset entirely, and because of the age of the model, everything would be wiped. 'Are you happy to take that chance?' the guy asked her.

'Yes.'

'Are you sure?'

'One hundred per cent,' Rebekah assured him, then took the girls to an ice-cream parlour on 13th Avenue, where she bought Kyra a milkshake and, as Chloe slept in the stroller, listened to her gabbling about a book she'd had read to her at daycare.

Forty-five minutes later, she returned to the store.

'I've managed to save *some* emails,' the guy told her, 'but, as I warned you, a lot of the other stuff has been wiped with the reset. This type of cellphone, nothing's backed up to the Cloud, because it doesn't have that feature – *but* there's a quirk where the email app sometimes retains random messages.'

She took the phone from him. 'Random messages?'

'A mix. You've got emails going back two years, but there are also some that are only a few weeks old. Individual email chains will have been disrupted during the reset, so you might have an email *you* sent, but not the reply you got. That sort of thing. Like I say, the model's old and that means it's got some weird, sometimes unpredictable functionality.'

Once she'd worked out where the Email icon was, she slumped: only eleven messages had made it beyond the reset and, at first glance, none appeared to be of any immediate interest. Her eyes switched to the address for the account, whodges@pyremail.com, then to the name alongside it.

Willard Hodges.

Who the hell was that?

She thanked the guy and headed home. As soon as she got through the door, she set the girls up in the living room with some toys, then retreated to the kitchen and started going through the cell. Most of the emails seemed to be marketing messages: loyalty programmes for clothing stores in the city that Rebekah had never heard of; an email about conference facilities at a vineyard upstate; another from a ticket company with availability for Giants games; confirmation of a sign-up to a porn site. She looked at the porn sign-up: that certainly wasn't beyond Gareth, but the rest seemed less likely. His company paid for a corporate suite at the Giants stadium, and he went to a ton of games every year with clients, so why would he bother trying to source his own tickets? He didn't drink wine either, so the vineyard seemed like a write-off, and the clothes stores were all high end, not the type of places he would normally shop. That didn't mean it *wasn't* him – he could be using an alias – but Rebekah's certainty had started to fade.

She put down the phone and grabbed her laptop, just as Kyra wandered through to the kitchen.

'Hungry, Mommy.'

'Okay, sweetheart, just give me a sec, all right?'

Kyra started pulling on Rebekah's leg, her foot, anything she could get her small arms around, and when that failed, her mom's attention still fixed on the Google search for Willard Hodges, she simply stared Rebekah down. Eventually, Rebekah stared back. *If looks could kill.*

She broke into a smile, the moment giving her a brief respite from the phone, from the burden of suspicion, and she lifted Kyra onto her lap and kissed the top of her head. Through the kitchen door, she checked on Chloe: she was on her mat, staring up at her mobile, her legs and arms going. Kyra started bashing the laptop's keyboard with her hands.

'Hold on, sweetheart, hold on,' Rebekah said, and set Kyra down again. Onscreen was the Willard Hodges search: the top hit was a Wikipedia page about a politician from the 1820s. The rest were just as irrelevant: ancestry websites, a few Facebook pages, defunct blogs.

I've got to stop before I drive myself crazy.

She snapped the laptop shut.

But she couldn't stop.

That night, Gareth arrived home late again. She rolled over to face him, but didn't open her eyes, smelling the whisky and cigarettes on him.

Inside ten minutes, he was snoring.

She lay there, determined not to do what she was telling herself she should: she didn't want more suspicion, more mistrust. She just wanted to forget she'd ever found the phone.

Except she couldn't.

Eventually she sat up and flipped back the covers. Gareth didn't stir. Padding into the girls' room, she checked they were both asleep, then wound her way downstairs. His jacket, his wallet, the keys to the house, and his work cell were on the table near the front door. She picked up the phone, popped out the charging cable and started to hunt around on it. She'd done it once already, in the weeks before she'd found the cellphone in the car, but she spent longer going through his Contacts this time, through his recent calls, through his email, internet and camera. There was no one called Willard Hodges in his address book, no emails from the account on the phone, no texts from the number. Gareth used Dropbox for work, which she checked, and then she went through his calendar to see if anything stood out. Just meetings, one after another. He could have used the names of the people he worked with to disguise something else: a non-work meeting; an hour in a motel; a woman; an affair.

Or maybe I'm just being paranoid.

The cell she'd found in the car might belong to someone he was doing business with, or one of his friends, or someone to whom he'd given a lift. Gareth would drive the Cherokee over to Giants games once or twice a month with clients. He often talked about giving rides there and back to people who lived along the route, in Jersey City and Hoboken. What if the phone had innocently fallen out of a pocket at some point?

What if it hadn't?

It was the age of the phone that bothered her most: she seriously doubted any of the slick-suited assholes Gareth worked with would have been caught dead with a cell as old or as basic as the one she'd found, but it also made no practical sense. So much of his job, so much of the work he did with clients and that they did with him, was reliant on the Cloud.

The phone she'd found barely even had the web.

Defeated, she headed back to bed.

13

Rebekah looked at the padlock on the floor, barely daring to believe she'd succeeded, then flipped back the hasp on the hostel door.

Ahead of her, a corridor extended out, dusty, semi-lit by the building's windows.

She hurried inside and stopped at the first door. It was a plain bedroom: two beds, two wardrobes. But the beds had blankets on them. She would never have guessed that the sight of something so simple would elicit such a profound sense of relief, but she let herself breathe it in before she checked the wardrobes. They were empty.

Returning to the corridor, she discovered that two of the doors led into poky identical bathrooms, and one at the end into a simple kitchen. In the corner, there was a generator, but it looked like it had been disconnected for the winter: it was sitting away from the wall and part of the back had been removed. If it had been working, she could have fired up the hot water and taken a shower in one of the bathrooms, but any disappointment she felt soon dissolved: when she checked the cabinets, she found teabags, coffee, some cans of chicken soup, two rows of canned clam chowder, some beef barley soup and a pack of root beer. She started to gather them up, feeling another intense rush of elation: these discoveries were so small, so perfunctory, but it felt like she'd struck a vein of gold.

After she'd loaded all of the food into the Cherokee, she went back for blankets, then switched her attention to a mattress. She pulled one off the nearest bed and dragged it out to the car. Once it was loaded, a second thought came to her: what about Johnny?

He'd need a mattress too.

This time, because of everything else she'd put into the Jeep's trunk, she couldn't get Johnny's in. She shoved at it as hard as she could, face red, but it kept folding and springing back to her. Eventually, she paused, watching the second mattress slide out, over the tailgate onto the damp grass.

Did she need a mattress for Johnny?

Am I really going to find him alive?

She pushed the thought down before it could take hold, and began trying again, getting under the mattress this time and using a shoulder. It worked. It wobbled one way and the other, then finally slid over the headrests into the back seat.

She stopped for a second, getting her breath back, before returning inside and taking the stairs to the first floor.

The rooms were almost an exact match to their counterparts on the ground floor, but in one of the last, she spotted something different. A wedge of paper, bent in half and placed under a leg on one of the beds.

Something printed on it had caught her eye.

She bent down and rocked the paper out from under the frame. As the bed tilted towards her, uneven now, she unfolded the piece of paper, its faded surface covered with years of dust and grime. It was an old leaflet, printed for tourists back in the eighties – and on the back there was a map.

It was of the island before Hurricane Gloria had changed its entire topography, but it would do just fine. It showed its layout, some of the routes around it, the beaches and dunes, the estuaries and marshes, and the full extent of the forest where she and Johnny had last been together.

As she left the hostel with a microwave and a kettle, for the first time in forty-eight hours she was feeling vaguely positive. She still needed to check out the second hostel, but it was getting darker and it could wait for now.

Today had been enough of a success.

All of a sudden she felt she could exist on the island for a few days, maybe even a week. If she could somehow get the electricity working at the store, if she could find a supply of drinking water, if she could get some heating going, a kettle boiling, a microwave cooking, she could survive until a rescue came.

Because it had to arrive soon.

Noella was her best friend. Gareth was the man she'd spent twelve years with and she was the mother of his children. They would have reported her missing by now.

Well, Noella definitely will have.

She thought about Gareth, about their turbulent history, about the phone she'd found in the Jeep. She thought about where the name Willard Hodges had eventually led her.

And, as she did, she wondered to herself: Would it be easier for Gareth if she never made it home alive?

Before

The morning after Rebekah had checked Gareth's work phone and found nothing, she went to see Noella.

Growing up, Noe had lived in the same neighbourhood, and had dated Mike for a time in high school. Even after they'd split, she would still hang around at the house, and when Rebekah finally made the move to New York, they began spending more time together, and quickly grew close.

These days, she was more like a sister than a friend.

'Why don't you confront him about it?' Noella asked.

They were standing on the front steps of her house, which she shared with her boyfriend, a UPS delivery driver called Tommy. Noella's ex-husband had been a malicious prick and, as well as having to contend with him, she'd also had to deal with cysts on both ovaries, which had made attempts to start a family a long, torturous journey, mapped with heartbreak and, ultimately, failure. It always seemed cruel to Rebekah that Noella had had to endure such a struggle: she would have been such a great mom, and had been so good with Kyra and Chloe. Any hardness she carried, calcified in the fallout from some of the awful relationships she'd had, and in her inability to have children, never showed when she was around the girls. In those moments, it all clicked, like puzzle pieces falling into place.

'Bek?' Noella pressed. 'Just ask him about it.'

'I want the truth.'

'Exactly.'

'I want to know more before I confront him.'

Noella frowned, her blue eyes narrowing, her coarse dark hair shifting in the breeze. 'Are you scared of him?' She paused, watching Rebekah. 'You're not scared of him, are you?'

'No.'

'You said he's never hit you.'

'He hasn't.'

'Because if you're scared of him, I'll come with –'

'He doesn't scare me, Noe.'

'So why go to the trouble of doing the detective shit? Just wait until he gets home, then tell him you found a phone, and have him explain his way out of it. If he's stumbling around even for a second, you'll know he's guilty. Take it from me. Most cheaters aren't good liars.'

'He might not be lying.'

Noe shrugged. 'How are you going to know if you don't ask?'

'I want to catch him in the lie.'

'Why bother?'

'I'm not going to destroy my marriage on the basis of a hunch, Noe.'

She grimaced. 'You've had that phone for nine months. Think about that. Nine *months*. It's time you knew the truth – about him, and about the woman he's seeing.'

'I need to be absolutely sure.'

'How are you going to be sure if you never confront him? The facts are staring you in the face, Bek. Gareth's a good-looking guy. He's confident, he's charming. He's getting home late at night, stinking of booze and perfume. The guy's cheating on you. You know it, I know it.'

'I *don't* know it. Not for sure.'

Noella looked at Rebekah as if she was the most naïve woman on the planet. 'Bek, he's getting home in the middle of the night –'

'I know. I heard you.'

Noella eyed her, clearly conflicted as to whether she should say anything else, then shrugged and waved at the girls in the back seat of the Cherokee. 'Just promise me this,' she said, from the side of her mouth while smiling at Kyra. 'If he's cheated on you, don't forgive him.'

'Of course I won't.'

'Yeah, well, I've said the same thing a few times. You catch a man in the act, whether it's in the emails he's sending or with his dick out in some motel, you always go off like a firework. You think, *Screw him.* You think, *That son of a bitch is never going to darken my doorway again.* Then some time passes and you discover how lonely it is on your own, and he's turning up at your house, crying, begging you to forgive him, and this little voice in your head suddenly says, "Maybe he really means it. Maybe he's changed." You still tell him no, but by then the doubts have kicked in. And when the girls –' she pointed to the Jeep '– are up crying at two in the morning because they've got colds or a fever or whatever, and you can hardly function because you're just so damn *tired*, I bet the idea of someone's support – especially someone who knows the kids, whom they're comfortable with – will be pretty welcome. And, before you know it, you let him in again, start to believe he's changed, and then he's acting like nothing ever happened. But here's the thing: something *did* happen. And if it happened once, Bek, it'll happen again.'

'I get it, Noe. I do.'

'You don't know how hard it is.'

'I can take a guess.'

But Noella was already shaking her head. 'I'm not talking about having some asshole cheat on you.'

'So what are you talking about?'

'I'm talking about surviving on your own.'

2

Break

Before

Rebekah first told her dad that she wanted to be a doctor when she was fifteen. He said she'd be better off following him into a career as a cop, because she was – in his words – 'tough and liked asking questions'. After he'd left the army, being a cop was all he understood, so it wasn't a surprise he saw it that way, but Rebekah often wondered if the seven years she'd spent apart from her father, in a different country, had also clouded his view of what she was capable of: he didn't think she had the endurance to make it as a doctor, because he wasn't aware of her potential. Or perhaps there was a much simpler reason: her father loved her – and he never wanted her to feel the disappointment Johnny had.

From as far back as Rebekah could remember, Johnny had always wanted to be a writer, his bedrooms constantly stacked with old paperbacks. He loved science fiction and horror stories, but his real passion was history: his heroes were James Michener and Ken Follett, and his favourite novel was *The Pillars of the Earth*. After high school, he went on to study English at Brooklyn College; once he graduated, he returned home and wrote the great American novel on the veranda at the back of the house, a 700-page epic set in 1624 when the Dutch first landed at the southern tip of modern-day Manhattan. And after it was written, after he'd imagined himself on the bestseller lists, on tours around the country, at a table in a store signing copy after copy, he began to accumulate a pile of rejection letters a foot high. For Johnny, the reality had been crushing: eighteen months after it was finished, he consigned the novel to a dusty box under his bed, and began working behind the counter of an electronics store in Bay Ridge that made the same every year as Radio Shack made in an hour. At the time, Rebekah didn't understand how her father must have felt, but when she finally became a mother she did: we want our kids to have the best jobs and the perfect life – but we don't want to see them fail while trying.

In the end, though, Rebekah didn't fail.

A year after she met Gareth in a bar on Madison Avenue, she was accepted to NYU's School of Medicine. Four years after that, she began a residency at New York Presbyterian, and just before her first Christmas as a resident, Gareth took her to a restaurant with views over Central Park and asked her to marry him.

During their five-year engagement, they often talked about setting a date but they were both so focused on their careers it was a conversation that tended to disappear into the background. But then, after Mike died in the car accident, it was as if something had shaken loose: the wedding became far more important, something definite in a time of great uncertainty.

They were married in a church in Dyker Heights. Rebekah's father always maintained he was Irish Catholic, which was partly true in as much as their surname was Murphy and his grandparents had come from Donegal. But there had never been much celebration of Henry's heritage at home, and their mother's family, according to what Johnny had overheard their father saying on the telephone one night, were Jehovah's Witnesses from Essex.

Even so, a Catholic ceremony made Gareth and his family happy, and it made her dad happy too. Rebekah hadn't thought much about it at the time, but it seemed so obvious when he fell sick soon after. Perhaps, on some deep level, he'd felt the illness in him, an eel writhing inside a net; perhaps he'd suddenly caught a clear vision of his impending mortality, and returning to church was the first step to whatever came next.

'It's been so long since I've been,' he'd said to Rebekah, as they arrived in the car. 'I hope he can forgive me.'

Rebekah looked at him from beneath the veil, uncertain whom he meant. 'Who are you talking about, Dad?'

She could hear the panic in her voice, as she wondered if her father was losing it, just seconds before he walked her down the aisle on the most important day of her life.

But then, when he didn't reply, she followed his eyeline towards the spaces above the main doors and saw who he was referring to.

He with a capital H.

A statue of Christ was gazing back at them.

'Don't worry,' Rebekah said, and squeezed her father's hand, wondering if it might be nerves. He'd told her in the days beforehand that he wasn't concerned about his speech, but maybe that had been a lie to protect her and stop her worrying. 'You've got nothing to ask forgiveness for, Dad.'

It occurred to her then that she had no real idea if that were true or not. She didn't know how many men he'd killed in Vietnam. She didn't know how many people he'd shot as a cop. She didn't believe he would ever seek any pleasure in either, but she knew there had been a lot that Henry had chosen not to bring home when she was growing up. He would tell them enough about Vietnam, enough about being a cop to keep them sated, but in his eyes, their mother leaving had always been enough for them to cope with. That, too, was a story Rebekah knew her father had downplayed – the real tale of her parents' marriage and why her mother had left. She often wondered if *he* was the reason Fiona had walked out on them, but she'd never found any evidence of that. Her father had always said Fiona's decision had come out of nowhere, and eventually it became much easier for Rebekah to blame the whole thing on her.

In the end, the wedding was perfect. At the reception her father gave a warm, funny speech that everybody loved. He didn't do much public speaking but Rebekah remembered thinking how good at it he was, how natural. He was witty, warm, his jokes a little predictable but delivered with love. He talked about Fiona, but only in passing, which was fine by Rebekah, and when they were eating afterwards, Gareth turned to her, kissed her cheek, and said, 'I'm so lucky to be a part of your family.'

That was the kind of thing Gareth would say a lot, especially in the early days of their relationship. He got on well with his own parents, even though his father could be tough, but he really connected with Henry. After the wedding was over, they'd found Rebekah's father asleep in the corner, drunk, exhausted, and Gareth was the one that helped him to the car.

It was easy to forget those times.

After Rebekah and Gareth's marriage fell away beneath them, it was simpler to believe those moments had never been there between them. But they had. For a long time, their relationship had been good, loving, its foundations stable.

But then the rot had set in.

And, before long, she'd realized she didn't know Gareth at all.

14

As soon as she got back to the general store, Rebekah spent ten minutes awkwardly trying to open the main door from the inside, so she didn't have to keep going through the window. Once she was done with that, she dragged in the mattresses, the blankets, the kettle and the microwave, then noticed something else: the leak in the ceiling had stopped.

She felt good: she had a bed, she had food lined up on the counter, she'd managed to find a faucet at the back of the bait-and-tackle place, hidden by grass, and – by the time the sun had gone down – she'd filled a bucket with water.

But, before she went to sleep, the adrenalin wore off, and she was back to thinking about the girls again. As that began to overwhelm her, she pictured Johnny, and spiralled even further. It was the end of her second day alone, and her third full day on the island. It was two nights since anyone, except a brother she couldn't find, had seen her. No one was coming to rescue her. *If they were coming, they'd already be here.*

I'm trapped.

She got up and went to the door, the ocean just about visible in the darkness, everything else imperviously dark. Somewhere, she thought she saw a flicker of light – there, and gone again – and she stayed exactly where she was for an hour, watching the blackness, just in case it came back.

It didn't.

But, still, she couldn't quite let go of the idea, the hope that a boat might be close by, or in the channel somewhere, within sight of her, so she grabbed the flashlight and headed out. Johnny had told her that Main Street and the harbour were wired into an old electrical grid, built back in the seventies when the island was still a tourist trap, with the original intention of expanding it out into other areas. That was why there was no diesel generator at the store. The power came from somewhere else. She just had to find the switch.

If she could get the lights on in the store, she could leave them on through the night, as a kind of beacon. Then she thought of something else: she'd noted on the map that there was an old lighthouse out on the east coast. Could the lantern be working in *that*? If not, could she get it going?

She dismissed the idea.

Most lighthouses were operated remotely now, and if it was still working, Rebekah would have seen it. The island, for the most part, was flat. As soon as it got dark, nothing – even Nuyáhshá – could obscure a glow as bright as a lighthouse lantern.

She moved to her right, in the direction of the harbour, following the back of the store. She found herself behind the bait-and-tackle place and, for the first time, wondered whether there were any fishing rods inside. She hadn't considered it before, because she didn't have a clue how to fish, but if, and when, she ran short of food again, maybe she'd have to teach herself.

Yeah, because fishing is so easy, she thought dismally.

For now she didn't have to worry about it, so concentrated instead on the road that sloped down from here to the harbour, the entrance to the wharf padlocked from the other side. Rebekah believed she could probably get over if she had to – the dividing line between the rest of the island and the harbour was a simple chain-link fence – but there was just an empty parking lot, the long jetty and a harbourmaster's shack beyond.

She moved back along Main Street.

The switch for the grid had to be somewhere close. She shone the flashlight right and left, but it didn't have as much impact out in the open, and it started to dawn on her how little of her surroundings she could make out.

She thought again about the gas station, about the clicking noise she'd heard, and the memory sent a cold finger up her spine.

I don't want to be out here any more.

She hurried back to the store.

I hate this darkness.

15

That night, she dreamed.

She'd had a recurring nightmare for a while, didn't remember when it started, only that it had arrived and never gone away. Sometimes it would slide into the background and stay there for a time – but, eventually, it always crept back into the light.

It started with Rebekah in a corridor, many floors up in an apartment block, an unobtrusive tan carpet beneath her feet, cream paint on the walls.

The door to an apartment was open. It was always on her left, always a pale blue, and always open just a crack. Faint light leaked out into the corridor from inside, and she saw the same *127* halfway up the door, its *7* fractionally askew. Most people wouldn't have noticed it, but Rebekah did. Every time she approached, she looked at the *7* and thought, *Seven is meant to be a lucky number.*

It was an expensive apartment, open, with huge windows looking out at the Manhattan skyline. There was a mezzanine level on her right, a glass and steel staircase leading up to it, and a black and chrome kitchen below that. Off to her left there was a wall of glass bricks, the distorted shape of a bed behind it.

Music started playing.

As soon as it did, everything changed. She stood in the doorway and felt a sudden overwhelming sense of fear, as if she'd wandered into a place she was never meant to. Now it was a fully fledged nightmare: she could feel herself struggling to breathe. When she tried to turn around she couldn't. Her feet had sunk into the carpet, and she suddenly had no shoes on, and the fibres were clawing at her toes, wriggling like the whole thing was alive, wrapping around her feet and ankles, pinning her to the floor.

I think you should stay.

Always the same voice.

Not male or female, just there, behind her.

I think you should stay, Rebekah.

She couldn't turn, couldn't see who was speaking to her, but she didn't want to stay. She so desperately didn't want to stay. Not here, not ever.

I think you should stay.

Please let me go.

I think you should stay.

Please.

And then she was crying.

Begging. Screaming.

Please let me –

She woke up.

It was morning. She'd sweated beneath the blankets, and as she threw them off her and shuffled to the edge of the mattress, she looked around the store and tried not to think of the dream. It had been the worst version of it that she'd had for a while: more desperate, more lucid, as if she could still feel its residue in her skin, even awake. *It's over now*, she told herself, but the thought didn't bring her any comfort.

Rebekah knew that, sooner or later, it would be back.

Like the island itself, there was no escape.

Before

Rebekah did nothing with the cellphone for a couple more days, trying to figure out how to play things. Frustrated, she tried to remember why she'd waited nine months to get the phone unlocked, but just one look at her daughters, both of them so small, so innocent, so reliant on her and Gareth, reminded her. She hadn't wanted to take the chance of destroying her marriage before Chloe had even arrived in the world.

So, was it better to live in denial?

Maybe it was then, but not any more. She couldn't stop thinking about the cellphone now, couldn't help wondering if it belonged to Gareth, and the not knowing was tearing her apart. The problem was, if she left it somewhere for him to find, just so she could gauge his reaction, he could deny everything, anyway, because there was nothing to tie him to it. No emails, certainly no texts or calls. Even the name associated with it was a dead end.

Rebekah still had no idea who Willard Hodges was.

It was also possible that it really *wasn't* Gareth's phone, but she knew she needed to know either way, even if she hated the idea of what the wrong answer might do to them. The thought kept coming to her that, if it turned out as she feared, Chloe and even Kyra would never know a time when the four of them had lived together. The portrait of a fractured family would be normal to them, how it was, how it had always been.

In the end, though, none of it really mattered.

At the start of April, four days after Noella had told Rebekah that she needed to confront Gareth about the cellphone, Rebekah arrived home from taking the girls to a market at Prospect Park, and found Gareth slumped at the kitchen table. He'd already opened a bottle of bourbon.

Rebekah frowned. 'What are you doing here?'

'I took the afternoon off,' he said quietly.

Kyra ran over to her father before Rebekah could ask why, and he took her in his arms, sitting her on his lap. He leaned into her, smelt her hair, listened to her as she described eating cotton candy, smiled when he was supposed to and asked her questions. Eventually, he glanced at Rebekah for the first time since they'd got home: he had tears in his eyes. The sight of them hit her, like a punch. She backed up, bumping against the countertop.

'You wanna watch some TV, sweetheart?' he said to Kyra. His voice was small inside the kitchen. In the stroller, parked in the space between them, Chloe was sleeping soundly. Gareth went into the living room with Kyra and set her up in front of the television. When he returned to the kitchen, he was wiping his tears with the edge of his sleeve. He sat down in the same chair.

'What's going on, Gareth?' she asked, the words like dust in her mouth. She knew exactly what was going on.

She'd seen him cry only once in all the time they'd been together. That had been a shimmer, like a change of light, in the moments after Kyra had been born. She'd put it down to his upbringing, to the blood in his veins: although she'd always liked his father, he was hard on Gareth, a perfectionist, uncompromising.

'I'm sorry,' he said quietly.

'Sorry for what?'

He swallowed, said nothing, just stared at her.

She was carrying a bag on her left shoulder, the strap passing between her breasts. The pockets were overflowing with creams, loose rubber teats for the bottles, nappies. As she thought of the word *nappies*, she thought of the last time the two of them had talked like this – standing in virtually the same places in the same room, four months before – as Gareth had told her, pettily, that they were called *diapers* in America. She'd traded so many British words for US versions since moving to the States, but just as many – like *Mummy* – she'd never quite let go of, even when Kyra called her *Mommy* in return. She lifted the strap of the bag over her head, set it down, and – slowly, as if pulling old bones out of a burial site – she went into the pocket of her coat.

Cell, not *mobile*.

That had been one change she'd made.

She put the phone down on the table between them.

'Is this what you're sorry for, Gareth?'

16

An hour after getting up, she finally found the switch for the electrical grid: it was in a fenced area, cut into a bank, a quarter-mile out of Main Street.

Something had been removed from it.

A battery of some kind.

Rebekah broke the locks on the security fence, anyway, and tried pulling and resetting the switch – but there was no buzz, nothing came to life. Without the power source, she couldn't turn on the lights in the store. She couldn't use a heater if she ever found one. Worse, she'd hauled the kettle and microwave from the hostel for no reason.

She looked down at herself, despondent, in the same clothes for the fourth day running, and thought of her girls. What would they be doing now?

Who would be looking after them?

She jumped into the car and headed back to the forest, trying to keep her mind occupied. She walked its trails for the entire afternoon, using the map from the hostel to find new areas she hadn't explored. At one stage, she became scared of getting lost, and then – for a while – actually did, but in the end she found her way back to the parking area. She got into the Jeep, tired and ground down, the sun burning out in the sky. Her legs were like lead. She was starving. Her voice was hoarse from repeatedly calling Johnny's name.

And she still hadn't found him.

*

She spent all of the next day outside the store, watching the sea.

She hardly moved from sunrise to sunset.

That night, after eating from one of the cans, the leak in the ceiling slowly returned, and she became convinced she could hear the faint chug of a boat. Springing to her feet, she rushed to the window again and stared into the blackness, forcing herself to see something. The harder she stared, the more she remembered from two nights before when she'd thought she'd glimpsed a light in the ocean. Could it *really* have been a boat?

Or am I seeing and hearing things now?

She definitely couldn't *see* anything tonight, and the noise she thought she could hear kept fading in and out with the wind, making her even more uncertain that she'd actually heard anything at all. After forty minutes, she retreated to the mattress, and felt like she was going to cry.

But then she heard it again.

She jumped to her feet and, this time, ran for the door. Yanking it open, she sprinted to the back of the store, which faced out to the ocean, and peered into the night. When the chug of the boat failed to materialize, she began furiously waving her flashlight from side to side above her.

Nothing.

No sound, no light out to sea.

Finally, she gave up, feeling ridiculous, and retreated inside. And then, after a while, she thought she heard the boat again and rushed out to the back of the store for a second time. And for a second time, there was no boat and no lights in the water.

She went back to bed, tried to sleep, to close her eyes and tune out the rhythm of the sea – but then she thought she heard the boat again.

She raced back outside.

Still nothing.

It went on like that all night.

Before

Rebekah pushed the cellphone further across the kitchen table, until it was right under Gareth's nose, but there was no reaction in his face.

He played with the glass of bourbon in front of him. The liquid rocked towards the rim of the tumbler, some of it spilling over his fingers. 'You weren't supposed to find that cell,' he muttered quietly.

'No shit. How did you know I had?'

'Kyra told me she overheard you talking to Noella. She asked me if I had a secret phone that Mommy wasn't supposed to know about.'

For some reason, Rebekah smiled. She'd been worried about the ways in which confronting Gareth might affect the girls in the future – but, in the end, Kyra was how Gareth realized he'd been caught.

'When did you find it?' he asked her.

'Ten months ago.'

He frowned. 'Why did you hold on to it for so long?'

'Why do you *think*, Gareth?'

Because of our girls.

Our marriage. Our life together.

'I'm sorry,' he said again.

'For what?'

His eyes pleaded with her not to make him say it. Rebekah's head was buzzing. She was hot, could feel pain in her chest and tears coming, a wave gradually washing into shore.

Don't cry.

'I never meant . . .' He stopped.

'You never meant to hurt me? It's a bit late for that, isn't it?'

'She was just . . .'

Gareth paused, but those three words were enough to cut Rebekah in two. *She.* Did Rebekah want to find out who she was?

Did it even matter now?

'I was just so consumed by work. It happened without me . . .' He swallowed, unable to look at her now. 'It just happened. I kept thinking, You need to put an end to this. This has to stop. But I couldn't.'

Rebekah blinked. *Don't cry.*

Not for him.

Not for this.

'We worked on this project together and . . .' He faded out again.

You're such a cliché, she thought. *You worked on a project together. It just happened. You tried to stop it but you couldn't. And now, months later, you've finally got the balls to tell me – but only because I found your phone. Only because you knew you'd been rumbled.*

She didn't say any of that, just looked at him. It was clear that her silence was eating him up, so she prolonged it, enjoying the narrowness of his face, pinched by the pain and guilt of what he was being forced to drag out. She looked down at Chloe, sound asleep in the stroller, only weeks into her life and oblivious to everything.

This time, Rebekah couldn't swallow the lump in her throat.

It was obvious now why there were emails on the cell from clothing stores where Gareth had never shopped – because he wasn't shopping for himself. Rebekah had eventually googled the vineyard he'd had a message from and discovered it was also a hotel, which explained that too.

'Did you two have a nice time upstate?'

He couldn't even meet her eye.

'The hotel looked *very* posh,' she said, twisting the knife. 'I was trying to remember when you took me there.'

But they both knew the answer.

He hadn't.

Before Chloe, she'd talked to him about getting away for a weekend, the two of them and Kyra, somewhere far out of the city where there was no traffic and no noise, and they could forget about their jobs for a while. But he always had some excuse. Too tired. Too much work. Too expensive.

'And she was a Giants fan,' Rebekah said, a final jerk of the blade. 'That must have been great for you. I mean, I never *did* understand American football, did I?'

'I'm sorry, Bek,' he said, scarcely audible now.

'Why Willard Hodges?'

He shrugged.

'Where did that name come from?'

'I just made it up,' he said, but something lingered in his face, and she couldn't tell if it was contrition or if he was concealing something else.

This time, she didn't have the will to find out.

'You need to leave,' Rebekah said, steel back in her voice.

'Bek, hold on.'

'I want you out of the house.'

'Look, Bek, we need to –'

'I want you out of the house by tonight.'

'Bek, come on.'

'I don't want to see your face, Gareth,' she said, and sucked in a long, painful breath. 'I can't bear to look at you any more.'

17

The warning light pinged into life.

Rebekah was heading back out to the forest to look for Johnny, and had been so consumed by thoughts of her brother that she'd overlooked something else.

Gas.

The needle was already below the quarter mark. There might be enough to get her through another day, maybe two at a stretch, but she wouldn't get beyond day seven or eight on the island without filling up. That meant she had no choice: she had to figure out a way to get the pumps working at the gas station – and that meant breaking more locks on more doors.

The prospect weighed heavily on her and, as she drove, she struggled to stay awake. She hadn't slept at all during the night because she'd kept hearing the boat – or thought she had – and now the fatigue was like carrying an extra body strapped to her back. Even on the short drive from the store, out to the gas station, she could feel herself drifting, eyes getting heavier, body sinking. In the end, after her head tipped forward for a split second, she decided to pull over.

She crawled onto the back seat.

Almost immediately, she fell asleep.

By the time she woke up it was early afternoon, and the sunshine of the morning had been replaced by rain. It tapped gently against the roof and, for a while, Rebekah lay there listening, wondering what Kyra and Chloe would be doing now. It was Thursday, 4 November, according to the readout on the Jeep's dash. That meant they should have gone to daycare, or Noella might have had them, or maybe Gareth had taken some time off from work to look after them. Since October, she'd taken the girls to the park every day, so Kyra could kick around autumn leaves. She loved the crunching sound they made. Maybe Rebekah would have been doing that with the girls if she was home right now. Maybe she and Kyra would have been playing games in the living room while she bounced Chloe on her knee.

Maybe.

She wondered what Gareth would do with the girls at night. Would he have moved back into the brownstone, as if Rebekah had never kicked him out? She pictured him in their bed, playing with the girls, making them laugh, the three of them already starting to forget Rebekah existed. She knew it was absurd – she'd only been away from them for six nights – but she couldn't stop. A parade of images passed in front of her eyes, snapshots of normality in which the girls were grown-up: she saw Kyra on her graduation day with only Gareth alongside her, his hair salt-and-pepper grey; she saw Chloe as a ten-year-old playing soccer at school, looking around for Rebekah and finding only Gareth on the sidelines; and then she pictured a moment, equally irrational, when they forgot her altogether, the mention of her name meeting nothing except blank expressions.

In her head, the girls didn't remember their mother at all.

Just as Rebekah didn't remember hers.

18

At the gas station, she left the car next to one of the pumps and walked to the back of the office. Again, she took the jack with her and, again, she attacked the door's lock, her technique refined after her efforts at the hostel. After a couple of minutes, it pinged off and landed in a patch of weed-broken asphalt.

As she picked it up, she glanced to her left.

That was the direction the clicking sound had come from.

. The abandoned properties, built on a slope between the gas station and the sea, looked like they'd once been vacation homes. The windows that weren't boarded up were dark and smudged with salt, like eyes with cataracts. Trees grew wild and untamed in the yards. Grass swayed long. From a certain angle, it was as if the houses were old wooden ships sinking in an ocean of green, their exteriors pitted with holes that might have been barnacles. Was it something on the houses clicking? Dislodged guttering? Loose clapboards? Her eyes lingered: she could look inside them if she *really* wanted to find the source of the noise, and maybe there would be supplies too. But, hard as it was to explain, she didn't want to. Something about the island, its ruin, its crushing sense of loneliness, was written into it. It was as if tragedy was chained to every empty property, like a ghost.

She moved inside the forecourt building.

There were two rooms.

The first looked out at the pumps, where there was a sliding window, a counter, a cash register, and some metal shelves stacked thinly with goods.

Oil. Brake fluid. Antifreeze.

No food or water.

Rebekah moved further in and saw, on a shelf under the counter, an old manual credit-card imprinter, and a pile of carbon receipts. She'd found a similar one in the general store. It made perfect sense out here: with no phone lines, there was no wired internet, and outside Helena, the cellphone signal was patchy. A digital card reader would have been useless.

Backing out, she moved into the second room.

It was larger but equally plain, a desk in one corner, a huge bookcase in the other, its shelves weighed down with manuals and reference tomes about everything from cars to aeroplanes. To Rebekah's surprise, the rest of the room had been turned into a bedroom-cum-kitchen: a torn mattress lay on top of a bed frame; next to that a cardboard box doubled as a nightstand; there was a lamp, a fold-out camping table, an old television, a DVD player and a stack of discs. Beyond all of those there was a portable closet, the front zipped up, and a rusty outside grill that had obviously been brought inside for the winter.

Rebekah stared at the bed, at the books, at the pile of action movies, and wondered why a person would choose to live like this, in such isolation, for seven months every year. *Maybe it's not the same person who comes back*, she thought, but even if the person manning the gas station changed for every new season, this must have been a tough existence. On many days, even in June and July, when the island might get some day-trippers coming to see the whales, or between August and October when the fishermen arrived to trawl for salmon, it was likely the person manning the gas station wouldn't see anyone. How did they bear it? Why would they want to? Were they escaping something back home? Or were they drawn to the island for some other reason?

Did this place harbour a secret?

She stood there for a while, thinking of her own secrets, her home – then switched her attention back to the portable closet. She unzipped it. Inside, all the clothes were male – a set of dark overalls, a couple of old wool sweaters, two T-shirts, oil-stained pants.

It would do. She could now wash all the clothes she'd been wearing for six days and not have to sit naked as they dried. She took the sweaters, T-shirts and pants off the hangers, then turned her attention to a red switch on a white plate, just inside the door. A ribbon of masking tape had been stuck under it, with 'GEN' written on it.

She felt a flutter of excitement and flicked it down.

There was a clunk somewhere in the walls, a sound like an old engine firing up, and the lights buzzed into life. She rushed through to the room at the front and looked at the pumps.

The readouts had blinked and reset.

It works.

Something actually works.

She hurried out, popped open the Jeep's gas cap, and grabbed the nozzle from the pump. For a second, she held it just short of the Jeep, scared that it wouldn't work after all, nervous about even trying. But then she inserted the nozzle and squeezed the trigger.

Gas hummed beneath her hands.

She smiled, saw her reflection in the pump's readout, felt crazy for finding such joy in the simple act of pumping gas, but hung on to it. Since that first night, there had been so few of these moments.

Afterwards, when the tank was full, she headed back inside to switch off the generator – and, as she exited, something caught her eye.

She'd almost missed it.

It was on a shelf, above her eyeline, obscured behind some oil containers. She dragged a stool out from under the counter, climbed onto it and shifted the oil to one side.

There, hidden, was what looked like a cellphone from the nineties.

Except it wasn't.

It was a handheld radio.

Before

For the first couple of months, Gareth lived out of a suitcase in a Jersey hotel. He would call Rebekah every night, or he would text, but whenever she saw his number flash up, she ignored it.

In response, he started coming to the house.

He'd stand there on the front steps, jabbing at the buzzer until she was forced to answer the door, worried that the noise would wake the girls.

'You've got to stop this, Gareth,' she said one night, three weeks after he'd moved out. His car was parked awkwardly against the kerb, the front tyre almost mounting it, and he looked like he'd just crawled out of bed.

'Please, Bek.' His eyes glistened.

Please take me back.

In spite of herself, she felt a flicker of anguish for him. 'You made your choice, Gareth.' She swallowed her emotion. 'This is your fault.'

'I know,' he said, beaten down, defeated. 'I know.'

'You can see the girls any time, I've told you that, but only when you stop calling me all day, every day. I don't want to keep picking up my phone and finding a hundred missed calls from you, asking for forgiveness. If you want to see the girls, that's when you text or call me. That's how it's got to work now. You text or call and we arrange a time. Is that clear?'

He nodded.

She pushed the door shut and stood there, listening to his footsteps fade away. Then, although she fought the urge, she began to sob uncontrollably.

The new arrangement worked for a few weeks, and whenever he came to the house to see the girls, she tried to leave him alone with them. But the more time he spent with them, and the more times he returned to the house, the angrier he seemed to get.

A month and a half in, on a steamy night in the middle of May, he turned up just before midnight, stinking of booze, and barged inside the brownstone, demanding to see the girls, even though he'd spent a couple of hours with them earlier in the day.

This time, it was easier for Rebekah to maintain control of herself. 'What the hell are you doing, Gareth?'

'What does it look like?' he slurred, stumbling into the hallway, his arm pressed flat against one of the walls for support.

'You're drunk. No way are you going upstair—'

'They're my girls,' he spat, and headed for the staircase. As Rebekah followed, telling him to keep his voice down, she thought of all the times over the weeks and months leading up to their split when Gareth had got home and never bothered to look in on his daughters. By the time she got to their room, she could feel the anger like heat on her skin. But then she watched him stand by the girls' beds, dropping to his haunches as they slept, taking their tiny hands in his, and couldn't bring herself to say anything. To do so, to shout and scream at him, to wake the girls and scare them, would have been to destroy the sanctity of the room. The animals on the mobile, gently turning above Chloe's head. The fairies dancing across the wallpaper where Kyra slept. Her pink giraffe, on the floor already.

So she left him there and went downstairs, and when he finally emerged, she was in the living room, waiting for him. He paused in the hallway, peering in at her, like a spirit haunting a place where it didn't belong. It made her wonder what he would look like after three months, or six. Would he be an even paler reflection of the man he'd once been? Or was this just a stage for him, just a stopping-off point on a journey that would end in more resentment?

'Thank you,' he said.

They stood there, staring at each other.

And then he left.

As it turned out, things got better, not worse: Gareth stopped drinking and they began to get into a routine, and in early June, he found an apartment only four blocks from the house. Rebekah prepared herself for when he'd begin resenting the arrangements, for bitterness and blazing rows, but it never happened. If anything, finding the apartment, and Rebekah allowing him to take the girls out whenever he called to arrange it, seemed to galvanize him. He picked up Kyra and Chloe, always had them back on time, and Rebekah never had to argue with him about financial support.

In the background, there was always the unspoken subject of divorce, the tension as to who would broach it first or move them closer towards a lawyer's office – but they never quite got there. And the longer they existed like that, in a separated partnership that shouldn't have worked, but somehow did, the more Rebekah let the rest of her life pull into focus. She went out for a drink occasionally with Noella. She went to the cinema a couple of times with Johnny. She saw friends for coffee while Gareth babysat, and she picked up more locum work. By the middle of September, six months on from their split, she and Gareth were still making it work. As odd as their set-up was, Rebekah felt as if she'd recaptured a little joy.

That was when her friend Kirsty Cohen called her.

And that was when Rebekah made a terrible mistake.

19

She powered the handheld radio on in the front room of the gas station. *Please work. Please work.* It did: the screen turned orange and the words 'FLOATING VHF' blinked a couple of times in the middle.

I've got a radio.

'I've got a radio,' she repeated out loud, frantic with excitement.

A big number *16* appeared on the left-hand side of the screen, a series of tiny icons on the right, and the kind of signal bar that a cellphone would carry at the bottom. The signal had greyed-out space for five bars, but only three were filled black. Did that mean she had reception?

Did VHF radios even work that way?

She looked at the buttons under the screen. An up and down arrow. An icon that looked like the Reload Page button on a web browser. Half-circles with 'CALL ENT SET UP' in one, and 'MEM ESC' in the other. One with 16/9 in it, and three more under that: 'WX', 'H-M-L' and 'SCAN'. She had no idea what most of it was shorthand for – but she knew what 'SCAN' meant.

She pushed it.

The screen dissolved and *Scanning . . .* appeared. Rebekah stared at it, not moving an inch in case the slightest change of position affected the signal. The wait was excruciating, the dots after *Scanning* disappearing and refilling one after another on repeat. *Come on*, she thought, *come on, please*, willing it to find something, anything – a channel someone else was using, a voice, a person she could talk to, just the vaguest hint of another human being.

The screen returned to how it had been.

'What?' She stared at it. 'What happened?'

She pressed 'SCAN' again.

This time she placed the radio on the counter, thinking that her hand couldn't have been steady enough. She leaned over it, watching the dots fill in and vanish, fill in and vanish. She tried not to bargain with it this time, tried not to will it to find something, in case she'd cursed it the first time around. In the seconds after that thought arrived, she realized its insanity: that a piece of plastic could be bargained with, that it might choose to play games with her.

The screen reset again.

'*Shit.*'

The signal icon had gone down from three to two bars – but if it worked like a cellphone that should still be enough to get a signal, surely.

She picked it up and looked at the top.

There was a dial marked CHANNEL.

She turned it one way and saw the number on the screen decrease to *1*. In the other direction, it went up to *26*. Double-checking that the volume was definitely on, she began cycling through each channel, stopping at every one.

Static.

She did it again, stopping for longer, giving each channel at least a minute. For almost half an hour, she simply went from channel to channel, waiting, and then, when she got no hits, no voices, she went back through them again. This time, halfway through, on channel 16, she heard something different: static, just the same as the others – but then a hint of a voice.

Words.

Indecipherable, but there.

She almost dropped the radio as she scrambled to reply. Bringing it up to her ear, she pressed the button on the side: there was nothing but static again now. She didn't let it deter her: 'Hello? Hello, is anybody there?' Clearing her voice, she tried again: 'Please. My name is –'

She stopped.

Should she give her name? She didn't know who the hell was on the other end. What if it was him?

What if it was the man with the green eyes?

Her mind went back to the forest, to the mound of freshly dug earth under the shadow of the exposed tree roots. Now she was hesitating, unsure whether to use the radio again.

But then she thought, *What if it really is a rescue boat?*

She had to take the chance.

She had to know.

'I'm calling you,' she said, and ground to a halt again. *Calling? Is that what they'd say on these things?* She decided it didn't matter. For now, she just needed to get the message out that she was trapped. No name, just details. She could suss it out from there. '*Please*. If anyone can hear me, I need help.'

She let go of the button on the side.

Waited. Nothing.

'*Please*,' she said again, pressing the speaker to her lips, gripping the handset tighter than she'd held on to anything in her life. 'If you can hear this, I need help. I'm trapped here. I can't get home. I need help!'

Again, she waited.

The static growled, just the same as before.

But, then, something else.

She tried to tune out the rain on the forecourt roof, the distant crash of the sea.

'. . . for the . . .'

Two words.

She grabbed it again. 'Hello? *Hello?*'

She let go of the button.

Static.

No other voices. No words.

'Hello?' she said, for what felt like the hundredth time. 'This is an SOS. Please, someone, help me! SOS! This is an SOS! *Please*. SOS!'

All that came back was the same wall of noise.

But then: '. . . westerly . . . a position . . .'

Did the voice say, *a* position?

Or *her* position?

She glanced at the handset, at the channel number. Had she just given herself away? Panic plunged through her chest. *It could really be him. Green Eyes. He could have been waiting for this. He could be listening out for anything to do with me and Johnny.*

She looked at the signal: it was still on only two bars.

Could that be why his voice kept fading in and out?

She rushed outside, onto the forecourt, holding the radio up in front of her. She did a circle of the building, trying to improve the signal, and, to her surprise, found something entirely different: a black, mud-spattered Ford Explorer – old and up on bricks – half concealed by weeds and scrub. She climbed into the bed of the truck and held the radio above her head.

Still two bars.

'Please,' she said, trying to speak clearly, slowly, 'if you can hear me, I need help. I got left behind here. Please come and help me.' And then, as she shouted, '*SOS!*' over and over, she got the hint of another response.

Words, barely intelligible, but there.

'. . . westerly . . . land . . .'

Land – or island?

Frustrated, Rebekah looked around.

In the distance, she could see Nuyáhshá.

She needed to get to higher ground.

20

Rebekah ran as fast as she could.

Nuyáhshá was only the height of a ten-storey building, but it seemed bigger because it was wide, a sprawling mound of grass, trees and mud trails.

On the eight-minute drive from the gas station, she tried the handset repeatedly – but she didn't pick up a hint of anything else. As she climbed, she started to feel the hopelessness of her search for life at the other end of a radio wave, but she pushed forward, struggling to breathe, hot – almost feverish – in all the layers she still had on.

Near the top, as the trail steepened, her lungs burning, images flooded her of when she had run for her school, when this would have been easy for her. It felt like another life. She battled to even recognize that girl.

At the top, the trail went through one final switchback before levelling out into what would once have been a picnic area. There were no trees up here, just a couple of wooden benches, coloured by old graffiti and scarred by names, hearts and messages. Rebekah looked at some of the dates: the marks were all made before 1985, some as far back as the early sixties. It seemed to underline how far the island had fallen: once, it had been a magnet for vacationers from all down the east coast; now it was just a phantom haunting the ocean.

Rebekah stopped, looking in all directions.

The ground under her feet was made up of concrete slabs, which rocked as she shifted her weight. She had an uninterrupted view of the ocean, a three-sixty-degree outlook from which she could see nothing but the grey Atlantic, and then – just a vague silhouette – the greyer outline of the mainland to the north. It was only a hundred and one miles away. A hundred miles was the distance she used to drive to Mike's house and back when he lived in White Plains. Now, though, as she stared out at the vastness of the sea, its surface completely unblemished by boats, a hundred and one miles seemed millennia away. It was too far for her to see any landmarks in Montauk.

She glanced at the radio.

Still two bars.

Hitting the button on the side, she said the same words yet again: 'I need help. Please, is anybody out there?' She stopped, listening.

Crushing, relentless static.

She looked at the *16* on the display. That was the one it had been set to when she'd powered on the handset. Did that mean it was the best channel for making contact? Could it be the emergency channel?

She only knew about emergency channels because she'd read about them once, or maybe seen something on TV. *I wish you were here, Dad. You'd know how this thing works.* Clouds scudded overhead, the wind picked up and died away, and she started cycling through all twenty-six channels again.

After almost an hour, she finally stopped.

Tears filled her eyes as she tried pressing all the buttons, tried swivelling the volume up and down, a last defiant move full of fury and frustration.

'Fuck!'

She launched the radio down the hill, watched it tumble and come to rest. It had been a stupid thing to do, but she stood where she was and let herself cry, before she trudged down, in the diminishing light, to pick up the radio again.

By the time she'd got back to the car, night was swarming over the island. She sat with the engine running, staring into the blackness, then headed back on the road she'd come in on. It wasn't until she passed the gas station and the dilapidated homes that the full, destructive weight of what she'd achieved – or hadn't – after six full days on the island hit her like a punch to the throat: she had a radio, but didn't know how to use it; she had a roof over her head, but didn't have any electricity; she had food, but it would run out long before the island reopened; she had spare clothes, but they were too big and would impede her movement.

Suddenly even the tiny victories felt like failures.

It was almost a week since she'd left home and there was no way her and Johnny's absence would have gone unnoticed. Johnny's boss at the store, his colleagues there, his friends, wouldn't have been able to get hold of him. And either Noella or Gareth would *definitely* have reported them missing. Rebekah not coming back to her girls was completely out of character. What reason would they have *not* to report her disappearance?

But when the question landed, it landed hard: she couldn't think of a reason why Noella wouldn't contact the cops, but it was easier to imagine why Gareth wouldn't, easier to imagine how he might benefit if Rebekah never made it home. As well as they'd been doing since the split, with Rebekah out of the picture the girls would be entirely his. He'd have sole custody. No more turning up at the brownstone at prearranged times. No court appearance when he and Rebekah finally decided to make things official. No chance that a judge might do something unpredictable in a settlement, like restricting Gareth's access to the girls.

It would be so straightforward.

But was he *really* capable of thinking like that? And even if he was, why wouldn't Noella go to the cops? As that second question lingered in Rebekah's thoughts, there was a brief moment when she and Gareth were back in the kitchen as Gareth admitted to cheating on her, and Rebekah realized something about that day, and all the days and weeks afterwards: she'd never asked for the name of the woman he'd been seeing. She'd never wanted it.

What if it was Noella?

Her stomach dropped.

It wasn't Noe. It can't have been.

But although she tried to push the idea away, she couldn't let go of it. Because now all she could think about was something Noe had said to her in the days before Gareth's confession: *Gareth's a good-looking guy. He's confident, he's charming. It's time you knew the truth — about him, and about the woman he's seeing.* And as the idea of Gareth and Noella ossified, the reality of Rebekah's situation hit home.

Maybe there wasn't going to *be* any rescue.

Home

At the end of the day, Frank Travis drove back to his place in Queens. It was a narrow home with red-brick steps up to the front door and a clapboard finish on the ground floor. Whenever he pulled onto the driveway and switched off the engine, he could see the echoes of the family that had once lived here. It had been four years since Mark had got a job on the west coast, two and a half since Gaby had gone to college, and many more since Naomi had told Travis she didn't want to be with him anymore, yet the reminders of them all remained.

Inside, the kitchen felt the same as it always did: in all the time he'd been living here, he'd barely changed a thing, not only because the cabinets and countertops were fine but because there were memories in all of it. A scratch next to the sink where, as a teenager, Mark hadn't used a cutting board. A hollow impression in the drywall where the kids had been fighting. Tiny pen marks, all the way up the door frame, where Travis had measured their heights every year until, suddenly, they were adults and gone. One of the many reasons Naomi had given for leaving — other than a two-year affair — was Travis's total lack of interest in maintaining the house. But the truth was, Travis wasn't disinterested in home improvement, or incapable, it had just never seemed important. At the end of every shift, he was beat, mentally and physically, his head filled with images he'd have given anything not to carry, so the idea of pouring the same energy into hanging a blind just didn't compute. In all his years as a cop, he'd never been able to forget what he saw on the job. So when he got home, all he ever cared about was hugging his kids.

Upstairs, he showered and changed, and then — as the snow started to fall again outside — he grabbed his cell and sent messages to Mark and Gaby. Mark was working in LA, doing something with video games that Travis didn't understand; Gaby was in her final year at Northwestern studying drama.

Once the texts were sent, he went to his voicemail and finally listened to the message Naomi had left him earlier. 'It's me,' she said, the sing-song quality of her South Carolina accent deliberately subdued. 'You still owe me the money for Gaby's last semester. I cut you some slack because I know you're struggling financially –' she pitched those last five words as exactly what they were: a putdown '– but my patience only stretches so far, Frank. You owe me that money. Don't force me to give Nat Stramer a call.'

Nat Stramer was her lawyer.

She was part of the reason Travis was still a detective, even into his fifty-ninth year: he'd originally retired at forty-five, after twenty-four years on the force, and had taken his pension while working a second career in security. But then the security firm had gone bankrupt and Naomi filed for divorce. A year after that, thanks to the efforts of Nat Stramer, Travis was ordered to pay his ex-wife one half of the amount that his pension fund had accrued during the time they were married, and that was why he'd returned to the NYPD – just not in Homicide this time, in Missing Persons.

His cellphone buzzed, a message from Gaby popping up.

Hey Dad. All good here. You wanna chat? x

He dialled her straight back. 'Hey, kiddo,' he said, when she answered. 'I don't want to stop you if you're in the middle of something,' but the second he said it, he thought, Please don't be in the middle of something. He wanted to talk to her. He missed both of his kids desperately.

'No, it's cool, Dad. What you up to?'

'Oh, not much,' he said, relieved. 'Just chilling out at home. I can't wait to see you over Christmas.'

'Me too. Are you by yourself tonight?'

'No, I've got some friends coming over later,' he lied, because he knew if he told her he was alone again, she'd worry, and he didn't need her mind on anything but the last months of her degree.

Even so, Gaby said, 'I worry about you in that house by yourself. Why don't you let me set you up on a dating site? You'd be a great catch.'

'That's sweet, honey.'

'I mean it. I just want you to be happy.'

Seven words that stopped him dead.

He swallowed, suddenly overwhelmed by her comment, the kindness in it.

He thought of all the times he'd sat on the porch in the backyard and watched Gaby and her brother play, and the moments in their teens, even as they'd argued with him, even as they'd stormed off after a fight, when Travis would think, I don't want them to get any older. I don't want them to leave. My kids and my work, they're all I have. It's all I am.

Maybe it's all I'll ever be.

The woman stared at the television without really taking in what was on. In her hands she played with a photograph, moving it between her fingers.

'You want some more wine?'

Axel's voice pulled her out of her thoughts.

'No,' she replied, still moving the photograph in her fingers. She could see Axel looking more closely at her now, at the picture she was holding. 'I'm good,' she said. 'You go on to bed if you like.'

Axel nodded, but didn't move.

'Are you sure you're okay?' he asked her. She looked at him properly this time, and he must have seen the answer, because as soon as he did, he was nodding again. 'I'll see you in the morning, then.'

She watched him go, watched him look back at her from the bottom of the stairs, worry in his face, and then he ascended into the darkness. She listened to him moving around above her, floorboards creaking, and then her attention returned to the photograph she was holding.

Taken on the front steps of a house in south Brooklyn, maybe ten years ago, it was a snapshot of a family.

A father.

His two sons.

And his daughter.

Before

Rebekah first met Kirsty Cohen at Columbia, where they'd both been on the same biology course. She was a sparky redhead who loved to go dancing, and they hit it off straight away. They had the same sense of humour, which made it easy, but there were other similarities too: Kirsty also came from a male-dominated family, except she had four older brothers, and two were already doctors, one a cardiologist at Johns Hopkins. Sometimes, when Kirsty's family came into town, Rebekah would feel intimidated and embarrassed to talk about her own, much as it pained her to feel that way: for three decades, Kirsty's mom and dad had jointly run a huge advertising agency in the city, and whenever they asked Rebekah about her parents, about her brothers, she would tell them her mother had died when she was still young, that Mike had been a successful app developer before his accident, and that Johnny was a writer of historical fiction. Only one part of that was accurate, and the guilt would eat at her afterwards, but it felt less disappointing than the truth.

The two women barely left one another's side until graduation, when Rebekah decided to stay on in New York to go to medical school at NYU, and Kirsty moved to Baltimore, following her brother's path to Johns Hopkins. As unlikely as it might once have seemed, eventually they stopped talking as often. But not entirely: over the years, they kept in touch by text and email – not frequently, but enough – and, every so often, whenever Kirsty was back in the city seeing her parents, they would meet up.

That was why they got together in the middle of September: Kirsty called and told Rebekah that three of the girls they'd been at Columbia with were all going to be in the city at the same time for the weekend, and she was thinking of organizing a reunion tour. 'Of New York's bars,' she joked over the phone.

'I'm a lightweight these days,' Rebekah responded.

Kirsty burst out laughing. 'Don't give me that shit, Murphy. You're Irish.' She'd always called her *Murphy*, even after Rebekah had married Gareth and changed her name. 'I'll ping you over the details.'

So, on a humid Saturday evening, Gareth came to babysit the girls, and Rebekah got an Uber into the city. Kirsty had booked a table at a burger joint on the corner of 114th and Broadway, where the five of them had gone all the time when they were students, and while it had been given a hipster makeover, and the burgers were now twice as expensive as they were in 2002, they still did peanut butter shakes, and the women still got to sit at the same window booth.

After they were done eating, they took another Uber south to the Renaissance on Broadway because one of the women knew the manager at the hotel bar and reckoned she could get them a round of free drinks. After watching her flirt outrageously for five minutes, to Rebekah's surprise it worked, and they grabbed a table with incredible views of Times Square, its billboards painting the night.

They left at about 11 p.m., after five more rounds, all of them drunk or most of the way there. Back in college, Rebekah had always been able to hold her liquor the best, and it seemed to her that was still the case, so when Kirsty came up with a plan to go to the Zee Club on 45th Street, Rebekah ran point, buzzed enough to think that doing a posh English accent would help convince the bouncers to let them jump the queue. It helped more that the five of them were attractive so, inside, they bought more drinks, then headed for the dancefloor.

Gradually, over the course of the next hour, as the bassline thumped through the building, Rebekah and Kirsty became separated from the rest of the women, and some time after that, Rebekah got separated from Kirsty as well.

The rest was a blur.

She woke up with an appalling hangover, the kind that pounds so hard at the front of your skull, it feels like your eyes are actually throbbing. To start with, as she moved in bed, nothing registered but the severity of her headache, the dryness of her mouth, the nausea simmering at the base of her throat. But as she became more aware of her surroundings, other things faded in: noises that didn't belong out on the block she and the girls lived on; the floral smell of the sheets beneath her; the feel of the mattress, its silence as she shifted, when her own pinged every time she changed position.

She opened her eyes.

She was in a room she didn't recognize.

'Good morning,' said a voice to her left.

A man she didn't know was standing beside the bed.

21

The clock on the wall showed 1.30 a.m.

Rebekah was wide awake, her head full of imagery she couldn't unsee. Gareth. Noella. The idea of them together. An awful thought lingered – that Noe had never had children, was scarred by years of infertility, and that she didn't want Rebekah to come back because she craved Kyra and Chloe for herself – and the moment she forced it away, something even worse took its place: memories of her and Johnny running for their lives through the forest. She could hear him calling for her through the trees. She remembered the confusion of those moments. And then she pictured him in the minutes just before that, when they'd still been together – terrified, tearful.

Where did you go after that, Johnny?

Outside, she heard the occasional caw, the flap of wings as the sea sloshed at the harbour walls. Once, she'd loved the ocean. She remembered the four of them going on their annual vacation to Union Beach, and she thought of how soothed she'd been back then by the sound of the water. It had been liberating, the perfect bedtime melody.

Now it was the sound of incarceration.

At two, she got up, thirsty. At two thirty, she got up again and went to the window. There was nothing to see, just an ebony swathe.

If she slept at all in this place, it was fitfully. Some nights, the fear was so overwhelming it was like a weight, a piece of clothing she couldn't unbutton. She'd jerk out of a dream in the middle of the night – a lot of nights, *the* dream, incapable of escaping it, her feet tethered to the fibres of the carpet – and she'd see the store and not recognize it. Briefly, the panic would fill her chest, blowing up like a balloon. She'd struggle to breathe. And then she'd remember.

I'm on the island.

I'm waiting for a rescue that isn't coming.

She got up and went to the door, double-checking it was bolted. There was no view out to Main Street and, deep down, she liked that. She didn't want to be able to look out because, as aberrant as it sounded, she didn't want anybody to look back in. The mind played tricks, especially after the sun had gone down. She knew there was no one else here.

But that didn't make her fear any less real.

Back in bed, she lay with the flashlight on, its glow painting a V-shaped wash on the concrete floor. She closed her eyes, her lids tinged red, and tried to think of something better, of Kyra and Chloe. It was their seventh night without her, but she tried to picture herself in their bedroom, listening to them sleep, their breathing faint.

I'm home now, she imagined saying to them. *I'm home.*

And then she heard something.

She opened her eyes. As the wind gathered outside the store, the noise came again. It was carrying in off the sea. Not a bird. Not the waves.

An engine.

She made a dash for the window, climbing up onto the counter, almost falling off in her desperation, then remembered what had happened when she'd thought she heard a boat the last time. But it took her just a second to realize tonight was different.

She could see a fishing trawler.

Shit. It's real.

It's actually real.

She grabbed a pair of pants, jumped into her sneakers and sprang the locks on the door while she was still hauling on her coat. As she got to the car, she checked again: it was still there, still heading in a northerly direction, past the forest out on the east of the island.

She fired up the Cherokee's engine, pulled a U-turn, and accelerated out of Main Street, back in the direction of the gas station. She caught glimpses of the boat way ahead of her, chugging along against the black of the water. But, very quickly, the trees grew thicker on either side of her – and pretty soon she didn't have a view of the trawler at all.

She kept going, past the turn for Nuyáhshá, past the gas station, her foot flat to the floor. She still couldn't see the boat, realized before long that ten minutes had passed and she hadn't glimpsed it once – but she tried not to let the lack of a sighting defeat her. *Keep going. Just keep going.* Eventually, she got as far across the island as it was possible to go in a car, a copse of three storm-damaged houses marking the easternmost point.

A beach ran to either side of her, wedged between the sea on one side and the forest on the other. The trees were straggly and gaunt, battered so hard by the wind that their branches appeared to be reaching inland.

She couldn't see the boat anywhere.

But she could see something else.

Torchlight, in the forest.

Before

The stranger took a step closer to the bed. 'Good morning,' he said again.

Rebekah grabbed the sheet and pulled it towards her, covering everything from her neck down. The man had a towel around his waist and was still wet from the shower. In one hand he held a cup of coffee, steam spiralling out of it. He put it on the nightstand, then stepped away from her, clearly recognizing her confusion.

'I can't remember if we even did introductions last night,' he said, but there was no bravado to him, no sense that he saw the lack of names as a form of conquest, a story to joke about. 'My name's Daniel.'

He held out a hand to her.

She saw there was no ring, but still hesitated, and when he realized she wasn't going to reciprocate, he drew his hand back, evidently hurt. Rebekah glanced around the bedroom again. 'What the hell happened?'

The man frowned at her.

'I don't . . .' Her voice trailed off. 'I don't remember.'

'We met last night at the Zee.'

She felt like she might puke. She'd never done anything like this before. She didn't do casual flings. She didn't have anonymous sex. She didn't go home with men after meeting them on a night out, especially not when she was thirty-nine years old and should know better.

Except I have.

That's exactly what I've done.

Shifting on the bed, she thought of Gareth. This was the first time she'd been out since their split. They weren't together, so it shouldn't have mattered who she shared a bed with – except, to her, it did. They'd gradually found an equilibrium, and Rebekah had been able to control the terms of it. Gareth's aberration, the months he'd spent taking another woman to vineyards upstate and to clothes shops in the city, and the fact that Rebekah had been unerringly loyal to him, gave her a certain level of power. She didn't use it often, but the promise of it was always there. The whole time she was saying to Gareth, *I loved you until you broke my heart. I trusted you. I would never be as primitive and crass as you've been.*

But what about now?

She hadn't cheated on him, but it felt like it. Waking up in a stranger's bed, with no idea of his name, getting so drunk she didn't even remember the act: it felt like the same kind of weapon she'd been using against Gareth.

'Are you okay?' the man asked.

He was older than her, maybe mid-fifties, handsome and square-jawed, softly spoken, physically fit. She double-checked his ring finger, not for a ring but for a mark, the evidence of a married man who had hidden his band. But there was nothing. That was a minor plus, and he seemed genuinely surprised at her reaction to him, which was another: if he was surprised, it meant he expected her to recall him and their night together. Somehow, he didn't seem the type of man who'd take advantage of a woman so crazy drunk that she was basically a blackout.

She tried to focus on what she remembered.

They'd turned up at the club, danced, and then Rebekah had gradually got separated from Kirsty. Her last memory was of searching the dancefloor for her friend, the restrooms, the cloakroom, then trying to call an Uber. But was that in the club or outside it? And then what?

'I love your English accent.'

Rebekah looked at the man. He was still in a towel but now he seemed conscious of it: he opened the wardrobe and grabbed a

T-shirt. Once he'd pulled it on, he ran a hand through his hair, pointing to a picture frame. 'My grandfather came from Portsmouth,' he said, and Rebekah saw he'd mounted an ancient map of Hampshire on the wall, dotted with names in old English. 'I love Britain. I've been over a lot.'

She just stared at him.

'Which part do you come from?'

'Look, Daniel, right?' She stopped, swallowed. 'I don't remember much about last night, and waking up like this . . . It's not something I do. It's not me.'

He nodded. 'I get it. It's not me either.'

She eyed him, trying to catch the lie.

'Honestly,' he said, holding up a hand. 'I never do this sort of thing so, believe me, I was as surprised as you when I woke up and found you here.' He smiled; it was warm. 'I know that sounds like a line, but it's not. It's the truth.'

She was still watching him.

'I don't blame you for being suspicious.'

'I just don't . . .' Rebekah paused.

'You don't need to explain.'

'It's just a blank, that's all.'

'If it makes you feel any better, I've got a few blank spaces too, although I *do* remember that we were absolutely *smashing* the shots at one point, so that'll be why my head feels like it's on fire.' He gestured to the coffee he'd brought her, still steaming on the nightstand. 'I've got some Tylenol if you need it.'

She looked around the room. The sheet was still tight around her, but the anxious knot in her stomach had begun to shrivel. 'Cambridge,' she said.

'Pardon me?'

'Cambridge. I was born in Cambridge.'

The man's face lit up. 'Oh, wow, I *love* Cambridge. Such a cool city. One of my friends did a doctorate there. I went over to see him a bunch of times. You sound like you've been in the States for a while, though?'

'Twenty-one years. I've lived here since I was eighteen.'

'Ah, that explains why we've managed to infect that beautiful accent.' He smiled at her again.

'My dad,' she said. 'He was from Brooklyn.' As she looked at him, his T-shirt damp, the towel around his waist, she started to feel disordered again. 'I should probably be going. I feel like shit, I've got a ton of things to do, and . . .' She thought of the girls. Guilt speared through her chest. Had she even sent Gareth a text last night to tell him she wouldn't be home? 'Look, I shouldn't have done this. I've . . . I've got . . . At home, I've got . . .'

The man held up his hands.

'Understood,' he said simply.

'I'm sure you're a nice guy . . .'

'I get it, honestly.'

'Thank you,' she said.

He seemed to realize she'd need privacy, and he got up and headed out of the bedroom, shutting the door behind him.

Rebekah let out a breath.

She just wanted to forget this had ever happened.

But she couldn't.

When she got back to the brownstone, Gareth was waiting on the front steps, watching Kyra bounce a ball around. Once she'd given the girls a hug, and they were out of earshot, he said to her, 'Why didn't you text me? I've been worried about you, Bek.'

'I'm a big girl, Gareth.'

'I know, but . . .'

She looked at him and felt another stab of remorse: he genuinely meant it. He'd been worried about her. He still cared about what happened to her.

She definitely couldn't tell him now.

'I stayed the night with Kirsty, and I . . .' *I don't even remember the name of the man I slept with.* 'We got a little drunk. I'm sorry.'

His gaze stayed on her. Could he see that that wasn't all?

'I think I remember now why I don't do this,' she added, and squeezed her eyes shut. She didn't want to have to look at him. 'I really am sorry. Have the girls been okay?'

When she opened them again, he was smiling, his gaze fixed adoringly on Kyra. 'They've been great. It's been awesome spending time with them.'

After Gareth had gone, Rebekah pushed the rest of what she was feeling all the way down. When Kirsty called and asked her what had happened to her at the club and where she'd disappeared to, Rebekah simply said she couldn't remember because at least, in that, there was a hint of truth.

And then, in the days and weeks that followed, when she was alone in the house, when she thought of how Gareth had cheated on her and she'd kicked him out, she'd feel the guilt burning inside her, like phosphorus. Sometimes she would defuse it by reminding herself that they weren't together any more, that he was the one who should be suffering, not her.

Mostly, though, she worried about how her actions might upset the balance the two of them had found.

She imagined the conversation that would follow any confession she made.

And, mostly, she would picture Gareth asking her who the guy was that she'd slept with – and Rebekah having to admit that, until the morning when she'd woken up in his bed, she'd had no idea at all.

22

Torchlight, inside the forest.

She killed the engine, and – leaving the door wide open – started running along the beach. As her shoes slapped hard against the sand, the line of the island began to bend around to her left and she spotted a jetty ahead of her. It was small, its rickety wooden frame perched over the surface of the water – but her attention wasn't drawn to that.

It was drawn to the fishing trawler that was moored there.

The one she'd seen out at sea.

Rebekah's adrenalin kicked in and she picked up her pace, shouting into the wind: 'Hey! Help me! Help me!' She wasn't certain if anyone could hear her, but she could still see flashlights, thin arrows of ivory switching direction inside the thickness of the forest. 'Hey!' she shouted again, waving her arm. 'Hey, I've been left behi–'

A noise tore across the night.

Instantly, Rebekah stopped running, her change of movement so hard and so sudden she stumbled forward and landed on her knees in the sand.

A gunshot.

Inside the forest, between the contours of the trunks, she could see separate spears of light, sweeping back and forth. She could hear voices as well.

Men. Two of them.

For a second, Rebekah didn't move. She couldn't, even if she'd wanted to. Terror gripped her, paralysing her. She didn't know whether to go forward or retreat, just kept thinking the same thing. *What if it's him?*

The man with the green eyes.

She got to her feet again, looking back in the direction she'd come. There was no view of the Jeep – it was disguised by the crescent of the beach and the colour of the night – and even when the moon drifted in and out of view and the beach shimmered between different shades of grey, she still couldn't see it. She was closer to the trawler, the jetty, than she was to her car.

Should she retreat?

But what if this *was* the rescue she'd been hoping for?

Again, she thought of the guns. Why would rescuers come armed? She started to move forward slowly, frightened but needing to know, following the direction of the flashlights. When she got to the edge of the treeline, she saw that the forest immediately pitched downwards, into a gully about forty-five feet below where she was. The men were among the knot of trees, deep inside them, beyond the top of a slope on the opposite side of the gully.

Rebekah hesitated again.

They definitely weren't coastguards: if they were, why would they have come in an unmarked trawler? They weren't fishermen either because the salmon run ended in October. Plus, what were fishermen going to find in a forest at 3 a.m.? And why would they be shooting?

Dread bloomed beneath her ribs.

Because she knew.

Deep down, she knew exactly who it was – and, as she slowly made her way down the slant of the gully, towards a trail at the bottom, she suddenly heard the soft crunch of a footstep.

She froze.

It had been close.

With a small step to her right, she found cover behind the mottled trunk of a tree and tried to follow the source of the noise. For a second, she couldn't see anything.

But then he emerged.

A man with a headtorch.

The light made it hard to see his face at first, but then he took out his cell and, as he checked the screen, a soft blue glow washed across his features — his jaw, his mouth, and finally his eyes.

Rebekah's heart hit her throat.

It was exactly who she knew it would be.

The man who'd tried to kill her.

23

Green Eyes.

It was definitely him.

His headtorch blinked like a heartbeat, dimming every time it registered the impact of a step. He stared at his cellphone, the brightness of his eyes illuminated by the screen, his olive skin softly lit in pale blue. In the week since he'd attacked her, he'd let his stubble grow thicker, maybe to cover the cuts and bruises – but she would have recognized him anywhere.

He followed the trail along the bottom of the gully, not looking up, his fingers moving across the screen. He had no idea Rebekah was watching, just twenty-five feet away, still breathing, still alive. He thought her body was further into the forest, decomposing, being picked apart by animals. Yet she was scared. She was so scared it was like a tremor in her bones.

He stopped directly down the slope from her.

His gaze was still fixed on the cellphone, but now it was vibrating in his hand, a muffled hum that carried across the stillness of the forest. *Please don't answer it here. Please go. Please just leave.*

He lifted the phone to his ear. 'Yeah?' he said, looking around him, turning towards her. 'No, I didn't hear it ring. This place is a total dead zone.'

'Did you just fire your gun?'

For a moment, Rebekah could hear the caller perfectly.

'Yeah, there's skunks out here.'

'Are you serious?'

'I don't want to go home with rabies.'

'*We're not even supposed to be here, you stupid asshole!*'

'Calm down, it's the off season,' Green Eyes said, then moved slightly – and, as he did, any response from the caller became muted by his body. 'No,' he said, 'I told you, she's not here.' A short pause. 'It wasn't this part of the forest. It was somewhere else.'

The man turned in Rebekah's direction again.

Either side of the tree she was using to hide herself, the ground burst into life, the foliage, leaves and branches lighting up. She flinched and closed her eyes, listening for him, her mind creating images of him tearing up the slope towards her, a gun out in front of him.

'I don't know where she is,' he said.

She let out a breath.

'I can't tell at night.' She saw him change direction again, could feel the wind pick up, carrying the conversation towards her. 'This place is like a maze. What do you want me to say?'

'*I don't want you to say anything,*' the caller fired back, as clear as if he were standing in front of them both. '*All I want is for you to remember where you last saw her.*' The man with the green eyes turned again, taking in his surroundings. '*Her body was supposed to be rotting in a fucking hole.*'

He started to move again, heading in the opposite direction to the way he'd come in. Soon, the other side of the conversation became impossible to pick up. All Rebekah could hear was the man with the green eyes, his faint Latino accent, the aggression in his voice, the threat.

'Even if I *can't* find her, by the time anyone comes back here – *if* anyone ever comes out this far – her bones will be scattered all over the forest by the animals.' He stopped, peering intently into the undergrowth. He'd seen something – or thought he had. The caller must have picked up on the silence. 'It's nothing.' Unhurriedly, carefully, he started walking again. 'If you want me to tell you where her body is, we're gonna have to come back in the day.'

He stopped again, half turned, his gaze back on the same spot he'd been staring into a moment before. Rebekah followed his eyeline: there must have been an animal there. 'No, I'm not saying we wasted our time,' he continued, still focused on the same spot, his voice dropping in volume as he searched the trees. 'But this forest is bigger than I remember and at the moment it's pitch black. If we come back during the day, it'll be easier to find her.' He began walking again. 'I disagree. It'll be fine. No one's going to be here until April.'

He was maybe a hundred feet from her now. Soon, he would be too far away for Rebekah to pick up anything – so, in response, she moved forward, automatically, trying to adjust her position to hear him more clearly.

As her foot lifted up and came down again she saw the crooked angle of a branch beneath it.

By then it was too late to pull back.

In the silence of the forest, the branch cracked.

Before

For a month Rebekah felt numb. In the evenings, after the girls had gone to bed and she was alone in the house, she would try to watch TV, or pick up a book, or distract herself with the laptop. She'd do anything to stop her mind slowly decamping to the one place she never wanted to go back to.

A stranger's bedroom.

She took the girls to Prospect Park, letting them kick around in the leaves as they started to fall, and met friends she worked with at the hospital who also had kids. She and Gareth even took the girls, as a four, to a movie – although it proved a disaster, because Chloe cried through most of it, and Rebekah and Gareth both ended up losing their temper, shouting at the girls, then turning on each other. Keeping busy worked, though: she didn't think about her mistake as often and, once she and Gareth had re-established the equanimity they'd entered since the split, her life drifted back to normal.

In the last week of October, as fall started to grip and the nights closed in, Rebekah invited Noella for dinner, and – as they were sitting at the table in the kitchen, drinking wine while chops sizzled under the grill – Rebekah almost confessed. She knew Noe wouldn't judge her, that she would almost certainly say it was good for Rebekah, important to go out and have fun, to spend time doing the things that a single adult *should* be doing. She'd say, 'Your daughters are the most important, most joyful thing you've done in your life, Bek, but when it comes to changing diapers and mopping up puke, everyone has their limits.' But something about that night, the anonymity of drunken sex, just made Rebekah flush with shame.

'Are you all right, hon?'

She looked up. 'Yeah, I'm fine.'

'You sure?'

Noe was eyeing her closely.

'Yeah, absolutely,' Rebekah said, and got up to check on the chops. When she'd finished, she glanced at Noe again. She was still looking at her as if she'd sensed something was up. Rebekah shrugged. 'I guess I've been thinking a lot about Dad lately. I mean, it'll be two years soon.' She paused, barely able to meet Noe's gaze, because it had been a lie, and a heartless one: she missed her dad so much, but she hadn't been thinking about the anniversary of his death. 'I can't believe it's gone so quickly.'

'I know, hon,' Noella said. 'Anniversaries can be hard. People think the worst bit is when someone dies – but it's not. I remember, after my mom passed, I cried my eyes out every time her birthday came round. I cried on Thanksgiving most years too, just cos I missed her mashed potatoes.'

Rebekah smiled, and then her gaze went to the doorway: Kyra had wandered in, her pink giraffe in her hands.

'Ky, you're supposed to be asleep.'

'I'm not tired, Mommy.'

'Come on, it's bedtime.'

But Kyra went to Noe and slid her arms around her, hanging on for dear life, because even at two and a half, she knew how to play the delay game. 'Hello, Aunty Noe,' she said innocently, and Rebekah and Noella stifled grins.

'Hey, honey.'

She squeezed Noe and Noe squeezed back.

'Your mommy's right, Ky. You don't want to be tired in the morning, do you?' Kyra buried her head even further into Noe's belly.

'Come on, missy, it's bed,' Rebekah said, and held out a hand.

Reluctantly, Kyra took it.

She left Noe to watch the chops and carried Kyra upstairs. A night light was scattering shadow animals across the ceiling. In the crib on the other side of the room, Chloe was sound asleep. Rebekah tucked Kyra in and, when she asked Rebekah to stay, she lay next to her daughter and began stroking her hair. It didn't take long for Kyra to go quiet, her breathing changing, but Rebekah stayed there for a while, enjoying being so close to her girls. She heard Noe in the kitchen, finishing off a dinner she was supposed to have been a guest at, but Rebekah knew she wouldn't mind.

Eventually, Rebekah slid off the mattress, kissed Kyra, pulled the door to and padded downstairs. As she did, she stopped at a photograph, mounted on the wall halfway down. It was of her, Johnny, Mike and their father, taken at the diner on Macdonald Avenue where they all used to meet, two weeks before Mike died. Looking at their faces, she felt another stab of guilt about the lie she'd told Noella earlier. When was the last time she actually *had* spent a moment remembering her dad? Maybe a week ago. Maybe two. But when was the last time she'd thought about Mike? A month ago? Two? Longer than that?

I need to forget about strangers, she thought, her gaze moving from her dad to Mike, and finally coming to rest on Johnny. *It's time to concentrate on the ones I love.*

24

The instant the branch cracked, the man turned.

His eyes pinged to a spot about three feet from where she was.

Shit. Oh, shit.

Instinctively she went for cover, to the tree she'd been using before, her back to it, her hands flat to the trunk, her heart in her throat.

Suddenly her lungs were like lead.

She could hardly breathe.

She squeezed her eyes shut, trying to hear him, but he was on the trail, not in the undergrowth like her, and the trail was mostly grass and hard mud.

He wouldn't make any sound.

Run.

You need to run.

She looked up the slope, in the direction she'd descended. Out that way was the beach. From there, she had a quarter-mile sprint back to the car. Could she make it without being caught? What would happen even if she did? They'd know she was alive. They'd know she was –

Crack.

Her body locked.

The noise had come from the other side of the tree, from the bottom of the gully. It was him. He was looking up in her direction.

Barely ten feet from her.

'*What is it?*'

He was so close, Rebekah could hear the caller again.

'*Have you found something?*'

Torchlight washed across the ground immediately to Rebekah's right. She didn't move. She watched out of the corner of her eye as the light began to sweep from her right, across the back of the tree she was hiding behind, to her left. As it did, she saw that a tree on that side of her had split, and part of it had toppled. The man's headtorch lingered on it, as if he was trying to figure out whether the tree had made the noise – or something else.

'*Are you there?*'

'Yeah,' Green Eyes said softly.

'*What's going on?*'

His silence felt like it went on for hours, pictures forming in Rebekah's head again: him creeping up the slope, her not even being aware of him, a hand coming out of the darkness and grabbing her by the throat.

'Nothing.'

His voice was still the same distance away.

She let out another breath.

'*We're not coming back here in the daytime.*'

'Why not?'

'*Didn't you listen to anything I said on the way down here? This whole area is patrolled by feds. It's a major coke route.*'

'So?'

'*So if they catch us here, it means questions.*'

'We can just lie.'

'*No, we can't just lie. We don't even have a permit to dock here – day or night. At least at night we got the dark. In the day, we got nothing. We can't lie our way out of being spotted and not having a permit. And, anyway, lies mean more questions. More questions mean more cops. I already got rid of one problem for that asshole. I don't need this thing escalating into another. Shit, why didn't you just bury her like I told you to?*'

'It was complicated. Things went wrong. I ran out of time.' The man sounded feeble, even to Rebekah's ears, and must have realized it because then he came back stronger: 'You don't know. You weren't there.'

'*No, I know I wasn't. That's the problem.*'

130

'Her and her brother . . .'

Rebekah stiffened at the mention of Johnny, anger swamping her fear. *What did you do to my brother?*

Did you kill him?

'Things just went wrong,' the man said finally. 'That's all.'

'*No shit.*'

'I'll make this right,' he said, and hung up.

Rebekah stayed exactly where she was, looking up the slope. But then she heard him, further out along the trail, clearing his throat as he walked. Eventually, she found the courage to lean out and take a look: he was so far away from her now that the darkness was swallowing him whole.

She replayed what she'd just heard.

Why didn't you just bury her like I told you to?

Maybe he would have done if she hadn't been at the bottom of a gully, even steeper and more inaccessible than this one. Maybe he would have done if he hadn't been working against the clock and had Johnny to deal with.

She tried not to linger on the idea of her brother being dead. The truth had fluttered in and out of her thinking ever since she'd been left behind and had started to coalesce after she'd spent so much time searching, fruitlessly, in the forest for him. But, perhaps, there was still hope. Did the fact that she couldn't find him mean he might still be alive? Could he, too, have escaped after they'd become separated? She'd found no body and no grave among the trees, and the man had said on the phone that things had gone wrong. Maybe Johnny really did make it out.

Reality dragged her back. If he was still alive, why couldn't she find him? The forest was dense, and maybe a couple of miles across at its widest point, but the rest of the island was a narrow, empty husk: fifteen square miles of broken buildings. There were no hiding places. And if he'd made it off, if that was why she couldn't find him here, why hadn't he raised the alarm?

She shut her eyes.

Forget it and concentrate.

She tried to imagine who the second man – the caller – was.

He'd said cops patrolled this area, and maybe they did, but until tonight Rebekah hadn't seen or heard a boat in a week, so if there were patrols out on the water, they were far away. That scared her, too, because it really *did* mean a rescue wasn't coming. Although there was one tiny crumb of comfort: the men were worried about being spotted on the island, even in the middle of the night. And if they were worried, it meant they wouldn't want to stay here long.

Lies mean more questions, the caller had said. *More questions mean more cops. I already got rid of one problem for that asshole. I don't need this thing escalating into another.*

She looked down into the gully again. What was the problem they'd got rid of? And who was the 'asshole'?

Rebekah still had no idea why someone wanted her dead, but she understood why they would have chosen this place. The man with the green eyes had called the forest a maze, and he was right: it was compact, crowded, easy to get lost in and incredibly hard to navigate once you were off the trails. He'd been right about something else too: if she'd been killed, if her body really was out here, by the time anyone found it – *if* they ever found it – she'd probably be bones. It would be a minimum of five months before any corpse was found, most likely more when you factored in how few people were on the island, even in season. That meant insects and animals would have finished their desecration long before anyone discovered her.

Except none of that mattered because she wasn't dead.

They just thought she was.

And, tonight, that gave her an advantage.

Before

The morning after she'd had Noella over for dinner, Johnny came to the house early, unexpectedly, cheeks flushed, holding a small parcel. Rebekah let him in, and whatever stress her brother had been feeling, he forgot about the second he saw Kyra. She ran towards him, arms out, and he scooped her up and whirled her around, singing 'American Pie', as he always did when they met, except he altered the lyrics from *Bye Bye* to *Ky Ky*. He hoisted her into the crook of his arm, Kyra playing with his red hair, and turned his attention to Chloe. He had a different song for her, this one made up because he always said he couldn't think of a famous song with lyrics that rhymed with *Chloe*. Chloe wasn't bothered, though: as he told her she was doughy, and showy, and loved to play in the snowy, she giggled. Rebekah set Kyra up with a xylophone in the living room, put Chloe in her bouncer, then took Johnny into the kitchen.

'Oh, I almost forgot,' he said, and handed her the parcel.

Rebekah looked at it. 'Is it my birthday?'

'I just saw it and thought of you.'

She untied the ribbon and lifted the top off the box. Inside was a tiny snowglobe: a runner was under the glass, partway across a miniature park.

'What's this?' she said, lifting it out.

'You used to have that snowglobe when we were kids, back in England, but it smashed. I think Mike knocked it off your desk when he was messing around. Anyway, there's a German woman who lives in my building who makes them – and I saw this and thought of you. That's supposed to be Central Park, by the way.' Johnny shrugged, as if the gesture were nothing, but Rebekah was already blinking back tears. She'd never forgotten the snowglobe she'd had as a kid. It had a woman with red hair in it, Big Ben behind her. Sometimes she'd asked God to make her small enough to go inside the globe, as the snow fell, to ask the red-headed woman why she'd left.

'It's beautiful, Johnny.'

'I know it's cheesy.'

Rebekah put the snowglobe down and threw her arms around her brother. 'It's amazing,' she said, and heard the surprise in her voice, but she shouldn't have been surprised at this small act of kindness. This was what Johnny was like. This was what he'd always been like.

'My car wouldn't start this morning,' he said, after they were done. His cheeks were no longer flushed, and seeing the girls – and Rebekah's reaction to the snowglobe – seemed to have curbed any frustration that might have been lingering. That was another thing she'd always loved about her brother: he rarely held on to things. Maybe it was the writer in him, the dreamer, the romantic, always convinced that whatever came next would be better.

'Do you know what's wrong with it?' Rebekah asked.

He shook his head. 'No.'

'So can't you just take it into the shop?'

'Oh, yeah,' he said, 'absolutely. It's not that. I've got the day off today, so that's fine, and tomorrow, for work, I can just get the subway. Or the day after. I can't remember when my next shift is.'

She frowned, unsure where this was headed.

'So what's the problem? Is it money?'

'No, no. It's not that.' He grimaced. 'I know it's probably a total waste of time, but I've been thinking about maybe starting a new novel. I can't get this idea out of my head.'

That wasn't what she'd been expecting.

For some reason, Rebekah thought of Kirsty, of her parents, of all the lies she'd told them down the years about Johnny being a novelist. She'd always played down his imaginary success, saying his books were out of print, because she never wanted them asking questions about where they could find his work.

'That's great, Johnny,' she said, and felt a stab of guilt. Was it great for him, because he was pursuing his dream again? Or great for her, because, if he got somewhere with a novel, she wouldn't be embarrassed about what he actually did for a living?

'You really think it's good?' he asked.

But she'd lost the tail of the conversation and all she could think about was how ugly she'd been, how distressingly shallow. Johnny was everything to her. She adored him.

'Bek?' he said. 'You don't think I'm making a mistake?'

'No, of course not. That's so great, Johnny.'

Her enthusiasm seemed to energize him.

'Have you ever heard of Crow Island?' he asked.

'Vaguely,' she replied, and she filled the kettle. 'Is that going to be the setting of the book?'

'Yeah,' he replied, pulling out a chair at the table. 'It's this island one hundred and one miles south-east of Long Island. Basically, three hours on a ferry from Montauk.' Rebekah enjoyed watching him, hearing the passion in his voice. She felt a charge of excitement for him that was completely selfless. It made her feel better immediately. 'It's actually called Cruys Island,' he went on, 'after the explorer Matthijs Cruys, who landed there in 1694, but when the British bought it from the Dutch, they couldn't pronounce "Cruys" so they called it "Crow" instead, because there were also these huge colonies of fish crow out there.' He saw her expression and rolled his eyes. 'Sorry, that's very boring. Anyway, these days, it's a ghost. It was a popular vacation spot for a while, but then a hurricane razed it to the ground in the eighties. Now it's only open from April to October to service the fishing industry. They get a few academics too – you know, marine biologists and those sort of people – because there are whales and seals off the north coast. But mostly it's fishermen.'

Now Rebekah understood where this was going. Academics meant potential interviewees for the research part of Johnny's book, and if he needed to get to Crow Island to talk to them, he wouldn't be able to do it in a busted car.

'Yes,' she said.

Johnny frowned. 'Yes?'

'Yes, you can borrow the Jeep.'

He laughed. 'Am I that predictable?'

'Yes,' she said, smiling, and started to make them some tea. 'Is that what the snowglobe was for? To butter me up?'

She asked the question, but knew the answer. Johnny didn't think like that. Thinking like that required cynicism.

'No,' he said, 'I promise it wasn't.'

'I know. Of course you can borrow the car.'

'Thanks, Bek. You're amazing.'

She hugged him again. 'I know.'

'I've got an interview lined up for this Saturday with a curator from the Museum of Natural History, and I just need a car I can rely on. I don't want to let this guy down. He's been out on the island since April, researching the Niantic people, and it's taken me almost three months of emails to get him to commit. I want to set the book on the island the year Cruys landed, and this guy is basically the world's foremost expert on that period, and that location.'

But then his expression clouded.

'What's wrong?' Rebekah asked.

'I just hope I'm not making a mistake.' He tapped out a rhythm with his fingers on the table. 'You know, chasing around, trying to pretend I'm a proper writer.'

'You *are* a proper writer.'

'Bek, I don't think it counts if you're unpublished and the only person who actually read your failure of a novel is your sister.'

She punched his shoulder playfully. 'Cheer up, will you? *I'm* the one who kicked her husband out so that means *I'm* the one who's supposed to be wallowing in self-pity, not you. So what if you don't have a publishing deal yet? So what if you're doing this on your day off from the store? Who cares? In a few years, when this book hits the shelves, and the *New York Times* is falling over itself to interview you, it'll be worth it. Right?'

He looked at her.

'*Right?*'

Johnny smiled. 'You're a bully, you know that?'

That night, Rebekah missed a call from Kirsty.

Or, rather, she chose not to pick up.

She just watched the cellphone buzz on the nightstand until, finally, it fell silent. Ordinarily, she would have loved to talk to her, but there was really only one reason why Kirsty would try to get Rebekah on the phone so soon after they'd last seen each other: she wanted to talk about the night out they'd had. She'd heard something about the man Rebekah had met at the club. She wanted the details, the gossip.

Rebekah turned off her phone.

25

She kept moving.

She had no idea which part of the forest this was.

Ahead of her, the man with the green eyes looked both ways, and headed right. Rebekah picked up her pace. He was weaving a path between a clump of withered oaks and, beyond him, Rebekah could see the beach and the ocean, then the trawler, to the right, bobbing at the jetty.

She slowed down as she closed the distance between them and then, gradually, became aware of something else.

Another shape in the shadows.

She ducked into some nearby beachgrass, the noise disguised by the crash of the Atlantic, and lay flat on her stomach, hoping she hadn't been seen. The grass was drenched with sea spray but she didn't move. Instead, with her chin in the sand, she picked out the shadow again, between her and the beach.

It was another man.

She could see the dome of his head, could see he'd shaved his hair – but couldn't tell which way he was looking.

'Anything?' he said.

He was the caller. She recognized his voice.

Green Eyes shook his head.

'You ever hang up on me again like that,' the caller said, taking a step forward, emerging from the night, 'I'll gut you like a fish. You're just a grunt, remember that.'

Rebekah tensed. The man had a New York accent and she could see he was shorter than Green Eyes, but he was wider – brawny and fibrous, like a wrestler. She didn't recognize him, but she could sense the type of man he was just by looking at him. She'd seen his type in emergency rooms, over and over again, as they waited around outside the OR. They'd pretend to be brothers or cousins in order to find out if the patient was going to live. But they were never relatives. At best, they were messengers or spies, sent to find out if someone had died. More often, they were the reason the victims had ended up on a table in the first place. They were the men who'd fired the bullet, or embedded the knife between the ribs.

'So we came all the way down here for nothing?' the caller said, obviously annoyed at the lack of comeback from his partner. He swivelled to face him this time, his expression carved in anger. '*Lima.*'

Lima.

Green Eyes, the man who'd tried to kill her, was called Lima. She was certain now that she didn't know him and had never come across him before – so why would a total stranger want her and Johnny dead?

'She's in there somewhere.'

'You already said that,' the caller responded coldly.

Lima looked behind him, his headtorch hitting a spot about five feet to Rebekah's left. Her heart lurched. She didn't move a muscle, just watched him: she could see his gun in his belt, a knife in a sheath at his waist. She wondered if that was the knife he'd used to slash the back tyre on the Jeep.

Wait. The Jeep.

It wasn't at the dig site any more. It was parked at the end of the beach, a quarter of a mile from here. What if these two decided to go back for it? What happened when they got to the dig site and didn't find it there? They'd know she was still alive.

Fuck.

Should she go back for the car?

No, wait, calm down.

They came in by boat and docked here, to the east of the forest. As it was, they could barely find their way through the trees in the dark, so they weren't about to hike through to the dig site. If they'd had a car with them, it might have been different – they could have looped around to it via the main road – but it was a long way on foot if they didn't know an exact route through the trees, and they'd already said they couldn't afford to hang around.

'I know I screwed up.' Lima's voice brought her back. It had unexpectedly faltered. 'I know I screwed this up for us.'

The caller paused. 'If you fix it, no one needs to know.'

'Fix it how?'

The caller turned, moonlight painting the top half of his face, eye sockets black as oil. He was scanning the trees, as if he sensed he was being watched.

'Hain? Fix it how?'

Hain.

Now she had both their names.

'We wait,' Hain said.

Lima frowned. 'Wait? What are you talking about?'

'We can't afford to get caught here: we're snooping around in the middle of the night, *without* a permit, in the off season. It looks suspicious because it *is* suspicious. That means we can't come back. If you and I get caught out here, we're gonna get charged and that puts us on the radar.'

Rebekah glanced at their boat.

For the first time, a thought came to her: could she make a break for it? Could she use the boat to escape? Would she even know how to operate it? There was a trail, running vaguely parallel to the beach, that she could use to come at the boat from further down the sand.

'So what do you want to do?' Lima asked.

Hain didn't reply, and in the silence Rebekah looked again at the boat. It would be an insane risk.

And they had guns.

'Hain?'

'Wherever her body is, she ain't going nowhere between now and next spring. It gets like the Arctic here with the wind, but this close to the ocean, there's moisture in the air, so that means she'll still be rotting the whole time. Even so, even if the animals scatter her, like you say they might, even if all that's left of her by next year is earth and bones, if someone comes down here and we *don't* get rid of her, there'll be enough of her left to make things hard. We can't leave her out in the open permanently. It's too much evidence.'

'So you want to wait until next year?'

'April first next year. We get here minute one, day one.'

'You want to wait until the island reopens?'

'Exactly.' Hain nodded. 'In five months, this place'll be open again and that means the ferry will be running. If we get the ferry, we don't have to worry about the feds stopping us out in the channel and asking questions we don't want to answer. We don't have to worry about IDing ourselves. We do it that way, we also don't have to worry about applying for a permit. We just come over, we find her in the forest, and we bury what's left of her. We can bring the pickup and the trailer too. After all, we need to dump her car because you didn't think it would be a good idea to take the keys from her before you killed her.'

'How was I supposed to bring back two cars, plus ours?'

'You weren't. You were supposed to bring back yours and *hers*, not yours and that other one.'

'In everything that happened, I just –'

'You forgot to get her keys. You screwed up.'

The tension between them simmered again.

'Whatever,' Hain said. 'Point is, her car's still where she left it. When we come back in April, the same rules apply as they should have done when you were here last week: if it's too risky to take her Jeep back to the mainland, we burn it right here. If we think we can get it to the mainland without raising any flags – and that's the preferred option – we drive it back to the city and crush it like a tin can.' He paused, looking at the forest, at Lima, a grim darkness lingering in his face. 'We're gonna make it like this bitch never even existed.'

Before

The day after Rebekah agreed to loan Johnny her car, New York Presbyterian called, waking her from a dead sleep at 6 a.m., before either of the girls was up. They asked if she could come in and cover the day shift: through a combination of vacations and ill-timed sickness, they were short of orthopaedic surgeons.

Gareth was away with work and Noella was at her dad's, and although Johnny was great with the girls, he'd never had both of them for a whole day. That meant, if Rebekah was going in, the only real option was daycare. She hated leaving Kyra and Chloe for so long, good as the staff were with the girls, but she wanted to keep the hospital sweet: now she was on her own, she'd need the money — and that inevitably meant taking on more shifts.

In the end the day turned out to be fairly routine.

She'd done her residency at NYP so she always liked returning, even if it brought back memories of her constantly pulling midnight-to-midnight shifts. Restrictions meant she wasn't supposed to have worked more than eighty hours per week or thirty hours in a single shift, but she'd quickly learned that the rules didn't mean much on the ground. Some weeks she'd clocked a hundred hours, a lot of her nights filled with so-called 'scut' work: monotonous tasks like IV line replacements, stat blood draws, and accompanying patients to CT scans and X-rays. She liked the hospital and its staff, but she didn't miss those years.

An hour before she was due to leave and pick up the girls, she was asked to check on a patient with a suspected broken wrist. It seemed straightforward, but when she got to the ward, the injury was more complicated than it had initially seemed, and she left the hospital late. By the time she arrived at the daycare facility, it was after 8 p.m. and they'd already been closed for thirty minutes. The staff were pissed off at having to hang around, the girls were over-tired and agitated, and although she tried to feed them quickly and get them into bed, neither Kyra nor Chloe would co-operate, and Rebekah had to put up with an hour and a half of screaming.

By the time they finally fell asleep, it was almost ten o'clock.

Absolutely exhausted, Rebekah crept out of their bedroom and simply slumped onto a step halfway down the stairs. It took her a full ten minutes to uncoil, and when she did, she found herself staring at the picture of her, Johnny, Mike and her father in their favourite diner.

This time, she reached up and took it off the wall.

She remembered the lie she'd told Noella: that she'd been think-ing about her dad a lot lately. Her eyes switched between him and Mike, and then she said a silent apology to them both for letting them slip so far from her thoughts. Johnny and she were either side of them in the same booth they always took in winter, when it was too cold to sit outside.

Whenever they met, conversations would often wheel around to Mike because his was by far the most interesting life and he was a born storyteller. Between them, they had such a weird mix of accents – Johnny mid-Atlantic, Rebekah diluted English infused with countless American expressions – that people often wouldn't believe they were related, but because Mike always sounded like a born-and-bred New Yorker, his stories somehow seemed more exotic. Their father would often ask him questions like, 'What happened to that blonde you were dating?' – knowing some anec-dote would be attached – and Mike would seize the moment. His self-deprecation offset any charge of arrogance. He would fre-quently joke about how bad he was with relationships, or about his most recent app only being a success because no one had yet real-ized what a fraud he was.

The last time the four of them had gone out, it was cold, trees reduced to bones, steam rising out of subway grates, as if the earth itself was breathing. Johnny brought their father, as he always did in those last years, and Rebekah arrived shortly after, completely fried, not just because she'd pulled an eighteen-hour shift but because she was seven months pregnant with Kyra at the time. Mike didn't get there until thirty minutes later, by which point the others had ordered for him and were into a second round of drinks – or Diet Coke in Rebekah's case. As soon as Mike slid into their booth by the window, the elevated train tracks outside like the belly of an immense beast, he said, 'Any of you remember that girl I dated? Alice?'

They all stared at him blankly.

'This would have been ten, maybe twelve years ago.'

Rebekah looked at Johnny, who shrugged, and it was clear it wasn't just her who didn't recall Alice. Mike looked shocked, ran a hand through his thick black hair, turned to their father. 'What about you, Pa? You remember Alice?'

Their father didn't reply, but his mouth was turned up in amusement. He always looked like that before Mike launched into one of his stories.

'No one remembers her?' Mike asked.

Johnny smiled. 'Mikey, in fairness, the last official count put your number of former girlfriends at one million, six thou–'

'I'm *serious*, Johnny.'

They all stared at him, taken aback, the smile gone from their father's face. Mike stared at his beer bottle, condensation running down it.

'What the hell's the matter with you?' Rebekah said to him, annoyed at her brother's sudden turn, cranky from the shift, from the fatigue of carrying around twenty-six pounds of extra weight.

'What the hell's the matter with me?' He looked up from the bottle, and his eyes shimmered briefly in the dull light of the restaurant. 'I went out with her for six months and you don't remember her. How can that be right?'

'Why does Alice matter so much, son?' Their father spoke softly, his thin, veined hand moving across the table to Mike's.

'I'm sorry,' Mike said quietly.

'What are you sorry about?' their father replied.

Rebekah saw the same reaction in Johnny and Mike that she felt in herself: a memory stirring, a shape awakening in the dark. As kids, their father would say that to them when they'd done something wrong. He'd forgo telling them off for a prolonged, disappointed silence, and when they finally returned to him to apologize, he'd always pose the same question.

What are you sorry about?

'She died today,' Mike said, almost a whisper.

'Damn,' Johnny responded. 'I'm sorry, buddy.'

Mike looked up at him. 'She jumped off a building.'

'*Shit.*' Rebekah gasped. 'I'm so sorry, Mike.'

'She called me up out of the blue about a week ago, and I could barely even remember her.' Mike had now removed the label from his bottle. He started folding it on the table, creating smaller and smaller squares. 'I think she was calling up anyone who'd ever hurt her,' he said, his voice like a low hum. 'I hurt her, and I barely even remember her.'

'You're not responsible for what she did,' Johnny said.

'Maybe I am, John.'

'No, Mikey. You can't go through life wondering if every single decision you made is going to have repercussions for someone ten years down the line.'

'Johnny's right, son,' their father said.

But it wasn't the answer Mike wanted – or not one that brought him any comfort. 'I don't want to be the type of person who just forgets the people who pass through their life,' he said, and in that second, Rebekah recalled thinking that she'd never seen her brother so shorn of bravado, so burdened by an act, a choice, its consequence. 'I've got to start making more of the moments I get. I don't want to be a person who forgets what's important.'

When she picked up the phone the next morning, Rebekah was still thinking about that evening, about what Mike had said to them, about what she had promised herself in the aftermath of her night out with Kirsty. *I need to forget about strangers. It's time to concentrate on the ones I love.*

'Bek?' Johnny said, when he answered his cell. 'Are you okay?'

'Yeah, I'm fine. I've just been thinking a lot about Dad, and Mike, and I realized I couldn't remember the last time you and I spent more than an hour together. Just the two of us, I mean. I think it might have been the day of Dad's funeral when we drove to Union Beach. You remember that?'

'Of course I do.'

'That's almost two years ago.'

She thought of what Mike had said at the diner: *I've got to start making more of the moments I get.* Except he'd never really got the chance. Two weeks later, he was dead. But Rebekah was still here, and so was Johnny.

'I've asked Noe to have the girls on Saturday,' she said.

A confused pause. 'What are you talking about?'

'Your trip to Crow Island in two days time.' Rebekah paused, looking at Chloe in a bouncer at her feet, at Kyra playing with her blocks. 'Why don't we go together?'

That night, after she'd put Chloe down and spent fifteen minutes with Kyra while she played with Johnny's snowglobe, Kirsty called again. As she watched her cell shimmy across the living-room table, Rebekah felt annoyed at her friend's persistence. She didn't want to talk about the night out they'd all had.

She didn't want to talk about what had happened.

It wasn't fun gossip to Rebekah.

After the phone had stopped ringing, she saw that a voicemail had been left. Rebekah thought about ignoring it, or deleting it. But Kirsty's calls would never stop coming until she rang her back.

She played the voicemail.

'Uh, hi, Murphy, it's me. I, uh . . . It's awkward. I just . . .' She stopped, the line filled with nothing but silence. 'I wanted to talk to you about someone.'

And then she told Rebekah who.

The Call

As Travis dozed in front of the television, his phone started buzzing. It took him a second to get his bearings, even though he'd been aware of the TV in the background the whole time, the dull sound of cars out on the street, dogs barking, planes heading south to JFK and into LaGuardia. He scrambled around for his eyeglasses – he'd got into the habit of wearing them whenever he answered a call, just in case he needed to write something down – then scooped up his phone.

It was Amy Houser.

'Ames?' He checked the time. It was 1 a.m. 'You okay?'

'I'm good, Trav.'

She was still at the office: he could hear phones, voices, the sounds of a squad room, and then he remembered she'd told him earlier that she was working late this week. 'I might have something for you,' she said.

He frowned. 'What do you mean?'

'That case you were talking about earlier.'

'Louise Mason?'

'Yeah, the artist.' Houser paused, her movement and the crackle of the line reverberating back to him. 'The phone kept ringing on your desk tonight – like, incessantly. I was starting to get real pissed, as was everyone else on my team – I mean, we both know nights are bad enough without phones still going like it's nine a.m. – so, eventually, I walked over and tried to switch the damn thing off. But then it started ringing again. So, I thought, What the hell?'

Something big was coming.

Travis could feel it.

'Who was the caller?' he asked.

'Male. That's all I know. I came right out the gate and asked him if he was

147

the one who kept calling. He said he was. I said, "If you want to speak to some-one on the Missing Persons Squad, you're gonna have to call back in the morning." But he wasn't looking for a conversation. He just said, "I heard he was searching for the artist. Tell him to take a second look at the boyfriend." '

Travis felt a surge of electricity.

' "Him" being you, it would seem,' Houser added.

'Did he say anything else?'

'Nope. Straight after that, he hung up.'

Travis grabbed his notebook.

'Why wouldn't he call you in office hours?' Houser said.

'Because he didn't want me to answer.'

Houser paused. 'That makes no sense.'

'It does if he thinks I might recognize his voice.'

Travis whipped through the pages of his notebook until he got to a section at the front that dealt with the guy Louise had been seeing before she'd dis-appeared. The boyfriend. Travis had dismissed him early on because he'd had a rock-solid alibi: he'd left her at the fundraiser early to head to the ER because a close family friend had been taken ill; later that night, he'd messaged her from the hospital to apologize, but by then her cellphone had gone dead. But what if this boyfriend had lied?

'Trav?'

'I really appreciate this, Ames.'

'Sure.'

Travis hung up, then started rereading the notes he'd made after interviewing the boyfriend first time around, back in October. When he was done, he retreated a few pages to the guy's personal details. His DOB, social security number, employment history and criminal record.

Except there wasn't a record.

There wasn't much of anything.

Johnny Murphy was spotlessly clean.

3
The Prison

26

Rebekah hardly slept for a week.

Whenever she shut her eyes, the walls of the store would close in and she'd be back at the beach. She'd be looking at Hain and Lima as they talked about how they were going to come back on 1 April to find her body and bury it. But what would happen when they *couldn't* find her?

She spent days thinking about it, turning things over in her head, the different reactions they might have. She was awake for so long, she began to lose her focus and clarity, and in her exhaustion, her thoughts became more irrational, more naïve, and she began entertaining possibilities, like the two of them forgetting to take the ferry on that first day, or making it over and then getting lost in the forest.

In the dead of night, frightened, confused, alone, the kind of rudimentary mistakes she knew, deep down, they weren't capable of, began to feel conceivable, even likely. But then, on day twelve, wrapped in blankets from the hostel, Rebekah closed her eyes as the sun set – unable to keep awake any longer – and didn't stir again until almost eleven the next day.

After that, she was thinking more clearly.

When a search of the forest didn't turn up her body, Hain and Lima would wonder why. If she returned the Cherokee to the parking lot at Simmons Gully, it might buy her some time, but sooner or later they would realize she was still alive. Lima had made mistakes that day, he'd admitted as much to Hain, so that would help reinforce the idea of her survival. After that, they'd surely head back to the harbour. They'd go there and wait. They'd watch passengers boarding the return ferry at the end of the day. They'd look at every single face until they found the one they'd come for.

Hers.

But then something else struck her. She'd started taking pebbles from a beach on the west coast, one for every day she'd been on the island, collecting them in a pile at the front of the store, not only to remind her of how long she'd been away from home but to help her keep track of time. So far, she had fifteen pebbles for fifteen days. But by the time Hain and Lima came back, by the time the new season rolled around, she'd have 152.

Day 15 to Day 152.

She had to survive another four and a half months.

Depression hit, and it hit hard.

She barely went outside, frightened that somehow Hain and Lima might come back and catch her wandering around. When she did go out – looking for food, for a kerosene heater to warm the freezing-cold store – she never went far, and she was constantly looking over her shoulder, paranoid, on edge, startled by every sound, spooked by every flicker of movement. A week later, she stopped going out at all. She'd clamber onto the counter and just stare at the sea. Sometimes, she would become aware of how unclean she was, the stench of sweat on her skin and in her clothes; she would understand that she was spiralling. Most of the time, though, she didn't care: she'd just stay there, in the store, staring into space.

Whenever she thought of the girls, she'd crash. She didn't even have a photo of them to look at. Her purse, where she always kept a picture of the three of them, taken at the market in Prospect Park a month after Chloe was born, had been stolen from the Cherokee by Lima and, by then, he'd already had her cell. She began to worry that she was forgetting them: their eyes, their smiles.

She tried to remember what it felt like to lie next to Kyra, stroking her hair as she dropped off to sleep, and couldn't. She wasn't sure if Chloe's bouncer had been yellow or red. One night, she stayed awake for four hours trying to remember if there were zebras or lions on her mobile. It became so unreasonably important that her skin started to itch. It got so bad her nails ended up tearing open her forearm.

The next day, she trudged out to the car to see if she'd left the Band-Aids in it because she couldn't find them in the store. She didn't even bother getting dressed, although the air was like ice: she just went out in her T-shirt, underwear and sneakers. She searched the Jeep and couldn't find them.

But then she noticed something else.

The date.

When she'd opened the car, it had appeared on the central display, and she'd been so focused on finding the Band-Aids, so adrift in her funk, she hadn't even noticed. But now she did.

25 November.

Today was Thanksgiving.

Until that moment – until her reflection looked back at her from the windshield – she'd never realized how much like a ghost she'd become, how quickly it had taken hold. But caught there, half dressed, hair a tangled mess, teeth unbrushed, she was so gaunt, so shadowed, she was unrecognizable to herself. When she'd first arrived on the island, she'd still been carrying some weight from her second pregnancy, but after almost a month, it was gone. Her body had become pinched, her skin taut against her bones, and its hue had changed. She'd always had colour before, a gold-brown, like the first hint of fall. Now she was pale and frosted.

She burst into tears at the sight of her image, at the date staring back at her. She imagined the girls eating with Gareth, *with Noella*, and once she'd pushed that image away, still unwilling to accept it was true, she went over and over what Kyra would be saying about Rebekah not being there, what Chloe would be thinking even though she was still too young to know her mother was gone. It welled like a storm, physically dragging her to the ground, until the images she had of her girls became choppy and disordered, and melted away, like old film.

There, on her knees, she wailed like an injured animal.

She'd finally hit the bottom.

Before

The ferry out to Crow Island left at 8 a.m. It was a three-hour journey, the boat winding its way out of the harbour on Montauk's north side, east around the Point, then south-east across the Atlantic for one hundred and one miles. Johnny told Rebekah that the island was on the same parallel as Philadelphia, but after a while it became hard to imagine it on the same parallel as anything, because, before long, they were surrounded by nothing but ocean.

Rebekah sat in the passenger lounge and watched land fade from view behind her, the coastline slipping into the sea. It was the penultimate day of the season and the ferry was almost empty. Inside, there were only two other men, one dressed in overalls, the second in oilskins, and then a bored girl, in her late teens, who was manning the concessions stand. Outside, on deck, there was a guy smoking a cigarette whom Rebekah had watched drive a U-Haul truck onto the ferry.

Johnny wove his way back, laptop bag on his shoulder, coffees in hand, a plastic-wrapped cookie in his teeth. 'Here we go,' he said, handing Rebekah a cup. He sat down next to her. 'How are you feeling?'

She watched him unwrap the cookie. It wasn't the first time she'd left the girls, but it was the first time she'd been so far away from them.

'I'm fine,' she said, although the way Johnny looked at her suggested he knew it was a lie. 'Honestly,' she added, not wanting to spoil the day before they'd even got there. He'd been so excited about the trip when she'd picked him up that morning, about

writing again, at the idea of research and the opportunity to interview a bona-fide expert.

'Is Noe having the girls all day?' he asked.

'Yeah, and then Gareth will look after them tonight.'

'What time did you say you'd be back?'

'I didn't. I'm going to call Noe later, just to check in on how it's
going, and I'll update her then. We didn't really have time to get
into it this morning.'

Rebekah winked at Johnny, making light of the early start, but it
had been stressful and upsetting, and was another reason she felt a
little disjointed: to get to Noe for 4.30, and then Johnny's for 4.50,
she'd had to wake both girls from dead sleeps at 4 a.m. They'd
hated it, were tired, grumpy, whined almost the entire way over to
Noe's, and Rebekah had had to leave them in floods of tears to
make it to Johnny's: if she'd been late picking him up, they wouldn't
have had enough time to get across Long Island to Montauk for
the eight o'clock ferry.

'The ferry gets back to Montauk at eight p.m.,' Johnny said gently, offering Rebekah half a cookie. 'You should be back home by
ten thirty. Ish.'

'It's cool,' Rebekah said. 'Noe's brilliant with the girls.'

Johnny sipped his coffee, still looking at her. 'I really do appreciate
this, Bek. All the garbage you've gone through this year with Gareth,
your job, the girls, all of that, and you can still find time for me.'

Rebekah thought of Mike again, of what he'd said that night in
the diner. *I've got to start making more of the moments I get.*

'I want to be here, Johnny.' She propped her head against his
shoulder and he put his cheek against her hair. 'So this place shuts
tomorrow, right?'

'Halloween, yeah.'

'Just like you to wait until the last minute, big brother.'

'You know me,' he replied. 'Always organized.'

'Always.'

'So are you and the girls going out trick or treating tomorrow?'

'Oh, yeah,' she replied. 'A whole group of us from the neighbourhood are getting together. Kyra's *very* excited. Chloe . . . I'd say

she's indifferent.' She smiled. And then she thought of something else: 'Oh, I almost forgot. Kirsty called me and left a weird message.'

'Kirsty Cohen?' Johnny stared at her.

'She said she wanted to talk to me about someone.'

He frowned.

'And that someone was you. Any idea why?'

'No,' he said.

'Could it be to do with the woman she set you up with?'

'Louise?' Johnny looked away from Rebekah, out of one of the windows. 'I doubt it. I haven't heard from Louise in weeks.'

'Oh.' Rebekah tried to see his face. 'Sorry, John.'

He shrugged.

'Maybe Louise wants to get back in touch with you.'

He still didn't look at her.

'I doubt it,' he said quietly.

It only occurred to Rebekah much later on that, in the rush of the morning, she'd never told Noella *exactly* where she and Johnny were heading. On the phone, when she'd arranged it with Noe, Rebekah had told her that Johnny and she were going out for the day, then had quickly moved on to what time she'd drop the girls off, because that had seemed more important. They hadn't had time to get into anything else on the call because Noe had had to hurry out to a work function. Rebekah hadn't been in touch with Gareth about the trip either, other than to explain that she and Johnny were going out for the day and that Noe would drop the kids off in the evening. And that morning with Noella, at four thirty, it had been so fatiguing and the girls so upset that, again, she'd never had the chance to talk about their plans.

'We're going out to Long Island first,' Rebekah had told Noe, as she'd removed the girls from their car seats. Chloe had been bawling her eyes out and Kyra kept asking the same question over and over again: *Where are you going, Mommy? Where are you going, Mommy? Where are you going–* 'I'm going out with Uncle Johnny, Ky. *Please.*'

She handed Chloe to Noella, then hurried around to the other side of the car, checking her cell for the time, flustered, worried about missing the ferry.

'Once we get to Long Island,' she said, as she popped Kyra's seatbelt, 'we're going to get –'

'Bek.'

'We're going to get the –'

'*Bek*,' Noe said, reaching across the back seat, putting her hand on Rebekah's arm. 'Calm down. Just call me later, okay?'

Rebekah had nodded then, smiled at her friend, and looked at Kyra, her daughter's eyes welling with tears. 'I'm sorry, my angel,' she said to her daughter, then leaned in and kissed her. 'Mummy loves you so much.'

In the minutes after that, as she got back behind the wheel of the Jeep, she waved to the girls from the other side of the windshield.

They were both crying again.

'I'll try to call you from Montauk,' Rebekah said, through her open window, but all Noella did was wave at her.

Over the engine noise, she hadn't heard her.

And then, as she reversed out of the driveway, as she got her last glimpse of the girls, Rebekah remembered the worst bit: Kyra.

It wasn't her tears.

It was the way she reached out – as if Rebekah were about to topple into some deep, dark hole.

27

Rebekah woke suddenly, the image of Kyra – arms out to her on the morning she'd left Noella's house – burned onto the back of her eyes.

She rolled onto her side. Everything hurt, but not from working so hard: from doing so little. Her weeks of inactivity were petrifying her, seizing her limbs. She flipped back the blankets and watched the leak in the ceiling for a while, dripping into a bucket she'd set under it.

The image of Kyra flashed in her head again.

Would that be the last time she saw her daughter? The vague hint of her face on the other side of a car window? Why the hell hadn't she told Noella exactly where they were going? Why hadn't Noe listened when Rebekah said they were going to Montauk? *Maybe because she did listen, but pretended not to hear. Maybe because she's not the woman you think.*

No. Rebekah squeezed her eyes shut. *No.*

She forced through an image of the Noella that, in her heart, she knew was real. Her best friend. Her sister. After that, she thought about what Noe definitely *did* hear that morning, and about what she and Gareth would actually be able to tell the police. The only thing Rebekah was certain that Noella had heard was 'Long Island' – so that was what she would tell the cops, and that was where the cops would start.

Rebekah's heart sank.

Long Island was a search area of more than fourteen hundred square miles. That made it three times bigger than New York City.

Not only that, but the disappearances would have been reported to the NYPD but worked by police departments in Nassau and Suffolk counties, which relied on the sort of co-operation Rebekah had seldom seen as a doctor. She'd rarely heard about it from her father either, and as she thought of him, his voice formed like an echo: *Cops are the most selfless and selfish people I know. The case you're working, it's everything to you. Anyone else's, it's irrelevant.* And even if there *was* some level of co-operation between cops, what were they going to do? They could try following street cameras. Maybe, in Johnny's house, they might find research for the book he was planning, or the name of the curator from the Museum of Natural History he was due to meet. Maybe, after that, they might realize that Long Island wasn't the ultimate stop-off for them.

But it felt like a long shot.

If the police knew where Rebekah and Johnny had ended up, why hadn't they come yet? And, anyway, was a beat cop really going to piece together the journey of a car from Brooklyn using traffic cameras? Were they going to *keep* following it along 128 uninterrupted miles of freeway? Was it more likely they would gain access to Johnny's house and turn the place upside down – or that the missing persons report would get written and filed, then put in a cabinet along with thousands of others? In the world of missing people – from what Rebekah had seen as a doctor – two adults, with no red flags in terms of their mental health or criminal record, would be left to drift if there were no fast leads.

It was just the cellphones that bothered her.

Johnny and Rebekah had had phones on that first day, and before they were taken, they'd made calls on them, or had tried to. Those calls would have pinged the tower on the island. So, had the cops not checked the cellphone records? Surely even beat cops would have done that much. The second they did, they'd have seen the cellphone activity and they'd have had a last location for Rebekah and Johnny.

Yet they still hadn't come.

Her thoughts were shattered by the squawk of a fish crow. She watched it pass the windows – a black blur – her heart thumping in her chest. It had been two and a half weeks since Hain and Lima had come to the island, and she was still jumpy. But it couldn't go on.

Something had to change.

She had to try to move forward.

She needed to wash her clothes, and it would be too cumbersome and awkward in the bucket that was catching the leak. She needed to go down to the sea and get them clean. She needed more food as well. She was down to five days' worth of cans – a week, if she was conservative – and she'd cleaned out the first hostel. She could try to find a fishing rod, but that really was a last resort. It could take her days – *weeks* – before she was proficient enough to catch the amount of fish she'd need to feed herself, even longer before she got to know the best spots for bagging the most fish. Before it came to that, she was going to try to raid the second hostel for more cans, and cover the rest of the island too: she still hadn't searched whole swathes of the north coast, the west coast – where the lighthouse was – and big areas of the centre. Deep down, she didn't expect to find much in any of them: even on the old map, created at a time when the island was still doing well, there appeared relatively few places of interest in those parts. But she had to try.

Hiding was no longer an option.

She had to fight.

28

She scaled the gates that segregated the harbour area from Main Street. They were chained and padlocked from the harbour side so, even armed with the jack, there was no way she could break them open without climbing the fence.

It was relatively straightforward to get over and onto the other side, the chain links in the gates providing ideal footholds. Once she had her feet back on solid ground, she worked at the padlock with the jack. It was the third time she'd tried to break one like this, and each time she was getting a little more efficient. Within a couple of minutes, it pinged open.

Aside from a small, empty parking lot and the pockmarked concrete of the quayside, there was nothing except the wooden harbourmaster's shack. She wanted to take a look, but first she wandered down to the slipway, to the water sloshing against its slant, and started to remove her dirty clothes.

It was absolutely bitter, but she took everything off.

When she got down to her underwear, she paused automatically, hands ready to unclip her bra, and turned back in the direction she'd come. It felt so bizarre stripping down like this, in a place that would have been so public in the summer. As her eyes went to the boarded-up buildings on Main Street, the wind stirred the trees. It swivelled an old weathervane on one of the roofs. Nothing else moved.

No one's watching.

She thought of Hain and Lima, then looked across the water to the smudged line of the mainland on the horizon. The wind came again, even colder than before, and she started to shiver. Slipping off her underwear, she climbed into the clothes she'd found at the gas station. They were old, musty, and smelt of mildew. The wool of the sweater was abrasive against her breasts, even with a T-shirt on, but she put up with it, climbing into the pair of oil-stained pants.

She slipped her sneakers back on, without her socks, washing some of the mud off the sides and toes, and then she went through each piece of clothing, dipping it into the water, soaking it, scrubbing it with half a bar of soap she'd found in the hostel, then squeezing it out. By the time she'd finished, her hands were blocks of ice. Scooping up her wet clothes, she made a beeline for the store, before remembering the harbourmaster's shack.

It had been locked with a key, not a padlock.

That made access trickier.

If it was even *worth* trying to access it. There were metal signs fixed to the exterior – IN CASE OF EMERGENCY CALL 911 and FIRST AID – which gave her a temporary burst of hope, but when she got up onto a cinder block beneath the only window, she couldn't see much worth making the effort for.

It was cramped inside, shelves everywhere, jars full of nails and screws, tools, boat parts. She could see a first-aid kit fixed to the wall but otherwise there was nothing. Before Hain and Lima, before she found out their plans to come back, she'd have prayed for a radio that she could understand how to use, unlike the one she'd found at the gas station. But now she felt weirdly conflicted: what if she did find one, and she successfully sent out an SOS message, and the two of them *were* listening in? She knew it wasn't feasible for someone to man a radio channel every hour of every day for the next four months, but that didn't stop panic gripping her. Because it wasn't irrational to believe that they might be listening to the audio traffic for this part of the coast. It wasn't irrational to believe that, at some point, they might hear her if she managed to establish contact with someone.

She rocked from one foot to the other, looking again for evidence of something to communicate with. In her turmoil at using a radio, she'd thought about alternative ways to make contact with the outside world, like gathering wood, heading up to Nuyáhshá, and starting a fire there. If she lit it after sunset, and kept it going all night, there had to be a pretty good chance that someone somewhere on the mainland would spot it.

But what if Hain and Lima had people in Montauk?

What if that was where the islanders retreated to in the winter, dotted along the coastline in their houses, always within sight of this place?

She thought it highly unlikely that Hain and Lima would have told anyone exactly what they'd done out here – they'd be admitting to murder – but it wasn't implausible that they might have slipped someone some cash and asked to be kept informed of boats heading in the direction of Crow Island, or people turning up and showing an interest in it. The two men would be thinking about cops, maybe coastguards, but a fire would probably be an even bigger question mark. Why would a fire suddenly start on the island's highest point in winter?

Screw it, just radio again, because you're running out of options unless you want to be here until April. But then she felt that same sense of hesitation, the fear so paralysing it was like she was drowning in it. She wanted to live. She wanted to get back to her girls and, at the moment, she had one big advantage: Hain and Lima thought she was dead.

Radios and fires were out.

She had to find another way off.

Before

The island edged closer. Rebekah dug into her pocket and got out her cellphone. No bars. Johnny had assured her that she'd be able to pick up a signal once they'd docked. She'd call Noella then to see how the girls were because she hadn't had a chance at Montauk harbour: they'd been late getting to the ferry, thanks to traffic on the Expressway, and the boat had left about a minute after they'd boarded – and about a minute after that, her signal had vanished.

For a while, it had felt liberating to be doing something other than changing nappies and making meals. But, soon, she was feeling confused, worried about being so far away from them, and as she glimpsed a peeling sign reading HELENA on the jetty up ahead, she started to wonder if she'd done the right thing in offering to drive Johnny all the way out here. What if the girls were still crying and Noella couldn't settle them?

But a moment later her signal returned and the handset buzzed in her palm. It was a text from Noe. There was a picture attached of her and the girls at Coney Island, the Wonder Wheel visible over their shoulders.

> Cold at the beach! But not too cold for early morning
> ice creams. Yummy! Everything good. Have a nice
> day and say hello to J. AND RELAX. Noe x

Through the windows, as the boat slowed, she could see a man standing on the jetty, some vehicles in a parking lot beyond, and another man moving around in Helena's narrow main street. With one last look at the picture of Noella, Kyra and Chloe, Rebekah pocketed her phone.

'Okay, big brother,' she said. 'Let's find your curator.'

She felt better, more positive: after Johnny had done the interview, they could sit on a beach, or – if she was feeling brave – paddle in the cold ocean water; they could get ice creams from a store and breathe in the smell of the sea. They could do anything they wanted for a few hours, be spontaneous, break loose. And, in that moment, Rebekah vowed to soak up every minute of her adventure out of the city – and out of her routine – alongside the brother she loved.

Johnny told her the curator had rented a room in a hostel full of fishermen on the north side of the island but worked in the forest, where he was researching the Niantic tribes that had once called Crow Island home.

'Do you even know what this guy looks like?' she asked, as they headed out of Helena.

'No, but he said to call him when we're near.'

She nodded, gazing at the scenery through the windshield.

'When did you last come here?'

'Years ago,' Johnny replied, 'way back in my Columbus days.'

He meant Christopher Columbus: in their early twenties, Johnny, Mike and a few guys from the neighbourhood had started exploring abandoned buildings. Most of them had done it for a dare, but Johnny's interests were more substantial: he was a fan of history, always looking for inspiration, and found a strange sense of place in the silent, empty corridors of old structures. Eventually it must have led him to the buildings left behind after Gloria had torn through.

'It could be really nice here,' Rebekah said.

Johnny didn't reply.

'I mean, I bet it *was* nice before the hurricane.'

Johnny was going over his notes – questions he'd prepared for the curator, things he needed to tick off, a succinct synopsis of what his book was about. Rebekah didn't take offence at his lack of response. She could see he was starting to get anxious now, his expression marked with worry. He looked old for a moment, his red hair flecked with grey, the lines around his eyes dense, as if a sculptor had carved them with a hammer and chisel.

'He's not going to think you're a fraud,' she said.

Johnny looked up. 'What?'

'I know that's what you're thinking. If he cared about whether you were published, he wouldn't have agreed to meet you, would he?' When, again, he didn't answer, she glanced at him. 'Would he?'

'I just don't want him to think he's wasted his time.'

Rebekah frowned. 'Do you think he's letting you drive all the way out here so he can tell you you'll never be as good as Ken Follett?'

Johnny smiled. 'I just want this to work.'

'It will.'

The curator's name was Karl Stelzik. Johnny tried calling him as they followed the main route around the island, a circular road called the Loop, but the calls kept going to voicemail. He left one message, then another, but the further away from Helena they got, the worse the cell service became.

Ten minutes later, they found the hostel Stelzik was staying in, a boxy utilitarian building covered with a gossamer sheet of sea salt.

There were no lights on inside.

'I hope this isn't a sign of things to come,' Johnny muttered, as he left the car and trudged down to the front door. He tried pulling it open. When it didn't move, he buzzed the intercom and waited for a response.

Rebekah switched on the radio while she waited. She twisted the dial, cycling through the stations, but there was no reception. Switching it off again, she returned to the picture of Noella, Kyra and Chloe at Coney Island, to three smiles, to the ice cream on Kyra's cheeks.

Unexpectedly, she felt another flutter of panic. Her eyes moved over Kyra's face, the glimpses of Gareth in it, the curls in her hair, and then to Chloe, her features scrunched up as she lay in the stroller, swamped in a snowsuit.

Before she knew it, she was outside the Jeep, the cellphone raised in her hands, doing circles of the car, trying to find a better signal. The instant one flickered into existence, she dialled Noella's number.

'Hey, Mommy,' Noella answered.

The reception was poor, crackly and distant.

'Hey, Noe, is everything okay?'

'Sure. Why wouldn't it be?'

'I, uh . . . I don't know, I just . . .' Rebekah swallowed. *What the hell is the matter with me?*

'You all right, honey?' Noe asked.

'I just . . . I just wanted to see how you guys were doing, is all.' She tried to keep her voice even and upbeat. 'I loved the picture you sent me. Thanks.'

'What's going on, Bek?'

Noe had seen through the lie.

Rebekah looked towards the hostel, to where Johnny was waiting. Their eyes met and he held out his hands, shrugging in frustration.

'I don't know,' Rebekah said, almost to herself, and let out a hard breath, as if she'd been holding it in for days. 'I just had this stupid feeling.'

'Feeling?'

'Like I needed to call you.'

'Well, you can stop worrying,' Noe said, voicing it like an order. 'We're fine. Aren't we, honey?' A brief pause. More wind turning to fuzz on the line.

'Mommy?'

Rebekah's heart swelled. 'Ky?'

'Ice cream, Mommy!'

Rebekah burst out laughing. *Everything's fine. They're fine. It's a few hours and then you'll be home again.* 'I know you're having ice cream, baby,' she said to Kyra. 'I bet it's yummy.'

There was no reply this time, just the sound of smacking lips.

Rebekah smiled. 'You must be good for Aunty Noe, okay?'

'Okay.'

'Mummy will see you tomorrow.'

'Okay, Mommy.'

'I love you, baby. Give your sister a kiss for me.'

Noe came back on the line. 'Relax, Bek. I've got this.'

'I know you have. I'm sorry.'

Johnny was on his way back, so Rebekah said goodbye to Noella and hung up. He pulled open the car door, eyes still on the hostel. 'No response,' he said, 'and he's still not answering his phone.'

Rebekah could see he was pissed off.

Back when they'd been kids, Mike was the hothead. 'Mike the Psych', as Rebekah always called him. He was the one who bit back most, and stewed over angry words. Often it was because he lacked patience, the ability to allow others to make mistakes. To him, it was all much simpler just to tell someone what they needed to know, needed to hear, or needed to accept. There was a kind of irony in the fact that those flaws in his character had ended up being the reason he was so successful. Rebekah loved him so much, even when they argued. He was brilliant, funny and irritating, but he was so different from Johnny it was sometimes impossible to imagine they could be related. Johnny rarely lost his temper. He always listened to what you had to say. Rebekah couldn't remember him saying anything bad about anyone, even the kids at school, who'd picked on him for a time, making fun of his mid-Atlantic accent, his dress sense, and the fact that he preferred to paint rather than play sport.

'What do you want to do?' Rebekah asked him, watching as the colour slowly drained from his face, the ire, the frustration.

'I guess he must be busy somewhere,' Johnny said.

He was gracious too – and always kind. Not that Mike wasn't, it was just that Johnny's goodness came from somewhere different, a place that was unspoiled by the type of anger and outbursts that Mike would sometimes unleash.

'So what's next, big brother?'

He looked at the hostel and then at her.

'Next is Plan B,' he said.

29

She headed into the forest.

It had been almost four weeks since she'd looked for Johnny properly, and it felt like a betrayal. Yet a part of her didn't want to pick up the search again. She was into December. She was into her second month. She was on day thirty-four and, despite all the effort she'd put into looking for him, she'd never found a hint that he was alive.

There was only one way this was going.

It was complicated, Lima had told Hain that night on the beach. At the time, Rebekah had entertained the idea that *complicated* meant Johnny had escaped, got away and made it out. Now it seemed like the hope of a child, simplistic and artless. It had been complicated that day because Lima hadn't had time to get back and bury Rebekah's body, not because of something that had happened to Johnny. There was nothing complicated about Johnny.

Lima killed him, and then buried him.

Admitting it with such candour stopped her dead. She gazed out at the forest. She'd brought the map with her because it had some old trails marked on it. But as she looked around her, she saw the truth: whatever trails had existed in here had long faded from view.

She was never going to find him.

She checked off parts of the island, one by one, using the map. She'd drive to them, get out of the car, wander around looking for food, for clothes, for things she could use – she found some old flares in a derelict house on the north coast – and if she came up with nothing, she put a cross through it and moved on. It was tedious work, relentless and repetitive, not helped by the map being over thirty years old: most of the landmarks – like an old sawmill she found near the lighthouse – had either been abandoned or wiped out entirely.

Eventually, she arrived at the other hostel.

Its exterior was the same design as the one she'd already cleared out, just a lot smaller: there was one floor, with four windows on either side.

The building had another difference too. Both entrances, front and back, were key-locked, not padlocked. The windows were exactly the same as the ones at the other hostel – barred, the glass reinforced – but if she wanted to gain access, she wasn't going to be able to rely on her strategy of smashing a lock until it snapped.

She did a loop of the building.

Neither of the doors appeared particularly strong – they'd peeled and warped, presumably because of the spray coming in off the ocean – so she felt confident she could lever them open. But she'd need something like a crowbar to do it.

She got back into the Cherokee, grabbed the map and drew a square on the north coast, approximately where the hostel was. It must have been built sometime after Hurricane Gloria: on the map, where she was standing now, there was a blue-grey outline of a different building. It was marked 'Museum'. There was an arrow coming out of it to an information box describing how the museum had housed *an impressive collection of Niantic and early European items, including coins, bone-handled knives and period clothing.*

The museum was gone, and so was its collection.

Next to the square she'd drawn on the map, she put a question mark, reminding her to come back.

So far, she had nothing.

But her luck was about to change.

30

The lighthouse sat at the end of a sliver of land called Schooner Point. It had discontinued operation long before the hurricane had hit, but they must have been doing tours of it back then because times and prices were listed on the map. Rebekah imagined it must once have been painted such a stark, clean white, it was almost luminescent, even during the day, but now its paint had sloughed away, like old skin, and it was a finger with frostbite, blackened and decayed. As she approached, she could almost smell the rot on the wind.

She parked the Cherokee on a slash of cracked blacktop and took in the lighthouse through the plastic wrap on her broken window.

Grabbing a flashlight from the trunk, she followed a wooden boardwalk across the surface of the dunes. The sun was still out, drifting behind clouds, but it was winter and already the light was dwindling. She zipped up her top and moved onto a red-brick path. It was loose beneath her sneakers, and shifted, like a floor in a funhouse.

To her surprise, the door was open.

Nothing, so far, had been this easy, so she stopped for a moment and took it in. When, finally, she reached out and pulled it towards her, she realized she'd tensed, bracing herself for whatever surprise was coming.

But there was no surprise.

Someone had just forgotten to secure it for the winter.

She stepped into old living quarters, stripped bare of anything that might have proved helpful, then shone her flashlight to her right, where a staircase spiralled upwards. Somewhere above her, a bird flapped its wings as the glow skittered across the white-painted walls.

She started the climb, all the way up to the lantern room.

It was hexagonal, and about forty feet in diameter, although it felt smaller inside because of the huge size of the light. Floor-to-ceiling windows gave an uninterrupted view of the island, the immensity of the Atlantic rolling out on all sides of her. A hundred and one miles north-west, the mainland was a smear in the distance. But it was alone. In every other direction, there was nothing. It was infinite ocean and the curve of the earth.

She looked for any sign of life out on the water, circling the lantern, taking in each part of the island: it was different seeing it from an elevated position, a way to reinforce her knowledge of what she'd already figured out or checked and, potentially, parts she might have missed.

And that was when her eyes locked on a set of small buildings off to her left, all with corrugated steel roofs.

They were on the opposite coastline to the mainland, at the end of a mud trail coming off the Loop. Somehow, as she'd driven from the hostel down to the lighthouse, she'd managed to miss them.

But it wasn't the buildings that had caught her eye.

It was something stored at the back.

A motorboat.

Before

Rebekah followed Johnny's directions, but they still almost missed the entrance to Simmons Gully. His Plan B was to go to the dig site Karl Stelzik was working at.

The track down was full of potholes, sprinkled with frost, and almost entirely obscured by trees, but at the bottom, Rebekah swung the car in next to a dirt-spattered Chevy Traverse, and knew straight away that they'd found him. The rear seats had been folded down, and the cargo hold was full of tools and equipment. There was also a Museum of Natural History sticker on the front windshield with 'STAFF' on it.

'Well, Plan B already looks better than Plan A,' she said.

'Let's hope so,' Johnny replied, and after Rebekah had locked the car, he led them into the trees. She'd worn an old pair of sneakers, and an older pair of denims, so it didn't matter how muddy the path got, but as they trailed further into the woods, she could see that most of it was frozen hard anyway.

Fifteen minutes passed, then ten more, then another ten, and finally Rebekah asked, 'Have you any idea where this dig site is?'

'I don't think it's too far,' Johnny said, but he sounded unconvinced.

A second later, his foot plunged into a puddle, disguised by the roots of a tree, the water coming all the way up to his ankle.

'Oh, you gotta be kidding me,' he muttered, stopping, his boot, his pants, both soaked.

'You okay?' Rebekah asked.

Her brother flushed with irritation.

'This is frustrating,' he said, typically underplaying it.

She guessed he wasn't just annoyed about his wet foot or the search for Stelzik, but feeling guilty about accepting her invitation to drive him all the way out here. She wanted to reassure him but, in truth, she was starting to feel pissed off herself. This wasn't sitting on the beach, listening to the sea. They hadn't started the day in a quaint coffee shop with views of the ocean, nursing an elaborate pastry while a fire roared in the corner. She'd known the island would be basic, but not this basic. And she hadn't thought they'd be doing a hike.

'I'm sorry about this,' Johnny said.

'Why don't you try giving him another call?' Rebekah asked.

He showed her his cellphone. 'No signal.'

Rebekah checked hers. It was the same.

'I think we should go back,' she said then.

Johnny eyed her.

'We don't know where the hell we're going. We don't know where the hell this guy is. We're just following a vague path into the middle of nowhere.'

'He said the dig site was down here.'

She looked past Johnny to where the path disappeared. 'Down where? We've probably walked a mile and a half already. It's almost the end of the season, and the hostel where he was supposed to be staying is totally dead. How do you know he's even still here?'

'If Stelzik has left already,' Johnny said, 'why's his car back there?'

Rebekah just shrugged.

Johnny took a step towards her – and, as he did, his boot squelched comically underfoot. He broke into a smile. 'Oh, come on, Bek. Are you saying we're not having a great time?'

She couldn't help smiling in return.

He rocked back and forth on his foot, the wet sound repeating. 'How about we make a deal?' he said to her, in the soft voice he'd always used when they were kids – when he was warning her not to rub Dad up the wrong way, when he used to talk about their mother. 'Ten more minutes and, if he isn't here, we turn ba–'

A noise erupted around them.

They looked at each other.

'What the hell was that?' Johnny said.

But he knew exactly what the sound was.

They both did.

It was someone screaming.

31

It was ten minutes back to the buildings she'd seen from the lighthouse.

As she drove, she thought about the motorboat she'd spotted there and started to feel frightened. It wasn't *using* the boat that scared her – even though she had no experience of boats – it was the thought of taking it out into the Atlantic. The vastness of the ocean, its ferocity, its unpredictability.

When she got to the buildings, she could see that all but one were wrecks: the one still standing had been converted into some sort of workshop, and, behind two unsecured gates, there were some benches and tools.

And then the boat.

It looked intimidatingly huge out of the water.

It was red and had *Chrysler Marine* written along its side. The top was open, there was no covering, no roof, just a half-window at the front, where the wheel was. In a stroke of good fortune, it was already mounted on a trailer.

She opened the gates fully and found a rowboat inside too: it looked like it was in the middle of being painted. Dragging it out of the way, she reversed the Cherokee in and tried to lift the trailer up and onto the hitch at the back. The trailer was heavy, but after a couple of attempts – muscles straining – she managed to slot it into place. She checked the time.

Almost four.

It was thirty minutes to sunset, and inside an hour, she'd have no light left. As she looked at the boat on the back of the Jeep, her choice seemed clear.

She'd have to wait until morning.

The next day, it rained from sunrise to sunset. She watched from the store's windows, waiting for the weather to clear, but there was no break.

The day after that, it was still wet, relentless. She took a drive in the Cherokee, the boat and trailer still attached, looking again for food and clothes, but didn't find any of either.

On the third day, the sun finally came out.

She got up early and drove the short distance to the harbour. It took her a couple of attempts to line up the trailer with the slipway, but once she did she started to inch the Jeep back, and the wheels of the trailer broke the surface of the sea, followed by the boat.

She had no idea how much of the hull was supposed to be in contact with the water, so she stopped when it was just past half-way in, killed the Jeep's engine, and unclipped the boat. She felt it shift against the rollers and inch a little way back, then start to slide.

The boat hit the water.

Immediately it was drifting in the wind, anchorless. Rebekah hurried forward, first soaking her shoes, then her pants, and tried to grab at the sides. She missed, almost lost her balance and landed in the water. At a second attempt, she missed again, and by the time she'd finally grabbed hold of the boat, she was forty yards from the slipway, waist-deep in the ocean, and her skin was like ice beneath her clothes.

She grabbed hold of a swim ladder that had been added, and climbed into the cockpit. There was no cover in the boat, so there was nowhere to keep out of the wind, but she found a compartment with a windbreaker, a blanket and another first-aid kit. Zipping up the windbreaker and putting the blanket around her shoulders, she returned to the stern. At her feet was a tube, unattached at one end, which must be the fuel line. Kneeling at the outboard engine, she detached a lever and dropped the engine into the water, then connected the fuel line to it.

She cranked it.

Nothing happened.

She tried again, and again, kept repeating the action. Every time, the motor would wheeze for a couple of seconds, like an old man gasping for air, then die. She kept going, but after a while it ceased doing anything at all and she figured she'd flooded the engine – or, worse, there was no fuel in the boat in the first place.

She collapsed onto the bench.

Trying to think straight, she got down into the freezing cold water again and used one of the ropes – extending it to its full length – to tie the boat to a cleat welded at the side of the slipway.

She then went back to the general store to change.

She was still wearing the clothes from the gas station, but now she slipped back into hers, which were dry. She didn't have any other shoes, so she had to pull on the soaked sneakers.

After that, she returned to the boat.

Except something had changed.

The boat was gone.

Before

Rebekah and Johnny sprinted through the trees ahead of them, following the sound of the scream. Soon, they reached a clearing. On the opposite side, where the path headed into more trees, there was a holdall, tools spilling out of it.

An archaeology kit.

'Dr Stelzik?' Johnny called.

There was a strange kind of hush to the forest: the birdsong had died out; there was no breeze. Rebekah had lost her bearings, felt disoriented.

'Dr Stelzik?' Johnny repeated.

He glanced at Rebekah. It was obvious they were thinking the same thing: was it Stelzik they'd heard screaming?

They crossed into the next swathe of forest.

It was dense, the trail awkward to follow, but a minute later, they suddenly found themselves in a second clearing, at the crest of a steep slope.

At the bottom was a man.

He was on his front, motionless.

'Dr Stelzik!' Johnny shouted.

Rebekah felt her muscles harden, a chill passing through her. Could he be dead? Johnny, alarm in his face, led the way down a bank at the edge of the excavation site.

'Johnny . . .'

He didn't stop, his focus on helping the man, but as Rebekah looked around the site, enclosed by the forest, it felt like something was off.

'*Johnny,*' she said again – louder, fiercer.

'What?'

She didn't know how to explain herself. 'Something isn't right,' she said, her eyes scanning the maze of trees that encircled them, branches creaking in the wind, like the hull of an old wooden ship. Johnny was already moving again, bridging the distance between him and the curator.

Get your shit together, she told herself – but then images of Kyra and Chloe strobed in her head. *I shouldn't have come here, I shouldn't have –*

'Bek!' Johnny shouted.

He was rolling the man's body over. 'Bek!' he called. 'What are you *waiting* for?'

She hurried down, heart beating fast, moving Johnny aside. Instinct and training kicked in, as if she were under the searing white lights of the OR, not miles from home in the middle of a remote forest.

'Do you think this is him?' she said to Johnny, trying to listen for sounds of gurgling in case there was vomit or fluid in the man's airways. 'Do you think this is Stelzik?'

Johnny nodded, holding something out to her.

'This was on the ground next to him,' he said.

A wallet with ATM cards and receipts in it. Rebekah slid a couple of bank cards out – *Dr K. Stelzik* written on them – and then her attention switched.

There was blood in his hair.

'Is he alive, Bek?'

She reached down and felt for a pulse.

'He's alive,' she said.

Johnny heaved a sigh of relief. 'So what's wrong with him?' She looked him over, examining the areas of exposed skin, before using a hand to adjust his clothes, searching for evidence of wounds or more blood.

There was nothing else.

Just a cut on his head.

She shifted forward onto her knees, leaning right over his face, and opened his mouth to double-check his airways. His breathing was regular, steady. There was no obvious sound of fluid. She had no equipment – no way to check his vital signs properly – but he didn't seem to be struggling, and as soon as she began to initiate the standard procedures for motor response, squeezing the trapezius hard, Stelzik flinched.

Grabbing her cell, she used the flashlight function to check his pupils: they constricted immediately and identically on both sides. When she removed the light, they dilated. There was more she might have done but, without the right equipment, a lot of the procedures were harder to carry out, and experience told her those checks weren't going to be needed.

'I think he'll be okay,' she said.

Almost as soon as the words were out of her mouth, Stelzik started to come round. Rebekah moved back from him, giving him room, and watched as his eyelids flickered. He moved, then opened his eyes. As his gaze found her, he moaned.

'How are you feeling, Dr Stelzik?'

He moaned again, wincing, and Rebekah glanced around the dig site. 'We need to get him some water,' she said to Johnny.

'We passed a stream on the way here,' he replied, and took off, back up the ridges of the site to where they'd seen an old bucket.

'How are you feeling, Dr Stelzik?' she repeated.

He'd hauled himself into a sitting position.

'Okay,' he said groggily. He rubbed a couple of fingers against his right eye. 'I've got a bit of a headache.' He looked out at the dig site, to the forest beyond, then back to Rebekah. 'I'm sorry. I'm afraid I don't recall . . .'

'I'm Rebekah,' she said. 'My brother's John Murphy. You were supposed to meet him at the place you're staying at, but, well . . .' She gestured to the fact that he was lying on the ground. 'I guess we know why you weren't there.'

He managed a smile. 'I must have blacked out,' he said.

'Do you remember why?'

He swallowed, a slight wheeze in his throat.

'Dr Stelzik?'

'Karl,' he said. 'No, not exactly.'

'You've got blood in your hair.'

He touched his fingers to a cut on his scalp.

'It looks like you might have fallen,' Rebekah suggested.

'If I did, I don't remember.'

She took him in properly. He was younger than she'd imagined – late thirties, early forties – and, despite the mud on his cheeks and the untidiness of his hair, he was athletic and handsome.

A moment later, Johnny emerged at the top of the dig site, a bucket in his left hand, his body leaning to the right to counter-balance its weight.

'Are you starting to feel any better, Karl?' Rebekah asked Stelzik.

'A little,' he said, although he didn't sound convinced.

And then: a noise.

It was coming from the forest.

'Johnny,' Rebekah said, 'stop.'

Her brother came to a halt, halfway up the site. 'Why?' he responded, confused. 'Bek, what's going on?'

And then something emerged from the grass.

Yellow teeth exposed.

Slowly, Rebekah got to her feet, hand out in front of her. It was a dog, a golden retriever: there was blood at one of its ears, the trail running in a thin path to its jawline.

'It's okay,' she said softly. 'It's okay.'

It growled.

'It's okay. Take it easy.' At the sound of her voice, the dog seemed to shrink a little, its hind legs closing in against its body in an act of submission. Rebekah stole a look at Johnny, told him to stay put with her eyes, and returned her attention to the dog. 'It's okay,' she said again. 'Take it easy.'

A long, muted silence.

And then a split second later, the dog charged her.

32

The motorboat was gone.

How could it just disappear?

But then she saw it. It was partly obscured by the jetty, drifting on the ocean, rope trailing behind it, like a stray thread, two hundred feet further out.

As fast as she could, she began taking off her outer layers, stripping down to her underwear and T-shirt, kicking off her wet sneakers, but as the wind crashed in off the water, she had a moment of clarity: she'd been on the island five weeks, it was December, below zero, she had no idea what the tides were like in this part of the world, or how much of a current there was.

And even if she swam to the boat, what then?

The Atlantic would be bitter – and there was no guarantee the engine would start because she didn't know if it even had fuel in it.

Still only partly dressed, she dropped to her haunches at the edge of the water, her skin rinsed pink from the cold, and tears blurred her eyes again.

But then she remembered the rowboat.

She pulled on her clothes and drove back to the workshop in the Jeep, dragging the rowboat from inside, up onto the incline of the trailer. By the time it was secured, her hands were scarred with rope burns, and she'd sweated through her top. She stopped, her muscles sore, and looked out at the ocean: the skies were clear and the water seemed calm.

Back at the harbour, she dragged the rowboat off the trailer and down the slipway, trying to focus on the job of getting into the boat, not on her fear of the journey that lay ahead of her. It rocked from side to side as it hit the sea, rocked again as she got into it, and one of the oars almost escaped its rowlock before Rebekah managed to grab it and haul it back in towards her. But then, finally, she was seated, had hold of the oars, and was moving.

Driftwood slapped bluntly against the hull as she rowed, jamming the oars into the water to avoid the motorboat she'd had to abandon. Eventually, she got beyond that, the wood, the harbour too, and the only thing in front of her, around her, was ocean. For a second, she felt exhilarated.

The feeling didn't last long.

The further out she got, the choppier the water became, jolting the boat so much it seemed to be fighting her. The wind was nothing more than a whisper, but the boat rocked hard, tilting from side to side as the swells of the Atlantic pounded against the hull.

She pulled harder, faster, straining every sinew. Slowly, the water began to change colour, green to blue to grey, and she looked behind her, across the vast sweep of the ocean, desperate to see the mainland, a small reminder that it was there. How far would she have to go before she could start to make out Montauk?

After a while, even though it was still bitter, her hands started slipping on the oars as her palms became slick with sweat. She was unfit, struggling to breathe, her muscles on fire, and she was far enough out that she'd begun to feel vulnerable: a mote of dust compared to the immensity of the ocean.

She looked towards Helena. She'd come half a mile now, maybe more, and – into the distance, on the other side of the island – clouds had begun to twist and form. Rebekah stared at them. She had no food with her and nothing to drink. She didn't have a life-jacket. She'd been so desperate to escape, she hadn't even brought the bare essentials. *What the hell am I doing?*

'I just want to go home,' she said quietly.

The ocean was silent.

'I just want to see my girls.'

She exhaled the words as if they were her last. And though she wanted to cry, she didn't this time, feeling the emotion as a ball in her chest. It seemed to come from somewhere deep, a hidden part of her. It began to throb so hard that her entire body hurt.

She let the feeling come, wave after wave of it, until finally she was back in control. By that time, the weather was changing. The wind had picked up and the clouds had changed again, their colour darkening.

This isn't an island, she thought.

She turned the boat around.

It's a prison.

Before

Rebekah stumbled back as the dog darted forward, the soles of her shoes clipping the edges of the barrier tape, immediately knocking her off balance.

She reached out behind her to break her fall and saw Johnny move. 'Bek!' he called, and as he took off, the bucket fell from his hand and hit the ground.

But the dog wasn't coming for Rebekah.

Stelzik thrust up an arm, protecting his face, his neck, as the animal leaped at him, its jaws clamping onto his wrist. He yelled in pain, the noise crashing through the trees like a wave, agonizing and terrible. He tried to shake the dog off, to free his arm from the vice of its jaws, but the animal wouldn't let go. Its paws were trying to get purchase on his body, its claws tearing at his shirt. But just as Rebekah scrambled to her feet, the dog's jaws snapped open and, a second later, it made a dash for the trees.

Stelzik rolled around on the ground, blood along his arm, and moaned. As Rebekah dropped to her knees beside him, checking his wounds – seeing they were bad, but not as bad as they might have been – Johnny looked for the dog.

'Roxie,' Stelzik muttered, nursing his bloodied arm against his body, as if it were in a sling. 'That was Roxie. She's my dog. I don't know what's wrong with her.' He tried to gather himself. 'I've brought her here every day for seven months, but today she just . . . She went absolutely nuts . . .'

Rebekah peered into the forest.

They'd been drawn here by the sound of screaming. But maybe

it hadn't been a scream at all, just Stelzik trying to call Roxie back.

Rebekah asked, 'Has she had her rabies shots?'

'They're all up to date.'

'Any injuries during the last few days?'

'No.'

'Hasn't been in any fights with other animals?'

'No, nothing like that.'

'So she hasn't been sick during your time here?'

'No, she's been fine.'

Johnny had gone to retrieve the bucket from the top of the dig site and now set it down next to Stelzik. He started ladling water out with a cupped hand and used it to wash down the arm. Tooth-marks were evident along the ridge of the radius, like black pennies, and there were scratches all down his chest, revealed in fine red lines by the gaps that had been torn in his shirt.

'I think I slipped,' Stelzik said quietly.

'Slipped?'

He looked at Rebekah. 'That's why I blacked out. Roxie started acting all crazy, took off into the forest, and I tried to follow her but slipped on all this mud. My head feels sore on the crown here.' He touched the cut again.

'We need to dress your wounds,' Rebekah said.

'I don't have anything like that here.'

'It's okay. I've got some basics in my car.'

He studied her. 'You sound like you know what you're doing.'

'Eight years and a residency teaches you how to dress a wound.'

'You're a medical doctor?'

She nodded as she and Johnny helped Stelzik into a sitting position.

'What do you think's wrong with Roxie?' he said.

'I don't know,' Rebekah admitted, 'but we should probably find out, and that means going and getting her. Is there a medical facility on the island, Karl?'

'No. Just a cabinet with some medicines.'

But that would likely be better than what she had in the car.

'Where's that?' she asked.

'At the hostel I'm staying in.'

'Are you all right to stand?'

He nodded. 'I think so.'

They helped Stelzik to his feet and Johnny stepped forward. 'We haven't been officially introduced, Dr Stelzik. I'm John Murphy.'

'Hello, John,' Stelzik replied, slowly starting to move. 'I'm only sorry you both had to find me in this terrible state.' He looked between them. 'I left my Chevy in the parking area. I assume you have a car too. Maybe you could drive mine, John, and the two of us could talk on the way to the hostel.'

'I wouldn't want you to feel any pressure to –'

'It's all right,' Stelzik said, attempting a smile. 'Honestly. It's the least I owe you for the help you and your sister have given me.' The smile fell away as he glanced at the trees again. 'What are we going to do about Roxie?'

'We'll take you back to my car and get your arm patched up,' Rebekah said, 'then Johnny and I will come back and try to find her.'

'Thank you so much,' Stelzik said, and Rebekah smiled in response, but she didn't want to go back into the trees. She didn't want to go searching for a dog that might be dangerous.

She just wanted to forget this day had ever happened.

Daybreak

Unable to sleep after Amy Houser's call, Travis headed into the office early. First he got hold of the recording of the call that Houser had picked up the night before, and had it transferred to his work station.

'Tell him to take a second look at the boyfriend.'

Before Houser had even had a chance to respond, the line went dead, and the recording ended. Travis immediately played it again: it sounded to him as if the caller might have been trying to adjust his voice – or disguise an accent. His words were artificial, too enunciated.

The logs said that the call had come from a payphone in Greenpoint. Travis returned to his desk and did some ringing around, trying to work out what level of camera coverage there was in that area of Brooklyn. The answer was not much – certainly nothing that might get him a decent image of the person. That, in turn, likely meant one of two things.

One, the caller was trying to deflect, to alter the course of the case, because he knew what had happened to Louise Mason, and feared that Travis might recognize and ID him, if they actually spoke.

Or, two, the caller was shit-scared.

Travis pulled his notebook towards him and flipped through to a page he'd filled off the back of his initial conversation with the man Louise had dated.

Johnny Murphy.

Could the caller be frightened of Murphy? Could he be a witness to something that Murphy had done? If the caller was frightened of a reprisal, a 1 a.m. tip-off, when Travis wasn't around to ask questions, made perfect sense.

Travis grabbed his notebook and the Louise Mason file and headed to the video suite two floors up. As he waited at the elevators, he went back through some of his notes, reminding himself again about Johnny Murphy – and then the doors pinged open and he was suddenly face-to-face with the chief of detectives, Katherine McKenzie.

'Morning,' she said.

She must have been heading for the top floor.

'Morning, Chief,' Travis replied, and stepped into the elevator. He pushed the button for eight, and glanced at McKenzie again. She was in her early fifties, tall and slim; Travis had always thought she was attractive, but she didn't smile a lot, so that could sometimes make her look severe.

'Early start?' she asked.

'Just trying to finish some last things off.'

'So you've been in all night?'

'No,' Travis said, smiling, realizing what she thought he'd meant. 'No, I'm sailing away into old age in a matter of days, so "finishing things off" is in the more permanent sense.' He held up his notebook. 'All I've got left is one pain-in-the-ass case that refuses to let go.'

She eyed him for a moment and a half-smile flittered at the corner of her lips. Travis thought it suited her. 'You're Travis, right?'

He nodded. 'Yes, ma'am.'

He'd never worked with her directly but he'd heard she was smart and had a good memory for names. People said she was a hard-ass too. Some detectives, very quietly and out of earshot, called her 'The Dyke' because she was single, had never been seen with a partner at any NYPD functions, and – in their eyes – being a lesbian explained why she was always busting balls. Travis had no idea whether she was gay or not, but she was a woman in a majority male environment, so the nickname was entirely predictable. For his part, Travis preferred to listen to people he trusted: Amy Houser had been coming through the ranks at the 40th Precinct when McKenzie was already commanding officer there, and she'd told Travis that McKenzie was no-nonsense, but if you worked hard and did the right things, she didn't care who you were, where you came from or what your story was, she'd always have your back.

In the 40th, Houser told Travis they used to have a phrase: 'The Mac Don't Crack.'

'I was sorry to hear you were leaving us, Detective Travis,' McKenzie said, bringing him out of his thoughts.

When his eyes met hers, he could see she meant it, and he could read between *the lines to what she was actually telling him: he was taking retirement, not because he'd wanted to but because there was a new, younger, brass at NYPD's summit, and Travis was seen as an expensive relic. McKenzie was saying she didn't agree with it, and that it had been a decision taken above her pay grade.*

'I appreciate that, Chief.'

The doors pinged open on the eighth.

'Good hunting, Detective,' McKenzie said.

Travis headed along the corridor to the video suite, his thoughts back on his retirement and how he would spend his days after this. He'd thought about moving south a few times: a couple of his old NYPD buddies had migrated to the Carolinas, or he could have gone even further to Florida, where he didn't know anyone but where winters were never like New York's.

But he'd done nothing about it.

That was another thing Naomi always said about him, another reason she'd given for leaving: he lacked drive. He lacked the will to see ideas through, or to try new things. You're scared, she used to shout at him. You're scared about doing anything that isn't this. She'd meant his job. She'd meant New York. But the truth was he was never scared. How could he be a cop — how could he look at a murder, at the terrible things one human being could do to another — if he frightened easily? No, he wasn't scared: he'd just come to understand that he didn't want to move to another state and start another life with Naomi. And after she'd left him, after the kids had both flown the nest, he didn't want to do it alone either.

He reached the video suite and, even though no one else was around, he pushed the door closed behind him so he wouldn't be disturbed. After that, he rolled a chair to a small TV monitor in the corner, flipped open the case file, and fished out a DVD he kept in a sleeve at the front.

From the moment video cameras had come in, every first interview that Travis had ever done he'd tried to record. There was no legal obligation to do so, and most cops didn't bother hitting Record until the first formal interview, but — if the person agreed to it — Travis had done it. While the notes he made were extensive, you couldn't see someone's manner on a page: the way they reacted to new questions they couldn't prepare for, their body language, their expression. Some of the other cops laughed at him, and not always behind his back; he'd heard them say it was because his memory was going, and without the videos he got confused about who was who in his cases. But he ignored it all.

In moments like this, when you felt like you might have screwed up, the videos were invaluable. There was no ambiguity.

They were perfectly preserved time capsules.

He put the DVD into the tray.

After Louise's disappearance had been kicked up the chain to him, he'd gone out and interviewed anyone who might have come into contact with her on the night she vanished, and in the days preceding it. That included Johnny Murphy, her parents, friends, people she'd attended the charity fundraiser with, and staff at the hotel – the Royal Union in the East Village – where the event had taken place. The fundraiser was the last place she'd been seen, and the last image of her alive was the one Travis felt like he'd spent three months staring at: Louise, talking to an unidentified man in the hotel bar less than twenty minutes before she disappeared.

The interview on the DVD had taken place in Murphy's house in Bay Ridge, on 81ˢᵗ Street. He'd told Travis he and his sister had been left the property by their father, but that his sister lived in a place in Windsor Terrace. That had all checked out. In fact, everything had checked out. But that was the thing about this guy. Maybe it was all just a little too perfect.

Onscreen, an image of Murphy appeared.

He was just staring into space.

'Okay, Mr Murphy,' Travis heard himself saying off camera, and still Murphy didn't look at him. 'I need you to tell me about Louise Mason.'

Before

Back at the Cherokee, Rebekah used up the remainder of what was left in a first-aid kit she kept in the trunk. The bites on Stelzik's arm were nasty, though not as deep or as severe as they might have been, and it was impossible to check for infection without the proper equipment. Whatever happened, the search for Stelzik's dog would have to be truncated: Rebekah thought it unlikely that Roxie had rabies, despite her aggression, but in the forest there were skunks, bats and raccoons, all of which carried the virus, so she couldn't write it off entirely. It was possible Stelzik was infected – and that made him a ticking time bomb.

He'd need a shot, and quickly.

All the way through the dressing of his arm, he kept offering to go and find Roxie, telling Rebekah it wasn't her fault the dog had escaped, but she knew it would be quicker if she and Johnny went alone. Stelzik was still shaken, so after he'd opened his Chevy, turned the ignition on and fired up the heaters, they left him there to warm up and headed back along the same path.

'He'd better give you a damn good interview,' Rebekah said.

'Do you think he's got rabies?'

They entered the top of the dig site, the grass at the bottom of the excavation still tainted red from where Stelzik had bled. 'I don't think so,' she responded.

'So what was wrong with the dog?'

Rebekah looked around them. 'Maybe she was scared.'

'Of what?'

Once they'd got beyond the dig site and were back inside the forest, the light seemed almost subdued, the brightness of the day piercing the canopy in just a couple of places, lancing through it in thin arrows of light. It gave their surroundings an uncharted feel that Rebekah wasn't certain she liked.

'What was the dog scared of?' Johnny asked again.

She glanced at her brother. He was looking at her differently now, his face shadowed by the trees, his expression one that she couldn't quite interpret.

'I don't know, Johnny,' she replied, and then a compulsion to call Noella hit her: she needed to know the girls were okay, as irrational as that seemed to be. 'Have you got any reception?'

'One bar.'

'That's more than I've got,' she said, and looked past the treeline into the depths of the forest. As Johnny handed her his phone, she kept her eyes on the interior, searching for the dog, while she dialled Noe's number.

'This is Noella. Leave a message.'

Voicemail.

Rebekah felt herself sag. *This whole trip has been an absolute shitfest.*

'Noe, I, uh . . .' She stopped. 'Give me a call when you get this, okay?' Rebekah's thumb hovered above the End Call button. *Everything's fine. You can hang up now.* But she didn't. She said, 'I need you to call me on Johnny's phone.' She waited, as if some part of her were expecting Noella to answer. 'I just want to . . .' She cleared her throat. 'I'll speak to you later, then.'

She hung up, searching the trees again.

Johnny had gone ahead of her.

'Let's get this over with,' she said to him.

But this time her brother didn't respond.

He just led her deeper into the forest.

4
Roots

Before

Rebekah saved the lives of a lot of people, but she always remembered Ramón.

His full name was Ramón Alejandro Cortez. He'd just turned nineteen, was dark-eyed and handsome, and in the States on a soccer scholarship. When the hospital staff had been through his pockets in the hours after he'd arrived at the ER, they'd found a Costa Rican driver's licence and a phone packed with photos of his family. A mother, a father, brothers, sisters. Ramón was in most of them, his eyes bright, with a smile full of white teeth. Rebekah was always reluctant to read too much into pictures, because mostly they were lies – false smiles, staged appearances, people bunching together unnaturally – but there was something genuine about Ramón's. She often thought it was because his family portraits were reminiscent of her own, the ones of her father, her brothers and her. There was just a truth in them, a legitimacy, something unexplainable but there, that – even before the split – Rebekah had never been able to find in the pictures of her and Gareth.

Ramón had been levered out of a car wreck on the Long Island Expressway. His French friend, also in New York on the same scholarship programme, was driving too fast, hit a patch of ice and lost control of his Toyota. Eyewitnesses said it spun three times and flipped onto its roof, rolling into the path of a truck that braked – but not quickly enough. Ramón's friend was crushed in the impact, killing him instantly, and Ramón's girlfriend – who was travelling in the back, without a seatbelt on – suffered severe head injuries. She made it as far as the ER but died an hour later.

Ramón arrived with a broken hip, broken ribs, a punctured lung, and a right leg severed at the knee. Rebekah had spent her fellowship in the OR looking at a parade of lurid trauma injuries, and nothing had been done to Ramón's body that she hadn't seen a hundred times over. Fast cars, and kids too young to handle them, tended to deliver a steady diet of lost limbs, snapped bones and deformity.

But it wasn't Ramón's injuries that stuck with her.

A few days after he arrived at the hospital, he woke up for the first time, wrapped in bandages and wired up. He looked out into the room, blood vessels thick in his eyes, and tried to say something. In the time he'd been out, his mother and father had travelled up from Costa Rica, and – at his bedside – they began speaking in Spanish, his mother thanking God he was awake, his father clutching Ramón's hand, tears gathering in his eyes. When Ramón tried to speak again, his father used his other hand to touch his son's arm gently, reassuring him they were both there.

But it wasn't them Ramón was talking to.

His eyes blinked, then found Rebekah, the woman in a white coat on the edge of the room, watching the Cortez family, clipboard to her chest.

'Foot?' he said.

It was clear he could feel something the moment he awoke: a sense of loss, of forfeiture. And then he saw the reality for himself, halfway down the bed, his toes, his ankle, his shin, his calf, everything below the knee – gone.

There were ways for him to become mobile again, artificial limbs that would allow him to disguise the truth in a pair of pants if that was how he felt. He would still be able to walk, run and get around, drive, sail, climb. He could even play soccer again. He'd be able to kick a ball around the yard with his kids.

Yet his physical loss was really the smallest part of what had happened to him. That was what Rebekah learned that day, what she came to learn over and over. That was why she always remembered Ramón, because it was the first time she ever saw it play out in front of her, as a person, not as words on a page in a psychology textbook. He was a sweet kid who, in the days after, would talk to Rebekah and the nurses, always quietly, politely, in heavily accented English, thanking them for looking after him and asking them how they were.

But whatever ambitions he'd held before the car crash, whatever he'd allowed himself to dream of, was just debris now: fans, money, playing in gigantic European stadiums that rose from the ground like floodlit coliscums.

She remembered Ramón, not because his was a young life reduced to rubble but because, after he asked about his foot, it was the first time anyone had looked at her with the expression she came to know so well. The one that said, *You think you saved my life by doing this. You think this is better for me.*

You should have let me die.

I'd be better off dead.

33

The day after she'd tried, and failed, to escape back to the mainland using two entirely different boats, Rebekah thought of Ramón for the first time in months and especially the expression on his face. She hadn't seen her daughters for five weeks. No rescue had come, or was coming. Every way off the island – whether she radioed for help, set a fire, or tried to row one hundred and one miles – carried an immense risk. It carried the risk not just of failure but of any brief success being cut down when Hain and Lima found out she was alive. Would it have been easier if, like Johnny, she'd never made it out of the forest?

She pictured Ramón, his expression. *Could death be any worse than this purgatory?*

By now, Kyra and Chloe, Noella, Gareth, any friends who'd heard about Rebekah and Johnny leaving home on 30 October and never returning, would have assumed they were gone for good. All of those people, including her daughters – perhaps, *especially* her daughters, given their age – would have begun to move on, maybe so slowly it was hardly visible, but each day Rebekah wasn't there was another day on the road to recovery. They were moving forward, but she was stuck: she was five weeks into a twenty-two-week prison sentence, she'd already run out of food, and even if, by some miracle, she made it to the last day of March, twenty-four hours later two men would be boarding a ferry to come back for her. How long before they realized she was still alive? And then what? Would she fight them?

The idea was laughable. She knew nothing about outsmarting

killers; she couldn't even fire a gun. So what was the point in trying to endure if, at the end of twenty-two weeks, she was dead within hours of the island reopening? Better not to give her killers that satisfaction. Better to end it before it got worse.

Better to be dead now.

For two days, she barely moved from her mattress. Another low hit her, like the world had fallen in: she hardly ate any of the little food she had left, she just slept, her recurring dream returning on the second night. It was so vivid, it was like the island had ceased to exist: she passed from the corridor into the apartment, looking at the skewed 7 on the door, and when the carpet began to move beneath her feet, when its fibres began to crawl up her ankles, she could feel everything, every physical sensation, every touch, every smell.

I think you should stay, Rebekah.

When she woke, sweating, heart pounding, it was a relief, but the relief didn't last long. She stared into the semi-lit store, at its half-empty shelves, full of crap that was neither going to help her survive nor help her escape, and her spirits plummeted even further.

Yet at no point did she seriously think she was capable of ending it all. She thought about the ways in which it could be done – a knife to the wrist, smashing a window in the lantern room of the lighthouse and leaping out – but she didn't ever feel she had the guts to follow through on it. And somewhere, just below the surface, there was the reason why: her daughters.

If there was a chance – however distant it seemed now – that she would get to see them again, to hold them, go home to them, she had to go on.

A day later a storm passed through, a blast of thunder and rain that felt like the end of the world, and after that, the leak in the roof got so bad, part of the ceiling fell away, landing on the floor of the store in a dull thump.

The temperature, already sub-zero, dropped even further.

I need to find somewhere else, Rebekah thought.

She looked at her map and saw a few areas along the north coast – old trails she hadn't explored – then got dressed and headed out in the Cherokee.

She needed to fill the car up too.

She'd planned to head west, around the Loop, and start at the north-western end of the coast, but instead she went the other way, so she could go past the gas station.

It was a decision that seemed so insignificant at the time.

But it was one that changed everything.

34

Rebekah watched the numbers on the pump spiral upwards. She had no idea what reserves were left and, in truth, hated having to think about it. Perhaps the only thing she'd found any enjoyment in on the island was her ability to travel around. It gave her purpose and a minor sense of freedom. She'd almost forgotten what real freedom was like – the ability to go anywhere, the comfort of absolute safety, the chance to be with the people you loved whenever you wanted – but the car was a modest taste of it, and she'd cherished it.

As she filled the Cherokee, her eyes fell upon the mud-spattered Ford Explorer, raised on bricks, at the side of the forecourt office. She'd found it the first time she'd come here, half disguised by rampant vines and grass, and every time she returned, she'd try to imagine who it might have belonged to. Some days, she even found herself building an entire back story.

Because the mud was as thick as paint on the tyres – the windshield dusty, the licence plate unreadable under grime – she told herself the owner had lived somewhere there were no paved roads. She'd wiped a patch clean on the driver's side window one day and had looked inside: crushed soda cans on the floor, chip packets and sandwich wrappings. There was an empty duffel bag too, and on the zip there was a keyring with a photograph: it was of a good-looking man in his forties with a woman of about the same age in some mountains somewhere. There was no sign of any kids, in the keyring or anywhere else, so Rebekah had decided the owner hadn't been able to have them. In her head, she'd named him Steve, because he looked vaguely like a doctor with the same name she used to know.

How you doing today, Bek?

That was the other thing she'd started to do.

Imagine conversations with him.

Morning, Steve.

He was working under the hood, his sleeves rolled up, a New York Mets baseball cap on his head. He always wore the same cap; he wore it in the picture on the keyring too. He'd grown a beard since they'd last talked, and Rebekah thought how good it looked on him. He was handsome, like his picture, but sometimes – outside the stillness of the photograph – it was hard to see just how handsome because he could come across as tough, made you work for that smile of his, and a lot of people wouldn't have had the patience.

But Rebekah did.

She'd put in the hard yards with Steve already and so, whenever she came back to the gas station, he would smile at her straight off the bat, and he would mean it, and when they talked, he was open and honest with her because, over time, she'd gained his trust.

A crow squawked.

Sometimes, like now, Rebekah would catch herself embedded in the fantasy. She'd become aware of how ridiculous it was for a grown woman to build an imaginary life for a man she'd never known. Other times, she ran away with it, mapping out every elaborate detail of Steve's life, because the alternative was standing in a gas station, surrounded by nothing but corrosion and weeds.

I was thinking about something, she said.

Steve didn't look up, just carried on with what he was doing. *Thinking, huh?* he replied, teeth pressed together in a grimace as he levered something out of the engine. *That ain't such a good idea.*

Rebekah smiled.

I was thinking about that keyring of yours.

He looked at her now.

How come you never had any kids, Steve?

He paused for a moment, as if frozen in time, then slid out from under the hood. *Well,* he said, putting down a wrench, and letting out a long breath. There was sadness in his expression now, but Rebekah could tell he was trying to suppress it. He didn't like becoming emotional: it was why he was always rubbing his face, using his hand to disguise his mouth and eyes.

You don't have to talk about it if you don't want to.

No, it's not that . . . He shrugged. *I guess it's just, it's a sad story.*

Rebekah nodded. She'd thought it would be.

Me and April – that's my wife – we tried for a long time. Boy, did we ever try. That smile again, but marked with pain this time. *We both came from big families, and kids – that was all we wanted. I mean, we started when we were just kids ourselves. I was twenty-three, April was twenty-one, and we never had any doubt that it would happen. We were young, healthy, we were at it all the time – it just seemed impossible that it wouldn't happen. But a year went by, then two. In the third year, we finally went to see a doctor about it.* He rubbed at his mouth again and pulled the peak of the cap down, so that the sun didn't show his eyes. *You ever heard of endometriosis?*

Rebekah felt a twist in her guts. *Yes.*

That's what April had. Makes it hard to get pregnant. Damn near impossible if you've got it bad, and April had it bad. She used to have these terrible monthlies. It would hurt when we were, you know . . . having sex. *All the warning signs were there, but we knew nothing about it. Like I said, we were just stupid kids. Back then, the world was so simple. You had sex without protection, you got pregnant. Nine months later, you had a little one in your arms, this perfect little thing that was everything you ever wanted in life.* He paused, swallowing down the break in his voice, trying to pretend it had never been there. *They said we could do IVF.* He shrugged again. *They said that was a way around it, but where were we gonna come up with seventeen grand from? I was a mechanic, April was a school teacher. Our parents were dirt poor. We had nothing. We didn't have no savings. When we got married, we knew we'd never be rich, but we didn't care because we loved each other. You think love is all that matters at the start. I mean, April and me, we loved each other to the ends of the earth. You ain't ever seen a love like ours, Bek. And our kids, we would have loved them even more. So much. I'd have been there at Little League with my boy and playing dress-up in the yard with my girl, and I would have breathed in every second of it. But then your whole life comes crashing down around you and you realize something. "Love conquers all", that's just a Hallmark card. It's Santa Claus. It's a thing people say when –'*

The nozzle clunked.

Rebekah was back in the gas station. A gentle wind passed across the forecourt, rocking the abandoned Explorer on its axle, and she realized she had tears in her eyes. Feeling foolish, she wiped them away and looked at the readout on the pump: $61.44.

As she put the nozzle back, she wondered what her father would make of her stealing sixty bucks' worth of gas in this way. There were two pumps and they both worked, but she was keeping to the same one for now, eking out what was left in it as best she could. She figured her dad would understand. He'd want her to survive, for her to have the meagre sense of freedom that the car had brought her. *I'm more concerned about you talking to imaginary people, sweetheart.*

Her gaze slowly drifted back to the Explorer and Steve was back under the hood.

I'm sorry, Bek, he said. *I got a bit heavy there.*

He wouldn't look at her.

He was embarrassed.

It's okay, Steve. I don't blame you.

It got bad, that's all. When we discovered we couldn't have kids, April and me, we got a little crazy. We lost our minds there for a while. Like, we'd be really fucking nasty to people who had kids. We were even nastier to the ones we didn't think deserved to have them. Sometimes . . . He paused, finally looking up at her, his cap and the hood of the Explorer keeping most of his face in shadow. But Rebekah could see enough. What was coming was bad. *Shit, I can barely even admit to this, but sometimes we saw these babies, saw the moms and dads they'd been lumped with, and we thought, We could give them a better life. We could take them now and give them everything they deserve.*

His gaze stayed on her.

What? Rebekah said.

Nothing.

No, what? Tell me. Please.

It's nothing, Steve said, *just a dumb idea.* He stopped again, and then pulled up the peak on his cap so Rebekah could see his eyes. There were tears in them. *I'm just worried about you, Bek, that's all. Cos maybe the way me and April were thinking — y'know, these crazy thoughts about snatching a kid, about creating a new life for them away from parents who didn't deserve them and couldn't handle them — maybe that's what Noella thinks about your girls.*

She snapped back to the forecourt.

'No,' she said quietly, and then again more forcefully. She screwed the cap back on and checked the plastic wrap was still secure over the passenger door and window frame, then slid in at the wheel of the Jeep. Her eyes strayed back to the Ford Explorer. It was empty. Dusty. Forgotten. It was just a dumb fantasy. Steve wasn't real. None of it was real.

Except you made it real.

He only thinks what you feel.

But she didn't really believe Noella was trying to steal her kids from her, did she? She thought about Gareth again, about both of them, about the fact that there had been no rescue, not even a hint of one, in five weeks, and then her thoughts snared on something else.

An image of her and Johnny in the forest on that last day.

What they'd found as they'd searched for Roxie.

And the last call she'd ever made to Noella.

Before

Rebekah called Roxie, more in hope than expectation, and Johnny joined in, the dense, unyielding forest gathering around them. 'Roxie!' they shouted, but it felt as if their voices were instantly lost.

Half a mile in, the ground started to drop away. It was full of broken, stunted trees. They looked like melted bodies.

'This place gives me the creeps,' Rebekah said.

The further Johnny led them into the forest, the less comfortable she felt: the hairs on her arms were on end and she could hear her pulse in her ears. They moved off in different directions – not so far that they couldn't see each other, but far enough to cover more ground. After five or six minutes, they returned to each other, breathing harder.

'So what do you want to do?' Johnny asked.

'I've had enough. I just want to go home.'

'What about Stelzik?'

'We'll go and see what medicine there is at that hostel, but he'll need some tests, maybe a shot, so that means he'll have to come back on the ferry.'

Johnny nodded. 'Okay.'

Suddenly, his phone was buzzing in the pocket of his pants. Clearly surprised he had any reception at all so deep in the forest, he held it up for Rebekah to see. 'It's Noe.'

Rebekah felt a wave of excitement, of relief.

'Noe?' she said, grabbing the cell from Johnny.

'Hey, Bek. You okay, honey?'

The line was lousy.

'You sounded panicked in your message.'

'I know. I'm sorry.' Rebekah rubbed an eye, then looked out to the forest, the trees, the frozen ground. 'I'll tell you all about it when we get home but, basically, it hasn't been the relaxing day trip I was hoping for. We should have gone to a spa.' It sounded like a joke, but it wasn't. She thought of how she'd felt as she'd waited for Johnny outside Stelzik's hostel, in the seconds before she and Johnny had come into the forest looking for the dog – it was as if, in being so far away, the tether binding her to her daughters had spiralled loose.

'Bek?'

'I think I realized today that I'm not ready to be this far from the girls yet. I know it sounds nuts. They're exhausting. But it's true. It's got nothing to do with you, Noe, I promise. I trust you with their lives. I just . . . I . . .'

Rebekah faded out. *I can't function without them.*

'I get it, honey.'

But was there something in Noe's voice? A flicker of disappointment? Had Rebekah upset her? She didn't want to hurt Noe. She'd been a rock.

'The girls are fine with me, Bek,' Noe said.

'I know they are.'

'They'll always be fine with me.'

Rebekah glanced at Johnny. He was just looking at her, waiting.

'Do you want to talk to Kyra?' Noella asked.

Yes, Rebekah thought immediately. *Yes, I desperately want to talk to her.* But she hesitated in her reply. *Noe needs to believe that I trust her. She needs to know.* 'No, that's fine. I don't want to disturb her.' And then, as she swallowed the disappointment of not speaking to her daughter, a thought came to her. 'Wait, I keep forgetting to tell you where we are. You know, just in case . . .'

Just in case what?

But Noella didn't reply.

'Noe?'

No response.

'Noe, are you there?'

There was just silence on the line now.

'Noe, can you hear me? We've come to a place called Crow Island. It's about a hundred miles from Montauk. Johnny wanted to –'

The line went dead.

Rebekah looked at the phone and then at Johnny.

Had Noella just hung up on her?

'You all right?' Johnny asked.

No, it must have been the reception in here.

'Yeah,' she said, although as she handed him back his cell, even to her own ears she didn't sound convinced. She sighed. 'Whatever. Let's go. I just want to go home to –'

A dog barked.

'Come on,' Johnny said, and hurried towards the sound, following it even further into the forest. Rebekah tried to keep up. But after a couple of minutes they came to a halt again. The barking had stopped.

They couldn't see Roxie anywhere.

'This is so dumb,' she said. 'We've got no idea where the dog is.'

Johnny said nothing, his back to her, looking off into the trees. She followed his eyeline and noticed a gully to their left, ten or twelve feet down, its slope half hidden from view behind a row of grey, emaciated trees.

'What are you looking at?' she asked. She couldn't see anything in the gully. 'Did you see the dog?'

'No,' Johnny said.

She rubbed her eye again, feeling bone-tired. Then her gaze was drawn back to the gully, this time to its right-hand edge: a tangle of exposed roots was surfacing out of the sloped bank on that side. Directly above them, the canopy of leaves and branches was much thinner so frost had been able to settle on the forest floor. There wasn't much, just a lone circle.

White, thick as spilled flour.

'Do you want to go, then?' Johnny said.

'Yeah,' she replied. 'Yeah, let's get out of here.'

But she didn't move.

She just kept looking at the same circle of frost.

Because now she could see something else.

It was right on the edge of the circle, completely out of place there, so jarring, so discordant, it took her a while to even rationalize it.

'Bek?'

Finally, she dragged her eyes away and looked at her brother.

'John, I think there might be a body down there.'

35

Behind the wheel of the Cherokee, the gas station silent around her, Rebekah thought of what she and Johnny had found in the forest, and then of that last call with Noella. She'd tried to tell Noe where they were – *had* actually told her where they were – but Noe hadn't responded. Until now, Rebekah had convinced herself that it was because the signal had dropped out.

But maybe it wasn't.

Maybe Noella heard just fine. Maybe she –

Click click click.

Rebekah froze.

She stopped thinking about Noella and looked out through the windshield. On the opposite side of the road, the derelict houses were still.

But she'd heard it. She'd definitely heard it.

The same noise as before.

She swivelled around, her door still open, and slid back out of the Jeep, looking across the hood. The noise had come from the direction of the houses, she was certain. She listened hard, trying to ignore the faint hum of the wind coming off the ocean.

Click click click.

It *was* the same noise she'd heard before, weeks ago, except then it had been pitch black, her sense of direction off.

She walked around the front of the car, keeping her eyes on the houses, her hand tracing the arc of the hood, like a part of her was trying to hold on for safety. Beneath her fingers, she felt sand and grime gather. But there wasn't anything here. *Or anyone.* So what was she hearing?

Click click click.

Nerves fired under her skin as she heard it for a third time.

Then: movement.

Out of the corner of her eye.

She whipped around in time to see a shadow dart behind the house on the end. *What the hell was that?* Her heart felt like it was in her throat.

She wanted to get back into the car and drive away, but she knew she couldn't do that. Not now. If she wasn't alone, she needed to know.

But how can there be someone else here?

Rushing around to the trunk, she grabbed a hammer from a toolkit she'd cobbled together as she'd driven around the island, and then – gripping it so hard her fingers blanched – crossed the road towards the houses.

'Hello?' she said.

Her voice carried away in the wind. She passed through a broken fence into the long grass at the front of one of the houses.

'Hello?'

She looked along the narrow gap between two of the houses, into their backyards. Around her, grass swayed and warped.

'I saw you, so you can come out.'

She sounded small, pathetic.

Taking a breath, she moved slowly along the gap, pushing her way through a tangle of weeds and webs that had fused themselves to the flanks of the houses. When she reached the backyards, she stopped and looked out at the sea of grass, every branch of every tree laden with the gold of fall. Garden furniture littered the place: tables were tipped over, broken chairs, old rusted fire pits. A torn hammock was in the next yard along, only attached at one end so it hung there limply.

'Hello?'

She moved further in, along the back porches, past a white

picket fence that had once separated the properties but was now on its side, chewed up in one of the storms. In places, the grass came all the way up to her waist, opaque and impossible to see through. The further she went, the harder it got to judge her surroundings. The wind was picking up: grass leaned and bowed, leaves snapped, loose doors juddered against their frames, windows rattled.

'Stop hiding,' Rebekah said quietly.

She sounded like she was begging now.

She went to one of the porches, perched herself on the edge, and waited. After forty minutes, the colour was gone from the sky and rain clouds were moving in. She'd started to understand the weather on the island in a way she'd never bothered to in the city – had never *needed* to – and she could tell this was the start of another storm. She could feel it, like a current in the earth.

Was I mistaken? she thought. *Am I seeing things? Hearing things?* She thought of her conversation with Steve. *What if I'm losing my mind?*

She looked around her again, but there was no clicking now, nothing except the wind, the muted roar of the ocean, and the slow dance of the grass. Defeated, she headed back to the car.

And that was when she realized she wasn't losing her mind at all.

She was just seeing a ghost.

Before

Rebekah climbed down into the gully.

'If it's a body, shouldn't we call the cops?' Johnny asked, from behind her.

She glanced at her brother and saw the same reaction in him that she felt: the prickle in her skin, the quickening thump of her heart behind her ribcage.

It wasn't the idea of a dead body that frightened her – she saw bodies all the time: she'd seen them all the way through her training, on gurneys, in morgues, in the minutes after the lungs stopped, the heart failed, and the brain died. It was that it was here, in this remote place, far from anywhere.

She kept going, gaze fixed, even though something was telling her to stay back. It was a man. There was blood at the top of his forehead, a dull red along the fringes of his thinning hairline and against the ridge of one eyebrow. From the distance she was at, Rebekah had an idea of what had caused the blood to spill, and as she moved along the trail of leaves, she saw that she was right.

A bullet wound.

'This is fucked up,' Johnny said, panic in his voice as he saw the body more clearly. She rarely heard him swear. 'We should call the cops, Bek.'

'I know.'

'Like *now*.' His voice was trembling.

'Okay, call them.'

Johnny removed his cell and started reaching above his head, trying to get the bars to kick back in.

'Damn it,' he muttered. 'We need to go back to the spot where Noe called you.'

The dead man was dressed in a checked shirt and tan pants, black work boots and an unzipped coat, which had twisted around him, encasing him on the side of the bank. His colour was grey, and there was fluid leaking out of him, blisters on the skin: decomposition had started but still mostly appeared to be internal. His bloodstream had filled with carbon dioxide, the toxicity poisoning his cells, enzymes eating away at them. As Rebekah edged closer, she could smell him, and see that one of his eyes was open and had misted.

'He's been dead for a while,' she said. 'Maybe a day.'

She heard Johnny fall into line behind her, the crunch of leaves under his feet, but still she didn't take her eyes off the man: he looked to be in his sixties, silver-haired and bearded, the skin of his hand mottled and veined. Parts of him were still obscured behind the snaking, exposed tree roots that broke out of the sides of the gully but she could see enough. There was a kind of natural platform ten feet above him, along the high edge of the gully, and Rebekah guessed he'd been standing there before he'd ended up where he was.

This is all wrong.

The second the words came to her, she realized how stupid they were – they'd just found a corpse with a bullet in his head – but it wasn't only the body. She'd felt the same way even before they left the dig site.

'Bek?'

She looked across at Johnny.

'Are you listening to what I'm saying?' he pleaded, coming towards her, his eyes scanning the forest, his gaze moving quickly between the trees. 'We need to go back to where we had a signal.'

'Give me two seconds,' she said.

'We need to call 911, Bek.'

She stopped within reach of the man. The foot she hadn't been able to see until now was caught inside a coil of roots, reversed to an impossible angle. It was shattered, the ankle broken. His other arm was broken too, the elbow inversed, the wrist bent under the forearm. He must have fallen hard, hit the ground even harder, the only tiny comfort being that he was probably dead by the time he had.

The bullet was still somewhere inside the skull: there was no exit wound. When she went around to the other side of his head to double-check, she saw his cranium was partially crushed, indented at the dome, the skin bloodied, split, which seemed to confirm that he'd landed as a dead weight.

'*Bek*. Let's get the hell out of –'

Something snapped at the top of the gully.

They turned quickly, looking upward, to the platform that Rebekah had seen earlier. Now, at its broken edge, someone was staring down at them.

'Dr Stelzik?'

Johnny's voice was confused, anxious.

But, above them, Karl Stelzik didn't respond.

He just kept staring at them, hair straightened, clothes changed since they'd left him at the Cherokee. As he raised his right arm, Rebekah saw the ends of the bandaging she'd put there, sneaking out from under the sleeve of his parka, dots of blood close to where the bites had been. She glanced at the man lying dead next to them, then back up the slant of the gully to where Stelzik was, a gun in his hand.

Except, she now realized, he wasn't Stelzik.

He was simply pretending to be.

The real Karl Stelzik was lying next to her with a bullet in his head.

36

As Rebekah emerged from between the houses, she heard the sound again.

Click click click.

This time, it was coming from somewhere else.

The gas-station forecourt.

Raising the hammer, she edged out of the long grass, stepped over the collapsed fencing that marked the former edges of the lawns, and back onto the road, never once taking her eyes off the building. If someone was there, they had nowhere to exit, except out towards her.

She had them trapped.

'I know you're there.'

She sounded more confident than she felt.

The windows of the building were all misted with sea salt, making it difficult to see in, but if the person was inside, that meant the door should have been open – and, as far as she could see, it was still closed. That meant they were where the Explorer was.

'There's no point in hiding,' she said. 'You might as well –'

A shape emerged from behind the building.

Stunned, Rebekah stumbled to a halt.

The shape paused, half covered by shadows, but clearly looking in her direction. There was a wound in the space next to the ear, and the injury had swollen that side of the face, closing the left eye. But with her working eye, she found Rebekah and stared at her.

'*Roxie?*'

The dog moved, her claws making the distinctive *click click click* on the polished concrete of the road, then stopped again, looking away from Rebekah, back towards the houses.

'Roxie? Do you remember me?'

She seemed unsettled, spooked by Rebekah's presence, and it was clear she was in pain. But, for now, she was still, at the edge of the forecourt.

'It's okay,' Rebekah said. 'It's okay, girl.'

She started crossing towards Roxie, placing one foot in front of the other, like she was walking a high wire. The moment she moved, Roxie stiffened and Rebekah stopped, not wanting to scare her.

For a moment, they were frozen, facing one another, and then Rebekah shivered in the wind, and Roxie seemed to do the same, her fur prickling and shifting, like a wave had passed through it.

'Are you real?' Rebekah said.

Roxie blinked at her.

'Where did you come from?' She looked up and down the road. 'How have you survived for so long?'

Roxie remained, an image of an animal that Rebekah worried might be a mirage, a clear and undeniable sign of madness.

'I thought you were dead.'

The dog flinched, whining a little.

'It's okay, girl,' Rebekah said, holding a hand out to her. 'You remember me, don't you? I won't hurt you. I want to help you.' She took another step. 'I'm a doctor, I can . . .' She faded out.

She's a dog, Bek.

Suddenly, Roxie flinched.

Rebekah didn't know why, but then she looked down at her feet: she'd unwittingly taken a big step forwards, drawn closer without realizing.

'Wait,' she said, and the movement sent another jolt through Roxie's body. 'Wait,' Rebekah repeated. 'Wait, Roxie. Wait, girl, I don't want to h–'

Roxie made a break for it.

'No!' Rebekah screamed after her. 'No, no, no!'

She hurried after her, taking the same route between the houses, Roxie disappearing into the grass ahead of her.

'Roxie!'

She'd guessed right earlier: a storm was coming, the sky swelling with cloud, the wind picking up. Broken wood rattled on the houses. Grass ballooned and shrank. Everything was moving as she looked desperately around the backyards – but she couldn't see the dog anywhere.

Roxie had vanished.

'Please, girl,' Rebekah muttered, forlorn. '*Please* come back.'

But the dog didn't reappear.

And then, a moment later, things got even worse.

37

Between the houses, halfway back to the car, as she took a step to her right to avoid a loose piece of clapboard rattling in the wind, the toe of Rebekah's sneaker glanced off something.

She stopped and looked down.

It was half concealed in the grass.

Dropping to her haunches, she picked it up. It was a dirty wallet, the leather washed-out, a bifold design that fell open in her hands to reveal a horizontal pocket, three empty credit card slots and a window for a photograph. There were two dollar bills inside and a driver's licence, long expired. There were some business cards too, old and creased.

Paul Connors.

Mechanic – East Hampton / Montauk.

In the window was a picture of a young family – the man who must have been Paul Connors, then a woman, in their late thirties, and two angelic kids: a boy and a girl, both of them white-blond.

They were all standing in front of a black Ford Explorer.

Steve.

She felt a tremor in her throat as she slid out Connors' driver's licence. It was three years past its expiration date, lost here for all that time. He was thirty-eight. He'd been six two, 190 pounds, and had blue eyes, the same as his children. He was listed as a veteran and an organ donor.

He hadn't battled to have kids.

His name wasn't Steve.

Deep down, Rebekah had never believed any of those things

were true, but saying them, playing around with them in her head, had been a way to anchor her to some kind of normality. Steve had been a step away from the abnormality of her existence. He had been her ballast.

But now he was gone.

Just like Roxie.

Just like everyone else in her life.

Her eyes searched the empty road as she crossed the Loop, back towards the gas station, silently willing Roxie to reappear. When that failed, she started calling her name again.

It was hopeless.

After a while, she started to doubt herself. Had she really seen Roxie? What did it mean if she hadn't? *Could* she be going mad? *Could* this be the beginning of some mania, brought on by the seclusion, and the silence?

She looked to the Ford Explorer, but there were no answers there, and as she got to the Cherokee, its door still open, she stared at her reflection in the windshield. It was like gazing into the face of a stranger, her eyes smeared with the weight of so much time alone, the skin on her face carved so close to the bone, it was like she was shrinking.

'You're losing it,' she said softly.

Her reflection mouthed the same words back to her, which seemed to break the spell. As she got back into the car and pulled the door closed, then started the engine, she thought of the famous quote about insanity, about doing the same thing over and over again and expecting a different result. That was what she'd been doing as she called for Roxie. For twenty minutes, she'd just repeated a name.

She squeezed her eyes shut.

And then, from the back seat: a noise.

It took her a second to find the source. Rebekah looked down, into the space behind the passenger seat.

Two eyes – one swollen shut – looked up at her.

The Interview

'Okay, Mr Murphy. I need you to tell me about Louise Mason.'

It was 12 October and Travis was in Johnny Murphy's house on 81st Street. Murphy nodded in response, but didn't seem to know where to start.

'It's a nice place you got here,' Travis said, looking around the living room. He'd told a white lie: the house was okay, nothing special. He was just trying to get Murphy to settle and engage.

'Thank you,' Murphy responded politely, looking up from his lap.

'Have you lived here long?'

'Yeah, this is where we all grew up.' He glanced around the room, then turned to Travis again. 'My dad was a cop, like you.'

'Really?'

'Yeah. The 68th Precinct on 65th Street.'

'I didn't know that.'

Murphy nodded. Travis made a mental note to follow up on that, just in case there was anything worth exploring, then checked the camera to make sure Murphy was correctly framed. In the corner was a date-stamp.

'Okay,' he said. 'Are we all set?'

Murphy nodded again.

'Mr Murphy, can you confirm for the camera that you're happy to be recorded?' Murphy said he was, and told Travis to call him Johnny. 'I appreciate that, Johnny. Okay, let's kick this off properly, shall we? How did you meet Louise Mason?'

'Through a mutual friend.'

'Who was the friend?'

'Her name's Kirsty Cohen.' Murphy glanced between Travis and the camera, as if unsure for a moment where to look, and Travis wondered if it was a shift of discomfort, an attempt to conceal something. 'Actually,' Murphy continued, 'maybe "mutual friend" is a bit of a stretch. She used to come to the house a lot at one time because she and my sister were at college together, studying to become doctors. So that was how I got to know Kirsty. She moved up to Baltimore after that, to medical school there, and Bek went to NYU, and whenever Kirsty comes back to the city, Bek and she meet up, and sometimes she'll drop by the house.' He stopped, frowned, as if he were confused. 'I don't know, I guess we are friends, but she's definitely more Bek's friend.'

'Bek is your sister?'

'Yes, sorry. Rebekah, with a k and an h.'

'So it was Rebekah and Kirsty who set you up with Louise?'

'More Kirsty. She's quite social – she goes to a lot of parties, society stuff, so she knows a lot of people, and somewhere along the line, I guess she met Louise. Bek said she and Kirsty spoke at the end of August, and Kirsty mentioned to Bek that she had a friend called Louise she wished she could set up with someone.'

'And Rebekah suggested you?'

Murphy nodded. 'She gave Kirsty my number. I guess Bek thought we might be a good fit.'

'Why would she think that?'

'Louise is an artist. I'm a writer.' But then Murphy paused, his head dropping slightly. 'Well, I'd like to be a writer,' he admitted. 'I suppose that's more honest.'

'You work in an electronics store, right?'

He nodded, seeming disappointed that Travis had brought him back down to earth. He glanced into the camera. 'We just sounded pretty similar. We were the same sort of age. When Bek found a picture of Louise online, I thought she was really pretty, and although I didn't really know her work, I soon found out she was this successful artist. Actually, I was surprised she'd even consider dating someone like me – but, in the end, I figured what do I have to lose?'

'When was your first date?'

'Uh, first week of September, I think.'

'And where did you go?'

'She only lived five miles from here, in Park Slope, so we went to an Italian place she suggested on Fifth Avenue. It was nice. We had a good time.'

'What happened after that?'

Travis watched as Murphy tried to recall: he had a quiet demeanour, spoke softly, seemed nervous – the last didn't raise any alarms for now, because Travis had long since accepted being put in front of a camera might create a certain level of anxiety with some interviewees. But the benefits outweighed the losses: nervousness wasn't the same as evasiveness, and so far Murphy's responses felt benign.

Travis repeated the question. 'So what happened after?'

'We texted a few times, and spoke on the phone,' Murphy said – and Travis quickly referred to the cellphone records he'd pulled for Louise; it tallied – 'then we went out again the next week for another meal.'

'And after that?'

'We went out a third time on the weekend that followed. This time we went to an exhibition at the Guggenheim,' Murphy said, 'about the golden age of Hollywood. "Hollywood Babylon". It was brilliant.'

'So everything went all right?'

'From my side, it went great.'

'From hers?'

Murphy shrugged. 'I didn't get any sense it didn't. I mean, if it had been a total disaster she never would have invited me to that fundraiser.' Travis checked his notes again: the exhibition had been on Saturday, 18 September. The fundraiser – and their fourth date – had been the following Thursday, the twenty-third. Murphy rubbed at his eyes, disguising his face for a moment, and it was the first time that Travis didn't have a clear view of his expression. 'I picked her up and drove us both to the hotel, and then I got a call on my cell.'

'From who?'

'The next-door neighbour of a friend of mine,' he said. 'Noella.'

Travis asked for her full name and contact details, and then – watching Murphy more closely now – said, 'What did her next-door neighbour want?'

'He said Noella had been rushed into the ER.'

'Why?'

'Stomach pain. Suspected appendicitis.'

'So this neighbour called you?' Travis asked.

'Noella's boyfriend, Tommy, was away. The neighbour had tried Bek first, but she was bathing the girls and didn't hear the phone – so, yes, he called me.'

'And you decided to go?'

'I told Louise I was really sorry, made sure she got to the hotel safely – and then I headed back to Brooklyn. Noe had gone to the ER at Langone.'

'Did you speak to Louise again that night?'

'No.'

'Just a text?'

'Yes,' Murphy said. 'After the doctor said Noe was going to be okay, I went outside and sent Louise a message to tell her I was sorry for running out on her like that. When I didn't hear back from her . . .' He faded out, his face carrying the rest of that sentence: *I guess we know why.* 'I tried texting her again the next day, and again didn't hear back, then called her and left a voicemail. When I still didn't hear from her, I just . . . I figured . . .' A shrug of the shoulders.

'You figured she didn't want to see you again?'

'Yes,' Murphy responded, his eyes back on his lap, the camera recording the top of his head. He laced his fingers together. 'I just assumed that, when I dropped her at the hotel and left her like I did, I'd really upset her.'

'Okay,' Travis said, and paused, watching Murphy. Murphy didn't move, just stared into space. It was a look Travis had seen a million times in interview rooms: he was remembering something. Travis just had to work out whether it was something he'd already admitted to – or something he'd held back. 'You got anything else you want to tell me about, Johnny?'

Murphy looked up, his expression harder to pick now, and shook his head. 'No, I don't think so,' he said softly.

But was there something?

'You sure?'

'Yes,' Murphy said.

Travis eyed him for a moment longer, then broke into a smile. 'Well, okay,' he said, 'then I think we're done here.' But he didn't get up from his seat, just remained still for a moment, pretending to make some notes. It was an old-school tactic: prolonging the silence, making it uncomfortable so a suspect would start speaking just to fill the quiet, and – flustered, made to feel awkward – say something they hadn't planned to. Travis was absolutely convinced that Murphy – introverted and modest as he appeared to be – would be someone who hated the unease of a situation like that.

But he was wrong.

Murphy just sat there quietly, saying nothing and staring at Travis, until eventually Travis had no choice but to call time on the interview.

Before

'What the hell's going on?' Rebekah said, her voice betraying her.

But the man pretending to be Karl Stelzik didn't respond: he stepped off the platform of mud and roots, and onto the slope of the gully, never taking his eyes off Rebekah. It was the first time she'd appreciated how green they were, and how incongruous they seemed in his face: like bright gems buried deep in the dirt.

He kept coming, step by careful step, until he reached the trail. As soon as he did, his gaze switched to the dead body Rebekah had discovered in the tree roots.

Skin crawling, heart racing, she looked at the man's wrist, at the blood that had soaked through from the bite marks, and put it together: Roxie had attacked the fake Stelzik at the dig site because he'd killed the real one – and the real one was her owner. The only thing that didn't make sense was why, when Rebekah and Johnny had first arrived, they'd found the man out cold, because it hadn't been an act.

She didn't need to be a doctor to know that.

'Look, I'm not sure what you think we've done,' Johnny started saying, sidestepping closer to Rebekah instinctively, 'but we're just tourists. We don't know anything about . . .' He stopped, glancing at Karl Stelzik's dead body, and Rebekah thought she could see the rest of the sentence, unspoken, in his face: *about this, about violence, about murder. This is so far from our world, it's a different universe.* Until now, Johnny had been surprisingly still, outwardly calm, but now he began blinking nervously.

'This is a mistake,' Rebekah said to the man, a hand up.

'You're damn right it's a mistake,' he replied.

He was from New York. He'd suppressed his accent when they'd first met: Rebekah had even thought she'd heard a hint of eastern European in line with Stelzik's name. But if she had, it had been a performance, part of the lie.

The man came a step closer.

They were maybe ten feet apart now. Rebekah had never been so close to a gun before. Her brothers had occasionally gone to ranges growing up, learning how to use weaponry. Their dad had thought it was a useful thing to know in America, and holstering a gun was as natural a part of his daily routine as buttoning up the blue uniform and pinning the badge to his chest.

But Rebekah had been in England until she was eighteen, a country where people were shot and killed sixty times a year, not sixty times a day, and she'd had no interest in learning once she arrived in New York. Guns scared her. They scared her even more now than when she was younger because she'd seen the effects of them in the OR: the way they shattered bone and punctured tissue, the way they lacerated, ruptured, destroyed.

'We won't say anything to anyone.' The frenzy in Johnny's voice returned her to the forest. 'Whatever it is you think we've done here, we haven't. I swear. So if you just let us go, we'll walk away from this –' he glanced briefly at Stelzik, at the grotesque angles of his body '– and we won't say anything.'

The man just looked at them.

'Please,' Johnny muttered. 'This is crazy.'

'You must have made a mistake,' Rebekah said, trying to back Johnny up, her words coming out as quickly as his. 'You must have us mixed up with someone else. We're nobodies. We don't have any idea what's going on.'

This time, the man gave a hint of a smile, as if entertained by what he was seeing. 'You look – what's the word? Befuddled.' He said *befuddled* in an English accent, in an obvious approximation of how Rebekah spoke.

'This is insane,' she replied. 'I don't even know you.'

'You don't *need* to know me, sweetheart.'

The man looked between them both.

'I messed up.' He gestured with the gun in the vague direction of the dig site. 'I've been trying to find that friggin' dog since I offed Stelzik and, this morning, I see it in the trees, and I go after it, and I slip like some old man.'

He looked at them both again, a *Can you believe that?* expression on his face, as if he was talking about some minor mishap. The fear ripped through Rebekah, her entire body trembling. He didn't care what he was saying to them, didn't care what he admitted to, and the casual way in which he talked about killing, about hunting, told her why: they were going to die out here.

'I hit my head on this old piece of rock Stelzik was digging up, and – *boom* – blackout.' He rubbed his skull, fingers at the point of impact. 'Anyway, it *could* have been a problem, because it *could* have meant I didn't get to do what I came all the way out to this dumb fucking rock to do. I mean, look at this shithole.' He waved the gun at the trees. 'What sort of backward-ass place doesn't even have the internet or working phone lines? I'm surprised they've got a cell tower. Hell, I'm surprised they've even got running *water*. But whatever. When I woke up, and there you both were, you know what I felt?' He shook his head. 'Just relief. Pure relief. You never realized I was after you because you'd come to *me*. I didn't have to go chasing round trying to find you. I didn't have to spend one second longer in this cesspit than I needed to.'

Rebekah dragged her eyes back to the body of Stelzik.

'I don't understand.' Her voice was breaking up, the words getting lost in her throat. 'What have we done? What did Stelzik do?'

'Stelzik? He's just a loose end.'

His expression changed instantly. It was like a light going out. Rebekah noticed again how green the man's eyes were, but the rest of his face was as opaque as night. Rebekah looked at Johnny, saw that he was on the verge of tears, and immediately started to sob too. 'Please,' she begged, 'I don't know what you thin–'

'Shut up,' the man hissed. He jabbed the gun towards the tree roots. 'Climb up there, both of you. Let's get this over with.'

38

Over the next few days, Rebekah dressed and treated Roxie's injury, washed her, made her a bed, walked her, and took her out for drives in the Jeep. She carefully rationed what food was left, dividing it into two piles, but by the fourth day after they'd found each other – Rebekah's Day 45 – they were down to just two cans of soup. Rebekah knew she had to find a way to get into the hostel that Stelzik had stayed in, otherwise they would both starve – but as they were out walking a trail, inaccessible by car, her plans changed.

She suddenly lost Roxie.

She disappeared so quickly into the bush that she was gone before Rebekah had even realized. 'What are you doing?' she shouted after the dog.

But no sound came back, no barking.

Rebekah sprinted after Roxie but, before long, she'd wandered onto another trail, snaking into a clearing. The wind moved, the trees making a gentle whisper, and when it died away again, she heard something.

A series of muted slaps.

It was early morning and the light was subdued, so she returned to the Jeep, grabbed a flashlight and headed back the way she'd seen Roxie go. She soon arrived in the clearing again: the grass had been compressed by the cold, creating a kind of corkscrew pattern, and off to her right an outcrop of rock sat against the trees, like a series of granite towers. In its middle was a cave with a thin, vertical mouth.

Rebekah shone the flashlight in the direction of the entrance and moved in closer, trying to angle it so she could see inside.

'Roxie?' she said, uncertainly.

The light quivered against the rock, expanding the closer she got, but the interior remained dark.

'Hello?' she said, her voice sounding loud in her ears. 'Rox? Are you in there?'

Nothing.

'Rox? Is that y–'

It swooped out of the dark, striking her in the chest like a bunched fist. Stumbling back, losing her footing, Rebekah hit the ground hard, the frozen forest grass like concrete against the base of her spine. Before she had a chance to understand what had happened, something else swept out of the cave, then more, one after the next, shadows against the mellow light.

Bats.

They kept coming, individually at first, and then in groups. They circled the clearing, the noise of the island replaced by the *whumph* of wings – and then, like the swirl of a cape, they all plunged back into the cave again.

Rebekah stared into its mouth.

'Rox?' she said again. 'Roxie?'

A thought hit her, cold as a hand on her throat: what if Roxie had gone in there, disturbed the bats and one had bitten her? Instinctively, Rebekah started shaking her head, hating the idea of it.

Not rabies.

Please not rabies.

But then, from her left, Roxie reappeared.

She wandered into the clearing, looking between Rebekah and the cave, as if she didn't know what all the fuss was about, or why Rebekah was on her backside in the middle of a patch of frozen grass. Rebekah clambered to her feet as Roxie pushed her head against her leg, and started laughing when she saw what the dog had returned with. 'You're a genius, girl, you know that?'

Roxie had a dead rabbit in her mouth.

*

Rebekah had been so preoccupied with what Roxie had found – a fresh source of food – that she hadn't noticed how the sky was changing. By the time they reached the Cherokee, the heavens had opened.

She sat in the car, wipers going, and considered going on to the hostel – that had been the original plan after the walk – but decided against it. When the storms came to the island, they came hard: this one felt like it was going to be more rain than wind, but if the wind got up, that was when things were dangerous. She'd lost count of the times – in the six weeks she'd been on Crow Island – when huge objects had been tossed around, like toys. One night, as she'd watched a storm unfold from the window of the store, a wooden picnic table had been lifted off a bank and launched at one of the buildings.

Once Roxie was beside her, Rebekah pulled out onto the Loop and headed in the direction of Helena instead.

'I wouldn't normally condone killing a rabbit, Rox,' Rebekah said, rain pummelling the windshield, 'but desperate times call for desperate measures.' She rubbed Roxie's belly but kept her eyes on the road: every second they were out, it got a little worse. Eventually, the wipers couldn't go fast enough.

Unable to see properly, Rebekah slowed right down and glanced out at the ocean, hoping to find some relief out there, some light in the sky. But the Atlantic was a swirling wall of mist, except for one black dot, like a pinprick in the fog.

She slowed some more, looking closer at the dot.

It was getting bigger.

39

It was raining so hard that, for a second, she lost sight of the dot. But then it broke from a thick curtain of rain, bigger than before.

It's a helicopter.

She shoved open the door of the Cherokee, telling Roxie to stay put. The dog seemed confused, moved from the passenger seat to the driver's side, but did as she was asked. Rebekah slammed the door, making sure Roxie couldn't run off, then raced around to the trunk. Inside were the old flares she'd found in the house on the north coast. She'd never fired one, but there was no time for a dry run.

Grabbing one, she raced further along the Loop, towards a more open section of the highway. The whole time the rain was relentless, pounding off the asphalt, the storm drains choking on dead leaves. As she got into position, already drenched, she focused on the flare she was holding: both ends were capped, one white, one red, but only the red one came loose. She wriggled it free and tried to work out the rest: an igniter was built into the flare, an abrasive patch that felt like sandpaper, and a similar one was embedded in the outside of the cap.

The helicopter was still way out over the sea – forty miles, maybe more – and she didn't want to fire the flare too soon, so she began to wave her hands above her head, jumping up and down on the spot.

'Hey!' she screamed into the rain, even though she knew her voice would never be heard. 'Hey! Look over here!'

The chopper kept coming.

She waited.

Waited.

But then, suddenly, it began to bank.

'No!' she shouted. 'No, wait!'

It was still at least thirty miles from the shoreline but now she couldn't afford to hold on: she began to jab the red cap hard against the igniter button.

It wouldn't light.

'*Shit.*'

She tried again. Still nothing.

'Come on, come on.'

Again, again, again.

'*Come on!*'

Finally, with a fizz, the flare bloomed.

She shot her arms up, above her head, and moved them back and forth, the red tail of the flare forming momentary lines in the air. For a second, she lost the chopper – but then she found it against the granite sky.

As she did, she felt herself wither.

It had already turned so far around that she could no longer see the front, even its windows. Its entire shell was just a narrow blur against the whirl of the storm.

'Hey!' she shouted, the flare still fizzing. 'Wait! *Wait!*' She screamed the words so hard she almost choked, waving the flare more furiously than ever, her shoulders scorched with the effort.

But the helicopter was just a dot again.

'Please come back,' she muttered, finally dropping her arms, the flare slipping from her fingers to the ground. 'I'm still alive.'

Before

'Move.' The man with the green eyes gestured with the gun. *'Move,'* he repeated, when Rebekah and Johnny didn't respond – and, slowly, with their feet barely able to cross the ten feet between where they were and the place in which the man was going to kill them, they started to inch forward. Johnny went first, still in front of Rebekah, still trying to protect her.

'This is a mistake,' Rebekah said again. 'We don't even *know* you.'

'Shut up and get over there,' the man said, using the gun as a pointer. They'd reached the base of the gully, where the slope slanted upward. From where they were, Stelzik's body was almost level with Rebekah's eyeline.

'Is this about money?' Johnny asked, trying to make his voice steady. 'Because if it's about money, we can organize something. When we get back–'

'She ain't going back, John.'

The entire forest seemed to lurch, but when Rebekah looked at Johnny, he was frowning, his expression odd. It was like he was confused.

'Johnny? What's going on?'

'I don't know, Bek,' he said quietly.

Rebekah looked between her brother and the man with the gun. Had Johnny just lied to her? 'What's going on?' she repeated. 'Johnny, what's –'

'I don't know what's going on!' he said, with a surge of frustration.

Rebekah tried to reach for her brother's hand, but she couldn't grab his fingers. He'd taken a step away from her now and was looking at the man again.

'Please,' he was saying, '*please*. Let my sister go. She's a mom. She has two little girls. This isn't right.'

'Shut up,' the man said again, checking his gun.

'*Please*,' Rebekah begged.

'Don't plead, honey. It ain't becoming.'

'But *why*? Who are we to you?'

And then his eyes snapped back to her. 'You're no one to me. That's the whole point. Now climb up to those roots there and let's get it over with.'

They dragged their legs up, their bones heavy. Both of them were crying now. It hurt Rebekah more than anything she could ever remember to see her brother so vulnerable. Halfway up the side of the gully, she reached out to him for a second time and this time she was able to grasp his hand.

For some reason she thought of their old house on 81st Street, to which she'd come back after leaving London. She pictured her and Johnny on the front porch, sun glinting off the windows. Rebekah saw her dad too, at the grill, steaks sizzling. She saw Mike, laughing at something.

And she saw Kyra and Chloe.

The girls had never been to the house on 81st Street. They'd never met Mike, and Chloe had never met Rebekah's father. That house had come before them, when Rebekah's life had moved on, when she was a doctor, and a wife, and then an ex. But, in her head, she could see the girls clearly, Kyra nine or ten, Chloe walking around, their smiles lighting up.

'Keep moving.'

The man's voice ripped her out of the memory. They were almost at the tree roots now: maybe only a couple more feet.

Rebekah squeezed her brother's hand even tighter.

'I love you, Johnny.'

'Me too,' he said softly.

She couldn't remember the last time he'd got as close to saying *I love you* as that. Maybe because he never had. 'This is all my fault,

Bek,' he said. 'This is all my fault.' And then he hugged her so hard it muffled the sound of her tears, raw, and desperate, and final. When he let go, she heard him exhale, felt his whole body contract, and then they were there.

At Stelzik's corpse.

They turned and looked down the slope, hands still laced together. The man was much closer to them now, feet away.

'Gimme your phones,' he said. Johnny reached into his pants and got out his cell, tossing it towards the man. He let it land at his feet and then his attention switched to Rebekah. 'You hard of hearing?'

Rebekah put a hand into her pocket.

She didn't want to give him her phone: it was like a cord binding her to the outside world, her family, her girls. But what difference did it make now?

They were both going to be killed here.

And, by the way the man was looking at her, she understood something else.

She would die first.

40

Roxie watched Rebekah from the passenger seat, obviously sensing a change in the mood, but uncertain how to make it better. As rain pounded against the roof of the Jeep, the dog pressed her muzzle into Rebekah's breast. She looked down at Roxie – at the brown flash of her good eye, at the white dressing on the other – and slid an arm round her, bringing her in closer.

Roxie whimpered a little, then settled.

Once they got back to the store, Rebekah managed to get a fire started outside, under a slant of overhanging roof, using some old wooden fence panels and the Zippo lighter she'd found on the first night. And that evening, she and Roxie ate rabbit.

After almost seven weeks of tinned food and candy bars, it tasted amazing, even if it was tough and overcooked. Skinning the rabbit had been horrible, not because it had made Rebekah squeamish, but because it had taken her so long – yet it was worth it. Again, she divided up the meat, trying to make it stretch for as many days as possible, and managed to supplement it with some marked brown apples: she'd found an old orchard not far from the lighthouse, and although all the trees had largely emptied for winter, and what had fallen had turned to mulch or been eaten by worms, there were enough to fill half a bucket.

As Rebekah sliced some, cutting out the bruises, the brown flesh, insects that had lodged in the skin and the core, she knew that if she'd been at home she would have dumped apples this bad straight into the trash. But here, on the island, they tasted sweet as honey. She'd found a bowl of sorts for Roxie – really just a mesh cover for a fishing bucket – and they ate at the back of the store, on the Main Street sidewalk, both wrapped in blankets.

'Today was shit,' she said, rubbing Roxie's belly, still feeling tearful about the helicopter turning back, 'but at least the food tastes better.'

Roxie was too busy chewing rabbit to reply.

Rebekah stroked her head and her ears. 'You know,' she said, 'there's a couple of little girls back in the city who'd love to meet you one day.' Roxie looked at her, blinked, then Rebekah began to feel the drag of that statement.

Roxie nuzzled her leg.

Her bad eye was still covered with gauze, which she kept trying to shake off, but the swelling was down, and in a day, Rebekah would be able to remove it. She'd had a thorn on her lower eyelid, and the skin around it had blown up, but it was healing. As she continued to stroke Roxie, Rebekah let herself return to her daughters, to hold them in her mind.

'You'd love my girls, Rox,' she said, her hand resting on the dog's head now. 'Kyra's almost three, and she's super-smart. I know I'm biased but it's true. I mean, she's her mother's daughter, what can I say?' She winked at Roxie. 'Chloe, she's a little sweetheart, but she's going to be boisterous. The day before I got here, you could tell by her face that she was already thinking about escaping the bouncer. It was like she was staring at the living room and saying to herself, "I can cross this. You just watch me."' Roxie's fur beneath her fingertips felt warm, comfortable – reassuring somehow – but, still, a sadness weighed on her as she pictured her daughters. 'You're the reason I'm still here, Rox, you know that?'

Roxie looked at her.

'Have you even got the first idea?'

She blinked, her eye searching Rebekah's face.

'I don't know if I'll go home alive after this is all over,' she said, running her hand across Roxie's belly again, feeling its rise and fall. 'I don't know if I'll even survive until this place reopens. I mean, we've got to get through – what? – another three and a half months.' She blew out a breath, a cloud forming in front of her face. 'Look how cold it is already. You're going to have to find a hell of a lot more rabbits if we're not going to starve.'

She smiled at Roxie.

'But I know something with absolute certainty. There's still a chance I'll get home to my girls alive – and that isn't anything to do with me.'

Rebekah dropped closer to the dog, sliding an arm around her.

In return, Roxie moved her head to Rebekah's thigh.

'It's all because of you.'

Before

Rebekah threw her cell towards the man and closed her eyes.

Her fingers were laced through her brother's.

She was waiting for the shot, for the sound to rip across the forest, for the force of the bullet to tear her away from Johnny's grip.

But it never did.

She heard Roxie before she saw her: a brief patter on her left, the crunch of frozen grass, then a pained wail from the man who'd come to kill them.

Rebekah's eyes snapped open.

The man hit the ground. She heard the rustle of his body rolling down the slope, the dog following him, teeth bared, one of her paws embedded in the side of his face. As soon as the man hit the trail, the dog came again, scratching at him, ferocious, unrelenting. Rebekah glanced at Johnny, he at her, and could see they were thinking the same thing. This was it.

This was their chance.

Run.

Rebekah grabbed her cellphone off the ground and they sprinted in the direction from which they'd entered the gully. Behind them, the dog growled, the grass crunched, the man said something – a shout, almost a yell, unintelligible – and then, suddenly, there was a gunshot.

He just killed Roxie.

Rebekah couldn't look back. Instead, she accelerated, heading up the side of the gully, back towards the main path that would take them to the dig site. As they did, another shot rang out, hitting a tree to their left. The trunk detonated, spitting bark into her eyes, and as Johnny broke through to the main path at the top, Rebekah stumbled and hit the ground four feet behind him. She started crawling on her hands and knees, her eyes shut, sore from the dust, her palm piercing on broken branches.

She felt Johnny grab her under the arm and drag her the rest of the way onto the main path, then another shot rang out. Johnny grabbed her a second time, and as she cleared her eyes, she saw him, just ahead of her, in a crouch. A third shot, a fourth. One hit another tree, the other disappeared into the forest. Rebekah looked back again, over her shoulder. One eye was still closed, the other blurred, watering, but she could see enough.

The man was coming.

She scrambled to her feet and started running hard, following Johnny back along the trail. Her eye was still watering, but it had cleared, and she remembered all the running she'd done as a kid. Her performances for her county had got her the scholarship to the private school. Another shot rang out. But she wasn't running for the finish line any more.

She was running for her life.

Another gunshot. Another.

Was that six now? Seven?

She tried to think how many bullets were in a gun, how many would be in the type of gun that the man had, and how many he would have left. But it was taking all her focus and energy just to run, to put one foot in front of the other, to watch where her feet were landing. In front of her, Johnny batted away a succession of branches, but his eyes were constantly flicking back to check that Rebekah was still with him.

Another shot.

And then a second almost instantly.

This time, Rebekah was knocked off balance.

It took her a split second to react, to process and understand what had happened. Then she looked down and saw a hole in the outer edge of her coat. A bullet had passed right through it, millimetres from her left hip. White insulation spilled out of the hole, black marks scorched the circumference – and, in the moment it took her to look, she'd taken her eyes off the contours of the path. Her foot caught on a stray tree root. She tumbled forward, smashing into a tree.

Black.

It lasted a couple of seconds.

As Rebekah pinged back into focus, confused, she saw the man – fifty feet away – looking in her direction. She glanced, to see if Johnny was nearby, but he was gone. He didn't know she'd fallen.

Where Johnny had gone, the trees formed a kind of mouth, the trail darkening, the canopy drawn together. She looked again at the man, even closer now, his gun up in front of him, then to the path. When Johnny came back for her – because he would, she knew he would – he'd be a sitting duck. The way the path wound and closed, he would never even see the man until it was too late.

Don't come back for me, Johnny.

Please don't come back.

But then she heard him calling for her.

'Bek?'

His voice, short and desperate.

'Bek!'

She sprang to her feet.

The instant she did, the man caught sight of her. He fired into the trees, the bullet fizzing past her and hitting a pale, scrawny oak to her right. She headed away from the path, away from Johnny, deeper into the forest, looking over her shoulder to make sure the man was following her. He broke from the path into the undergrowth, kicking and chopping his way through a maze of vines and scrub. Rebekah heard Johnny calling her name again, further off now – his voice like a cry from another room – and then, finally, the sound changed: it was just the noise of Rebekah, stumbling, and her pursuer, breathless, behind her.

He shot at her again.

It came close, a low hiss in the air to her right, but then she veered left, making use of a break in the scrub and tried to alter her direction. Somewhere – so far off she wasn't even sure if she was hearing things – Johnny called her name again, and then the ground became uneven. As trees clotted around her, the forest floor pocked, and her ankle jammed into a hole, five inches deeper than the rest of the terrain. It jarred the whole side of her body, ankle to hip. She'd barely even lifted it out when she hit another, less deep but much wider, and this time her ankle rolled into the empty space.

She fell.

Her hands cushioned her, but the impact still hurt. Every part of her hurt. She was so scared her bones ached. She pushed herself up, stumbling forward, hitting a tree, bouncing away from it, then hitting another.

She fell a second time.

Beneath her, the ground had altered again: it was starting to slope away from her, and she could hear something. She could smell it too: salt.

She was nearing the coast.

Maybe I can find help there, she thought, clambering to her feet. *There might be people or fishing boats.* She looked behind her, to see where the man was, to see how much distance he'd gained on her, and faltered.

Where was he?

A shot rang out.

The bullet came so close it was like she could feel the air move in the spaces beside her head. Her immediate reaction was to shield herself with her arm, protect her eyes, her skull, even though it was too late, even though the flesh and bone in her arm would be as effective as paper if he got the next one on target. As she did, she wobbled, the lunge of her arm shifting her weight – and she took a jolting step into another hollow. Her cellphone fell out of her pocket. Loose change went with it.

And then she started to tumble.

This time, there was nothing to stop her.

The ground dropped away beneath her: she'd been on the edge of another gully, but this one was smaller, much deeper, and disguised by a swathe of scrub. She went straight through the scrub, taking some of it with her as she tried to stop herself falling, and hit the sides of the gully hard. One roll, another, another, each one faster, each turn of her body pounding so hard against the frozen ground it was like a series of grenade blasts going off inside her. Halfway down, she pierced her head on something sharp – a branch, a root, the pain an immense flare along her face and neck – and then she landed so hard in a bed of dead, dried leaves it sucked all the breath from her. Leaves puffed up around her. Her body became cocooned by them. And then she became still.

She stared up at the sky.

It was grey, like dead skin.

Is this it?

Is this the end?

She tried to reach a hand to her face, to the injury she could feel next to her right ear, but it felt like everything had disconnected. Her arms weren't doing what she was asking them to do. Her chest was on fire. Her breath was catching, and when she tried to clear her throat, she wheezed. Seconds later, everything smeared. There was blood in her eyes.

Briefly, her vision went red.

And then, once again, everything turned to black.

Missing Hours

Travis paused the DVD of the interview with Johnny Murphy.

There were a couple of moments in it that he hadn't paid much attention to the first time around, and hadn't placed any great emphasis on in the times he'd watched the footage since: the pauses between words or after sentences; Murphy's head dropping, his fingers coming together; his eyes flicking between Travis and the camera. It was all tiny, possibly insignificant, stuff but Travis wrote down the time codes for all of them so he could easily refer back to them later. Once he was done, he turned back to the monitor, to the frozen image of Johnny Murphy.

Take a second look, the caller had said.

But a second look at what?

Travis opened his notebook again.

He'd been through the computer on day one to see if Murphy had a record, any markers in his history, but he'd been clean – not even so much as a parking ticket. His alibi for the night was backed up by cellphone records and security cameras: he'd dropped Louise at the fundraiser at 6 p.m., and GPS data showed him heading to the ER at NYU Langone in Brooklyn, as he'd stated. Travis pulled video from cameras at the hospital to make sure, and Murphy had appeared on film, at the entrance; that, in turn, coincided with a text received by Louise's cellphone, from Murphy, a minute later, apologizing for 'abandoning her'. Back in October – following the interview with him – it had been enough for Travis to dismiss him as a suspect.

But two months on, perhaps there were potential gaps.

The video that Travis had pulled of Murphy at the ER covered only a very brief time period – 9.29 p.m. to 9.51 p.m. – when he was visible at the entrance. Before that, the information was much less overt; in fact, Murphy's cellphone appeared to have been switched off completely between the time he arrived at the hospital, at 7.01 p.m., and when he first appeared on camera at 9.29 p.m. Travis had spotted the anomaly shortly after the interview, and called Murphy about it, and Murphy had given a credible reason: he was in a hospital, in an environment where certain areas of the building, and certain equipment, might have been sensitive to the presence of a phone, and therefore he'd been encouraged to turn it off by hospital staff.

But what if that had been a lie?

What if he'd turned it off because he didn't want to be traced — and that was because the two hours and twenty-eight minutes that his cell was off coincided with the last time anyone had seen Louise at the fundraiser? It coincided with the split-second glimpse of Louise that Travis had found on one of the cameras at the Royal Union Hotel too: she'd been in the bar at 9.01 p.m. Ten minutes later, her cell had died. Both of those fit into a timeline where Murphy could have headed back to the fundraiser. Those two hours and twenty-eight minutes would have given him more than enough time to drive from the hospital back to the hotel, then make it back to his friend Noella's bedside in order to send the apology text to Louise. The question was why? Why do it that night, when his friend was sick? Why do it at all?

Travis still couldn't answer any of those questions because Murphy still felt like an empty space. So the next step seemed obvious.

He had to speak to Johnny Murphy again.

Nick Tillman sat in the corner of a deli in Sunnyside, watching the time. On the table in front of him was a notebook. He'd filled most of its pages already.

He preferred paper to a phone because paper was easy to dispose of. Phones weren't. They melted, they shattered, you could throw them into a river or bury them in the ground, but they still left a trace: a single text or the briefest of internet searches, and suddenly you were on a server somewhere, for ever. He hated that idea.

Sinking the rest of the coffee he'd ordered, he headed to the counter to pay. The woman at the register tried to engage him in small-talk, which he forced himself to take part in — in his experience, it was easier to remember someone who was rude to you than someone who was pleasant — then exited the deli, heading out into the snow.

There was a payphone a couple of blocks to the south.

The woman answered after four rings.

'Travis is going around in circles,' Tillman said.

She didn't reply.

Responding to her silence, he said, 'Is something up?'

'Give me a second,' she told him.

Another wait.

'Okay,' she said finally, coming back on. In the background Tillman thought he could hear a door closing. 'I just had to wait for Axel to leave,' she explained. 'I don't want him hearing this.'

Axel.

He was going to be a problem if they weren't careful – but Tillman didn't say that to her. For now, as always, he just kept quiet.

'Nick, I'm looking at these things you sent over,' she said. The sound of paper being leafed through. The tap of a keyboard. 'What about Johnny?'

'What about him?'

'Is he really capable of this?'

Tillman looked up and down the block. 'When it comes to beautiful women like Louise Mason,' he said, 'men are capable of anything.'

Snow flurries skirted across the windshield as Travis made his way south on the interstate. To his right, somewhere under the steel girders of the freeway, he saw the flash of lightbars, their colour painting nearby buildings, sirens screaming to a crescendo and fading again as they headed away from him.

All the way from the office, he'd been thinking about Louise Mason, trying to line up what he knew with what he suspected. Images of her blinked in his head, photos her parents had given him, footage of her he'd watched that her father had filmed at an anniversary dinner. Louise had made a toast to her parents, her words warm and witty. It had drawn Travis even closer to her. Mostly, though, when he thought of Louise, he thought of the terrible error he might have made in dismissing the man she'd been dating.

He got off at the exit for 86th Street and headed for Third Avenue. There, squeezed between a grocery store and a nail spa, was Bay Ridge Electronics.

The place where Johnny Murphy worked.

He found a space a block away. It was less than a week until Christmas Eve so lights and decorations blinked everywhere. It was almost the same amount of time until Travis retired: at 5 p.m. on 23 December he would walk out of the front entrance at One Police Plaza, straight across the road to a retirement party. And after it was done, he'd go home to the emptiness of his house and never return to the office.

To his desk. To his cases.

To Louise.

He upped his pace, walking faster, the city in deep freeze.

I've got five days, he thought. *I've got five days to solve this.*

When he got to the store, he paused, looking through the ice-speckled glass. There was a CLOSED sign up, but he could see someone moving around inside. Travis rapped on the door and, after a while, an Asian guy in his thirties approached.

'We're not open until ten,' he mouthed.

Travis placed his shield against the glass.

The guy's face changed — surprise, then confusion, then worry: why would the cops be calling so early? He unlocked the door and pulled it open.

'Can I help you, Officer?' he asked.

'Detective. I'm looking for Johnny Murphy.'

The guy frowned.

'I couldn't get him on his cell or at home,' Travis pressed. He smiled at the guy, reassuring him that there was nothing for him to worry about.

'Johnny's not here,' the guy replied.

'He didn't turn up for work?'

'No.'

'Did he give a reason?'

'No. I mean, he hasn't been in work for seven weeks.'

It was Travis's turn to frown. 'Seven weeks? What are you talking about?'

'I thought you people would have known.'

'Known what?'

'Him and his sister,' the guy said. 'They disappeared.'

5
The Storm

Before

Blackness gradually gave way to a vague grey light.

When the muscles of her face moved, they felt starched, and Rebekah realized it was because her blood had congealed and dried. The wound was above her jawline, close to her ear; every time it throbbed, it sent a spear of pain across her nose and forehead, and into her neck and shoulders.

She tried to blink.

That didn't work either.

She could smell the blood, taste it, but mostly it was in her eyes. When she tried to open them, she couldn't: the blood had acted as an adhesive, binding her lashes together.

Finally, she wrenched them open, and as she saw where she was, she remembered falling, the ground giving way beneath her, her last desperate attempt to cling to something as she tumbled. The whole thing was over in seconds, but that had only disguised the distance she'd come. This gully was deeper than the one in which they'd found Stelzik, the sides much steeper, almost vertical. If she'd been descending on foot, she would have had to do it leaning back, with a hand pressed behind her, or on her ass.

And then she thought of something else.

Why was she still alive?

Where was the man who'd tried to kill her?

Rebekah froze as she pictured him, his green eyes, as she remembered what he'd done to Stelzik, to Roxie, how he'd tried to march her and Johnny up to the spot in the tree roots to kill them. And then, as her head filled with an image of her brother, she panicked. Where was *he*? Had the man gone after him?

Was Johnny dead?

The idea sent a tremor through her throat.

Slowly, she raised a hand, her muscles stiff, then tried to shift the rest of her body. Pain on her left side, in her skull, her neck, right the way down the centre of her chest. After a couple of failed attempts, she managed to sit up and tried to move her legs back and forth. She was looking for sprains, fractures, breaks. Miraculously, the only injury was on her face. She touched a couple of fingers to the wound.

It felt bad.

Skin was flapping like paper, and as she moved again, trying to get onto her knees, she felt a trail of fresh blood break free from the cut and trace the outline of her cheekbone. Out here, in the middle of a forest, and especially because of how she'd fallen, there was a good chance the cut was dirty, filled with debris. She needed to get it cleaned and dressed.

Using a nearby tree as an anchor, she hauled herself up. Bones creaked. She paused, checking her pants for her phone. *Shit.* No phone – but she still had the keys to the Cherokee in her pocket.

As she started to look around, at the floor of the gully, at the scrub and vines and swathes of thick brush, she remembered why she didn't have her cell: it had spilled out of her pants as she fell; all her loose change had gone too. The phone was still at the crown of the slope somewhere.

Slowly, she headed up there on her hands and knees.

She felt a hundred years old and heavy as concrete. Her hands became filthy, coated in mud, and leaves, and chips of ice. She wiped more blood away with her sleeve as she got to the top, still breathless after the climb, and started scanning the area for her cell. Eventually, she found the place at which she'd gone down the slope into the gully, the ground disturbed, her footprint visible. Close by, loose change was dotted like jewels.

But there was no cellphone.

He must have taken it.

She looked around the forest, suddenly worried that this was all part of the game, that the man might still be somewhere close by, watching, but she couldn't see him. So why had he left her alive?

Picking up her change, she scanned her surroundings again. The trail she'd broken away from, the trail she and Johnny had been following back to the dig site, was just about visible through the trees. It looked quiet. The whole *place* looked quiet: in the time she'd been out, the wind had died right down and the weather had changed. There was no blue sky now, just an infinite grey ceiling of cloud. And it was even colder than before, the air raw. In desperation, she began searching for her phone again, not just so she might be able to make a call, but to find out the time.

She had no idea how long she'd been out.

A minute? Five? Longer?

I need to find Johnny.

She got back onto the trail and tried to pick up her pace. She wanted to run, but what if the man heard or saw her? Under the canopy of trees, inside the section she'd last seen Johnny pass into, she realized how cold she was. Her coat and hoodie were both wet from the ground, muddied from the leaves. She could still feel blood and dried saliva on her face. She wiped at her cheek with her sleeve, smearing blood across her lips, and – briefly – thought of calling out for Johnny. But she stopped herself, thinking of the man once again. If he was close by, he'd instantly know that she'd made it out of the gully.

She headed back in the direction of the car.

It took her twenty minutes to get to the Cherokee, with no sign of the man or Johnny on the way. *Where are you, John? Please don't be dead.*

I can't handle this on my own.

Then she noticed that Stelzik's Chevy was gone.

Had the man taken it?

Or Johnny?

She looked around her, and as she did, she caught sight of herself in the windshield. She took a step closer to the glass. Blood covered one side of her face, an eruption of it from a hole-like injury next to her ear. The cut looked worse than it had felt when she'd been poking around with her fingers – blacker, deeper – and when she tried to wipe blood away from her cheek, most of it had dried solid. When she used a little saliva, all it did was spread. The whole area was like an explosion of red dye.

Leaning further in towards the glass, she turned her head to get a better view of the injury and something occurred to her.

Her mind spun back to the moments before she'd tumbled into the gully: one of the bullets had passed so close to her face, it was like she'd felt the air move. It was what had knocked her off balance and triggered the fall.

As she'd descended into the gully, she'd injured herself.

She'd smashed her head on something.

And then she'd hit the ground and she'd bled across her face, and she'd lain there – with that side of her head showing – absolutely and perfectly still.

She'd been that way because she was unconscious.

But if the man had come to the edge of the gully, if he'd looked down and seen her lying there – and especially when he'd seen all the blood, and the shape and appearance of the wound next to Rebekah's ear – it would have looked like something else: a kill. Instantly, he would have switched his attention to going after Johnny because he'd have believed that the reason Rebekah fell, the reason she ended up in the gully, was him.

That was why the man wasn't here.

That was why Rebekah was still breathing.

He thought he'd shot her in the head.

41

Rebekah returned to the second hostel, armed with tools. She'd managed to find a claw hammer and an old chisel to use as levers on the door.

The day was bright, the sun out, but two weeks into December, the temperature had dropped like a stone: as she stood outside the hostel, Roxie beside her, panting impatiently, all she could see in front of her was her breath.

Wood splintered as she attempted to rock the hammer back and forth, the claw wedged into the space between the door and the frame. She could feel how rotten the edges were, damp and soft, and it didn't take much effort to break off small chunks of the door at its edges. The more difficult part was the area around the lock: it had been treated and repaired at some point.

Please let there be food in here.

She renewed her attack on the door, Roxie moving in half-circles at her legs, as desperate to get inside as Rebekah was. She could feel herself sweating, hot under her clothing, but any moisture that formed on exposed skin instantly felt like ice. After a while, she shrugged off her coat, but then a glacial wind cut in off the water, and she was no longer sure if she was hot or cold. It felt like a fever.

Roxie started to scratch at the door.

'Out of the way, Rox,' Rebekah said, frustrated.

She kept going but, after a few minutes, the door remained intact, and she'd made precisely no headway on the lock plate.

'How the hell are we going to get in?'

And then an idea came to her.

Returning to the Cherokee, Roxie trailing in her wake, she reversed the car onto the grass at the front of the hostel, all the way to the door. Getting out again, she opened the tailgate and grabbed some rope from the trunk. She managed to push it through a tiny welded loop on the door's lock plate, then knotted the other end to the Jeep's tow hitch.

With Roxie on the back seat, obviously sensing something was about to happen, Rebekah put the car into Drive and began inching forward. It took a few seconds for her to feel the resistance kick in.

Once the rope was at its full extension, she gently touched the gas.

The grass was wet under the tyres and, for a moment, they spun as the car went nowhere. She kept the same amount of pressure on, her eyes flicking to her mirrors to see if anything had changed. Roxie didn't know where to look: at Rebekah or at the rear windshield, her head pinging back and forth.

'Come on,' Rebekah said softly.

The wheels spun again.

'Come on.'

Roxie barked.

'Come on, you stupid bloody —'

She heard the ping above the sound of the engine, and then — a second later — something crashed against the back of the car. For a moment, she didn't know if her plan had worked, or if the tow hitch had simply broken off.

She got out.

On the ground, below the Cherokee, was the metal plate, as well as a fresh, ugly scar — carved out of the fender — where the plate had struck it.

Rebekah didn't care.

She hurried over to the door. Screws hung loose, no longer attached to the plate, and the door handle had broken into two pieces. More wood had cleaved away as well.

The door was open.

Rebekah let Roxie explore while she hurried straight for the kitchen. As she passed the bedrooms, she could see they were exactly the same design as the ones in the other hostel – plain and undecorated, blankets on the beds.

In the kitchen, she started opening cupboards.

She felt an instant wave of relief at seeing the cans there, knowing – even from a quick glance – that they now had enough for at least another six weeks, maybe a couple of months, if she continued to ration what they ate. She grabbed ravioli, tuna, corned beef, more clam chowder, and a lot of beans: refried and pinto, chilli, beans with pork and with chicken franks. She'd never have eaten any of this stuff if she'd still been at home – but right now the cans meant survival.

Roxie started barking. It sounded like she was upstairs somewhere. 'Rox?' she called. 'What's up?'

More barking.

Rebekah headed to the first floor and found Roxie in the last room on the left.

She stopped in the doorway.

In the middle, Roxie was doing circles. She was worked up, confused, and it was obvious why: she could smell someone in here.

Someone she'd loved.

This was the room Stelzik had stayed in.

Rebekah dropped to a crouch, trying to reach out to Roxie. 'It's all right, Rox,' she said softly, 'it's okay,' but even as she said the words, her mind had skipped ahead to what she might find in Stelzik's room.

Maybe a clue as to why he was killed.

Maybe the reason they'd tried to do the same to her.

Before

Rebekah stared into the window of the Cherokee, at the image of her head injury, at the wound that looked like a bullet hole, then noticed something else, on the other side of the car.

The window on the opposite side wasn't there.

It had been smashed.

She'd totally missed it, the shock of seeing her reflection over-powering everything else, but as she hurried around the front of the Jeep, she looked in through the passenger window and found glass all over the seat.

Something was missing from inside too.

The dashcam.

It had been stuck to the windshield, without ever being switched on, but now all that remained of it was a vague circle on the glass. She couldn't remember the last time she'd run it. Gareth had bought it in the weeks before the split, telling her everyone was using them, that in the event of an accident it would save a ton of hassle with their insurers. He'd framed it like an insult, a comment on her driving, but in those final days and weeks, she hadn't had the energy to fight him on every tiny thing. Now it had been taken, and she had no idea why.

Why would someone smash a window to get at it?

She slid in at the wheel and fired up the Jeep. The moment it rumbled into life, she looked at the clock on the centre console: 14:58. She'd lost track of time, didn't even know when she and Johnny had entered the forest, so she had no idea how far behind Johnny she was, or if Johnny had left at all. She looked out through the dust and mud, speckled on the windshield, into the tangle of trees, and worried that trying to go for help was the wrong move. What if Johnny was still in there somewhere? What if he was injured? What if he was dead?

She focused on the thing that mattered: finding him. And she could only find him with help. The forest was far too big for her to cover by herself, its trails too difficult to understand. She needed local knowledge.

Jamming the Jeep into reverse, she began backing out. But the second the wheels started turning, she knew something wasn't right. The car felt imbalanced, as if something was weighing it down on the left side.

Getting out again, she looked towards the trunk.

The back rear tyre had been slashed, cut so deeply that the rubber had folded over on itself. In her hurry, she hadn't noticed it.

She wanted to scream into the trees.

Popping the trunk, she began looking for a spare tyre, even though she was already certain that there wasn't one. When they'd bought the car, she remembered overhearing the salesman telling Gareth how the tyre-inflator kit worked – but it was worth less than nothing when the damage was to the side wall. Sure enough, a kit was all she found.

She slammed the tailgate shut.

What now?

She had no cellphone and no vehicle and it was at least a mile back up the track to the Loop. But it was her only choice.

The track was hard going, full of ruptures and holes, and half-way up, it began to rain. It didn't take long for the cracks in the mud to split, and Rebekah was slipping, the wind gathering and scattering leaves from the trees.

When she finally got to the top, the clouds were even denser than before, knotted together like clumps of wool. Out to sea, a leaden wall of rain hung like a stage curtain – and then the entire sky blinked white.

A storm was coming.

She looked both ways along the Loop, hoping to see a car close by, a truck, a person, anything. The road was empty, save for the flickering shapes of buildings, drifting in and out of the rain, and debris, perhaps from a truck: she could see wood chips and plastic fasteners dotted across the road.

The most direct route to Helena was to her right, but the buildings she could see were on her left, so she headed there first. If just one was occupied, that meant people, and people meant help.

The rain jagged in towards her, needles against her face. She was already wet from the climb up the track, but now the cold came too: her clothes were stuck to her, like a skin she couldn't shed, and as the first of the buildings edged closer, she started shivering.

It was ugly, crumbling, with a gunmetal-grey roof and no windows at the front. She tried the door. It was locked. She started banging on it and – when there was no response – moved around to the back. It was full of junk, a graveyard of old machinery and mangled vehicles. It was clear no one had lived here for years.

Lightning flashed again.

The next building was a couple of minutes away but, before she got there, she could see it was a dead end. It was boarded up, part of its roof collapsed. The next house was the same. The only difference this time was that the front yard had a mobile home in it. Rebekah stopped outside the trailer and banged on its walls. They vibrated against her fist.

'Hello?' she shouted against the rain. 'Hello?'

She tried the house too, but everything was locked. No one was at home. No one was anywhere.

She needed to get to the ferry.

There would be help there.

She set off again. All the time the rain kept coming and now it was getting dark. That meant it must be after 4 p.m.

The day before, Chloe in one arm, Kyra at her legs, she'd opened the doors of the brownstone and remembered seeing the sky through the back windows, starting to colour. She remembered Kyra asking if she could watch TV, then the sound of the *Dora the Explorer* theme coming from the living room. *Dora*, Rebekah had learned, through routine, through repetition, started at four every day, and it was like a rescue boat. It was a thirty-minute pause on a videotape that never stopped. For that short period every day, her girls would sit and watch *Dora*, and Rebekah would get to cuddle them. She didn't have to make anything, didn't have to prepare any food; they didn't wriggle away from her; she wasn't telling them off or kissing them better.

It was just the three of them.

She tried to think of other things about her life, memories that would give her momentum, that would energize her muscles and bones as if she wasn't already soaked through, freezing and exhausted, and for a while, it worked: she pictured Kyra playing with her building blocks on the living-room floor, Chloe reaching a hand up to the toy bar that arced over her bouncer.

Rebekah was thinking of Kyra, of the structures she used to build with the blocks, of the sound they would make as the tower finally collapsed, when the images of her daughters began to flicker. And as the storm intensified and the rain lashed against her, desperation began to overwhelm her.

Why is this happening to me?

She tried to calm herself, going over what Johnny had told her earlier, using it to reassure herself: the ferry back didn't leave until five o'clock, so she still had time. If she missed it, it would be bad, but not irretrievable. The island didn't close until tomorrow. She could still get home then. And if she had to wait until tomorrow, she had time to find Johnny.

She looked out to sea, through a wall of rain. A few seconds later the entire horizon bloomed with white light. The storm was still a long way out, but it was getting closer, sailing towards her, to the island, like a warship.

But then, something else slowly tilted into focus. Not a memory, but something real, here – *now* – up ahead, faint and imprecise.

She broke into a run.

42

Stelzik had set up a desk in one corner and his laptop was still on top of it. There was a pile of books in the corner, stacked waist-high, and a folder of notes, hole-punched and clipped to a binder. Rebekah went to the closet first: inside, there were rows of dog-food cans, and above, Stelzik's clothes. Stelzik, the *real* Stelzik, hadn't been a large man, so Rebekah suspected his clothes would be a decent fit for her – better, certainly, than the ones she'd found at the gas station.

The whole time, Roxie kept doing circles.

Rebekah beckoned the dog towards her while trying to focus her attention on Stelzik's desk. But she was finding it hard to con-centrate: Roxie just kept moving, stopping only occasionally to sniff the bed, the mattress, the unmade sheets and blankets. 'It's okay, Rox,' Rebekah said. 'I understand.'

The room wasn't much, but Roxie had known it for almost seven months. She'd been here with Stelzik every day. Now he had simply gone.

Except not entirely.

She could still smell him in everything.

Roxie finally came to a halt. Rebekah had removed the dressing from her face: her eye remained a little pink, even though it had healed, but Roxie had been blinking a lot, as if it were irritating her. And, in that moment, in the slump of her body, she was so human.

Inconsolable. Heartbroken.

Rebekah put a hand on her. 'I get it,' she said again. 'I get it more than you can ever know.'

She started going through Stelzik's desk.

In it, she found three notebooks. He'd already filled one and had been on his way to filling a second, but the third was blank. Rebekah fanned through the empty pages.

At the store, she'd been using the inside of a cereal box to make lists of food and supplies, to keep track of what she had, what she needed, and how long the canned food would last. But the notebook would be better – *and* it would allow her to do something else.

For the entire time she'd been on the island, she'd been trying to work out why she and Johnny had been targeted. Why had Hain and Lima wanted them dead? What could they possibly have done? Rebekah was a doctor and a mother. Johnny was an unpublished writer and the assistant manager at a failing electronics store. It made no sense. Rebekah had lain awake at night, trying to set it out in her head, but too often it dissolved into chaos. It was the kind of chaos in which her friends and family had never reported her missing; in which Noella took her kids from her; in which Gareth cried crocodile tears whenever people asked where Rebekah was and he told them he didn't know.

She kept thinking about Johnny on that last day as well, the little things that had embedded in her memory. Like when her brother had begged Lima to spare them, offering to pay him when they got back to the city, and then Lima had cut him off, gun raised, and said, *She ain't going back, John.* She, not you. Not you and your sister. Not both of you. Just Rebekah. *She* ain't going back. Did that mean Rebekah had been the main target? And what about the look Johnny had given her after that – like he'd been confused somehow?

Like he'd been betrayed.

Had she *really* seen that in his face?

Or was it just the terror of the moment?

Roxie brushed against her legs. Rebekah ran a hand through the dog's coat, switching her attention back to the empty notebook, trying to dismiss the thought about Johnny. Instead, she concentrated on what the pages of the notebook would allow her to do:

write everything down, slowly, meticulously, and try to make sense of it. And then she looked at Roxie again, and a different idea landed.

It took a couple of journeys back and forth, as Rebekah took blankets up the stairs to Stelzik's room, and the supplies she'd gathered over the course of seven weeks. Every minute, Roxie got more excited and, by the time they'd finished, she didn't know what to do other than sprint from one end of the corridor to the other.

Rebekah had only remained at the store to watch the ocean, to watch for the rescue she had hoped would come. Now that seemed forlorn. It was possible a helicopter might come back and, if it did, she'd have a pretty good view of it out of the hostel's first-floor windows. But there seemed little hope of a boat – at least one unconnected to Hain or Lima – passing so close to shore that they could see her waving them down. She'd come to the conclusion that the fishing lanes must be much further out, because she'd seen nothing on the water in seven weeks, which meant that, at this time of year, trawlers didn't come close enough to the island to register her as a person, let alone to instigate some recovery.

Nevertheless, after Rebekah had locked up the store as best she could and placed board at the window she'd smashed, she wrote *SOS* on the wood using some paint she'd found at the gas station. Once that was done, she collected some rocks, rubble and old pieces of masonry from a patch of scrub just out of town, and brought them all back to the harbour. As Roxie waited patiently, Rebekah created a series of messages in the empty parking lot – *HELP ME* and *NEED RESCUE* and *LEFT BEHIND*.

She got back to the hostel as it was growing dark.

Using the rope from the car to secure the door from the inside, she tied it to a metal railing on one of the interior walls, then moved through to the kitchen to double-check the generator. Just as when she'd checked earlier, it was obvious that, like the other hostel, everything had been disconnected. She spent a while trying to reconnect wires, just in case, but something had been removed from the front panel, a battery or a power source, so any fantasy she'd had about a warm shower soon ended.

She headed back up to the room.

Roxie was curled up at the end of Stelzik's bed, completely ignoring the one Rebekah had made for her. 'I'm not sleeping on the floor, if that's what you're thinking.' She smiled, and went to the desk.

There was a calendar on the wall above it: she could use it to replace the pebbles she'd been using at the store to count down the days.

There was a laptop too.

She flipped up the lid, expecting it to be dead after going months without use – but, to her surprise, it sprang into life.

There was still nine per cent battery left.

Grabbing a blanket, she wrapped it around her shoulders, sat down and used the trackpad to open some folders. Luckily, Stelzik hadn't used a password, so she had access to everything, but it soon became evident there was nothing of any real interest. Most of the documents were scans of textbooks, notes he'd made, or papers he'd been writing.

She opened his email.

No new messages loaded because there was no internet connection, and as she searched the room, she saw no phone line, and no router. It probably meant Stelzik had been using his cellphone as a hotspot whenever he needed to fire off an email. She spent a couple of minutes digging through his things to see if she could find his cell, but she couldn't. Most likely, Lima had taken it, just as he'd taken Rebekah and Johnny's.

She looked at the Inbox again.

This time, something caught her eye.

Slowly, she began scrolling down. The further she went, the more she realized what was missing. She checked the Trash, just to be sure – but there was nothing in there either.

Dread slithered through her stomach.

She leaned away from the screen as if a part of her didn't want to have to look at it, and as she did, her mind spun back to the day

Johnny had come to the house, when he'd first asked to borrow her car: *I've got an interview lined up for this Saturday,* he'd told her, *with a curator from the Museum of Natural History. It's taken me almost three months of emails to get him to commit.*

Except there were no emails from Johnny.

Not even one.

He and Stelzik had never been in touch.

Before

Helena. Rebekah could see a hint of it in the distance now.

She pushed herself harder, running faster, the Loop empty ahead of her, like a road at the end of the world.

Keep going.

Thunder rumbled. She tried to count the gap between claps, tried to work out how far away the storm still was and how much time that gave her.

Keep going.

She kept repeating it to herself, dropping her head against the rain – but, as she did, she saw that, in the dark, she'd strayed off the road.

She stopped, exhausted: the road was about fifty feet from where she was, but even such a small deviation felt like a defeat.

She dragged herself back, keeping her focus on the yellow lines, but she'd lost her rhythm and was shivering uncontrollably. A minute later, lightning forked across the clouds above her – terrifying, beautiful.

That was when she spotted the bicycle.

It was leaning against an old shack. The back wheel – raised off the ground – turned every time the wind roused, each revolution bringing a muted squeal. Rebekah hurried to it, almost losing her footing in the water that was running out of the overflowing storm drains.

Yanking the bike away from the shack, she wheeled it back to the road. She could feel one of the tyres was soft, the movement of the bike slightly off, but she didn't care, just started cycling.

Rain was coming at her horizontally and, as thunder exploded directly above her, she wobbled, almost losing control. But then, suddenly, the road started to drop away. It was subtle at first, then became steeper, and she could see the town clearly: grey roofs, the harbour.

Her adrenalin spiked.

I'm almost there, Johnny. I'm almost in Helena. I'm going to find someone here who knows the forest and I'm going to come back for you, I promise. Please don't be dead, John, please don't be dead, please don't be d—

She hit the brakes.

The bike screeched. The sound was so loud she heard it over the snarl of the wind and the machine-gun crackle of the rain on the road.

There were no lights anywhere in Helena.

No cars, no vehicles.

Nothing at the harbour.

It had been ninety minutes, maybe more, since she'd got to the Loop, ninety minutes of being out in the rain, so she'd expected to miss the ferry back. It wasn't a surprise to see no boat waiting for her. But where were the people who worked here? Why were there no cars in the parking lot?

Why was there no sign of life?

She hadn't noticed it at a distance, in the darkness, but she did now: the buildings were already shuttered, wooden boards fixed at windows and doors.

It wasn't protection against the storm.

It was protection against winter.

'No, no, no,' Rebekah muttered into the rain.

She swung her legs off the bike and let it roll away from her. It clattered to the ground. By then, she'd already broken into a run, sprinting down Main Street, the buildings on either side boarded, any sign of human life gone.

At the bottom, the gates to the harbour had been pulled all the way closed, chains binding them together.

On the other side, a padlock taunted her.

'No!' she screamed, her voice instantly lost in the rain. *This must be a mistake. It must be a trick. It can't be right. It can't be.* She yelled into the night, and as a vibration moved through her chest, a faint wail escaped from her throat, like the moan of an injured animal.

Everyone's gone.

Everyone's left already.

She looked back along Main Street.

Johnny had told her that *tomorrow* was the last day of the season. He'd talked about it on the ferry that morning. Even though it felt like centuries ago, she remembered exactly what he'd said: Halloween was the last day. But now she could see the truth: the island didn't close tomorrow. It closed today.

Which meant Johnny had been mistaken.

Or something much worse had happened.

He'd lied.

43

Stelzik's laptop died fifteen minutes later.

Rebekah stared at the black screen, the whole room dropping into darkness as night settled outside. Reaching for her flashlight, she flicked it on, her gaze returning to the computer. Why were there no emails from Johnny in Stelzik's Inbox? Had Stelzik deleted them? If he had, why weren't they in Trash? Rebekah glanced at Roxie, saw her staring back, and muttered, 'Do people delete emails *after* putting them in the Trash folder?'

Maybe some people did, maybe *Stelzik* did, but it seemed a weird and very deliberate thing to do. Johnny had told Rebekah the day he asked to borrow her car that he'd been chasing Stelzik for three months. Had Stelzik become pissed off with Johnny's requests? Would that explain why he might go to the trouble of completely erasing Johnny's emails from his laptop?

No, that didn't make sense either.

If he was so pissed off, why agree to be interviewed at all?

She looked at Roxie again and a deep, pervading sense of unease spread inside her, like an oil slick.

Could Johnny *really* have lied to her?

Why?

She closed her eyes, hating the idea, an image forming in her head of the snowglobe he'd bought her. She could see Kyra tilting it and letting it settle again, over and over, the night before Rebekah had come to the island. She could still see her brother, with the gift box in his hands, a couple of days before that, when he'd handed it to her. *I saw it and thought of you*, he'd said.

Her mind went even further back, digging through her best memories of him, trying to bathe in the certainty of them, and one in particular lodged with her.

When Rebekah was seventeen, in her second year of A levels, Johnny had flown to London to visit her. He'd managed to sell a 5,000-word short story to a literary magazine on the west coast – the one and only time he had sold any of his writing to anyone – and had been paid $400 for it. When he talked to Rebekah on the phone, elated at the idea of being published, he told her he was going to use the cash to come and see her. She told him he didn't need to, that he should spend the money on himself – but he insisted. 'I miss you,' he said, and the more she and Johnny talked, the more excited they became. She'd show him the city again, all the things that had changed since the family's move to America; and when she was at school, he would go and see all the literary sights – the British Library, Baker Street, Highgate Cemetery, the homes of Keats, Dickens and Samuel Johnson.

He landed on a rain-soaked morning, and Rebekah met him in the arrivals hall at Heathrow, both so glad he had come. They laughed on the Tube, catching up on the things they'd missed in each other's lives. They dropped off his bag at the cheap, dreary B&B he'd paid for, close to where Rebekah boarded at school, laughing about the sinister-looking woman on Reception and renaming the place the Bates Motel. Then they went into the city and straight to the pubs, Rebekah high on the adrenalin of being with her brother, Johnny slightly delirious with jet lag. He told her it was so good to be back in England, to be able to share those moments with her in the country they'd grown up in. He said exactly the things that Rebekah expected from Johnny: kind words, earnest, loving. He might not always be demonstrative, he might never say *I love you*, but he didn't need to: like their dad, he could convey what he felt in the way he looked at you, in the simple act of spending all the cash he had on a flight.

But then she came crashing out of the memory, and her thoughts darkened, and she remembered the last day of the season. She remembered how he'd told her that the island shut on 31 October when it actually closed the day before. Even though she'd been confused the night she'd made it to Helena in the rain, questioning her brother's motives – a man she thought she'd known better than anyone – she'd eventually put it down to a mistake, not deceit. Mixing up dates, forgetting the fine detail, those were traits of his, and always had been. He was a dreamer. His mind wandered because he was creative. She trusted her brother. He wasn't capable of deception, of cruelty, of such damage.

But then that trip to London crawled back into her head.

It had been perfect for two days, the pair of them as happy as Rebekah could remember them being. They went to museums, ate fish and chips beside the Thames, talked for hours and laughed even more. And then, on the third night, they went out with Rebekah's friends. She'd been so desperate for them to meet her brother. She'd been so proud of him.

It turned into one of the worst nights of her life.

The Stranger

'There didn't seem like there was anything up with Rebekah?'

Travis shuffled forward to the edge of the couch, pen poised above his notebook. Opposite him, Noella Sullivan shook her head and glanced at the camera he'd set up: 'Honestly, she seemed fine. She was a little stressed, I guess — you know, leaving the kids, having to make it over to John's for a certain time — but nothing that would have made me concerned.'

They were in Noella's living room, small but homely, paintings of Irish vistas on the walls. There were shelves with a few photographs, all of her with the Murphy family, and in particular her with Rebekah Murphy's girls. Travis gestured to the pictures and said, 'You were obviously the designated babysitter.'

He said it with a smile, but her reaction was small and stoic. 'Yes,' she said. 'I love those girls. It's important now for them to have some stability.'

Travis nodded, trying to work out if there was something to interpret in her choice of response, then took a sip of the drink he'd asked for. He winced. Noella had made him a mint tea. It was something Gaby had put him on to, and that he'd frequently lapsed from drinking, but four days out from retirement he was giving it another go.

'Why are you drinking something you don't enjoy?'

He glanced at Noella, who seemed amused now. He hadn't seen her smile before: she was pleasant, appeared concerned for the wellbeing of her friends, but it was clear she'd developed a tough hide. He knew she was thirty-six, but she was greying, looked older, more fortified. He wondered what had happened in her life to make her that way. He smiled again and said, 'My daughter tells me I need to cut back on my coffee intake.' He looked down at his notes. 'So Rebekah never said where she and Johnny were going?'

'It was such a rush, all I got out of her was Long Island.'

'If it was a rush, that suggests they had to be somewhere for a specific time,' Travis said, but it wasn't really a question, more a statement.

'Johnny had an interview lined up.'

'Did he say with who?'

'No. Bek just said it was for the book he was writing.' Noella paused, thinking, her expression pensive. 'I guess they had to leave early to meet whoever Johnny had set up the interview with.'

'And you said you heard from her later on?'

'Yeah, a couple of times.'

'And she didn't say anything then?'

'About where she was?' Noella shook her head. 'No. When I say that now, it sounds crazy, but it just never came up. She was having a hard time being so far away from her girls – the furthest she'd been from them was the hospitals in the city, one shift at a time – and I don't think it ever dawned on her that she might feel so heartsick for them. So we were dealing with that. And then there were a lot of problems with reception.'

'The calls kept dropping out?'

'Dropping out, or just dying.'

Travis was quiet as he made some more notes, trying to think about places on Long Island where the reception might be unreliable. It was hard to imagine there were many: almost three million people lived in Suffolk and Nassau counties, seven and a half if you factored in Brooklyn and Queens. The island was big. It was populated and connected. He tapped his pen against the notebook, thinking about the early start Johnny Murphy and his sister had made. 'Did Rebekah mention anything about getting a boat?'

Noella frowned. 'A boat?'

'Maybe a ferry?'

She shook her head. 'No, nothing like that.'

Travis put a question mark next to the word 'Ferry'. He'd have to look into it some more. He knew there were hundreds of islands in the Long Island Sound, but a lot of them weren't accessible, and even those that were you could normally only get to on ferries that sailed from Connecticut, not Montauk. Plus, so far, there was no evidence that the Murphys had got a boat anyway.

'Can't you just check her cellphone records or something?'

'Yes,' he replied. 'I've made a request for them.'

'Then you can see where she went.'

He nodded. 'That's the hope.'

He forced down more of his tea, then changed tack. 'You were rushed into the ER back in September, is that right?'

She frowned, thrown by the change of direction.

'And Johnny came to see you at the hospital that night?'

'He did, yeah. He was brilliant.'

Travis flipped back in his notebook to the timeline he'd written down, including the two hours and twenty-eight minutes that Murphy had had his cell switched off. 'Do you know if Johnny was there the whole time?' he asked.

She frowned again.

'He didn't leave to go anywhere else?'

'No,' she said. 'Not that I remember.'

'Were you conscious the whole time he was there?'

She was trying to think. 'I'm not sure,' she said eventually.

'Did any other friends or family come to see you that night?'

'My boyfriend was away and my dad is very sick and frail, so it was just Johnny,' she said, and a sadness seemed to press on her. Travis glanced at the photos in the living room again: her father was her only family. Rubbing the side of her face, Noella said, 'They put me out.' She shrugged. 'So I guess I was unconscious for a part of the time John was there. Why are you asking me that?'

'It's just a loose end, that's all.'

'A loose end to do with my appendectomy?'

Travis smiled. She was smart. 'I'm just trying to get an idea of the type of person he is.'

Noella eyed him, as if she still didn't really believe him, but then she gestured to a photograph on the wall, of her, in the centre, with Murphy, his sister and two other men – one younger, one older. Travis knew who they were because he'd already built a background on the entire Murphy clan. He'd even looked into the death of the younger brother, Mike, but there had been nothing suspicious in it, just stupidity: a young man driving an expensive car way too fast.

'You want to know what type of person Johnny Murphy is?' Noella said, a little distance in her voice now, her eyes locked on the photograph of her with the family. 'Just ask around. Everyone will tell you exactly the same thing. He's basically the kindest, gentlest, most generous person you ever met in your life.'

Travis got home and watched the interview with Noella, then cooked some pasta, because it was easy and he was tired. At 7 p.m., he set up his laptop and waited for a Zoom call. It came through at 7.15.

'I'm so sorry I'm late,' Kirsty Cohen said.

She was a plain-looking woman in her late thirties, with auburn bangs and a pale complexion. Travis remembered from the first time he'd interviewed her – in the weeks after Louise had gone missing – that she was also energetic, helpful, and talked a lot. She'd clearly come straight from work: she still had her ID around her neck.

'It's no problem,' Travis replied, and flipped to a fresh page of his notebook. 'What's the weather like down there in Baltimore?'

He'd asked the question to put her at ease, but Kirsty didn't stop talking for ten minutes about all the snow they'd been having in Maryland. Eventually Travis had to cut her off. 'Something's come up,' he said, 'and I wanted to talk to you about it.'

'Oh. Okay. Is there news on Louise?'

He paused, trying to figure out how much to tell her. He decided to give her the truth. 'I don't know if you've heard this, but your friend Rebekah Murphy, and her brother Johnny – they're both missing.'

Her face dropped. 'What?'

'So you didn't know?'

'No. No, I had no idea.'

'They disappeared seven weeks ago.'

'What?' she said again, and brought a hand to her mouth this time. 'Are you kidding? That's awful. What happened to them?'

'I've only been working their case for a day,' Travis said, his eyes drifting to a calendar on the wall, and he thought, I'm only going to be working it for three more.

'Detective Travis?'

He pulled himself back into the room. 'So, I take it you haven't heard from Rebekah?'

'No. No, not at all. I tried calling her a month ago, maybe more . . .' Kirsty faded out. 'Actually, it must have been around the time they went missing, if you're saying it's been seven weeks. I tried calling her and she didn't answer, so I called again a couple of times. I wanted to talk to her.'

'About what?'

'Well, you know . . .'

She was stumbling over her words.

Travis waited her out.

'Well, you know, about Johnny.'

'What about him?'

This time, there was a flash of guilt in her eyes.

'Kirsty?'

'You were asking me questions about him, about what Louise thought of him when they went out on those dates, and it only occurred to me after that, well, you must be thinking . . . you know, that he's a suspect in all of this.'

Travis let her carry on.

'I just wanted to talk to Bek about it.'

'Why?'

'I don't know. I guess I just wanted . . .' She grimaced a little, then the connection dropped for a second, her image juddering. 'I wasn't trying to warn him about anything, I promise. I just wanted to . . .'

Again, Travis said nothing, just waited.

'I wanted to hear what she thought, that's all. I mean, she knows him better than anyone, and for him to have possibly been involved in something like Louise going missing . . .' She stopped again. 'It just seemed totally crazy. I know Johnny a little bit, and I knew Louise would love him. I mean, I was right, because she told me after their first date that he was a really nice guy. He could be shy, quite introverted, but he was a real gentleman, to me, to Louise, to everyone. Rebekah always spoke real highly of him too. But, then, I don't know, I just kept . . . I kept going back to . . .'

She faded out.

Travis shuffled forward in his seat, wanting to hear what had gone unspoken. When she didn't say anything, he prompted her: 'What? You kept going back to what, Kirsty?'

'I don't know,' she said again. 'I just kept thinking about this one thing Bek told me, when she was really drunk, back when we were in college.'

Travis leaned even closer to the screen. 'What thing is that?' he said.

'There was this incident, way back in the late nineties.'

'An incident?'

'In London.'

'London?' Travis frowned. 'London, England?'

'Yeah,' Kirsty said. 'Bek said that Johnny went a bit . . .'

She faded out, grimaced.

Travis waited.

'She just said that something happened that night – and when she looked at him, it was like looking into the eyes of a stranger.'

Before

Rebekah had chosen the pub because she knew Johnny – as a big fan of the movies – would love it. It was on Holloway Road, less than a mile from her halls, and built into the side of a beautiful, grade-two-listed art-deco cinema called the Regal. The pub was housed inside the cinema's original foyer, and it gave the décor a wonderful bygone elegance, with its hardwood stairs, marble floors, and geometric and sunburst patterns. On the wall behind the bar, there were huge posters for *Double Indemnity* and *The Maltese Falcon*, which was another reason Rebekah had chosen the place: Johnny had loved both movies, watching them on repeat growing up.

'Wow,' he said, as they entered. 'This is so cool.'

'I thought you'd like it,' Rebekah replied. Because they'd arrived at the pub early it was relatively quiet and they got to pick the best spot: a curved booth with a metal table built from the bones of an old film projector.

'This is amazing,' Johnny said, as they slid into the seat. 'Thanks so much for bringing me here, Bek. I love it.'

Rebekah's friends started to arrive just after five, and although Johnny was never great in crowds, particularly with people he didn't know, he put on his best show for her. He was sweet, funny, let Rebekah tell stories of when they were young, listened politely as the conversation moved to school, to the teachers there, to gossip about other students. At one stage, maybe four drinks in, Rebekah leaned in and asked if he was all right, and he told her he was enjoying himself. That wasn't entirely true, she knew: a few of her friends would bring him back into the discussion sometimes, but most of them – like Rebekah herself – were seventeen, armed only with fake ID, bravado and a youthful belief that their story was the funniest, and most important, and the only one that deserved to be heard.

As the night went on, the pub became busier, eventually filling with Arsenal and Spurs fans. A north London derby was kicking off at Highbury at 8 p.m., and although uniformed officers were stationed all the way along Holloway Road, principally in an effort to keep the two sets of fans apart, some had scurried into the Regal unseen and were shoulder to shoulder at the bar.

Forty-five minutes before kick-off, Rebekah offered to get another round of drinks, because the Regal always stopped asking for ID once the crowds were two deep at the bar.

As she was waiting, a guy in his late forties, his gut straining against a Spurs shirt, backed into her, spilling his pint on his boots. 'Fuck's sake,' he muttered, turning, angry, his expression fierce. But when he saw Rebekah, his ire instantly dissolved. He looked from her breasts to her face. 'You all right, love?'

She just nodded.

'You going to apologize, then?'

'For what?'

'What do you think?' He gestured with the pint glass, lager sloshing around inside. 'I spilled half my beer on my shoes because you backed into me.'

'*You* backed into *me.*'

Behind him, a friend peered over his shoulder. 'What we got here then?' the friend said.

'A stuck-up bitch by the look of things,' the man said, and winked at Rebekah, as if she should lighten up. 'Just messing. You out with mates?'

'What's that got to do with you?'

The man looked beyond her, his eyes scanning the pub, trying to find the table where Rebekah was sitting. And then he spotted it: it wasn't hard because, aside from Johnny, it was filled with seventeen-year-old girls.

'Bloody hell,' the man said, catching his friend's attention and pointing at the table. 'Get rid of the queer boy and we'd do a bit of damage there, Woody.'

Rebekah shook her head. 'Piss off, will you?'

'What was that?' the man said, leaning in to her.

'I *said*,' she responded, facing him down even though he was almost twice her size, 'why don't you two just piss off to the football?'

The man grinned again.

'You got a filthy mouth,' Woody – the friend – said, but the man shushed him. He and Rebekah were still staring at each other, his smile still there.

'Just leave me alone,' she said.

'Women with mouths like yours are only good when you give them something to fill it with,' the man said, sinking his beer. As he drank, he didn't take his eyes off her. 'You good on your back, love?'

This time, Rebekah chose not to reply, hoping her silence would defuse the situation. She glanced over her shoulder and could see everyone on the table deep in conversation, unaware of what was going on. But then Johnny looked out across the pub, searching the crowd for her, and they found each other.

'I could teach you if you like,' the man said.

'Drop dead,' she muttered.

'Oooh, yeah,' he fired back, looking at his friend, deliberately creasing his face into an expression of faux-ecstasy. 'Oooh, dirty talk. I love it, darlin'.' The two of them burst out laughing. 'I bet you take it up the arse.'

The men wailed like hyenas.

Rebekah tried to get the barman's attention.

Please come and serve me.

'Seriously, though, do you take it up the arse, love?'

Please.

The men erupted into laughter again.

'You all right, Bek?'

Rebekah turned to find Johnny standing at her right shoulder. He looked at the men, then at her. Johnny was no fighter, but in that moment she would rather have him at her side than not. He shuffled into the space between Rebekah and the men.

'Cover your arse, Woody,' the man said.

They laughed again but the mood had changed.

'Looks like it's queer o'clock,' Woody chipped in.

'Why don't you guys just give it a rest?' Johnny said.

'Hello, it's GI Joe.'

He tried again: 'Just give it a rest, guys, okay?'

The man leaned all the way into Johnny, stopping so close to him that their noses were almost touching. 'I'll give it a rest whenever I fucking want to.' He pushed Johnny in the shoulder. Johnny stumbled back, into Rebekah, who stumbled into the people next to her. Straight away, she could tell that Johnny hated this, that it scared him, that he was so far out of his depth he could barely see dry land – but he did what he had to do as her big brother.

He stepped forward again, into their space.

'I think you need to calm down.'

'Or what?' the man growled.

'Just . . .' Johnny glanced at Rebekah.

'Or what? You gonna fight me?'

Saliva speckled Johnny's face.

'You gonna *fight* me?'

'Just leave her alone,' Johnny repeated meekly, wiping the saliva away from his cheek. 'Just go enjoy your soccer match and leave her alone.'

'It's *football*, you fucking bender.'

'Whatever. Just leave her alone.'

'Or *what*?'

'That's enough.'

'Enough? I'll tell you when it's enou–'

Johnny grabbed the man by the neck, clamping his fingers around his throat. It happened so fast, the movement so quick and unexpected, that for a second Rebekah barely processed what was happening. She didn't remember the last time Johnny had even so much as raised his voice – in twenty years, she was pretty certain he'd never raised his fists. When he was picked on at school, pushed

284

around, he never fought back. Mike would tell him he needed to, but he wouldn't. Except now he had: he was shoving the man to the floor, sending him crashing into a nearby table, stools toppling over, glasses smashing, the background music drowned in gasps and shouts from the bar staff.

Rebekah looked down at the man, splayed on the floor, his face a mix of shock and anger, and even as Johnny saw the bouncers rushing over, he wasn't done: he went for the friend, Woody, grabbing him by the hair, by the excess skin at his neck, and throwing his head against the bar. Woody folded, like a piece of paper, his pelvis hitting the hardwood, his face smashing against the counter top, nose breaking instantly, blood spattering.

Johnny leaned over the man on the floor. 'I'll fucking *kill* you.'

He spat the words – violent, destructive – and of all the things that stayed with Rebekah about that night, two faces remained most vivid, even years on. First Johnny's: there was corrosiveness behind his eyes, a rage that she'd not only never seen before but had believed he simply wasn't capable of. It so shocked her that, in the hours afterwards, she convinced herself she must have been mistaken, that the emotion of the moment had skewed her memory.

And then there was the second, that of the man on the floor: Rebekah saw the fury in him, the violence he was capable of – but the moment he went to get up, the moment his eyes found Johnny, it vanished.

Johnny had made him cower.

As soon as the bouncers arrived, one grabbing Johnny's arm, the other hauling the man up off the floor, everything altered, a fracture repairing itself: Johnny glanced at Rebekah and said, 'I'm sorry, Bek.' He was her brother again, panicked, worried, his voice small. He repeated himself as he was marched away, one of the bouncers already on the phone to the police.

But Rebekah never forgot that night.

Or the stranger who had been her brother.

44

The gas station was pitch black.

She flooded the forecourt office with light from the Cherokee, then hurried with Roxie around to the back. Once inside, Rebekah cranked on the generator, listened to it rattle out of its slumber, and then – as bulbs flickered into life above her – she went through to the front office.

She'd come armed with Stelzik's laptop.

There was no juice left in the battery, so when she tried powering it on after plugging it in, she got no response. Tapping out an impatient rhythm on the desk, she felt Roxie brush past her legs, sniffing her way around the floor of the office. Rebekah looked down at her, and then her eyes drifted back to the denims she was wearing: she'd returned to her own clothes and, for the first time, saw what a state they were in. Blood. Mud. Grass stains. She'd torn one of the pockets on her first day here, so that it just flapped against the top of her thigh. As she thought of that, her mind went all the way back to what Johnny had told her. *Tomorrow is the last day.*

She didn't know any more if it had been a mistake or a lie.

She switched her attention to the laptop and tried powering it on again. This time, it worked: the black screen turned white and it began to load.

As soon as it was done, she went to Stelzik's email. When she'd used the laptop at the hostel, his Inbox had already been open, presumably because it had been left that way the last time the PC had gone to sleep. Now, though, because she'd been forced to reboot the laptop, she had to wait for the browser to fire up.

Once it had, she clicked on the shortcut for Stelzik's Gmail and started scrolling through messages again. She wanted to make sure she'd been right the first time and there were no emails between Johnny and Stelzik.

There weren't.

She checked Sent and Trash, then went through some of the colour-coded folders that Stelzik had created, and in which he'd stored things like important messages, research and scans.

Again, she found nothing.

Next, she went to the browser history.

The last three entries were all related to his email, and there was one entry each for Inbox, Trash and Sent.

Rebekah looked at the dates and times.

Saturday, 30 October.

14:45 through to 15:03.

She flashed on a memory of getting to the Cherokee after being left for dead in the forest, and of seeing 14:58 on the car's clock. At that same time as she was bleeding, scared and confused, as she was wondering where her brother was, someone had come here, to Stelzik's room, and spent eighteen minutes in his email. Between 14:45 and 14:56, they were in the Inbox; 14:56 to 15:00 in Sent; and the remaining three minutes were spent checking Trash. Had Johnny's emails to Stelzik been deleted in those eighteen minutes? It made sense: if you were looking to delete emails, you'd go through the Inbox first, then check Sent, and then you'd make sure Trash was empty of them as well.

But who had deleted the emails?

Lima? Hain?

Johnny?

If it was Lima and Hain, why hadn't they just taken the whole laptop or, at the very least, wiped the browser history? That would have meant fewer questions. As it was, it was still possible to track what had been happening on the PC that day.

There was another mystery too.

Wasn't anyone missing Stelzik back in New York? He, like Rebekah, hadn't come home on the last day of the season, so why hadn't anyone he knew – or might have been in contact with – raised the alarm about him? Unlike in Rebekah's case, the people he worked with would have known where he was. He'd have told them he was going to Crow Island.

But then she got her answer.

She'd missed it the first time, but now, as she looked again, she saw an email in the Sent folder she hadn't paid attention to. It had gone out at 14:57 on 30 October. The timing coincided exactly with what Rebekah had already discovered in the browser history. More than that, it meant whoever had used the laptop hadn't just been deleting emails.

They'd been using the account to write them too.

45

The email was to someone called Gideon Burrows at the Museum of Natural History. Stelzik – or whoever had pretended to be him – had told Burrows he'd decided to extend his stay on the island for a while longer, into the winter months, because he was on the verge of making 'a big, very exciting discovery'.

> I've arranged transport back to New York for when I'm finished.
> I'll be in touch.

Sooner or later, when Stelzik didn't resurface, someone would start to ask questions about what had happened to him. But maybe that was the reason why the laptop had been left. If it was still here, browser history intact, along with Stelzik's clothes and belongings, it looked much less suspicious. His body was buried next to the tree roots in the forest, but if it was never found, there was no evidence he'd been murdered and, given his apparent decision to stay during the winter alone on the island, if he went missing the only logical conclusion was that he'd had an accident. She could hear her dad for a moment, ticking off the obvious outcomes people would reach: *He slipped somewhere and knocked himself out. He fell into the ocean. Maybe they might even think he killed himself.*

Rebekah found herself nodding, as if her father were in the room with her. Whatever Burrows and the rest of the staff at the museum *thought* was the reason Stelzik hadn't returned, it tied into something else Hain had said to Lima on the night Rebekah had followed them to the beach: *You brought the wrong car back.* He'd wanted the Cherokee, not Stelzik's Chevy: if the Chevy had been left behind, it would have played into the whole idea of Stelzik staying on, then perishing unexpectedly in some accident.

Rebekah checked through the Inbox again, through his address book, some of the folders he had with photographs in them, trying to figure out why no one except Gideon Burrows might miss Stelzik. But then it started to become clear: Stelzik wasn't married, and he didn't have kids. A family wasn't looking for him.

She leaned back on the stool, away from the screen, disturbed by what she was seeing. Could Johnny really have been involved in this deceit?

Rebekah shook her head, wanting to rid it of the thought. But she couldn't, not quite. There were just too many truths: she'd never seen her brother after she'd fallen into the gully; all the timings on Stelzik's laptop lined up perfectly with the idea of him coming here; and the memory of what her brother had done that night in London still burned brightly. There was something else too, something to which she'd barely given any thought since it had happened: Kirsty's call to Rebekah before she and Johnny had come out to the island. She'd said she'd wanted to talk about Johnny, and when Rebekah had asked Johnny about it, on the ferry over here, he'd told her he had no idea what Kirsty might have wanted. But was he lying about that too? Why would Kirsty want to talk about Johnny?

And then, as she looked at the laptop again, at the folders in Stelzik's email, she remembered she hadn't checked the Spam.

She opened it.

Inside, there was one message she hadn't seen.

It had been sent to Stelzik on the afternoon of 29 October, the day before Rebekah and Johnny had arrived on the island. When they'd found Stelzik in the forest that first day, Rebekah had guessed, from the condition of his body, that he'd already been dead for twenty-four hours – so it was possible that Stelzik had never read this message. That would certainly explain why it was still in his Spam.

Not that there was much to read.

The email was empty.

Confused, Rebekah's gaze went from the message window, up to the sender and their email address.

It took her a second to recognize the name.

And then her world fell apart.

Doubts

Travis had breakfast at his desk – his last ever Friday on the force – and spent three hours on the phone to the Metropolitan Police in London. Eventually, after being put on hold for what felt like the thousandth time, he landed up with someone who offered to help him. Inside a couple of hours, a copy of a two-decade-old arrest report dropped into his Inbox.

He started reading.

Johnny Murphy had never been charged, so the report was light on detail, but the bottom line was that he'd put one guy in hospital, and had told another that he would 'kill' him. Kirsty Cohen had told Travis that Murphy had been like a stranger, according to his sister, and the report backed that up. Murphy didn't deny things had got out of hand, and that he'd gone too far – even accepted the blame for everything – but said the two men had been 'aggressive and inappropriate' towards Rebekah, and 'it was clear that she was struggling to deal with it on her own.' For some reason, Travis thought of the moment – right at the end of the video interview he'd done with Murphy – when he'd tried the old trick of prolonging the silence. Travis had made it uncomfortable and awkward, feeling certain that Murphy was the type of person who would hate stuff like that. But all Murphy had done was sit there quietly and wait for Travis. He'd tried to play Murphy.

But maybe Murphy had played him.

The doubts had their nails in him now. There was no denying the arrest report, no denying that somewhere in Murphy there was a man capable of violence. If you accepted that, you had to accept that he might have abducted Louise Mason. Because that was what this was: an abduction. It had been three months since she'd last been seen at the fundraiser. There had been no sightings of her at all. It was impossible to believe that this was a decision taken of her own free will.

Yet Travis had dismissed Murphy as a suspect back in October. His instinct, at the time, was that Murphy was telling him the truth. Character witnesses then – and character witnesses, like Noella Sullivan, even now – all said Murphy was a good guy. Travis had spoken to the hospital where Noella had been taken, and they'd confirmed that they encouraged patients and their families to switch off their phones in certain areas of the building, which was exactly what Murphy had done. That explained the missing two hours as well. Something else bugged Travis too: why leave the hospital to go all the way back to the hotel? Geographically, it was a huge hassle. It didn't mean it hadn't happened – but Travis was wavering.

And, at the back of his head, there was something else nagging at him: all of this revised focus on Johnny Murphy had started with an anonymous call to his phone at work, in the middle of the night, from a man who didn't want to leave his name or stay on the line. But because Travis had been so desperate for a break in the case, and because he was so short of time, he'd run with it.

Now he didn't know who was telling him the truth.

He didn't know who was lying.

And he had only four days left to get to the answer.

46

Rebekah stared at the name of the sender, at the email address of the person who'd contacted Karl Stelzik with an empty message.

Willard Hodges.

That was the name Gareth had been using on the cellphone she'd found in the car. The same email he'd been using to book hotel rooms on wine estates and buy clothes for another woman in high-end stores.

His alias. His secret identity.

The name he'd used for his affair.

She stared at the email, unable to process what it meant, tears welling in her eyes. 'Are you really doing this to me?' she said quietly.

First Johnny. Now this.

'Are you really all *doing* this to me?'

She moaned the question into the silence of the gas station, then put a hand over her eyes, burying herself in the darkness.

But all she could see now was Gareth.

It was that day in the brownstone, when she'd got home and found him alone at the kitchen table with a bottle of bourbon. *I'm sorry, Bek*, he'd said to her. And then he'd told her Willard Hodges was just a name he'd made up.

Random.

Unimportant.

She opened her eyes again and looked at the screen.

Except it wasn't unimportant at all. Gareth had contacted Karl Stelzik. But why? How would he have *known* Stelzik in the first place?

She calmed herself, tried to get her thoughts into some sort of order.

It had to be through Johnny, surely, although she was uncertain of how. He and Gareth had never been close, even during the best times Rebekah had had during their relationship, and that had been exacerbated after Gareth had turned up late to their father's funeral. They definitely hadn't been in touch since the split.

That you know about.

She tried to shake her head free of interference. Could Johnny and Gareth *really* be working together? Why would either of them want to see harm come to Rebekah?

And what about the message?

It was empty.

There *was* no message.

So what was it? A test to see if Stelzik's email worked? What did that mean – that Stelzik was involved too? The day Lima had tried to kill her and Johnny, he'd told Rebekah that Stelzik was just a 'loose end'. That suggested Stelzik was ancillary to all of this, not central to it.

Or maybe it didn't.

She stared at the email again, then snapped the laptop shut. She didn't know what was going on.

But she was going to find out.

47

Over the next few days, while Roxie lay next to her, or roamed the empty corridors of the hostel, Rebekah wrote everything down on the pad she'd found in Stelzik's room. She put hours of effort into finding direct tethers between Gareth and Stelzik, but she could only get from Gareth to Stelzik via Johnny. She couldn't figure out if Stelzik and Johnny had been working together to lure her to the island – and, if so, why? – or whether Johnny and *Gareth* were plotting, and Stelzik was some sort of patsy. But that raised just as many questions, given the relationship between her brother and her ex. So if she discounted Johnny, Gareth was the person she should be looking at, which returned Rebekah to an idea she'd already had: that Gareth wanted her out of the way and Noella might even have been the reason he had invented the name Willard Hodges.

But did she really believe that?

Her husband was capable of deceiving her, that much was true, but did she really believe he wanted her dead? Did she believe Noella, her best friend, basically her sister, would be complicit in an affair with her husband *and* in a plot to get rid of Rebekah for good? And what about Johnny? Something held on inside her – a tiny flicker of light: a certainty that the man she'd grown up with, even the man she'd glimpsed in London that night, simply wasn't capable of something as insidious as this. And if she believed that about him, she must believe it about Noella too. So that just left Gareth.

That was when she saw her mistake, when she saw she'd overlooked two people in this jigsaw who were *definitely* involved.

Hain and Lima.

As soon as they pulled back into focus, she started to find a logical path through some of the questions, particularly the lack of emails to Stelzik from Johnny. Although a whisper of doubt about Johnny wouldn't leave her, two nights later she had paper all over the room, stuck to the walls, the front of the closet, even to the door when it was closed, and she could see clearly: it was far more likely that Hain and Lima had deleted Stelzik's email chain with Johnny, not her brother.

Stelzik had been dead for at least a day by the time she and Johnny had found him. And she remembered something else: as he'd pointed his gun at them both, Lima had said, *I've been trying to find that friggin' dog since I offed Stelzik.* If Rebekah was right, and Stelzik's body had been twenty-four hours old, it meant Roxie must have been loose in the forest for at least the same amount of time, and that Lima had been on the island the day *before* Rebekah and Johnny arrived. He must have come to take care of Stelzik first.

She looked at one of the notebook pages she'd mounted. It had a solitary question written on it, the question her father had always said was the starting point for every case he'd ever worked.

Why?

Number one, coming a day early gave Lima time to take care of Stelzik, the 'loose end'. If Stelzik had been left alive and was then questioned by cops looking for Johnny and Rebekah, he could have discussed the fact that he'd been in contact with Johnny. But there was more to it than that: after spending hours opening and closing different files and applications, Rebekah stumbled across an activity log on the laptop. It took her some time to figure it out – she was a long way from being any kind of expert – but she soon started to notice a regular pattern in it: Stelzik's IP address kept changing.

The reason landed hard.

His laptop was being accessed remotely.

He was being spied on.

And if Hain and Lima were watching emails between Johnny and Stelzik, it was just as likely – in fact, certain – that they were watching *all* of Johnny's emails. Perhaps even more disturbingly, they not only knew that Johnny had agreed to come to Crow Island to meet Stelzik on 30 October, they knew that Rebekah was coming too. And the fact they'd known that meant they'd been keeping as close an eye on Rebekah as they had on her brother, because she hadn't even *suggested* accompanying Johnny to the island until a day and a half beforehand. It had been a last-minute decision, and Hain and Lima had been able to react to it immediately. Even scarier, Rebekah had agreed to go with Johnny during a telephone call, not in an email. It meant that Hain and Lima hadn't just been looking at her Inbox. They'd been listening to her phone calls too.

On another piece of paper that she'd stuck to the closet doors, she'd written the words *perfect combination* and underlined them. That was what Rebekah's decision and Crow Island had turned out to be: Johnny's interview, and her offer to drive him out to it, had brought them to an island that was not only almost entirely unpopulated but more than a hundred miles from the mainland, and dominated by a forest – this dense, sprawling burial site – where they could easily be disappeared without anyone noticing.

And yet there was still the solitary question: why?

Roxie jumped onto Rebekah's bed, disturbing her train of thought, and nosed her way under the blankets. Since the middle of December, it had been bitterly cold, so Rebekah let her come in and returned her attention to the walls. For the first time, her gaze didn't land on the *Why?* but instead on Stelzik's calendar.

She looked at the days she'd marked off, at what day it was today, and everything else fell away. Instantly, she stopped thinking about why anyone would watch her and Johnny, much less try to kill them. In its place came a powerful, overwhelming and paralysing sense of loss.

Christmas Day.

In her head, she saw images of her girls around the tree, giggling with excitement, their new toys scattered around them – and, as she did, she crumbled. She was overrun by rapid, aggressive flickers of life at the brownstone, and all the doubts about Gareth, about Noella, flooded back.

She curled over, sank into herself. She sobbed, saying the names of her girls out loud, as if it would draw them closer, as if she was back home with them again, as if none of this had ever happened.

As if no one had tried to murder her.

And as if she'd never had to ask why.

Before

'Why?' She shook her head. '*Why?*'

They were standing outside the gates of Rebekah's boarding school, a tube train rumbling across a series of empty railway arches further along the street. There was a charge in the air that had nothing to do with the rain.

It was the morning after Johnny had been arrested.

'I'm so sorry, Bek,' he said, head down.

'You and me both.'

'I know I embarrassed you.'

'You embarrassed yourself, John.'

He nodded, looked up at her, didn't say anything.

'I didn't even know you were capable of that. Is this who you are?'

He frowned. 'No,' he said.

'Then how the hell do you explain what happened?'

He looked at her, then away, as if he didn't know how to articulate himself. The train disappeared from view.

'Do you remember my freshman year?'

Rebekah stared at him. 'What?'

'My freshman year.' He stopped and took a breath. 'When those kids at school picked on me. Do you remember I told you, Mike and Dad about it?'

'What has that got to do with *anything*, John?'

'The type of person I am,' he said, 'was forged in those moments. I told you guys some of it, but not all. Most of it I tried to forget. I was fifteen, with this dumb accent I've never been able to shake off, not American, not English, not one or the other. I came to hate it.'

His eyes flashed. He was hurting.

Why was he telling her this?

'You'd have been all right if you'd been in America, at school with Mike and me. Kids would have heard your accent and thought, *She's English*, and that would have been the end of the story. Maybe it would even have marked you out as cool. Mike, he always did fine because he sounded like he was born and bred in New York. But me, my accent got me noticed. Kids would accuse me of being a fake, of trying to put on an English voice or an American one. It got so bad, I stopped speaking some days. I kept my mouth shut and walked around school in total silence. But that got me noticed too. The things I loved doing – not sport, not math or science, but reading, writing, art – they became *another* difference. All I tried to do was fade into the background in everything I did – from the second I got into school – and none of it worked.'

He glanced at her, his eyes wet.

'Johnny, I –'

'It was just utterly relentless,' he said, the words catching in his throat. 'I got cornered in the bathrooms, I got pushed around at the lockers, I got my books stolen and ripped up, or they tossed them in the trash, or they flushed the pages down the can. I'd be walking home and they'd throw garbage at me. They'd dance around, mimicking my accent, calling me a "retard" and a "fag". It got so bad, no one wanted to spend time with me. I was a contaminant. If you ever got caught with me . . .' He faded out. 'I didn't really want to talk about it at home. I just wanted to *be* home. I wanted to be somewhere safe. So last night at the pub . . . it all just came out. There were so many times I wanted to do that, so many times I dreamed about it. I *always* backed down. I was always Johnny, the kid who took it on the chin. Johnny, the quiet one, or the arty one, or the lonely one, or the pathetic one.' He looked at her. 'Those two assholes, Bek, I didn't want to take it any more.'

'Johnny . . .' Rebekah stopped. 'I didn't . . .'

'You didn't know because I didn't *want* you to know. I didn't want any of you to know how bad it got for me.'

'Why?'

'I felt weak, I guess. Alone. The only times I ever felt normal was when I was with you, Dad and Mike, when we were a family. I didn't want to tell you because I didn't want you to treat me differently. The normality kept me sane. But as weird as it sounds now, I think a part of me . . . I was jealous of you, Bek.'

'Of me?' She frowned. 'Why?'

'You know what the difference is between you and me?' He waited for an answer, but she couldn't think of one: she had no idea why *he* would ever be jealous of *her*. 'You don't survive and flourish through luck, or some vague hope that it'll get better, or the occasional big idea paying off, like I do – you do it through logic. You get a problem, you work it out, you succeed, and you move on. You're so much like Dad, it's kind of scary. I think he was right: you would have made a good cop.' He forced another smile, but it was like it pained him to do it. 'So, you want to know why I'm jealous of you, Bek?'

The rain was getting heavier.

The city was louder than ever.

But all of it seemed to fade away.

'It's because you know how to fight back.'

48

It's because you know how to fight back.

She remembered Johnny's words just before she went to bed on New Year's Eve. By the time she woke up the next day, something had changed in her. It was subtle, but there: a determination she hadn't felt in a long time.

I need to be ready.

January was so cold she didn't go outside unless Roxie needed a toilet break. It barely crawled above zero for weeks, frosts and sleet almost every day. She used her time indoors to lay everything out, expanding into the first-floor corridor, sticking pieces of paper to the wall there as well. Every piece was a slightly different size, most taken from Stelzik's blank pad, but she found some coloured card downstairs too; when that ran out, she started using old pages from browning newspapers and magazines that had been left behind. She used the card originally in an attempt to colour-code her thinking but her system soon fell apart: there wasn't enough card and nowhere near enough colours, so she just wrote in big letters using the thickest pen she could find, so she could see everything clearly and precisely, even at distance.

In February, the skies brightened, but it was still freezing, the hostel like an icebox during the day and even worse at night. That was when it finally dawned on her why people abandoned the island during the winter: the caustic cold, the relentless wind, the storms that would roll in three or four times a week and feel as if they were about to lift the entire hostel from its foundations. It was brutal and ferocious. But the weather didn't stop her working.

If anything, being indoors so much helped her.

By the end of February, she'd filled one side of the corridor, end to end, with all the things that needed doing before the first day of the season. Most days, after supply runs, after she'd ensured they had enough food for another week, her focus would shift: she'd drag a chair out into the corridor, swathe herself in blankets, and go over the question of how. How was she going to get off the island on 1 April? How would she do it without being noticed? How far away should she get before calling the cops?

The idea of calling them straight away – of finding someone on the ferry who'd brought a cellphone with them – and not trying to make it off at all was magnetic. She kept coming back to it. And many nights, she'd wonder if she even needed a phone. After Hain and Lima had headed out to the forest to try to find her body, she could make a scene in Helena, scream and head to whatever passed for the authorities on the island. The way the two men had talked when they'd come back to the island together, it was obvious they didn't want anyone to know what they were up to. And yet she couldn't quite let go of the doubts.

What if they *weren't* working alone?

The idea that Hain and Lima had someone on the island they knew and worked with wouldn't dislodge once it had entered her head. If there was even a remote possibility that it was true, it meant asking for help was a risk.

So, in the end, she decided to stick to her original plan.

Get off the island.

Raise the alarm on the mainland.

Except, even then, even when it was clear in her head, she still couldn't relax. It wasn't just that two murderers were coming back to the island for her. It wasn't that she was so scared of their return she could barely breathe. It was that there was only one way to flee the island, and that was on the ferry.

When it left at five o'clock, Rebekah would be on it.

And, once they failed to find her body in the forest, once they knew she wasn't dead, so would Hain and Lima.

49

The corridor of paper wasn't Rebekah's only project.

She also started running again.

She used a pair of jogging pants that Stelzik had brought with him, one of his T-shirts, and the old woollen sweater she'd found in the gas station.

To begin with, she could manage a mile and a half, which wouldn't even have been a warm-up for her in her youth. But gradually, as the days and weeks passed, she got faster, going longer distances, running on the deserted, frost-peppered roads, knowing she had to get faster and stronger.

At the beginning of March, she cut her hair short, sitting in front of the mirror in Stelzik's room with a blunt pair of scissors she'd found in one of the kitchen drawers. It wasn't perfect, but it was good enough. It made running easier because her hair no longer got in her face when the wind picked up, and from there, she pushed herself further: on Sundays, she would run the entirety of the Loop – all twenty-three miles of it – because it made her feel in control of something, powerful and purposeful. For three and a half hours, she wasn't thinking about anything else. When she ran, she was just moving forward – and with one solitary goal in mind.

She needed to be unbreakable once the island reopened.

Sometimes, when she got back to the hostel, she could hear the echoes of her father, as if his voice were in the wind; she could picture her and Mike in the front yard of their place on 81st Street after they'd finished a run, and see their dad standing on the porch repeatedly telling Mike to stretch properly. 'If you don't stretch,' he would say, 'I promise you'll be walking like John Wayne in the morning,' and then Mike would stretch half-heartedly, and the next day, like clockwork, he'd come down to the breakfast table pretending everything was normal, even though he could barely move.

She upped her running again in March, going even further, making use of the milder weather, and the candy bars in the store for energy. She knew she needed to change herself, and prepare for what was coming. And the more she ran, the more it helped her focus when she returned to the hostel. Her heart pounding in her chest, her clothes soaked with sweat, she would sometimes sit and look at the paper she'd stuck to the wall of the corridor – mismatched and overlapping, sticky tape everywhere, scrawled, untidy writing that only she could understand – before she did anything else, including stretching. 'Sorry, Dad,' she'd say quietly, her routine pushed aside so she could study everything she'd collated.

Very quickly, the 'why' became the most important part of the corridor, the area she spent most time in, and the area she continued to add to. And within the 'why' section was the area she focused on most of all.

To a stranger, it would look like an untidy waterfall of names.

To Rebekah, it was a suspect list.

50

The list had started in January with just five pieces of paper, all torn from Stelzik's notebook by hand. The edges were imperfect and the sizes all slightly different, but it didn't matter. She'd knelt in the corridor, laid the pieces of paper out in a row on the floor in front of her, and written a name on each one. Johnny. Gareth. Noella. Hain. Lima.

Under each one, on a fresh piece of paper, she wrote a possible motive. For Hain and Lima, it was difficult. She still had no idea why they wanted her dead, didn't even know who they were and how or when she might have crossed paths with them, so instead she concentrated on what she *did* know: what they looked like, and what she could remember them saying the night they'd come back to the island. Beneath that, she posed the same question below their names: *Are they working alone – or with other people?*

She turned her attention to the other people.

Writing *Working with Hain and Lima?* under each of the three names, she set about coming up with possible motives for Johnny, Gareth and Noella. Using a ball of string she'd found in the general store, she began slicing off lengths of twine with a cooking knife, then mooring the suspects to one another, the string indicating a confirmed connection. That became easier as she added more names to the wall: there was a confirmed connection between Gareth and Karl Stelzik because of the email; there was one between Johnny and Kirsty Cohen, whom she added as well, based not only on the fact that Johnny had known Kirsty but that Kirsty had called asking to speak to Rebekah *about* Johnny the day before they'd left for the island.

Over the course of the days and weeks that followed, she added more and more names to the walls: doctors she'd worked with, other mothers she knew, friends from college, a few people she'd fallen out badly with down the years. She'd even written *Daniel* at the top of a piece of paper, and the names of other men she'd slept with before Gareth, trying to remember if there was anything that might be worth thinking about further. There wasn't. One of the last names on the list was her father's, although he'd already been dead for over two years, so it was hard to imagine how he could be connected to any of this. Maybe someone he'd arrested. Maybe someone out for revenge.

Even though some of it felt like a stretch, under each name she listed things she'd done with that person, major events or memorable occasions that might be linked to what had happened to her on the island. She tried especially to think of times when both she *and* Johnny had done something as a pair with that person. That looped back in Gareth and Noella, perhaps Kirsty as well, but Rebekah struggled to think of many other mutual acquaintances. But, still, it was reasonable to assume that the catalyst for Lima wanting them dead was something that Rebekah and her brother had done together.

After weeks of collation and study, she kept coming back to the same five names. The first three were the people she was closest to: Gareth, because of the email to Stelzik, and the affair he'd had with a woman Rebekah had never wanted to ask about; Noella, because she'd described Gareth as good-looking, confident and charming, and because of that weird last phone call in the forest, when she'd stayed silent on the line before appearing to hang up just after Rebekah had told her they were on Crow Island. And then there was Johnny. In her heart, she still believed her brother had had nothing to do with what had gone on, but there were small questions she couldn't answer or deny: the way he had simply vanished after Rebekah had fallen into the gully, or getting the last day of the season wrong, or the way he'd said to Rebekah, as they stood waiting to be shot, that everything was his fault.

The fourth name on the wall was a separate reason she couldn't dismiss her brother yet: Kirsty Cohen. Because, under both her name and Johnny's, pieces of string coming from each and joining at the top of a fresh piece of paper, there was another name: *Louise*. The woman Johnny had been dating, the woman he and Rebekah had, briefly, talked about on the ferry over. Rebekah remembered how reluctant Johnny had been to discuss Louise, although she knew it wasn't unusual for him to be guarded about his love life. In fact, it had happened many times before. He didn't make a big deal of dating until it looked like it might actually be going somewhere.

He and Louise hadn't gone anywhere.

Rebekah had never met Louise, didn't know anything about her, even her surname – but, still, for some reason she'd decided she didn't want to see Johnny any more, and it was Kirsty who'd originally set them up, so there remained question marks.

More often, though, her gaze would be drawn to the same part of the wall, to a fifth name she'd added much later than the others. She'd been awake one night, unable to get warm, a rainstorm buffeting the hostel windows, when she'd begun to think about the *Why?* again. And that was when she realized she'd missed someone.

Her mother.

Rebekah knew nothing about her, barely even remembered what she looked like, but that only added to her sense of disquiet. Was it more likely that all of this stemmed from the actions of someone like Johnny, whom Rebekah had trusted and known her entire life, or from the type of person who would just abandon three young children? *'With Sympathy' cards don't count*, Rebekah thought, remembering the envelopes that had turned up in the mail after Mike and her father had died.

She couldn't imagine where her mother's life, and whatever she'd done with it, intersected with hers and Johnny's, let alone why someone would want them dead because of it. But of all the people she'd put up on the walls of the hostel, all the names she'd added – all the theories she'd constructed and tried to shackle together into a cohesive argument – she knew the least about her mother.

To Rebekah, Fiona Camberwell was a total stranger.

Midwinter Pier

She watched Axel from the living room, all the lights off, the only glow coming from the television, which was playing reruns of old shows. He was letting himself into the house, being as quiet as he could, and he paused, the door still open, snow flittering inside, and looked up the incline of the stairs. He was trying to figure out if he'd woken her, seemed genuinely concerned about it.

Most of the time, that was what he was like.

'Hey,' she said.

He looked in her direction, became aware that the television was on, that light was dancing along the corridor towards him, painting its walls and floors, and he turned, the soles of his shoes squeaking on the parquet.

'Oh,' he said, 'hey. I thought you might be asleep already.'

'Just watching some TV.'

He came forward, stopping in the living-room doorway, the TV bleaching one side of his face so it looked like he was wearing half a mask.

'Have you had a good day?' she asked.

'Long.'

'Even though it's late, I thought we could get takeout.'

'Okay.' He smiled. 'That sounds nice.'

'You choose.'

But he eyed her: he could see something was up.

'Are you okay?' he asked.

'I'm fine.'

'You just seem a little . . .'

They looked at each other and he didn't say anything else, because he knew what was wrong with her and it didn't need repeating. Instead, he came further into the room, eyes switching to the TV, to the LA Law rerun that was silently playing. 'Oh, I love this one,' he said, eyes lighting up, looking at her as if they were in the middle of a conversation about something else entirely. It was like he didn't have any cares in the world. 'This is the one where Rosalind turns around and just steps into that elevator . . .'

She watched him.

'Oh, this is it,' Axel said, smiling again to himself, moving closer to the TV. Blobs of snow were melting on the hardwood floor now. 'This is where she drops.' He chuckled, perching on the edge of the couch. 'Here we go.'

Onscreen, the doors to an elevator opened and one of the characters — not realizing the car hadn't arrived — stepped into the empty shaft.

'Damn,' he said quietly. 'What a way to go.'

He glanced at her and smiled again, she smiled back, and when his eyes returned to the television, she kept looking at him, turning things over in her head. She started thinking about relationships, about how they evolved over time — and about how, sometimes, hard as it was, they left you no choice.

You just had to walk away.

Early the next morning, Tillman was waiting for her on a bench at the end of Pier 15. The city was in deep freeze, the sky gunmetal-grey and hanging like a ceiling on the verge of collapse. With the wind whipping off the river, and the snow straying in and out of existence, it was a smart place to meet: as she made her way off the esplanade and along the bleached wood of the pier, she didn't pass a single other person. No one was brave enough — or stupid enough — to be out here.

No one, except them.

She sat down next to him, pulling her coat tighter around her. Next to her, Tillman didn't move, just kept his gaze on the river. He had his coat collar up and a scarf over his mouth, but his skin was still scoured red and his eyes were watering. He said, 'Whoever made the decision to meet out here is clearly a moron.'

It was a joke. It had been his.

They stayed like that for a moment, because they both knew what they were here for and neither wanted to begin, but then Tillman shifted his weight on the bench, turned to her, and said, 'What do you want to do?'

'I want to try to pretend we aren't having this conversation,' she replied, then glanced at him out of the corner of her eye. She smiled, although it was sad, fleeting.

'We can wait,' Tillman said.

'Will waiting make it any better?'

Tillman shrugged. His silence was him being generous. It wasn't going to get any better. They had a problem and it would need to be addressed.

'Look,' Tillman said, 'after today, Travis has three days left as a cop. From what I hear, he's made absolutely zero progress. The whole case is in the swamp and he's up to his neck with no way out. There's no chance in hell this is going to be solved before he goes. So we can wait and see if anyone else picks up the reins. It might happen, and if it does, we can delay for now and make the decision then.' Tillman paused as the wind came again, colder and harder than before. He tightened the scarf around his chin. 'But, you know . . .' He looked at her. 'Even if Louise Mason gets filed and forgotten, it's still in a drawer somewhere. This whole thing will still be hanging over us.'

She watched as a plane dropped out of the clouds, like a dolphin diving beneath the surface of the ocean. It was banking in their direction, heading towards Newark. For a moment, she thought of escape, of taking a plane somewhere and disappearing for good. Then she said, 'What was she like?'

'Who, Louise?'

'No.' She shook her head. 'Rebekah.'

Tillman eyed her. 'I don't know.'

'You never met her?'

'No.'

'I hear she was a doctor.' She could see the concern on Tillman's face. He was worried she was losing focus. 'Takes a lot to become a doctor.'

'Takes a lot to become all sorts of things.'

He shut her down, maybe rightly. This was a discussion that wasn't going anywhere good, and even if she ignored him and kept asking questions, she'd end up the only casualty. She'd look weak and indecisive in front of him when she needed to be ruthless and single-minded.

Rebekah wasn't the reason they were here.

Neither was Louise.

This was about someone else entirely.

'Just give him a little longer,' she said.

51

On 10 March, the gas station ran out of fuel.

Rebekah had never expected there to be enough to last until her final month on the island, but even so, as the lever on the nozzle clicked empty, she felt an acute sense of loss. There were twenty-two days still to go until the ferry came, and during the awful, protracted nightmare of her enforced stay on the island, only the Jeep, her running, and Roxie had brought her any joy at all.

She had enough in the tank to get the car back to the dig site, so – as Roxie sat watching from the back seat, sensing Rebekah was upset – they took the Loop east, pulling off onto the potholed track that took them down to Simmons Gully.

At the bottom, she parked the car where it had been on the final day of the season, turned off the ignition and sat for a while. On the passenger side, the plastic wrap, bound to the door, popped in the wind.

'I know, Rox. It's dumb to be upset about a car.' Rebekah put her hand on Roxie's head. 'But . . .' *For a few short hours every day, as ridiculous as it sounds, being in the car felt like I'd been set free. I had choices.*

Small as it was, I had a life.

She got out and started ripping the plastic wrap off the window, then cleared the Jeep of debris, of things she knew hadn't been left inside on the day she and Johnny came to the island.

Then she and Roxie headed back to the hostel on foot.

Using the bicycle to get around, Rebekah began making repairs to the things she'd broken. Some were beyond fixing – like the padlocks she'd smashed – but she worked around them. She wanted things to look relatively normal for when Hain and Lima docked.

She got rid of the *SOS* sign she'd painted onto the board at the general store and gathered up all the messages she'd laid out at the harbour with rocks. She got rid of the pile of pebbles she'd been using to count the days off before she moved to the hostel. There was nothing she could do about the boats she'd tried to commandeer: the one with the engine had been carried out about half a mile, and had stayed there ever since; the rowboat had been tossed back into shore by one of the storms, part of its hull smashing as it crashed against the concrete walls of the harbour. She'd tried to drag it up the slipway, but it had been too heavy.

After that, she started preparing a backpack, the essentials she'd need. There were candy bars and bags of chips in the store that still had a couple of months to go before their expiry date, and she dumped a load of them in the side pockets of a bag Stelzik had left in his closet.

She emptied two bottles of Mountain Dew into a sink, and filled them with rainwater, which she'd collected in one of the fishing buckets. She added a first-aid kit, and some freshly washed clothes. They were *her* clothes, the outfit she'd originally come to the island in. For the trip back, she'd decided to wear Stelzik's pants and the sweater she'd found at the gas station.

There were two reasons.

Lima knew what she'd been dressed in on the last day of the season – her hoodie, her denims, her sneakers – or, if he didn't recall exactly, seeing her again would remind him.

And the clothes might act as a disguise. It was part of the reason why Rebekah had cut her hair short. It was why she'd pushed herself so hard with her exercise, running more, using bricks and old pieces of masonry as makeshift weights: she needed to appear bigger and more powerful because she wanted to disappear in plain sight.

She was going to try to pass herself off as a man.

52

But there was one thing she couldn't bring herself to sort out.

Roxie.

As much as it hurt her to admit it, the second Hain and Lima came off the ferry, the dog would put Rebekah at risk. Lima knew what Roxie looked like – she had attacked him and he'd never managed to locate her afterwards. He'd tried to shoot her, and failed. He'd searched for her, and failed. In all probability, as long as he didn't see her, he wouldn't even consider her: he'd just assume Roxie was dead, unable to survive by herself through the hard winter months.

Rebekah wavered for days, thinking about all the ways in which she could take Roxie with her, in which she could attempt to hide her, but as much as she'd grown to love her, Roxie was an animal, and that meant she was unpredictable. Unpredictability would get her caught.

It would get her killed.

And so the night before the island reopened, the evenings lighter, the air a little warmer, Rebekah called Roxie into the bedroom opposite the one they'd been staying in. In it there was a bed full of blankets, two big bowls of franks and a bucket of water. 'I can't do this in the morning,' Rebekah said quietly. She had tears in her eyes.

Roxie looked at her, at the food.

'I can't even stand to do it now.' She dropped to her haunches and held out her hands, and Roxie came to her. 'I love you, Rox,' she said, her face buried in the back of the dog's neck. 'Without you, I never would have made it this far.' Roxie turned her head and tried to nuzzle Rebekah's jaw. 'I'll come back for you . . .'

I promise.

But there was a reason she couldn't say the last two words out loud: she couldn't promise. She didn't know if she'd make it back. In all the preparation she'd done for when the ferry docked, all the things she'd repaired, all the ways in which she'd tried to disguise the fact that she was still alive, there was an unspoken truth that she could never quite bring herself to face: she'd survived five months, almost entirely alone, on an island one hundred and one miles from anywhere – and, by the next morning, it might all have been for nothing.

By the next morning she might be dead.

Crying, Rebekah stood again.

And then she locked Roxie inside.

Waiting Game

Before bed, Travis finished reading Cat on a Hot Tin Roof. *Gaby had told him on the phone the night before that she was studying it this semester and, in their production of it, she'd been given the part of Maggie. She'd sounded excited, so he'd told her that was great, even though he had no idea what sort of part Maggie was, or even what the play was about. At lunch, he'd walked a couple of blocks to a bookstore on Broadway, bought a copy, and taken the play, a shredded-beef sub and a soda to the break room. It turned out that Maggie was one of the two lead parts, so he'd sent Gaby a WhatsApp with a selfie of him, holding up the play, and wrote that he was so proud of her.*

She'd read the text about ten seconds after he'd sent it, but hadn't replied. Travis imagined she was busy, maybe in rehearsals, maybe out tonight in Chicago having a good time before she flew home for Christmas, so he didn't send her a follow-up. He didn't want to annoy his kids, especially as he saw so little of them. Mark still hadn't replied to the text that Travis had sent two days before, although, like his sister, he'd read the message. That wasn't especially unusual: he'd always been more independent than Gaby, much more flighty even when he'd been living at home, so Travis tried not to take it personally.

Even so, if there was a worse invention than the two blue ticks in Whats-App, he didn't know what it was.

He put the play down, removed his reading glasses, and watched the snow fall outside on the street. It had been cold today, the city freezing in the chill, subway grates breathing, vents spewing. Travis hated winters in New York, despite having lived through fifty-nine of them, and as he thought of that, he again thought of his retirement, of how he had friends in the south who would help him set up down there if he wanted to. For a moment, he wondered what Naomi would think if he did something as spontaneous as that, if he called her one day from Charleston or Myrtle Beach and told her she'd been wrong about him. But then he looked to the nightstand, to the play, to his cellphone, his texts still unanswered, and wondered what would be worse: being lonely here, or being lonely there.

His attention switched: next to his phone was a file with pale covers that he'd brought home with him. It was a missing persons report.

Actually, it was two.

One for Johnny Murphy. One for his sister.

Today was 20 December. They'd been missing since 30 October. Seven weeks and two days, and there had been no sign of them at all. Travis reached over and picked up the file, flipping open the front cover.

They'd left early that morning to head to somewhere on Long Island, where Murphy had an interview lined up for a new book he was planning to write. His sister had decided to go with him only at the last minute: Noella Sullivan had told cops in the 68*th* Precinct at the time that Rebekah had needed a break from being a full-time mom, and had been looking forward to spending time with her brother.

Travis didn't know whether to read anything into the sister's decision to go with Murphy, especially because it had been last-minute. He flicked through the pages of the file again, knowing the answers weren't likely to be there: the initial missing persons report was a box-ticking exercise, and the subsequent search had never got off the ground. The officer who'd taken the details had left the force two days after filing it, so the search instantly fell through the cracks. Neither Murphy nor his sister raised any red flags – they weren't vulnerable, and didn't have mental-health problems – so it had been treated as low priority from the go, and had only become less important over time.

Even basic due diligence hadn't been done.

Before Travis had got involved, not a single interview had been conducted, other than the initial one with Noella. No requests had been made for cell records, and there'd been no attempt to contact any of the Long Island police departments to see if they might have something. Travis had set all of those things in motion, and while he'd hit some walls already, especially out on Long Island, he'd at least been able to narrow the search. He'd even got a warrant for Murphy's house on 81*st* Street, where he'd found reference books and notes on the novel Murphy had planned to write, although no direct link to the person he'd gone to interview. There was no laptop, so Travis assumed Murphy had taken *it on the trip to Long Island, which would make sense if he was researching a book. He'd found very little in the life of the sister, Rebekah, either. Her ex-husband gave Travis access to a brownstone in Brooklyn where they'd both lived before their split, and he'd been through her emails, using a laptop she'd left behind. He'd found nothing. If Rebekah and her brother had discussed the details of their trip, it was over the phone or in person.*

That made it a dead end.

It was the same story with the lab.

Before Travis had got home, they'd called him. He'd swabbed toothbrushes for Murphy and his sister, but his contact at the lab said it could take up to twelve weeks to get DNA profiles completed for missing people, probably more. That meant three months, minimum, before their profiles could be compared to others in the system.

He didn't have three months.

From tomorrow, he didn't even have three days.

He put the file on the bed and thought about quick workarounds. He could call the Met again in London and ask if they had a set of fingerprints on file for Murphy that he could then compare with ones they might have on the local and national databases here. But he knew it was more than a long shot: Murphy was never charged, so that was one definite reason there would be no fingerprints retained on file; another was that Murphy had only been in the UK for a week – the week he'd spent with his sister – since the family had moved to New York, so there was no chance he'd been printed at some later date on another, similar trip; the last was that his arrest was over two decades ago, and the cop he'd spoken to at the Met had told Travis that the details of Murphy's attack on the men was only on their system because the man Murphy had punched in the pub that night had a rap sheet going all the way back to 1995. It was the reason the man had chosen not to press charges against Johnny – he didn't want the police looking too hard at his own life.

Travis tried to think and, as he did, reached to the nightstand for something else he'd been keeping there – a small red leather-bound journal.

Louise Mason's.

He began flicking through the pages again, as familiar with what was written there as he was with the case file. He traced the lines of Louise's hand, the quirks in it, the repetitions: she'd replicated all of this in her cellphone, all the meetings and social events, but her family had told Travis that she kept a physical journal in case she ever lost her cell, and because she loved to write. She was an old soul in that way, her mom had told him, tearful, unable to go more than a few sentences without crying, and when he'd walked the spaces of Louise's studio, then the rooms and hallways of her apartment, he saw exactly that: hundreds of pens — as many pens as paintbrushes — including antiques in boxes. He took photos of a couple and searched for them online. Some were worth a thousand bucks.

His phone pinged with an email.

He picked up the handset, not expecting much, but then felt an instant charge of electricity as he saw the subject line: he'd been warned the cellphone records for Johnny Murphy and his sister might take three to five days.

They'd taken thirty-six hours.

He didn't wait, didn't try to transfer them to his laptop where he'd be able to see them better, he just opened them there and then.

Taking a cursory glance at the actual calls that had been made in the two weeks before the disappearances, he then went straight to the last page. That was the one he really wanted.

It was where the cell-tower pings were listed.

And it would tell him exactly where the Murphys had gone.

53

Rebekah's recurring dream started to emerge from the dark in the week leading up to 1 April. It began in snatches, there and gone again, as she finally drifted off to sleep. She recognized the imagery but didn't feel any of the dread. The dream was more like blinks of light, never quite fully formed, as if a part of it were still growing and taking shape in the shadows.

It didn't help that, the closer she got to the first day of the season, the harder she found it to sleep. She would go to bed at night and lie awake for hours, listening to the creaks and groans of the hostel, plagued by images of failure, of not making it to the ferry, or of making it only to find Hain and Lima waiting for her inside. And when she did sleep, other nightmares filled her head, a torrid and dysfunctional stream she struggled to escape from: she saw Johnny, stumbling from the forest, bloodied and injured, and was never quite close enough to grab him; she saw Noella and Gareth lying in bed together, the sheets twisted around their bodies; and she saw her mother, little more than a blur except for a flash of red hair, and always running, even as Rebekah called for her to come back. One night, Rebekah dreamed she was in the house on 81st Street, a place her mother had never been to. She came in to find her at the kitchen table, talking to Johnny, and when they saw Rebekah, they stopped talking, and her mother, faceless, simply got up and left.

Rebekah would wake soaked with sweat and breathing hard, and the longer the dreams went on, the more they began to repeat, to merge with one another, then mutate into something else. And in the final few days before the ferry was due to return Rebekah finally knew what they were mutating *into*: something more familiar and more terrifying.

I think you should stay, Rebekah.

She was back in the high-rise building.

In Apartment 127.

Unable to escape.

The nightmare came on her last night.

Instantly, it felt more frightening than any version of the dream she'd had before. For a moment, Rebekah couldn't understand why. She was in the same corridor as always, looking at the same cream walls and tan carpets.

But then she realized what was different.

This time, Roxie was at the end of the corridor, half concealed in the gloom. The dog was looking at her, and as Rebekah approached, as she got closer to the open door of the apartment, Roxie began whimpering. It was an awful sound, the same sound she'd made when Rebekah had locked her into the room hours earlier, and now here, in this place, it was even worse. Every whimper squeezed Rebekah's heart.

I'm so sorry, Roxie, she heard herself saying. *I'm so sorry.*

But then Rebekah got to the door of the apartment. She glanced at the *127* on it, at the *7* that was askew, and she had the same thought as always, that seven was supposed to be a lucky number – and by the time she looked for Roxie again, she'd vanished. The corridor of the apartment block was empty.

Roxie?

Music started playing inside the apartment. She couldn't tell what type it was, had never been able to tell, it was just *there*, but this time it seemed louder, more obscure, and way more painful on her ears. As she pushed the door wide and stepped in, she felt the fibres of the carpet under her bare feet.

They started to squirm and move.

They wrapped around her feet, binding her to the floor, climbing up her ankles, inching up her calves to the inside of her thighs.

And then the voice behind her, genderless but ugly, started repeating those same words: *I think you should stay.* Except this time it wasn't just words, it was a harrowing rasp.

I think you should stay.

She so desperately didn't want to stay.

I think you should stay, Rebekah.

Please let me go.

I think you should stay.

Please let mc wake up.

And then, finally, she did, gasping for breath, as if she'd just climbed from the bottom of the ocean. She looked around the bedroom, expecting it to be a trick, a second nightmare concealed within the first. But she was awake, her skin slick with sweat. When she caught sight of herself in the mirror, she could see her vest was soaked through and there were fine tear trails on her cheeks.

Light poured in through the window.

Rebekah looked across the hallway to the other door, to the room she'd put Roxie in. She wanted to call out to her, to see her and put her arms around her, but she didn't. Instead, she planted her feet on the floor, her skin still tingling as it had in her dream. On her right hand, along her palm, there was an arc of tiny red gouges: she'd been clenching her fists so tightly, she'd drawn blood.

She closed her eyes for a second, breathing.

Relax, it's over. It's over.

She checked Stelzik's clock on the nightstand beside her. It was 8.56 a.m. She'd set the alarm for nine. The ferry was due in at eleven and, on the practice runs she'd done the previous two days, it took thirty minutes to get from the hostel to the harbour on the bicycle. That meant she had at least an hour to ready herself, change and check she had everything she needed.

Switching off the alarm, she climbed out of bed and started to prepare, washing herself, dressing, making sure her hair was styled in exactly the way she'd practised. She'd gone for a side parting, moulded into shape with some hair paste Stelzik had kept among his things. She knew her features didn't look particularly masculine, but the hairstyle disguised that just a little, and when she pulled on the men's clothes, they helped blur the lines even further.

She stood in front of the mirror and stared at herself, fear like a ball in her stomach. She'd pictured her death so many times in the lead-up to this, she wasn't certain if she was more frightened of dying on the island, before she ever got close to the ferry, or making it a distance, feeling a fleeting sense of success and of freedom, and having it torn away from her. There was even a strange part of her that was scared to leave the island: it wasn't home, it never would be, yet she'd made something of it in the end, especially after she'd found Roxie. There was a kind of safety in the routine she had here.

But then she thought of her girls, and she began checking her hair again, her clothes, her backpack, laying the items inside it on the bed.

That was when she glanced at the calendar.

It was pinned to the wall. Before today, for weeks, it had been circled by scraps of paper, a trail that had led out into the corridor, a pathway she'd built to help her figure out the why and the how. All of that was gone now. She'd taken it all down, her suspect list, her string tethers, her attempts to connect all that she knew, had folded it and put it into her backpack.

All that remained on the walls was the calendar.

It was from the Museum of Natural History and had belonged to Stelzik, and each month was represented by an animal. She hadn't turned the page to April yet, so it was still on March, a striped hyena. Except it wasn't the animal that had caught her eye this time.

It was the dates underneath.

It was something printed next to 13 March.

She hadn't noticed it nineteen days ago, not only because the print was so small, but because she'd been so deeply embedded in building her lists, in taping her pieces of paper to the wall, in moving string from area to area.

But as she stared at it now she froze.

Under 13 March were two words.

She glanced at the alarm clock and saw that it was 10.15 a.m. She should have had plenty of time to get to the ferry if she left now. She should have been able to get there well ahead of when Hain and Lima arrived on the island. But she'd made a mistake.

A terrible mistake.

She looked again at the two printed words.

DST starts.

Daylight Saving Time. She'd missed the switch on 13 March. And that meant it wasn't 10.15 a.m. right now.

It was 11.15.

Hain and Lima were already here.

BOOK TWO

6
Open Season

54

Ahead of her, Helena was being stalked by sea mist.

Rebekah approached from the north, using a series of off-road trails instead of the easier, smoother asphalt of the Loop. She didn't want to chance being seen by Hain and Lima. They were almost certainly at the forest by now, but she wasn't going to take the gamble.

As she crossed to the open road of the town limits, she tensed. She could see two people on Main Street – but neither were the men who'd come back to bury her. One was pointing towards the front of the store, the door Rebekah had broken, and another was gesturing in the direction of the harbour. She tried to steer clear of them, conscious of being seen, but then one looked over and away again. He didn't seem interested in her – probably assumed she'd come over on the ferry – yet every face she saw, every time someone glanced in her direction and made something as simple as eye contact, seemed like a huge moment. It felt like she'd been on the island for ever, trapped alone in this hinterland, silent, invisible, forgotten; a memory of a woman who went to Long Island one day and never came home.

She sucked in a breath, trying to focus on the only thing that mattered – getting home – and found a space on a sloping grass bank to the west of the town. She'd scoped it out in the days before: it gave her a clear, uninterrupted view of Helena, but it also had enough cover to step into, should she need to.

Her eyes fell on the harbourmaster's shack.

She remembered, months ago, looking through its window in

her search for a radio, unable to get inside. But now a man stood at its entrance, staring out at the docked ferry, the door propped open beside him. Rebekah followed his eyeline and glanced towards the ferry, its ramp open, its interior empty of vehicles, then back to the harbourmaster. He was in his fifties, silver-bearded, his belly resting on a belt that was holding up a pair of baggy denims. Then her eyes were drawn to his belt. Something was clipped to it.

She felt a flutter behind her ribs.

A cellphone.

She looked at the signs on the shack – IN CASE OF EMERGENCY CALL 911 and FIRST AID – and knew, even if he hadn't had the cellphone on his belt, the harbourmaster would have access to a VHF radio. He'd have multiple ways of contacting the mainland, multiple ways of calling the cops, without delay.

No, stick to the plan, she told herself.

You don't know who you can trust.

She ripped her eyes away from the harbourmaster and looked at the ferry again. It had emptied, foot passengers – if there had been any – gone, any vehicles, apart from two pickups in the harbour parking lot, already somewhere else. Was it possible one of the pickups belonged to Hain and Lima? She didn't see them anywhere, and she remembered them saying they were going to bring a trailer with them so they could transport her Cherokee back to the mainland if necessary. It seemed much more likely that the pickups belonged to the two men talking outside the general store.

Or the harbourmaster.

She looked at him again. He'd reached inside the shack and had brought out a coffee cup.

He was now checking his phone.

He's got a signal.

Rebekah looked along Main Street, out to where it connected to the Loop. There were no cars out there. No sign of Hain and Lima. She could make it to the harbourmaster, to his phone, in seconds. All it would take was one phone call for her to be rescued from this.

No. She closed her eyes. *Stick to the plan.*

A couple of minutes later, she unzipped her backpack and took out Stelzik's alarm clock: 12:17. The ferry didn't go until 5 p.m. Was she really going to wait almost five hours when there was a usable cellphone less than four hundred feet away? She looked at the harbourmaster again. She could call the cops on the mainland now. She could *already* have called them – and they could already be on their way. Fear, courage, indecision: it all hit her at once.

Hain and Lima aren't here.

Stick to the plan.

They're occupied on the other side of the island.

No. Stop it.

You're not going to get this chance again.

You could grab that phone and make the call.

No.

This could all be over already.

No. It's too risky.

This could be over and you could be speaking to your girls –

Her body was moving before her brain had caught up.

She sprang to her feet and took off, leaving the bike where it was on the grass bank, then headed down, onto Main Street, and in through the gates of the harbour. As soon as she did, the harbourmaster saw her. She was hurrying, almost stumbling. The closer she got to him, the more concerned he looked.

'You all right, sir?' he asked, but as she got closer, panic gripped her: she was disguised as a man, but the instant she spoke, her voice would give her away. She'd never practised for this. She'd never thought about having to make conversation. What was she going to do now? Put on an accent? Drop her voice an octave? *You idiot.* All of a sudden, she felt overwhelmed by her stupidity, her impulsiveness. *You fucking idiot. You should have stayed where you were.*

'Sir? Are you okay?'

She looked at the harbourmaster. As she stopped short of him, breathless, tears welled in her eyes. The kindness in his face, in the smile at the corners of his mouth disarmed her. She hadn't seen evidence of another person's kindness for so long she was barely even able to remember what it looked like.

'I, uh . . . My name's . . .' She stopped. Her voice had come out sounding exactly like her own. *What do I do? How do I speak?*

A frown bloomed on the harbourmaster's face, and Rebekah realized that – despite her clothes, despite the hair, despite all the hours she'd put into the disguise – the instant she talked, he'd known she was a woman.

'Uh . . .' He didn't know how to address her. *'Miss?'*

'My name is Rebekah,' she said.

It meant nothing to him, she could see that.

'Are you okay, Rebekah?' he asked.

'No,' she replied. 'I've been trapped here.'

He put his coffee aside. 'What?'

'I've been trapped here for five months.'

He looked like he wasn't sure if she was joking or not. 'You've . . .' He glanced out to the ferry. 'You've been on the island since Halloween?'

She nodded, swallowed.

The harbourmaster looked floored. 'Wha– How?'

Her breath stalled. Her eyes blurred.

Tell him.

You need to tell him.

'Someone tried to kill me.'

55

The harbourmaster told her his name was Caleb. Inside the shack, the shelves were laden, but her attention was drawn to a handheld VHF radio. It was on the desk, clearly brought over that morning, because it hadn't been there during the winter. An orange DISTRESS button was on top.

'We need to call the cops,' he said, watching her, curious, perhaps even wary, still struggling to comprehend the extent of what she was telling him. 'You've really been on the island this whole time?'

She frowned. 'Why would I lie?'

He held up a hand. 'I ain't accusing you of lying.'

'I know, I just . . .' Rebekah took a breath. 'I'm sorry. I came here with my brother and I don't know where he is.'

'You two got separated?'

'In the forest, when they tried to kill us. I don't know if Johnny's dead or alive. I don't know if he's in a grave out here – or if he made it back home.'

But the question she'd asked herself, every single day for five months, was, if he *had* made it back home, if he *was* still alive, why hadn't he sent help?

'The guy who tried to kill me, he's here right now.'

'On the island?'

Rebekah nodded, but there was something in Caleb's face. Was he just humouring her? Did he not believe her? Should she have trusted him at all? She started to panic again, her chest tightening, her throat shrinking, but then she forced herself to calm down, to breathe, to think. For now, she had to run with this, make it work. She'd made her choice by not sticking to the plan.

Caleb glanced through the window, to the empty lot and the ocean beyond. 'Okay, well, the most important thing is you're safe with me now.' Rebekah wasn't sure if that was true or not, and Caleb didn't seem entirely certain either. He was obviously trying to think about the best course of action. 'You said the guy who tried to kill you took your cell?'

At the mention of a cell, she switched on again: 'Can I use your phone?' she asked. 'I need to call home. I need to speak to my girls.'

Caleb unclipped his phone from his belt.

As he did so, Rebekah thought of Hain and Lima.

The ferry had docked almost an hour and a half ago so, given the fact that – unknown to them – they'd never find her body, it seemed likely they'd still be out there, among the trees somewhere.

Likely.

But not certain.

She glanced out of the window, into the mist that was hanging over the harbour, and then down, into her lap, at her hands. Dirt and grime – the stains of existing here for five months, of finding out how to survive with no help – marked her fingers, engrained in them despite a thousand washes. There were fine cuts every-where, bruises on her arms and legs. There was a constant throb in her head and neck, worse some days than others, from when she'd fallen into the gully. She'd repaired the cut, stitched it, dressed it, and removed the stitches after it had healed, but it was always there. And as she saw the blemishes, every reminder of what had happened, the doubt started to gnaw at her again. *This man can't protect me.*

I should have stuck to the plan.

'Miss?'

She looked up at Caleb.

He was holding out a cellphone to her.

She took it from him. 'Thank you,' she said, and as she looked down at the screen, her doubts vanished: the name of the network was in the middle; at the top were four bars.

This is real. It's actually happening.

She could finally call home.

And then someone knocked on the door of the shack.

A New Life

Travis woke to the sound of wind at the windows. For a while, he lay there, adrift on the edge of sleep, listening to the weather, its rhythm, the hum of the neighbourhood. Then he rolled over and checked the time.

It was nine twenty.

In a past life, he would have been at the office for two, maybe three, hours already. The early starts had been a part of his routine, one that went all the way back to his first days as a detective. The earlier the start, the longer the quiet lasted. The quiet had always helped him focus. Sometimes an investigation had taken him so deep in those first hours of the day, he would look up after what felt like thirty minutes, and it would be afternoon.

But not any more.

He moved to the edge of the bed, staring at himself in the mirror. His shoulder throbbed. He rolled it, feeling the normal spark of aches and pains in his hip, and then he stared at the sixty-year-old in the mirror. There had been a slow creep of excess around his belly and face for the last couple of months; his hair and beard were still mostly black, although the thicker he'd let his beard grow, the more grey he was starting to see. The biggest difference was less easy to pin down: he was diminished somehow, less impressive, as if he'd left a part of himself behind, or lost it entirely. If he were on the other side of a table in an interview room, the cop that Travis had been would have looked at this version of himself and seen a man who carried sadness like a bruise on the skin. It was as if he were grieving for someone.

Or something.

'Dad?'

He tore his gaze away from the mirror. Gaby was leaning against the door

338

frame, a frown on her face, and he realized she must have been there for a while, studying him. 'Morning, honey,' he said, trying to clear his expression.

'You okay?'

'I'm good. How are you?'

Gaby shrugged.

She was dressed in one of Travis's old robes, way too big for her, and her hair was damp. She was a tall blonde twenty-one-year-old who looked like her mother; only her smile belonged to Travis. Sometimes it was unerring, and was why he'd always liked to make Gaby laugh. Her laughter completely changed her face and helped erode the reminders of Naomi, the countless ways in which Travis's ex-wife had screwed with his life since the divorce.

It was a bitterness he'd let fester and flourish, even if he'd tried his best over the years never to articulate it in front of Gaby and Mark. For the last ten days, though, it had been especially important to gain control of it, to sink the enmity he felt for Naomi and try to forget it, because if he didn't, he knew it would drive a wedge between him and his children. Mark maybe not as much as Gaby: his son had already returned to LA and he was built more like Naomi — sober, pragmatic, sometimes a little aloof. Gaby was different, more like Travis, much more demonstrative and temperate. She didn't need to hear Travis recounting the ways in which Naomi had made his life a misery — how much of his money and security she'd taken, how every barbed comment hurt.

Not so soon after Naomi had died.

'I might go to the cemetery today,' Gaby said.

Travis nodded.

'Put some lilies on Mom's grave.'

'Sure, honey. She loved lilies. That sounds nice.'

Gaby eyed him. 'You don't want to come with me?'

'It's not that,' he said, though that wasn't entirely truthful. 'I'm happy to drive you down there, but I'm meant to meet Amy Houser for lunch at twelve.'

'Your friend from the force?' A smile twitched at the corner of Gaby's mouth. 'Is she attached?'

Travis laughed. 'I'm old enough to be her dad, kiddo. And, no, I don't know if she's seeing anyone. I don't ask about her love life — it would be creepy. But even if that wasn't the case, I'm pretty sure Amy — or anyone else under the age of fifty-five, come to that – isn't interested in an old man who spends his days watching *ESPN* in a sweet terry-cloth robe.'

Gaby laughed.

Travis enjoyed the sound.

'I just want you to meet someone,' she said.

It had become a familiar refrain over the years, and one that he never let annoy him. It came from a good place. He loved his daughter and he knew the thing that bothered her most was the idea of him being alone for the rest of his life. The truthful answer would have been that some people just weren't destined to be plural, only ever singular, but he reverted to his stock response: 'I'm happy, honey. You really don't need to worry about me.'

But every time he said it he was never sure if he was lying to Gaby or not: he didn't feel unhappy per se, just a little lost. He missed the work and he pined for the routine desperately. It was why he felt – and appeared to himself in the mirror – like a man in mourning. Because he was.

It was three months to the day since he'd retired.

He was grieving for the job he'd lost.

56

Rebekah was so consumed by the cellphone Caleb had handed her that, for a second, the knock on the door didn't even register with her – and, by the time it did, Caleb was already pushing the door open. She looked from Caleb, to the window, through the glass to the man waiting outside the shack, and then to a photograph he was readying.

'How you doing, pal?'

At the sound of his voice, time slowed down.

It was him.

Oh, shit, it's Lima.

'I'm doing all right,' Caleb replied.

'Cool. You recognize this woman?'

Rebekah's heart stopped. Lima's hand appeared inside the shack, the photograph of her out in front of him. She was close enough to see that it was the photo from her driver's licence. She looked from the picture to Caleb, and slid off the chair, onto her knees, shuffling as far under the desk as she could go. By the time she realized what a dumb move it was – she'd boxed herself in and made herself an easy target – it was too late: Caleb was replying.

'No,' he said. 'She don't seem familiar. Who is she?'

She glanced at Caleb. He didn't look back – not with his head, not even with his eyes. He didn't adjust a single part of himself.

He's trying to protect me.

'No one's been asking about her?' Lima responded. 'You haven't seen her car before? A blue Jeep Cherokee?'

He'd avoided Caleb's question but that wasn't the only thing that had lodged with Rebekah: why was he asking about the Cherokee when he would have already seen it parked in Simmons Gully?

'No,' Caleb said simply.

'You haven't seen her?'

'No.'

A pause.

Something had already changed: it was like the air had become heavy. *Lima knows something's up*, Rebekah thought. Her throat began to pulse, as if an insect was trapped in her windpipe.

And then she looked down at the phone.

Call 911.

She pushed *9* and it made a soft beep.

Inside the shack, it was like a scream. Rebekah muted the volume, but by the time she was done, ready to put the rest of the numbers in, Lima was talking again: 'You sure no one's come asking about her or her car?'

'I'm sure,' Caleb replied.

Her car again.

Why was he asking about the car?

But then, a second later, it hit her. *Shit. The tyre.* On the last day of the season, Lima had slashed it with a knife – but then Rebekah had replaced it. *That* was why Lima wasn't still in the forest. It was why he'd come back to Helena so quickly. It was why he was *here*: because it had taken one look at the new tyre on the Jeep to know something was up.

'What are you,' Caleb said, 'a cop?'

'Yeah, something like that.'

'"Something like that"? What does that mean?'

That's enough, Caleb, she thought. *Don't push him any further. Just let him leave.* Above her, through a window to her left, she could see the high point of the grass bank she'd been on before coming down here.

Why the hell hadn't she stayed there?

Why hadn't she stuck to the plan?

She pushed *1* on the phone.

'So, are you a cop or not?' Caleb said. He was trying to help, trying to get Rebekah some answers – but all he was doing was making it worse.

Stop asking him questions.

Another 1.

'If you're a cop, where's your ID?'

Her finger hovered over Call. She couldn't have a conversation with the cops without Lima hearing it.

She stared at the 911 on the screen.

'Where's my ID?' Lima repeated, from the doorway.

Rebekah looked around the room for a weapon. On the shelves between her and Caleb was a wrench. It wasn't heavy, but it would do enough damage if it came to that.

She started shuffling forward on her knees.

Halfway out, she stopped again. There was a set of shelves immediately to Caleb's right. Out of sight of Lima, his hand was moving.

No, Caleb.

No, please don't do that.

He was reaching for a hammer.

57

'Where is it then?' Caleb said again. 'Where's your ID?'

Rebekah had got far enough to see part of Lima's profile. As Caleb asked him for ID, he glanced behind him into the parking lot. It took her a second to grasp why: *He's making sure no one's watching.*

But, before she'd even finished the thought, it was already too late.

In the blink of an eye, Caleb stumbled back, against the shelves he'd been trying to grab the hammer from, and crashed into the far wall. Pots of nails emptied over him; chunks of old machine parts, oilskins. He'd barely hit the floor and Lima was inside the shack, bent over, grabbing hold of his neck.

His other hand was inside his coat.

He's going for his gun.

Rebekah rocked forward, springing to her feet. She saw the surprise in Lima's face as he looked at her, the horror, his bronzed skin blanching at the sight of a dead woman. Then his eyes went to the shelves next to her: he had no idea what was missing from them, he just knew she'd grabbed something. He tried to adjust, to turn, to pull out his gun. But Rebekah got there first.

The wrench connected with the side of his head.

It made a dull *slap*, like raw meat dropped onto a chopping board, then Lima lurched awkwardly to his right, collapsing into one of the shelving units. He had hold of the gun now, but he was dazed: he looked for her, eyes drifting and failing to focus, his hands unsteadily trying to gain purchase on the floor.

Rebekah kicked the weapon out of his grip, his fingers springing open; as it clattered against the wall, his arms gave way and he hit the floor. He landed in a blanket of roofing nails, crying out in pain as he pierced himself. Almost instantly, he attempted to get to his knees again, but he was woozy. He couldn't focus. Rebekah pressed her foot into his back and pushed him down.

She had no plan, no idea where to go from here and, for the first time, she remembered Caleb: he was still slumped against the shelves, motionless. In the frenzy, a chunk from an old boat engine had landed on his head and now he was bleeding from his scalp. He was unconscious.

Lima had started moving again.

Shit.

She looked between him and Caleb and the parking lot: coming down from Main Street, into the harbour, was a black Dodge Ram pickup, pulling a trailer, with another vehicle loaded on it: her Cherokee.

Her eyes met those of the driver inside the Ram.

Hain.

Rebekah grabbed her backpack and sprinted out of the shack. Behind her, she heard Hain's pickup gun into the lot – but she didn't look back. She scrambled up a concrete slope, a sea defence built to protect the town during storms, and – thirty seconds later, as she reached Main Street – began looking for help. To her horror, no one was around. Helena was deserted.

'Help!' she screamed in desperation. *'Help!'*

She headed towards the store where she'd slept for months, thinking of the men she'd seen outside that morning. She'd assumed they were the owners. She'd assumed they'd open the store on day one.

But she was wrong.

The store remained closed and neither man was around. She went to the bottom of Main Street where the bait-and-tackle store was.

That was shut too.

Panicked, she glanced out to the rest of the town, at the two rows of boarded buildings on either side of her. Nothing was open; there was no sign of life. It was just Hain, Lima, Caleb – and her.

But then she came out from behind the bait-and-tackle place and looked down the ramp to the harbour parking lot, two hundred feet away.

The ferry.

There were two men behind the glass of the bridge.

'Help!' she screamed, frantically waving her arms above her head. 'Help me, I'm being attacked!' Neither looked in her direction. They couldn't hear her from this distance. 'Help me! Please help m—'

She stopped, struck silent.

Hain had emerged, on foot, at the bottom of the ramp. Their eyes met, his expression dark as night. And then he mouthed something.

She couldn't hear him.

But she understood.

You're fucking dead.

She sprinted back the way she'd come, up the incline of Main Street, as Hain made a dash to his Ram. She could run, she was fit, she could go on for miles without stopping – but there was one thing she couldn't do.

She couldn't outrun a car.

Behind her, she heard the rev of his engine, heard the weight of the Ram's tyres hitting the harbour ramp.

And then an idea struck her.

A desperate, stupid idea.

The Fix

Travis showered and headed downstairs.

Naomi's funeral the day before was the major reason why he was so late in getting up: after dropping Mark at the airport for a 9 p.m. flight, he and Gaby had gone to meet a bunch of old family friends at a bar on Hillside Avenue, and had drunk too much. Booze didn't mix with bereavement, and Gaby had got home and burst into tears, crying about her mother's death. She'd already been sobbing pretty much non-stop for the previous two months when, completely out of the blue, Naomi had been diagnosed as terminal, and the kids had started having to travel back and forth at every new diagnosis, on every occasion when the doctors had said it wouldn't be long before Naomi passed, only for her to rally once more.

The three times Travis had been to see his ex-wife – because it had been the proper thing to do in her last weeks – she'd told him he'd been a shitty husband, airing the same criticisms over and over, and he'd sat there and let her talk, because another argument would have been worth nothing. It was the reason, even if he hadn't already arranged to meet Amy Houser, why he didn't want to be at Naomi's grave today, playing nice in a dreary cemetery on the shoulder of the Long Island Expressway.

After showering, he headed downstairs, sitting opposite Gaby at the kitchen table. They ate eggs and drank coffee and talked about everything Gaby had coming up, and at 10 a.m., Mark texted to tell him that his flight back to LA the previous night had been fine, that he was already in work and that he was missing them very much. Travis archived the text, putting it alongside some of the other messages Mark had sent over the years where he'd said unexpected things, or been uncharacteristically expressive. Travis had always had to work

347

harder with Mark than with Gaby but these moments, although small, made all of it worthwhile.

'Do you think people get what they deserve, Dad?'

Travis looked up from his cellphone.

'I mean, you had a lot of cases over the years, right?' Gaby shifted some egg around her plate. 'I don't know, with Mom and everything, it made me think about the kind of work you did.'

He watched her for a moment, waiting for her to continue.

'It must have had you asking some big questions about life,' she said, her words a little harder to form now, after the impact of the last week. She put down her fork. 'I mean, how do you rationalize it all?'

Travis shrugged. 'I don't think you do.'

'You never tried to?'

He reached across and took his daughter's hand, squeezing it gently. At first, he thought about planing the edges of his response to give her an answer that, twenty-four hours after she'd buried her mother, wouldn't entirely crush her. But he didn't want to lie to her. Not now, not today. So he squeezed her hand again, and looked her in the eyes, and said, 'I joined the NYPD in 1983, and in thirty-six years I did as a cop in total, I saw stuff that didn't make sense. I'd go into these places, these crime scenes, and you'd see some of the things one human being was capable of doing to another, and you'd have to take a moment to try to clear your head. Because it would be impossible to understand. I mean, all the rules we set out, not just on pieces of paper, but in life – laws we don't write down and make a big show of, we just know – in those crime scenes, they've all been broken. You're just standing there, thinking, How did we even get here? To start with, there was always a small part of me, a voice in my head, that said, "You won't solve this because you can't comprehend it. This crime is so heinous, so immeasurably, unfathomably awful, and you're too ordinary."'

'So you're saying nothing can be rationalized?'

'I don't know what I'm saying exactly, honey, but I can tell you what I learned as a cop, because I think it's pretty close to what I learned about life. It was incredible and terrifying. It surprised and delighted me, and then, in the next breath, it didn't just pull the rug out from under me, but collapsed the entire floor. I loved it and hated it. It made me feel like a million bucks and then would deeply and profoundly hurt me. In all those years, a ton of cases passed across my desk, and I think, overall, I did a pretty decent job. I made mistakes, but I did some good things too. But I'll tell you, it's a hell of a lot harder to remember the good things than it is to remember the things that caused you pain. The cases that got away and I didn't solve, they still hurt.'

After that, he told her he loved her and he knew what Gaby must have been thinking: the things he'd talked about, the things that being a cop had taught him about life, was all an allegory for the way she would feel about her mother. She probably thought his line about the unsolved cases – the way they still ate at him, the way they overwhelmed any successes he might have enjoyed – was really just an analogy for the grief she was carrying. The death of people we love hurt more than a million astonishing moments.

But it wasn't an allegory.

It was a literal description of how he felt: the frustration of failure, the way he'd had to retire before he wanted to, and how he'd left three people behind.

Louise Mason.

Johnny Murphy.

His sister, Rebekah.

The Murphy disappearances had fallen into his lap in that last week, and all he'd hit was roadblocks. Even their cell-tower pings – his greatest hope for finding out where they'd gone that day – were dead ends. He remembered the night he'd got that data through, the way he'd been so excited, so charged about it, then had crash-landed. The pings had charted a course for them both, from their homes in Brooklyn, out across Long Island to Montauk at its tip, and then to a small outcrop called Crow Island, a hundred miles off the coast. Travis had known then that the island tied into some of the cryptic research notes he'd found at Johnny Murphy's place. It had also confirmed something Travis had been thinking a lot about: the two of them had gone to Long Island to catch a ferry.

Yet later that day, Johnny and his sister had returned on the ferry and back along the Expressway. Then, for reasons that Travis couldn't work out, they had taken the I-95 north to Connecticut, where both of their phones went dead outside Stamford, approximately fifty miles from their homes. Why had they gone in the other direction? What was in Connecticut? They appeared to have no connection to the state. He'd put out a BOLO with state troopers for the sister's Cherokee, but it had never been sighted in or around Stamford, and neither of the phones came back on again after they'd gone off.

That night, three days before he retired, was when the case died. He couldn't figure out what had happened to either of them. He couldn't fix it.

Nor could he fix Louise Mason.

He'd tried for three months with her, and had tried even harder after Johnny Murphy disappeared — knowing, in his heart, the two cases were connected, that one fed into the other — but, in the end, he'd failed Louise. He couldn't find her and, worst of all, he never got to give her family an answer. Louise, Murphy, his sister — they just became three people he'd had to let go.

Until today, perhaps.

He got ready to go and meet Amy Houser.

58

A desperate, stupid idea.

It was so risky, so profoundly reckless, Rebekah almost tripped as she considered it, like her legs were fighting the images forming in her head.

Turning, trying to ignore the reasons not to do it, she kept to the side of the buildings on Main Street – obscuring herself from Hain, in the parking lot – and returned to the top of the ramp that led down to the harbour. At the bait-and-tackle store, she stopped and peered around the right angle of its wall.

The pickup was almost upon her.

She whipped back, pressed her spine against the wall, and waited. As she did, doubt put her in a chokehold, an almost hysterical fear following in its wake: she was shivering, there were tears in her eyes, her head was on fire. As she heard the Ram coming, the rattle of the trailer behind it, she realized she'd been pressing her nails so hard into the bricks, one had snapped off.

The pickup swung around the corner without stopping and headed in the direction Rebekah had been going. She launched herself off the wall and into a sprint, following directly behind the trailer so that – if Hain checked his mirrors – he wouldn't spot her.

She had to push herself hard to keep up.

Teeth gritted.

Heart pumping.

On the island, she'd been averaging six miles per hour tops – now she was having to do way more just to keep pace with the pickup and the trailer as it bumped its way slowly up Main Street, towards the crest of the slope.

She reached out, brushing the steel cage of the trailer with her fingers. *Come on.* Once the Ram hit the flat, it would be over. She tried again, tried to grab hold of a bar, breathing hard now, pulse crashing in her ears. *You can do it. Come on, you can do it.* She tried again, and again, her hand getting hold of the bar, then slipping. She felt herself stumble, thought it was over.

And then she had hold of it.

She almost lost her footing, the tug of the vehicle so strong – but she managed to use the momentum of the pickup to launch herself off her feet. She crunched the flats of both shoes against the back of the trailer. Her backpack slapped against her spine.

Climbing over the back gate, she paused, trying to gain control of her breathing again. To her left and right were slide bolts, keeping the rear gate of the trailer in place. She released one just as the Ram hit the flat at the top of Main Street. Inching across to the other, she swung her backpack around to her front and went to the zip pouch on top. Inside were her car keys.

She released the other bolt on the gate.

It hit the asphalt with a clatter, sparks kicking up, and immediately she felt the pickup brake: Hain knew something was up. He could feel it.

Rebekah didn't waste any time: she moved to the left-hand side of the Jeep, opened the door as far as it would go before it hit the sides of the trailer, and slid in at the wheel. She looked at the smashed passenger window, the glass still dotted in the footwell. She saw Kyra's pink giraffe and Roxie's hair on the back seat. And then she pulled her door shut and hit the ignition button.

The car fired up.

She glanced at the instruments to check just how low on gas the Jeep was. There was less than a fifth of a tank left. She tried not to let it weigh on her: *If I can get clear of the town, I can find the people I saw this morning. I just need enough gas to buy me time and get help.*

She slammed the car into reverse.

It lurched backwards and hit the road almost instantly. The impact was so hard, Rebekah crashed forward and smashed her head against the top of the wheel. For a second, she was dazed, could feel the car swerving, out of control.

She hit the brakes.

Again, she jolted forward: she watched the trailer's brake lights come on and everything whip to a stop. Then, in her mirror, a figure appeared behind her, at the top of the harbour ramp, by the bait and tackle place.

Lima.

She swung the car around, using the road and the grass either side of it to pull a full-lock U-turn, and hit the gas. The Cherokee arrowed back down the street, Lima not moving for a second – maybe disbelieving what he was seeing, maybe still unsteady – and by the time he understood what was happening, and started going for his gun, Rebekah had almost hit him.

He leaped out of the way, rolling across the blacktop, and when he was on his feet again and had the gun up in front of him, Rebekah was turning a corner. She was heading out of Helena the other way, in the opposite direction to the forest and the hostel, towards the lighthouse on the west coast.

She gunned the Jeep past the mist-shrouded echoes of old properties, knew she was driving too fast, knew it was foolish on these roads. But she kept going, her foot flat to the floor.

The further north she travelled, the more the mist thinned, until – finally – she broke from its grasp. Sun appeared, blue sky, the marbled sweep of the beach to her left, then the lighthouse. There were rock pools in a ragged line at its base and she could see that the door was still open, flapping in the wind.

She slowed slightly, leaning forward, eyes narrowing. She thought she'd seen movement at the door, inside the darkness of the lighthouse's interior.

But had she really?

Or was she just hoping?

She looked in her mirror, checking for any sign of Hain and

Lima, and then her attention pinged back to the lighthouse. Should she go and check? Should she ignore it? She was conflicted now, unsure what to do.

As she got to the turning, she made the decision: she bumped off, onto the peninsula the lighthouse was on, stones pinging off the underside of the Cherokee, and sounded her horn. She jabbed it to start with, but the further down the track she got, the longer she kept her fist to the centre of the wheel.

No reaction.

No sign of movement inside.

Then she heard something: a distant vibration, a hum, hidden behind the crash of the ocean. It took her a second to work out what it was.

She started turning the car around.

As she did, she glimpsed it in the mist, there and gone again, drifting in and out of existence, like a ghost. And then, finally, it emerged from the fog.

The pickup.

They'd dumped the trailer.

They were coming for her, faster than ever.

59

She hit the gas.

In her mirror, she watched dust kick up behind her, a whirlwind of grey-brown earth, and then she was heading back to the Loop. To her right, as the car bumped and shifted on the fractured ground, the Ram appeared out of focus, a blurry black shape – but she could tell they were moving way quicker now, could hear the growl of the engine behind the boom of the sea.

As soon as she got back to the Loop, she veered left, away from them, in the direction of the north coast. She didn't even brake. The car fishtailed, the turn too sharp and too fast, forcing her from one side of the road to the other. For one long, awful moment, she was unable to gain control, the engine vibrating like it was about to explode, its nose facing off towards a grass bank that dropped into a thin cluster of trees. If one wheel went over, the whole vehicle went with it.

At the last second, she saved it, righting the direction of travel. As soon as she did, she jammed her foot to the gas again, and the Jeep stuttered, jumped, then started to pick up speed. She'd lost precious seconds, could see the pickup had gained on her, but she was back in control of the Cherokee.

The faster she went, the more the engine began ticking, as if there were something defective under the hood, a bomb counting down to detonation. She tried to ignore it, checking her mirror. The Ram had gained on her again – it was close enough for her to see both of them clearly, their faces, their features – and something worse.

Lima was leaning out of the passenger window.

In his hands was his gun.

A shot rang out, cutting across the afternoon like the roar of a jet plane. She felt the Jeep buck under her, thought for a moment that a tyre had been hit then realized that, in her panic, her foot had slipped from the gas to the brake.

She looked again, saw him lining up another shot.

Do something. Do it now.

Ahead of her, the road was starting to arc to the right, looping around the lines of the old sawmill, long shuttered, that she'd been to once after she'd first found the map. In front of the mill was a narrow line of pine trees.

Another shot. A third.

Something pinged off the bodywork, the noise like the *ting* of a cymbal. When she looked back, Lima still had the weapon out in front of him, his wrist resting on the black frame of the mirror, trying to steady his aim. Rebekah knew that if he got one in the tyre, she'd instantly lose control of the vehicle.

She could hit the pine trees on her right.

She could flip.

She needed to stop Lima getting the shot in. She needed to disrupt the pursuit. Their car was faster, newer, more powerful. It was gaining on her the whole time. Her foot was flat to the floor. She couldn't go any faster.

And then a thought came to her.

Maybe I don't have to.

She slammed on the brakes.

She hit the pedal so hard, everything in the Cherokee propelled forward, the pink giraffe hitting the windshield in front of her. The seatbelt locked hard between her breasts. Pain lightning-forked across her.

Quiet.

And then it shattered: brakes screamed, tyres squealed, a car howled as it tried to change direction at the last second. They'd got so close to her, it was impossible to avoid her.

The Ram swerved violently to the right, smashing into the Jeep and exploding a tail light. A shudder passed through the cab, and the Cherokee lurched forward, rocking and resetting.

On her right, through the smashed window, she watched the pickup leave the Loop, and then, a split second later, it collided with a tree. Ten feet from the road, in the shadow of the sawmill, it stopped dead, its hood crunching and folding like paper. As it did, the two men slammed forward, airbags erupting into their faces.

And, like a video pausing, everything stilled.

Only steam continued to move, hissing from the crushed hood. Hain's head was slumped against the door, eyes shut. Rebekah didn't know if he was dead or alive, but he was definitely unconscious. Next to him, Lima was still awake, but dazed. She checked her mirror.

Should she turn around?

Should she head back into Helena?

She needed to call the cops before the men came around properly – and there was an easy way to do it. She could see a cellphone in a charging slot on the centre console of the Ram. It was still in place despite the crash: if she could grab it, she'd have her escape route; she'd have her immediate call to the cops.

No delay, no waiting.

But she'd have to get inside their car to take it.

Life Raft

Travis let Gaby have his car, so she could drive to the cemetery, and got her to drop him at the subway on 46th Street. As the carriage rattled through the earth towards the city, he thought about the conversation he'd had with his daughter that morning, and about where it had ended up.

With the cases he'd failed to see through.

He reached into his pants and wriggled out his old notebook, the one he'd used at the NYPD after starting in the Missing Persons Squad. It was full, first page to last. After he'd finished talking to Gaby, he'd gone up to the bedroom and dug through a tower of shoeboxes, and it had been there, buried in one, alongside every other notebook he'd ever bought and filled. They were a thirty-six-year record of success and failure, a testament to his life as a cop, engraved in black ink. He'd gone through a couple, recalling other cases he'd worked and closed, and then, wary of becoming distracted, had entombed them in the closet. All except one.

This one.

The one that contained his notes on Louise Mason.

And on Johnny and Rebekah Murphy.

Now, as people moved in and out of the train, as stations passed, Travis barely noticed anything else. It had started with Louise, and for now that was where he began again. So much of her case he knew off by heart, the details of her disappearance tattooed on him. Mostly, though, what endured in his mind was how close Louise had been to her parents, and how crushed they'd been when, in the days before his retirement, he'd been to see them again to tell them he still hadn't found their daughter. Often at night, when he couldn't sleep, Travis would look up into the dark of the bedroom and find himself in their shoes, and it would be Gaby missing, and he'd feel everything Louise's parents were experiencing. The failure felt immense.

Murphy and his sister he didn't know as well — but whatever had happened to them, Travis was convinced it was connected to whatever had happened to Louise. He still couldn't prove that Murphy wasn't behind all of this — but, in his gut, Travis knew he wasn't. It didn't feel right. Murphy didn't fit the profile, and his sister would never have abandoned her kids.

And then there were the cell-tower pings, the way they traced a path to Connecticut, for reasons he didn't understand. And the less he understood, the more the frustration burned.

After he'd ceased to be a cop, he'd thought about asking for a favour from someone, an old colleague who might be persuaded to do some hunting around for him, to chase paper trails and exhausted leads, but Louise and the Murphys were both long-term disappearances. They'd been missing for months. There were hundreds of other cases ahead of his, confirmed crimes, murders, rapes, robberies, that were way up the list. And perhaps, if he was honest with himself, there was another, more compelling reason that Travis couldn't pass the torch: no one knew the cases like he did — and he didn't trust anyone to work them like him.

But then Amy Houser had called.

She'd called him in the days after Naomi passed, in part to send her condolences to Travis and the kids. But that hadn't been the only reason. She'd also asked Travis if he'd be interested in some freelance work: they needed some cases reviewed, to see if anything had been missed, and Travis had been the first person Houser had thought of. Travis had said yes straight away: he needed the money and he wanted the distraction.

But he said yes for another reason too.

Amy Houser was going to be his life raft.

Travis waited for Houser on a bench at the southern end of Columbus Park, next to some kids playing on the jungle gym. It was cold but they were having a ball, and as he watched them, smiling as they squealed with delight, he wondered if he would ever be a grandparent. Maybe Gaby in a few years, but not Mark: he'd already made it clear that he didn't want kids, and when he'd told Travis that, Travis had felt a weird stab of guilt, as if the reason might be down to him: mistakes he'd made as a father, times he hadn't been home when he should have been, ways in which he'd neglected his children without ever knowing it. He'd always thought he'd been a good dad, even with the demands of his

359

job, but Mark's confession had stayed with him, started to embed itself, and a few times in retirement – as he woke up to another day on his own – he'd wondered if his loneliness might not be a kind of punishment.

'You okay, Trav?'

He hadn't seen Houser approach.

'How you doing, Ames?'

'All good.' She checked her watch. 'Sorry I'm late. Got caught up in the world's longest and most boring meeting. Let me pay for lunch to say sorry.'

Travis stood. 'You don't have to do that.'

'You got to help the elderly where you can,' she said, winking at him, and as they headed up Mulberry Street, into Chinatown, she slid a gloved hand through the crook in his arm, and started filling him in on all the office gossip. He loved it: it made him feel normal again, reattached to something he understood.

Eventually, as the snow continued to fall, Houser said softly, 'I was really sorry to hear about Naomi.'

Travis nodded. 'Thanks, kiddo.'

'How you feeling about it all?'

'I don't know . . .' He shrugged. 'Conflicted, I guess.'

Houser just nodded: Travis had told her about his marriage.

They ate dim sum at a place on Mott.

Over lunch, they talked a lot about the force, about the changes being pushed through by the brass, and then Houser surprised him with the news that she'd had a promotion, swapping Major Crimes for the Cold Case Squad.

'That's amazing, Ames.'

She smiled warmly at Travis. 'Thanks, Frank.'

'You're gonna kill it in that squad, you know that?'

She looked at him for a moment, the admiration clear in her face – and not just for his work as a cop – and Travis realized how much he missed the force, the people he'd worked with, and especially Amy Houser. He missed seeing her every day. Save for the one drunken night when she'd told him about the father she'd never known, Houser had never been big on sharing, but Travis had learned enough down the years: she was divorced, she liked going to the gym, she ran a kids' softball team for the Police Athletic League, and she had an almost encyclopaedic knowledge of eighties action movies. A part of him had always liked not knowing everything because, as time had gone on, they'd continued to learn new and interesting things about each other.

'Thirty-seven and already a lieutenant,' Travis said, and whistled for effect. 'You'll be running the whole damn place before long.'

'What can I say? I learned from the best.'

They carried on eating for a while, then Travis asked her more about her promotion. 'Is that what you've got lined up for me? Cold cases?'

'Yeah,' Houser said, picking out a sliver of prawn with her chopsticks. 'It's ninety-nine per cent signed off. I just got to take you back to the Plaza for introductions. You're going to need access to our system again, obviously, so a few people need to make sure you're not a total charlatan.'

She winked at him again, but Travis hardly noticed: his thoughts had lodged on what Houser had said about access. That was what he needed. That was how she was going to be his life raft. As much as he denied it, because he liked Houser, wanted the work, and felt guilty about carrying an ulterior motive into this lunch with her, access was the major reason he was here right now: he needed to be back in the system. He needed the police databases.

They were how he could find the Murphys.

They were how he could still find Louise Mason.

60

As Rebekah approached the Ram, neither man seemed to be aware of her.

Hain's head was still down, eyes on the steering column that had shifted towards him. Lima had a hand on the crushed dash, trying to swivel his legs to the door. The cellphone was between them, in a charging slot at the midway point of the centre console. To get it out, she'd have to lean over Hain. What if he grabbed her? What if Lima had his gun close by?

She stopped dead, but then forced herself forward again. They still didn't seem to have noticed her – but, with every attempt to exit the vehicle, Lima was getting stronger. After a while, he switched tactics: he leaned back and kicked at the passenger door with both feet.

She hurried towards the bed of the Ram, so that she'd be approaching Hain's open window from the rear of the vehicle. She could see him in the side mirror, head still down. He looked as if he'd slipped back into unconsciousness: his eyes were closed and blood was leaking from his shaved head, a perpetual *drip, drip, drip* that carried threads of it down the side of the car.

She'd almost got level with Hain's shoulder when Lima sprang his door. As it came back at him, he stopped it with his boot. The second he did, it was like something changed: he seemed to become aware of where he was and how he'd ended up here. He started looking at the damage around him, at Hain, then out at the Cherokee.

He's searching for me.

Rebekah dropped to her haunches.

Below the level of the windows, she was blind. She could only hear: he was shifting inside the car again, probably trying to haul himself out. She looked both ways along the Loop – all she wanted was to see another car now – then towards the sawmill, knowing help wasn't going to come from there. Further out there was a tangle of buildings, grey at this distance. They were a mile away at least. Could there be someone in them?

Lima was outside the car, in front of the trees.

If she was going to grab the phone, she had to do it now.

She crab-walked the rest of the way to Hain's smashed window and peered through. She had a clear view of Lima's midriff on the other side of the pickup. He was moving, shifting from one foot to the other, as if he was trying to get a better view of the Cherokee and of Rebekah. When he moved to his right, she could hear a slight drag of the foot. He'd damaged it.

She turned her head, double-checking on Hain. He was in exactly the same position as before.

Except his eyes were open.

It took her breath away and – as she froze – his arm came up from his lap and tried to grab her by the neck. She managed to lean away from him, hitting her head on the top of the window, but avoided his grasp, then jammed the flat of her palm into his face.

The impact vibrated through her wrist.

'Hain?'

Lima ducked, looking through the passenger door.

His eyes met Rebekah's.

'You *bitch*!'

He couldn't get around the front of the car without weaving through a knot of pine trees, so he started hobbling towards the back, dragging his foot.

Quickly, Rebekah leaned inside and tried to grab the cell.

It didn't move.

She tried again, realizing there were identical buttons on either side of the slot that the phone was clipped into. She pressed the buttons and pawed at the cell for a second time.

It still wouldn't come out.

Checking on Hain, she saw he was coming round again. She leaned even further in, her heart pounding inside her chest, and as she got her fingers around the phone, as she popped it from its station, she started to wriggle back out.

Hain tried to grab her again.

'No!' she screamed. 'Let go of me!'

'Don't let that bitch go!' Lima shouted from her right. He was at the back of the car somewhere. She could hear his foot dragging.

Rebekah thrashed at Hain with her spare hand, trying to hit his face, his throat, anything, and as she did, he jerked, avoiding her attempted blows.

He gripped tighter.

'No!' she screamed again, lashing out with her elbow – and, this time, she caught him in the throat. He instantly released her, his body pivoting sideways – but as his arms went with him, they connected with her hand, and the cell spun out of her grip. She watched it hit the wheel, bounce off the dash and exit through the open passenger door.

No.

It came to rest outside among the pines.

No, no, no.

She pulled herself out of the pickup, across Hain's slouched body, and searched for Lima. He was in view of her now, teeth gritted, at the tailgate of the car. In his hand was the gun.

She turned on her heel and looked at the Jeep. It was too far away. She would have covered barely half the distance between her and the Cherokee before Lima was all the way around the pickup. By then, she'd have a bullet in her back.

That meant there was only one option left.

Run.

61

She passed from the road to the grass and then into the trees, the light changing, the wind dying. Behind her Lima was shouting again – and then a gunshot rang out. Its sound was ruinous, a noise that ripped through the air. A second shot, a third, a fourth. He couldn't see her and had no idea where she was.

He was panicking.

Rebekah flashed on the mirror image of this moment – she and Johnny running for their lives five months ago – and then she picked up her pace again. She could feel electricity charging through her veins, the air against her face. She was back at school, between the white lines of the athletics track.

Just then, the pines began to thin out again, and the sawmill rose out of the ground, like a titan breaking from the earth. It was hardly standing, its windows shattered, its corrugated metal rusted. In front of her was a huge sweep of uneven, pockmarked ground, awash in tall grass – in places, almost as tall as Rebekah – and piles of moss-covered timber.

Before she became swamped by the grass, she looked out to the left of the mill, to the dirt track she'd driven down in the Jeep when she'd come here looking for dry wood in the winter. For a vehicle, it was the only way in and out of this place. It would also be a shortcut onto the Loop's northern flank. If she used it, she'd be closer to the buildings she saw earlier.

There might be someone in them.

She headed for the dirt track.

Please let there be someone.

That was when it appeared.

The Cherokee.

She stumbled to a stop. Lima had predicted her plan. He was coming down the dirt track, using her own car to cut her off.

Shit.

Rebekah looked around, scared, desperate. The last time she'd been here it was winter, when the temperature had been in the twenties, when anything the frost hadn't compacted was being blown sideways by the merciless squalls howling in off the Atlantic. Now, in spring, it looked completely different.

She headed back to the long grass.

It was so tall, the scrub so thick, it dragged at her legs and arms as she tried to hide in it. The further she went, the harder it became to see through and the more her sense of direction skewed. Without the snow and the frost, there was nothing to inhibit the grass: when everything stilled, she could just about see through to the dirt track, the Cherokee accelerating along it; when the wind picked up, the grass acted like a flash flood, washing around her, confusing her, trapping her.

Her stride stammered.

She tried to reassert her control: above the whisper of the grass, she could hear the ocean and the rattle of the Cherokee, and she knew she could use them to re-establish her sense of direction. The ocean was behind her, through the pines. The Cherokee was to her left, the north. The mill was straight in front of her and she could see a ramp at the side of it, old and collapsed, where the timber had once been moved to the lumber yard out front. It was a way inside. If she could go through the mill, she might be able to exit at the other end and get back onto the Loop further down, without Lima ever realizing.

But then, suddenly, she fell.

She'd hit the ground before she knew what had happened, the impact so hard it was like a fist to the centre of her chest. Winded, she looked back, retracing her footprints in the mud, trying to see what had tripped her. It was a log, half covered with grass, four feet away.

Her whole body hurt like hell.

She'd jarred her shoulder, her ankle.

She got onto all fours and scrambled to her feet, pain shooting up her leg. Along the crown of the grass, as the wind stirred it, she glimpsed the Jeep.

It was parked. Its doors were open.

No one was inside.

He's already looking for me.

She tried to hide, the grass moving around her. All she could hear was the thump of her pulse in her ears, a drum beat that overwhelmed every other sound. She didn't know what to do because she didn't know where he was. Those moments in the pines, the fleeting seconds of victory, the freedom she'd felt as she'd escaped from the car wreck into the trees – knowing she was faster than them – seemed a million miles away.

'Rebekah?'

She chilled.

It was him.

And he was right next to her.

Meetings

When they got back to Police Plaza, Houser had to sign Travis in. Even such a small act felt weird, a little dispiriting: he'd been coming to the building for eleven years, ever since rejoining the NYPD as part of the Missing Persons Squad, and he'd never had to stop at the front desk. Now he was just another member of the public. Some freelance work and a couple of database logins couldn't disguise that.

They took the elevator up to where the Cold Case Squad was based. It was a small team and Travis knew only one of its members. Houser introduced him to the rest. When she was done, she said, 'Time to go and meet the captain.'

They headed back to the elevators.

'Why's the captain on a different floor?' Travis asked.

'She's been in meetings all morning. She only joined a month ago, so she's playing catch-up. She's from Queens but she was a lieutenant over in Newark.'

Houser hit the button for the tenth floor.

'A female captain and now a female lieutenant,' Travis said, after the doors had slid closed. 'This is progress. No wonder they got rid of a dinosaur like me.'

'They shouldn't have gotten rid of you and you're no dinosaur,' Houser said, shoving his shoulder gently with hers. 'You're more like a Neanderthal.'

Travis was laughing as the doors pinged open. They headed down to an office on the right, all glass with metal blinds. Inside were two women of about the same age: one he recognized, the other he didn't.

'You know the CoD?'

'I met her once in an elevator,' Travis said, looking through the glass at Chief of Detectives McKenzie. She was at her desk, writing something. On a chair to the side of her was Houser's captain, talking to McKenzie but with her gaze already fixed on Travis. Even from where he was, Travis could see the fiery

368

colour of her red hair and how blue her eyes were: they were beautiful, like a summer sky, but they were at odds with the rest of her face.

She looked fierce.

'You said you met the chief once in an elevator?' Houser knocked on the office door, then wriggled her eyebrows comically. 'Travis, you sly dog.'

'Come in, Amy,' McKenzie said, before Travis could respond to the joke.

Houser and Travis entered, Houser closing the door behind her. She introduced Travis to McKenzie, then to Captain Walker.

Walker didn't offer Travis her first name.

'Please,' McKenzie said, 'sit down.'

Travis grabbed a chair next to Houser.

'I think we've met before, Frank,' McKenzie said. He remembered again the stories about her, the nickname she had among some of the male cops – The Dyke – and particularly the observation that she never smiled, or perhaps was physically incapable of it. 'A few days before you retired.'

Travis nodded. 'I remember, Chief.'

'It was early in the morning.'

'That's correct.'

'Did you manage to close the case you were working?'

Travis looked between McKenzie and Walker, and then, very briefly, at Houser. They all knew the answer, because they would already have been through his file, his history, the cases he'd worked and the ones he'd failed to see through. That meant they were just looking for the right response.

'No,' he said. 'Unfortunately, the day I left the force, I had to go to the parents of the woman I was trying to find and admit that I hadn't been able to locate her.'

This wasn't the time for reputation-saving bullshit. It was a test.

McKenzie just nodded. 'Captain Walker.'

Walker came forward in her seat. 'I know you were here a long time, Frank, but I appreciate you coming in like this. I've only been here four weeks so I'm still finding my feet, still getting to know everybody. I don't know you, other than what I've read on paper, and I'll be totally honest, at Newark PD, I wasn't a particular fan of outsourcing investigations, even to former cops with experience like you.' Her face barely moved as she spoke, like her skin had been starched, and Travis thought he could hear the faint trace of an accent. Not New York, even though Houser had said she was from here; not Jersey either,

*where she'd worked before this. It was an accent from somewhere further afield —
but it was so soft he couldn't be certain where. She went on: 'All that said, I
hear you were an excellent cop, I like your honesty, and Lieutenant Houser
says she trusts you, so for now that's enough. We've been given a federal grant
to pursue cold cases that stand a good chance of being cleared, which is obviously
positive news, but we've also got over twelve thousand unsolved murders in the
cabinets downstairs, going all the way back to the mid-eighties, which is not so
great. We need you to start closing some.'*

'Yes, ma'am.'

*Walker, like McKenzie, just nodded, and then McKenzie went over the
terms of the work he was about to agree to, including how much Travis would
be paid. It didn't amount to much, but that was okay with Travis. The money
wasn't the real reason he was here.*

*'Okay, thanks for coming in, Frank,' McKenzie said, putting an end to the
meeting. She got up and shook his hand, Walker opened the door for him and
Houser, and before he knew it the two of them were back in the elevator.*

'Well, she seems fun,' Travis said, once the doors had closed.

Houser smiled. 'Which one?'

'Walker.'

'They're both serious women.'

'No shit.'

'You've still got it, though, Trav.'

He frowned. 'What do you mean?'

*'You know that thing they say about McKenzie? Well, one of the things
they say about McKenzie, that she's physically incapable of smiling?' Houser
shrugged. 'Well, she smiled at you. I think she likes you.'*

He laughed. 'Bullshit.'

'I'm serious. Would you ever date a cop?'

The doors of the elevator sprang open.

'She's ten years younger than me.'

'So?'

'And she's the chief of detectives.'

'So?'

*He thought of McKenzie and remembered the way she'd smiled at him in the
elevator that morning, the week before he'd retired, how it had suited her, and
how she'd made clear that she didn't agree with him being forced out. She was*

attractive, smart and, despite his protestations, he had to admit there was some-
thing about her that he liked.

'I thought she was gay, anyway.'

'That's the assumption.'

'So she's not?'

'I don't know,' Houser said. 'No one's ever been brave enough to ask.'

They arrived back at the Cold Case Squad cubicles. Houser took Travis to
the filing cabinets and started digging through them.

'What about Walker?' Travis asked.

'What — you prefer her?'

'No, I mean, where's she from?'

'She told you. She came from Newark PD.'

'No, where's she from? *She's got an accent.'*

'Oh.' Houser pulled some files out of the drawers. 'I don't know. I think
someone said she moved out from England back in the eighties.'

62

'Rebekah?'

Lima sounded so close he must have been almost on top of her. Slowly, she put a hand flat against the muddy ground, steadying herself as the wind passed out of the pines, from the sea, and washed through the long grass.

'Rebekah?'

His voice sounded like it came from behind her this time, but when she turned back to where she thought he would be, she couldn't see anything.

'I can't let you go home, Rebekah.'

Now it sounded as if he was in front of her. What the hell was going on? She looked in all directions, realizing he was using the wind to his advantage, its ability to carry sounds and obscure their origin. She started moving, inching forward. Every time the breeze picked up, she went further in the direction of the mill; every time it calmed, she stopped, put a hand to the ground, not daring to move except to scan her surroundings.

She looked ahead of her, to the wooden track at the side of the sawmill, watched it flicker in and out of view every time the wind roused. It was about a hundred feet from her. Should she make a run for it – or stay put?

Terror spread, like wildfire.

She tried to stop the vibration in her hands, tried to claim back some of her composure, and – as she paused, almost on all fours – she happened to look to her left, through a V-shaped gap in the grass.

It was him.

He was less than thirty feet from her.

His back was to her, his profile in silhouette against the sun, which was casting butter-coloured light across the top of the saw-mill. At his side, facing down and pressed against his leg, was the gun. As the grass moved, it began to obscure him again.

She didn't shift a muscle.

She just watched, trying not to make a sound. A step to his right, then another – and, once more, he was gone.

'Rebekah?'

His voice was almost lost in the wind.

'You know I can't let you escape.'

She started to move slowly, lifting her hands off the ground – her palms perfectly captured in the mud, as if they'd been set in bronze – and inched away from where his voice was, away from the sawmill. She did the first part on her knees, because it kept her as low to the ground as she could possibly get, and then she got onto her haunches again.

As she moved, she spotted something lying in the shadow of a massive, trunk-sized piece of wood: a rusting piece of metal. It looked like a tool of some kind. There was what appeared to be a wheel at the end and a sharp-toothed blade along the underside. She didn't know what it had been and didn't much care: all that mattered was it was a weapon.

Sidestepping through the grass, she yanked at it.

Where are you, asshole?

Around her, the grass seemed to pulsate.

Come on.

It towered above her as she crouched on the ground.

Come on, I know you're . . .

She stopped.

Something was wrong.

The wind of a moment ago had died out completely. But if there was no wind, there was no way the grass could still be moving – and, yet, it was. It was still swelling behind her, on her shoulder.

Because someone was moving it.

She spun on her heel, propelling herself one-eighty with her hand, but it was already too late: he was right on top of her, a shadow in the grass.

A gunshot ripped through the air.

63

Rebekah staggered backwards. The second she landed, she expected pain – the excruciating agony of Lima's bullet tearing its way through her – but she felt nothing. When she looked down at herself, at her chest, her stomach, there was no bullet wound.

Had he missed?

From only four feet away?

She looked up, the grass like a wall around her. Lima was gone. She couldn't see him anywhere. She pushed herself to her feet, still crouched in case he was near.

What the hell had happened?

That was when she saw the blood on the grass.

A slather of crimson on some strands to her left. She saw footprints too: male, big, an eleven or twelve.

They looked like they were going backwards.

She glanced behind her, at the place she'd landed, and saw the rusted piece of metal she'd been about to use as a weapon. Scooping it up, she gripped it tightly, then faced the grass ahead of her again, the spot where the blood lay, like a marker.

Something moved.

She saw it out of the corner of her eye.

She swivelled on her heel, in the direction of the Cherokee, pulse throbbing in her ears. No sign of Lima there. No sign of anyone.

She looked towards the blood again.

Took another step. A second.

The blood was fresh, running in thin red tresses. She reached out, slowly parting the grass, gripping the weapon harder than ever.

As soon as she did, she saw him.

Lima was lying next to some rotting timber. He'd landed awkwardly, propelled backwards by the bullet that had passed through his face. Rebekah took another step forward, his blood swapping the grass for her arm, but she hardly noticed: it was him on the ground, his eyes like glass, the bullet wound a dribble of treacle an inch above his left eye.

Startled, she looked back the way she'd come and suddenly glimpsed the shape of another person. As it moved, she remembered how she'd never been able to get a handle on Lima's position, how she'd thought he'd tricked her, looped around her somehow.

But now she knew it hadn't just been Lima out here.

It had been Hain too.

She backed up slowly, one deliberate pace after the next, trying to make as little noise as possible, gripping the weapon so hard it was cutting her skin.

Hain was coming towards her.

She could see him now.

She raised the chunk of metal she was holding. She had to get him before he saw her clearly. She had to strike before he ever got the chance to pull the trigger.

Come on, you son of a bitch.

And then a hand pushed through the grass, an arm reaching out for her, a face, a body – and it wasn't Hain at all.

It was a man she'd never met before.

His gun was at his side, the barrel pointing down, and the second he saw her properly, he stopped dead and held up a hand to her.

'It's okay,' Rebekah,' he said, almost whispering it.

He slowly placed the gun on the ground.

'It's okay, I promise. I'm not here to hurt you, kiddo.'

The Crossing

That evening, after Travis had washed up the dinner plates and Gaby was busy FaceTiming a friend in Chicago, he sat at the living-room table with the ten cold cases Houser had given him. They were all murders.

With the temporary user ID that Houser had organized, he grabbed his laptop and logged into the NCIC, and found all ten replicated in the system. Most of what was in the physical files broadly mirrored what was on the computer, but some of the digital versions lacked the fine detail of the paper notes he had to hand. That wasn't unusual. Over the years, he'd worked alongside lots of cops who'd treated the physical file as a Bible, the absolute authority on a case, and the NCIC version as a simple box-checking exercise. Travis had always tried to do both well, but there was little doubt that there was a heartbeat to the paper records, a clarity, that the computer could never duplicate.

'You okay, Dad?' Gaby was in the doorway behind him.

'Yeah, I'm good, honey.'

'What are you doing?'

'Just looking at some of the stuff Amy gave me today.' He glanced at the TV remote in her hand. 'You watching something?'

'The Thing is on at nine.'

'Oh, man. A literal stone-cold classic.'

' "There's something wrong with Blair." '

Travis laughed. When the kids still lived at home, he'd carved out a corner of his home life entirely for the three of them by watching classic horror movies with Mark and Gaby. Naomi had never shown much interest in cinema, and that had been fine with Travis: when she was out, or even sometimes when she wasn't, he'd curl up on the couch, his son and daughter either side of him, and watch films like The Thing. *Even now the kids would talk about it: a couple* of nights before Naomi's funeral, the three of them had been talking about Stephen King novels, and it soon turned into a Misery, The Shining and Carrie *movie marathon that had gone on until 3 a.m.*

'Shall I make some popcorn?' Gaby asked.

'Oh, you bet. I'll be through in a second.'

Travis turned back to his laptop, closing the NCIC *login page, and going to a folder marked 'Montauk' on his desktop. He'd created it an hour earlier, after Amy Houser had come through for him yet again. Three or four years ago she'd worked a case – a rape and murder – with a detective from Suffolk County PD, but he'd only remembered it because she'd mentioned it at the first lunch they'd shared, four weeks after he retired. As soon as she'd started talking about working with the cop out on Long Island, Travis had thought about Johnny and Rebekah Murphy. So, before he'd left Police Plaza, after Houser had handed him the ten files he now had spread out in front of him, he'd asked her if she'd be prepared to call in a favour on his behalf with the detective at SCPD.*

'Why?' Houser had asked.

'I need some video.'

She'd eyed him suspiciously.

'It's okay,' he said. 'It won't affect what I'm doing for you.'

'So what's the case?' But almost as soon as she asked, the answer had come to her. 'Wait, are you still trying to work that thing with the artist?'

'It probably won't lead anywhere.'

'But it might?'

Travis shrugged. 'It might.'

Her eyes had stayed on him for a moment, a conflict playing out behind them. 'I gotta ask, Frank. You're not going to screw this up for me, are you?'

'No,' he said. 'I'd never do that.'

'Because I just took you up there to Walker, to McKenzie, and vouched for you. You know they'll have me on traffic duty if anything blows back.'

'It won't. You have my word.'

And he'd meant it, and that had been enough for Houser.

Travis refocused on his laptop. In the folder marked 'Montauk' there were two files. The first was labelled '10/30/21 a.m.' and, when Travis double-clicked on it, it opened onto a shot of Montauk harbour: the parking lot, a ticket office fringed with a green awning, a jetty extending out into the water, and a boat with CROW LINE printed on the side.

The video started at 7 a.m., an hour before the ferry left for Crow Island and, for the most part, the parking lot was empty. Putting the speed up to 2x, and then 4x, Travis watched the image: he could see the ferry's ramp, its interior big enough to take between twenty and twenty-five vehicles, depending on their size; he could see crew members milling around; and, at the edges of the shot, he could just about make out some cars waiting to get on.

At 7.30 p.m., he switched back to normal speed, pulled in his notebook and flicked through to a page, somewhere near the back, where he'd written the cell-tower ping locations for Johnny Murphy and his sister. They mapped a trail all the way along the Expressway to Montauk, then out to Crow Island.

Onscreen, the ferry started to load.

There weren't many vehicles going out, because 30 October was the last day of the season, which made it even easier to spot the one he wanted.

A Jeep Cherokee.

Using another temporary login that Houser had set up for him, so he could gain access to DMV records, he double-checked the licence plate, making sure the Cherokee was definitely the same one that was registered to Rebekah Murphy. It was. Her DMV entry listed her by her married name, Russo, but he knew – from talking to her friend Noella – that she'd switched back to her maiden name after splitting from her husband. The Jeep disappeared into the bowels of the ferry, and then, just before 8 a.m., the ramp was raised. Pretty soon, the ferry was chugging out of Montauk.

The video ended.

He opened the second, marked '10/30/21 p.m.' The timecode said it was 7.30 p.m. After a couple of minutes the ferry started its slow emergence from the darkness, forming like a monster from the sea bed. Just before 8 p.m., it began manoeuvring into its slot at the same jetty.

Travis slowed the video right down.

The ramp dropped, revealing all the cars and vehicles that had come back to the mainland for winter. He watched them emerge, guided out by one of the crew, and each time one appeared Travis would take a note of the licence plate. More had come back than had gone out: the last ferry of the season would have returned people who'd been staying on the island.

But there was no Jeep Cherokee.

This was what he'd spent his retirement thinking about, the hunch slowly forming at the back of his mind: Johnny Murphy and his sister had never come back. It was why the BOLO he'd put out had never got any hits in Connecticut. It meant, if they actually went to Stamford, it was in another car — but, more likely, they'd never left the island at all.

It was just their phones that had.

It was a set-up, an attempt to throw the cops off the scent, and have someone like Travis looking in totally the wrong direction.

And, for a long time, it had worked.

His blood hummed into life as he minimized the video and returned to his browser. He went back to the DMV records and inputted the licence plates for all of the vehicles he'd seen come off the ferry on 30 October. Every time he brought up a new person, he returned to the video to compare and contrast the photograph on the driver's licence with as much of the driver's face as was visible on the video. It was slow work.

After a few minutes, Gaby came through from the living room, TV remote in her hands. 'Are you coming to watch the movie, Dad?'

'Definitely. Just give me five more minutes, sweetheart, okay?'

The interior of some cars was clearer than others, but most he could see some of, certainly enough to match the driver to the DMV version of them with a fair degree of accuracy.

But there was one that didn't fit.

It was a white Chevy Traverse. The DMV said the vehicle belonged to a Karl Stelzik, but Stelzik was grey-haired and in his sixties; the man on the video, driving Stelzik's car, was younger — late thirties, black hair, bright eyes.

Travis switched browser windows.

Logging into the NYPD database, he put in a search for Stelzik to see if there had been any flags against his name — a record, an arrest, anything.

He found something else instead.

Stelzik was missing too.

7
The Secret

64

Rebekah sat with Frank Travis in the shadow of the lighthouse and watched as the police got closer, shimmering into existence fifty miles out. There were five boats, one carrying two patrol cars and an ambulance, as well as what Travis said was a mobile crime lab.

He was quiet alongside her, as if conscious of not crowding her. After he had shot and killed Lima at the sawmill, he'd guided her away from the body, back towards the Cherokee. But as he made the 911 call on his cellphone, Rebekah could hold back no more: she started to sob. Even though Travis was midway through a conversation, he came back, pulled open the door and placed a hand on her shoulder. And when his call was over, and the cops were on their way, he remained in the same spot, keeping his silence, letting her cry.

Eventually she asked if she could use his cell to call home. He handed it to her and told her he'd give her some privacy, going back to where Lima's body lay, and she sat there for a moment, just staring at the phone, not quite believing no one was going to stop her. *I get to talk to my girls. This is everything I've been waiting for.* She'd believed the same thing with Caleb, inside his shack, but that opportunity had been snatched from her. This time, there was no one to get in her way. All she had to do was dial.

Except she didn't know what she would say.

How could she ever explain a five-month absence in the lives of two girls too young to understand? For Kyra and Chloe, it would be black and white.

One day, their mother had walked out on them.

And she hadn't come home.

Just hearing their voices will be enough for now.

But she couldn't remember cellphone numbers for Noella, or for Gareth, and when she thought of Gareth, she kept thinking of the email she'd found in Karl Stelzik's Inbox. She looked up, into the long grass, and saw Travis wading through it. She didn't know him, but there was something about him she trusted, and that meant she didn't need to worry about what Gareth might or might not have done. Not for now. Travis would protect her from Gareth, from anyone else who might still want to hurt her, or why would he have come all this way? Why work her case? Why stop the men who were trying to kill her?

She looked at the cell again and put in the number for the brownstone. Her thumb hovered for a second above Call and then she dialled.

It just rang. No answer.

Heart beating fast, she hung up, wondering what the lack of an answer meant, panicking that it meant something bad, and then she calmed herself and called directory assistance. She didn't know Noella's number off by heart. The operator rerouted her, and Rebekah listened again to a long line of rings until, this time, it hit a machine.

'Hey, this is Noella. Leave a message and I'll get back to you.'

The sound of Noe's voice made her tearful again, but Rebekah hung up before the tone, not wanting a recorded message to be the way in which Noe – or anyone else in her life – found out she was still alive. As a last resort, she dialled assistance again and asked to be connected to Mendelson, the ad agency Gareth worked for. When an operator picked up, Rebekah asked for him.

'I can't connect you, ma'am,' the operator said.

'Why not?'

'I'm afraid we don't have anyone of that name here any more.'

Rebekah frowned. 'What?'

'Gareth Russo left the business at the end of February.'

'*What?* Where did he go?'

'I don't have that information, I'm afraid.'

Rebekah killed the call, her head swimming, a flutter of nausea in her throat. Gareth had left his job – for another? Or did it mean he'd left New York entirely? Had he taken the girls with him? She tried to recall the name of the place Noella worked at, tried to think of anyone else in the life she'd had before this one whom she could possibly call.

'You all right, kiddo?' Travis asked, as he got back to the car.

'I can't get hold of anyone.'

She didn't want to break down again. She knew she was so much stronger now, so different from the person who'd first been abandoned on the island. But now she was so close to going home, to seeing her girls – so close to this nightmare finally being over – her whole body felt like it was trembling.

'It's okay,' Travis reassured her.

'I just want to speak to them.'

'I know you do.'

'I can't get hold of my ex, or my best friend.'

'Don't worry, we'll get hold of them for you, okay?'

'They said Gareth moved, and I don't know if they mean –'

'Rebekah.' When she stopped, he smiled, told her to breathe. 'It's all right,' he said. 'You don't need to worry any more. You're going home tonight.'

Going home, just without my brother.

'Do you know where Johnny is?'

'No,' Travis said. 'Not yet.'

It looked like he was desperate to add something else, some theory that might explain what had happened to Johnny, some small sliver of hope – but he obviously couldn't come up with anything. Across five months, Rebekah had allowed herself to taste some of that hope. She'd even allowed herself to picture an escape – a courageous act of survival on Johnny's part – where he'd made it out alive.

Except it had always felt like a fantasy.

Once she'd made the decision to drop her suspicions about him – to embrace what she knew in her heart was true about her brother – she realized there was no way that Johnny would ever have left her behind, even if he feared she was dead. He would always have come back for her.

The reason he hadn't was obvious.

65

Travis told her they should go and fetch his car from where he'd left it – on the Loop, north of the sawmill – and then they drove back to the lighthouse, where he'd told the cops to arrive. Soon, the Dodge Ram emerged into view at the edge of the road, its crushed hood, its shattered windshield. As Rebekah saw the empty driver's side, she felt a sudden flash of alarm. 'What about Hain?'

Travis looked at her. 'He's missing.'

'Missing?'

'He was already gone from the pickup when I drove past earlier.'

Travis was right: there was no Hain, only the evidence of him. A faint trail of blood led away from the driver's side door, across the road in the direction of the lighthouse. When they parked up and got out, Travis swept the building for any sign of him, but all he found was more blood, heading past the lighthouse to the edge of the water.

'Was a boat ever docked here?' he asked Rebekah, clearly thinking Hain might have commandeered one – except Rebekah couldn't remember. She'd been past the lighthouse so many times, but she'd either never seen a boat or never thought to look for one: boats had quickly become a reminder of her failure and a symbol of her fear.

They stood there for a while, looking in the direction Hain might have tried to head, searching for any evidence of a wake, or a hint of a swell – but the sea was vast, and grey, and entirely untouched.

'He could still be on the island,' Rebekah said, horrified at the idea.

'And if he is, they'll find him,' Travis replied, gesturing to the water, to the police boats coming towards them. 'If he's injured, he won't be able to get far. And if he's hiding out, they'll use the dogs. His scent's all over the pickup.'

At the mention of dogs, Rebekah thought of Roxie, of locking her inside the room at the hostel, of her still being there, and her heart plunged. Barely able to get the words out fast enough, she told Travis about her, where she was, and Travis assured her they would go back for her, once the authorities had arrived. 'We've got to wait and see how the cops want to play it first,' he added.

They were quiet for a time, their silence comfortable, and then, slowly, they started talking about the island, about the events that had led up to Rebekah being left behind, about how she'd survived alone for so long. They talked about the night that Hain and Lima had come ashore, looking for a body to bury, and then of Caleb, and Rebekah remembered that she'd left him injured at the shack. Travis called one of the cops he'd been in contact with and told them to send a paramedic straight to Helena and, soon after, they saw one of the boats veer off towards the harbour.

'How did I get left here, Frank?'

He nodded, as if he'd been expecting the question. 'I called around and the people here at the harbour, they're supposed to keep records of the licence plates that enter and leave the island so they know who's gone and who still remains. I mean, that seems a pretty essential tool when you're this far from the mainland in a place that closes for five months a year. But, from the calls I made, it seems those records stopped being taken some years ago. The vast majority of people who come here are fishermen, and they all have their own transportation so the island authorities became sloppy.'

Rebekah's head dropped.

'I'm sorry, kiddo.'

'So how did *you* find me?' she asked.

'You heard of someone called Louise Mason?'

Her thoughts went to the corridor in the hostel, to the wall of paper she'd mounted. She'd never known Louise's surname until now, and she'd never been on Rebekah's suspect list, but a piece of string had branched out from Louise to a name that was.

Her brother's.

'She was the woman Johnny dated.'

'Right. She disappeared back in September.'

'She's missing too?'

Travis nodded again. 'Your brother was one of the last people to see her alive. For a time, I'll admit, I thought Johnny might have had something to do with it. I got this anonymous call that kind of turned everything on its head, so I went back in and looked at him again. That was when I found out that he – and you – had been missing since October thirtieth. Three disappearances, and two of the people unaccounted for – Louise and your brother – had a clear and obvious connection.' He grimaced, as if he didn't like having to remember some of the theories and decisions he'd made before this moment. 'I'm starting to wonder if my anonymous caller might have been one of the two men who came here to find your body today. I can't imagine why, but maybe they felt I was getting too close to them. Maybe they needed to shift the blame to Johnny to protect themselves.'

Travis then started telling her about the cell-tower pings: 'Something always bugged me about them – why Connecticut? You two had no links there, far as I could tell. I got no hits on your Cherokee up in Stamford or anywhere nearby – I even checked in with state troopers after I retired, and that was still the case in February and March – so I started to think it might just have been another diversion. I knew I was right when I got hold of some video from a security camera at Montauk harbour, taken on October thirtieth: Lima came off that boat behind the wheel of Stelzik's Chevy. He took both your cellphones to Connecticut to throw cops like me off the scent, knowing they'd ping towers all the way there. From what you've said, it sounds like Hain wanted him to bring *your* car, but Lima forgot to get the keys from you before he tried to kill you, so I guess he figured getting rid of Stelzik's Chevy was the next best thing. Either way, the plan would have been the same: ping the towers and lead the cops to a dead end in another state.'

He smiled, but it was sad, almost an apology. 'I watched that video from Montauk a week ago, and waiting a week to come out here, it felt like a year. I can't imagine what it's been like for you. If I was still on the force, I could have got boats in the water straight away to come here with the troops and find out what happened. I thought about alerting a friend of mine – she's a cop at the NYPD – but, I don't know, she was . . . It wasn't . . .' He seemed conflicted.

'Frank?'

'Sorry. It's nothing. Simply that this friend of mine, she'd trusted me with something unrelated to this, vouched for me in front of the brass back in New York, done a favour for me in getting hold of that video from Montauk, so I didn't want to drag her into this.' He stopped again, something remaining in his expression that Rebekah couldn't interpret. Was it to do with his friend at the NYPD? 'So, I've been sitting on my hands, waiting for this ferry, hoping for answers, for eight days. And do you know the first thing I saw when I drove out to Montauk harbour and pulled into the lot?'

Rebekah shook her head.

'Lima. I was sitting there in that parking lot, waiting for the ferry, and I saw these guys pull up in a pickup, towing a trailer. And one of them gets out to take a leak and, when he turns around, I see his face, and it's the same guy I saw in the security-camera video, the guy driving Stelzik's car . . .'

'So you followed them?'

'Best I could, without being seen. If one of them made that anonymous call to me about Johnny, then I figured there was a good chance they knew what I looked like. I'd been in newspapers, all the way back to my first spell with the department, and it was likely they would have done their homework. I knew I was okay in terms of my car, because it was a rental, but I couldn't risk them getting too close and seeing *me*. That was why I was last onto the ferry, and it was why I stayed in my car the whole time – I didn't go up at all during the crossing. And then, when we got to the island, they headed east, down to the dig site there. I'd planned to go to the harbourmaster first, to see if he recognized you, but that was before Lima turned up in Montauk. I had to switch plans. So I waited for them at the top of Simmons Gully, hid out behind this old building, and when they reappeared ninety minutes later, they had your Cherokee on the trailer. I felt sick seeing it, because I knew what it meant for you, and for Johnny. There was only one reason they'd be getting rid of evidence like that. They were arguing too. I saw it, even from where I was. Of course I know now that by then they were starting to doubt you were even dead.'

That was why Lima had come to the shack.

It was why he'd shown Caleb her photograph.

'Hain wanted to get some gas, so he dropped Lima on Main Street, then turned around and went back. That was why Lima was alone. I couldn't keep tailing Hain – the roads were so empty and it was so easy to spot me – and there was nowhere else in Helena to just sit in the car and watch what they were doing without them seeing me. I had no idea you were in that shack, or I'd have come.'

'I know you would,' Rebekah said.

He shook his head, as if the decision was still raw. 'There was no way they could leave the island until the ferry left, so I knew I had time on my side. And before I came to the island, I spoke to this colleague of Karl Stelzik's at the Museum of Natural History, a guy called Gideon Burrows, who'd eventually reported him missing, and Burrows said Stelzik was staying in a hostel on the north coast. So I thought I'd head out there, see what I could find. To me, it was likely Stelzik was buried here, but even though I knew that, even though I'd seen your Cherokee on that trailer – a very obvious sign that you and your brother were dead too – I still had nothing on Louise.'

'Did you find anything at the hostel?'

'No,' he said. 'I didn't even get that far. I was on the Loop, north of the sawmill, when I heard this deafening crash. That was when I pulled a U-turn.'

The crash had been Hain and Lima hitting the tree.

'Here,' Travis said. He was holding his cell out to her, a hint of a smile on his face. He knew where her head was at: now he was trying to haul her out of the hole she was in. 'That friend at the NYPD I was talking about, I texted her after you tried to call your girls earlier and asked her to find some numbers for me.'

He stared at the phone for a second, as if some unspoken message were passing between him and the handset, then handed it over.

Rebekah took the cell from him. Onscreen was a text from a woman Travis had logged as 'Amy'. Her text had two cellphone numbers in it.

One for Gareth. One for Noella.

'I bet there are some little girls who really need to hear from their mom.'

Her fingers trembling, Rebekah pressed her thumb against the number for Gareth.

As it started ringing, she checked the time: it was just before 4 p.m., so probably too early for Gareth to be home. The girls would still be at daycare and he'd be somewhere else. *If the girls even did the same hours, or went to the same daycare. If Gareth had even moved back into the brownstone in the first place.* Maybe he'd decided to start again somewhere different. What if he really *had* moved to another city? What if he'd moved in with the woman he'd been sleeping with? What if the girls now saw her as their mother, as the permanent fixture in their lives, as the only th—

'Hello?'

A voice at the end of the line.

66

For a moment, everything stopped.

'Hello?' the voice said again.

'Gareth?'

A long, agonizing pause.

'*Bek?* Bek, is that you?'

'Yes,' Rebekah said, elated, unsure, confused about how she felt. The call had rung for so long she'd become certain he would never answer.

Now he had, she didn't know what to say.

'Bek? Are you there?'

'Yes. Yes, I'm here.'

'Where the hell have you been?' His voice wavered, an oscillating lurch between anger and relief. 'We thought you were dead. You haven't called, y—'

'Someone tried to kill me.'

That brought him to an instant halt. 'What?'

'Someone tried to kill me,' she repeated, but the words were getting lost now, disappearing as she struggled to hold back the tears. 'Johnny and me, we came out to an island, and someone tried to kill us, and I don't know what happened to John, and I got left behind in this place. I couldn't get home to . . .'

She faded out, wiping her eyes.

'Bek?'

'I've been here alone for five months.'

'On an island?'

'Yes, off the coast of Montauk.'

'Shit, Bek. Are you okay?' He seemed to realize what a stupid question it was immediately after asking it. 'I mean, are you hurt? Shall I call the –'

'I'm okay. The cops are here.'

She glanced at Travis. They'd driven about a mile back down the coast in the direction of Helena, where a jetty crawled out into the ocean. It was the closest point to the lighthouse that the police boats could get to without running aground. Travis had left Rebekah in his rental and walked down to meet the cops.

'Shit,' Gareth said again. 'Bek, I'm so . . . I can't believe this . . .'

'I know,' she said.

'Shall I drive out to you or something?'

'No, it's fine. I'll be home soon.' She sniffed. *I'll be home soon.* Even now, it was hard to believe that was true, harder to *let* herself believe it. 'I didn't know if you'd be at work or not,' she said, and the ordinary nature of the sentence, its absolute banality and how much she'd longed to be able to ask something as simplistic and mundane, brought more tears to her eyes.

'Bek?'

'I'm sorry,' she said.

'It's okay. I got a new job and do afternoons from home now – you know, since you left, uh, since you disapp–' He stopped himself. He didn't know how to describe what she'd told him. 'Since last year. Since last November. The girls go to daycare in the mornings, and I pick them up and bring them back here, and they constantly interrupt me while I'm on conference calls.' There was humour in his tone, a profound sense of love for their daughters. 'It's actually worked out pretty well,' he added, but then paused, as if he understood how insensitive that might have sounded.

Rebekah thought of the email Gareth had sent Stelzik, of his place on the suspect list, of the questions she wanted answers to – but then it all faded into the background. 'Can I speak to the girls?'

'Yeah,' Gareth said. 'Yeah, of course.'

'Are they there?'

'Yeah, they're here.'

But now there was hesitation in Gareth's voice.

'Yeah,' he said again. 'Yeah, just give me a second.'

She heard him put the phone down and shout, 'Kyra! Kyra, come here, sweetheart!' And then she heard the faint creak of footsteps, of old floorboards moaning, of Gareth ascending the stairs, and after that there was a hush.

And, in the hush, she knew something for sure.

He's told them I'm dead.

That was why he'd left the cellphone behind instead of taking it upstairs with him. It was where the hesitation in his voice had come from, the thing that had distracted him. Eventually, maybe two or three months in, with no sign of her or Johnny, no indication of where they'd gone and why they hadn't come home, he'd realized he had to tell Kyra – because Chloe was still too young – the truth, or some version of it. He had to tell her why her mom wasn't living with them, why she wasn't at the breakfast table first thing in the morning – and why she wasn't there to tuck them in last thing at night.

So he'd told them she was dead.

Because that was what it had looked like.

'Hello?'

Her voice came out of nowhere.

'Ky?'

No response.

'Ky, is that you, baby?'

It was deathly quiet at the other end.

'Kyra? *Kyra?*'

Why wasn't she answering?

She's not answering because she doesn't know who I am.

I'm a stranger.

She doesn't remember my voice.

'Ky, it's okay, it's me. It's Mummy.'

An even longer, more terrible silence.

'Ky,' Rebekah sobbed, 'you remember Mummy, right?'

Again, there was no sound from the other side, not even the crackle of her daughter's breath on the line, and this time Rebekah completely fell apart. She leaned forward, against the dash, and everything hit her at once: tears as fierce as every storm that had ripped across the island; abandonment as brutal as every day she'd been alone; pain as real as every cut she'd made in her skin, every bruise, every sprain. Out of the corner of her eye, she saw Travis staring at her from the jetty. But there was nothing he could do.

There was nothing anyone could do.

'Did God send you back?'

Everything stopped for a second time.

'Ky?'

Rebekah wiped at her eyes, her nose.

'Did God send you back?' Kyra repeated, her voice small, reticent, her words edged with an uncharacteristic shyness. But it was her. It was the voice Rebekah had longed to hear every day for 152 days.

'Yes, baby,' Rebekah said. 'God sent me back.'

'Because Daddy said you were in Heaven.'

She swallowed. 'I know he did.'

'Are you still in Heaven?'

She wiped her eyes. 'No, honey,' Rebekah said gently. 'No, I'm not in Heaven any more. I'm on my way back. I'm almost home.'

67

Investigators cleared a space inside the general store and set up a table, some chairs and an interview kit. The roof was still leaking, the bucket Rebekah had left there to catch the water overflowing. Islanders had told the cops that the owner of the store didn't usually arrive back until May, but Rebekah overheard the cops talking to him on the phone at one point, explaining what they were doing. Later on, an early-season fisherman came in and made running repairs to the ceiling. The whole time, he kept eyeing Rebekah.

She watched through the door, a blanket around her shoulders, some water on the table in front of her, as – out on the street – Frank Travis talked to one of the detectives from Suffolk County PD. It had been four hours since he'd found her outside the sawmill, three since she'd got off the phone to Kyra and Gareth, and two since the cops had decided to move her down to Helena to be interviewed. Travis had told her forensic teams were still up by the lighthouse, working on the pickup in the molten orange glow of sunset; search teams were busy too, scouring the island for signs of Hain.

So far they'd found nothing.

The detective Travis was talking to was called Bowners, and was a slim, attractive woman in her late forties. Beside her, Travis couldn't have looked more different. He was over ten years older for a start, his body starting to go to seed, his hair just about more black than grey, his beard dark, except for the places in which it was thickest – at the chin, along his jaw – where it had tinted silver. Halfway through talking to Bowners, he'd got out a notebook and put on a pair of reading glasses, but the weird thing was, none of it made him seem old. There was an energy to him, a vitality. She'd often seen the same thing with doctors after they'd called it a day: they ended up missing the job, even the worst of it, and whenever they returned – to advise, to give lectures – it was like something lit up in them. They cast off retirement like they'd prised open the teeth of a trap.

Travis and Bowners broke off the conversation and disappeared from view. A couple of minutes later, Travis returned.

There was someone with him.

'Roxie!'

As soon as the dog heard Rebekah's voice, she was straining against her leash. Travis smiled, struggling to cope with how hard Roxie was fighting to get free, and Rebekah jumped up from the table. Roxie leaped at her, so excited she barely knew which part of Rebekah to start with. In return, Rebekah simply squeezed, closing her eyes, savouring it.

They stayed like that for a long time.

A while later, Bowners came in.

'Hey, Rebekah,' she said, sitting down next to Travis. 'We met earlier. I know you want to get home. Five months alone in this place . . .' She let the rest of the sentence hang. 'Problem is, we're a hundred miles from the mainland, on an island with one cellphone tower, no internet, and no police station. By the time we've got back to Montauk, we would have lost time and, potentially, recall. I want to get this first interview down before we leave. Is that okay?'

'I guess,' Rebekah said.

'I'd like to film it too, so I'm just going to grab a camera,' Bowners said, and went outside again, in the direction of the harbour, where Rebekah knew a police truck was parked. As she thought of the harbour, she thought of Caleb again and asked Travis how he was doing.

'It's too early to say, but they think he'll be okay.'

She nodded, eyes returning to the window, the two of them

quiet now. She had something else to ask – she just wasn't sure if she wanted the answer.

'Have they found Johnny yet?'

Travis pushed his lips together. 'Not yet. I'm sorry, Rebekah.'

But that wasn't all.

'Frank?'

His gaze was on an item that Bowners had brought in with her and left between the two of them. Rebekah couldn't make out what it was. When Travis looked up again, he seemed distressed.

'They found this,' he said, and placed the item on the table between them. It was a clear plastic bag marked EVIDENCE. Inside was a wallet.

Rebekah felt winded.

'This was Johnny's, I think?'

She nodded. 'Where did you find it?'

'At the lighthouse.'

'The lighthouse? Why would it be there?'

'We don't know yet,' Travis said.

'But his body's not there?'

Body.

Even now, she could hardly bear to describe Johnny in that way. She tried to think of how she might have missed him at the lighthouse, and the answer came soon enough: because she hadn't been looking for him there.

'No,' Travis said quietly. 'We haven't found him yet. Sorry, kiddo.'

After that, they were silent for a while.

'You know,' Travis said eventually, 'I didn't tell you this earlier, but when I was eight, my parents brought me here.' He was looking at Main Street, caught in a memory. 'I mean, I'm an old man, so you can imagine how long ago *that* was.' He grimaced playfully. 'Back in the sixties, Crow Island was the place to come. And I remember, one summer break, my old man surprised me and my mom. He drove us all the way to Montauk in his shitty AMC, rust all along the panels, the suspension like a tank's, and he told us we were getting the ferry out here. We were speechless. Crow Island was where rich people came. Don't get me wrong, we stayed in the cheapest, crappiest hotel on the island, because that was all my dad could afford, but my mom and me? We didn't give a damn. We were lucky if we got a vacation at all, so a vacation to Crow Island?'

'We were like that.'

'Yeah?'

'Did I tell you my dad was a cop?'

'No, but I knew he was. When I talked to Johnny last year, he said your dad worked out of the 68th Precinct.'

A brief pause at the mention of Johnny.

'Anyway,' Rebekah said, 'a beat cop's salary, three kids, you can do the maths. I lived in England until I was eighteen and, when I came back for the summer holidays, we used to go to the same place in Jersey, at Union Beach. The J, it was called. It was the only vacation Dad could afford, but we loved it.'

Travis nodded. 'Your dad passed a couple of years back, right?'

'Yeah.'

'And your other brother?'

'Mike?' Rebekah forced a smile. 'Yeah, he's dead too.'

And then the full, unadorned picture was laid bare in front of them. Rebekah's dad was dead. Mike was dead. And now Johnny was too.

She was all that was left of the Murphys.

'You wanna hear something weird?' Travis asked. He looked older all of a sudden, greyer, more beaten. 'When I pulled into Montauk this morning, I had this crazy, completely inappropriate sense of nostalgia about returning to the island. Despite everything, the dread in the pit of my stomach, my head was full of images of my mom and me building sandcastles on the beach.'

There was another flicker in his face.

'But, you know, the second the boat left, it all changed. Everything just pulled into focus. It wasn't just that I'd recognized Lima and knew, in my gut, that he and Hain were up to something. It wasn't even that I *knew* you, your brother and Louise, were connected somehow – even if I still can't prove it – and that if the cases are connected, it stands to reason that the same men are involved in both. It wasn't those things. It was more that I just kept thinking you and Johnny were going to be buried deep in some hole somewhere, and the men I was following would get away with it again, just like they did with Louise. The expectation of failure gave me focus, because I felt certain I was going to fail you, like I failed Louise.'

He glanced at Rebekah, and something moved in his eyes. To start with, she thought it was a kind of mourning for Louise, and maybe it still was that. Maybe it was some residual emotion, the echoes of him steeling himself for what he'd thought he'd find here. History repeating.

But it wasn't that: 'I drove out to Montauk this morning, thinking I'd never – not for a second – find you alive. But you are, because you fought so damn hard to be. The way you survived here, the fight you've got, it might just be the bravest thing I've ever seen in my life.' He turned to her, his eyes flashing. 'So I guess what I'm saying is, I know I'm asking a lot here – I know I'm asking a hell of a lot, more than I should be, I know all you want is for your life to be normal again, to be home with your girls *right now* – but I need you to be brave for a bit longer, Rebekah.'

Bowners was on her way back.

'You're the key, kiddo.'

'The key?'

He looked at her. 'I don't know why they wanted you dead. I've still got zero idea what happened to Louise. But there's one thing I *do* know.'

He leaned in a little closer to her.

'Somewhere in your head is the answer.'

Identities

She was in a cab, on the way home, when Tillman called her on her cell. The day before, he'd given her the number of a new burner he was using, and in the time since, she'd committed the number to memory, so she knew right away it was him. She knew as well that he wouldn't call without a reason.

She hit Answer. 'It's two a.m.'

'Yeah, well, we need to talk about something.'

'At two a.m.?'

'We might have a problem.'

'And this can't wait until morning?'

'It's about Travis.'

Her breath caught. 'What about him?'

'And it's about Axel too.'

She tried to retain her composure. 'Okay.'

'Maybe it's better if we do this in person.'

That meant it was big and potentially messy. She felt herself tense, then tried to think of the best place to meet. She didn't want Tillman at her house. As much as possible, she tried to avoid being seen with him, especially now. She'd worked her ass off to land the new job. The last thing she needed was questions being asked about her judgement when she'd barely got her feet under the desk. She said, 'I thought all of this shit was sorted.'

'It was a sticking plaster, that's all. I always told you that.' Tillman was on edge. She could hear it in his voice. 'And now I find out that Travis is back working cold cases. Have you got any idea how fucking dumb that is?'

'The Louise Mason case is dead.'

'And I guarantee you that, by bringing Travis back in from the cold, it's not going to stay that way for long.'

'I vetted the cold cases we gave him.'

'You just don't get it, do you? Travis isn't some asshole. He's smart. He knows what he's doing. And you've just given him access to the system.'

She felt a shiver of panic.

'I told you from the start. What we did that night with Axel, it was just to stem the flow. Sooner or later, this was going to come back and bite us on the ass. Axel is a big problem. He's always been a problem.'

She closed her eyes. She'd known this day was coming — Tillman himself had warned her the last time they'd met in person, on the bench at the end of Pier 15. But even though she'd asked for a delay that time, and Tillman had honoured it, she knew there could be no delay this time. It was inevitable.

When she opened her eyes again, in the window of the cab she briefly glimpsed a reflection of herself, phone to her ear. Except for her hair, she looked colourless, like a wraith, a pale, tortured soul, tethered to nothing.

No person. No home.

No family.

'You think Travis knows about me?' she asked.

'No.'

'You think he knows who you are? Your details?'

'No, definitely not.'

'How can you be so confident?'

'Because I switched identities after the fundraiser.'

She glanced at the cab driver, suddenly aware that he would be able to hear her side of the conversation. She lowered her voice and said, 'You never told me that. You switched the night of the fundraiser? Why?'

'Why do you think?'

It was a stupid question.

They both knew what had happened that night.

'The name "Nick Tillman" was confined to the trash the minute your precious Axel entered the picture.' A damning silence, loaded with the weight of the last six months. 'Axel is responsible. Axel is the reason we're still running around, months down the line, trying to plug holes in the hull of this sinking ship. Axel is the issue here.'

She looked ahead of her, through the windshield of the cab, into the darkness of the Holland Tunnel.

It was like a mouth about to swallow her up.

'Tillman, I know this has to be done but –'

'Hain,' came the response. 'From now on, you can just call me Hain.'

68

For the next hour, Rebekah told Bowners everything. By the time she was done, the street outside was black and silent, the ferry gone. The police activity had subsided too. From where she was, she could still see some marked cars, but their lightbars were off.

'I'm sorry you had to go through all that,' Bowners said, the nib of her pen making a soft scratch across the pages of a pad. Despite the camera, she'd made notes on pretty much everything Rebekah had told her. 'I mean it,' she added, and looked up. 'I've got kids myself. It must have been hell for you.'

Rebekah just nodded. It had. What else was there left to say? 'Is Hain still on the island?' she asked.

'No,' Bowners responded. 'We don't believe he is.'

Something twisted in Rebekah's gut.

'We believe he may have commandeered a boat.' Bowners held up a hand, seemingly recognizing the reaction. 'It's okay, we'll find him. And until we do, we'll make sure you and your family are protected. I've spoken to detectives at the NYPD and they've posted officers at your home already.'

Cops being posted outside the home in which her girls were sleeping: it would have been barely believable before all of this, something that happened to other people. Now it wasn't even the worst of what she'd been through.

'The names "Lima" and "Hain",' Bowners went on, 'are aliases. "Hain" we haven't managed to trace, although there appear to be some links to the stolen identity of a man called Nick Tillman. The real Tillman's been dead for ten years, so Hain – whatever his real name – was just using it. "Lima", we have a confirmed ID on: he was called Lorenzo Selestino. He was born in Lima, Peru, which is obviously why he chose that particular name. We're still running down some leads, but he had a record – he did five years for assault at Rikers – so our assumption is that "Hain" will have a similar background. He'll have a record. We just need to find it. Of course this whole thing begs the question of why they chose to use aliases, even when they were alone – or thought they were. The obvious answer was to minimize the risk of them being IDed, at any point.'

Bowners looked down at her notes. 'One thing I can't figure out,' she said, 'and I know it's been bothering Frank as well. Why did Lima come to the island by himself to kill you and your brother? We haven't found *any* evidence of Hain on the cameras in Montauk.'

Rebekah shrugged. 'I've no idea.'

'You said when they both returned to the island that night, you got the sense that Hain was in charge?'

'That's what it seemed like, yes.'

'So if he was in charge, why leave everything to Lima?' Bowners wasn't really asking Rebekah. 'It would have been a hell of a lot less risky if Hain had come along as well. You'd definitely never met either man before?'

'No, never.'

'And you never met Louise Mason either. Is that correct?'

'Not in the flesh, no.'

'So your only knowledge of Louise was through Johnny?'

'And Kirsty Cohen.'

Bowners wagged her pen at Rebekah. 'Right. Your college friend Kirsty. She played matchmaker for Louise and Johnny?'

'Yes.'

'But Johnny thought Louise wasn't interested?'

'I know he texted her a couple of times after leaving her at the fundraiser, maybe called as well, but never got a response. He didn't talk much about it.'

'About Louise? Was that unusual?'

'Not at all. Johnny kept things pretty close to his chest when it came to relationships. He didn't like to talk about them until he knew for sure it was real, and that the woman was genuinely interested.' Rebekah thought of the confession her brother had made to her the night after the incident in London. 'Johnny was always scared of being hurt. I *do* think he liked her, though.'

There was a brief, funereal quiet. He liked her, she seemed to like him, and in any other life they might have ended up together. But not in this one.

Travis shuffled forward in the booth.

'Okay, here's what I know about the night Louise vanished,' he said, a notebook out in front of him now. Every inch of it was crammed with scribbles in the margins, diagrams, phone numbers. 'On September twenty-third last year, she went with your brother to a fundraiser at the Royal Union Hotel in the East Village. It was for the children's charity One Life, Second Chance. Louise was one of its patrons and had offered to paint someone's portrait as part of an auction they were doing. Anyway, Johnny gets a call from the hospital about your friend Noella having appendicitis just as the two of them are arriving at the hotel, so he drops Louise at the fundraiser – makes sure she gets into the event okay – then heads back to Brooklyn. She goes inside . . .' Travis stopped: a flicker, a long breath. 'By the end of the night, she's vanished.'

'No one remembered seeing her?' Rebekah asked.

'Plenty of people remembered seeing her at the actual event, but no one remembered seeing her leave. Best I ever got was a possible sighting of her in the hotel bar.' He went to the back of his notebook, where there was a pouch, bulging with more paper. Snapping off a band, he pulled everything out. Most of the paper was folded, including a glossy printout, fuzzy and dark: a still from a surveillance camera. 'That's the hotel bar,' he said, pushing it towards Rebekah. 'The camera is out in the corridor, which doesn't help. But I think this might be her head.' He jabbed a finger at the indistinct top half of a face, obscured by people and the open doors of the bar. 'She's talking to someone.'

Travis's finger moved from Louise to a second face, even more obscured at the edges of the frame. It was a man, white or Hispanic, caught in the middle of a wide smile. She could see the vague profile of his face but, beyond that, it was impossible to be sure about anything else: the shot was zoomed in, blurry.

'Do you know who that is?' Rebekah asked.

'It could be Hain.'

Rebekah leaned in closer to the picture.

'Or it could be Lima.' Travis selected another piece of folded paper, opened it out, and set it in front of her. 'These are the best two shots we've got of the bar in the time before Louise disappeared,' he said, and pushed over the second.

It was another still from the same camera in the same part of the hotel. This one was showing more of the foyer, the bar only visible at the left edge of the frame. The camera must have been on a rotation. Elsewhere, guests milled around, or waited in line at the front desk, or spilled through the lobby doors.

The shot was bleached, the resolution mediocre, grainy.

Rebekah's gaze went to the left of the frame.

It took her a second to work out what had caught her attention but then it pulled into focus: a group of men were just inside the door of the bar – five of them, possibly more – a tangle of arms and legs. One had his hand on the door, holding it open, as if he were getting ready to leave. It was impossible to see who he was because, apart from the sleeve of a jacket, he was behind the partly open door; it was also impossible to make out the rest of the men, certainly as individuals, because their tuxedos and dark suits merged into one homogenous blob, or parts of them were cut off by the framing. All Rebekah could clearly see were two faces: a waiter in the foreground . . .

. . . and someone else.

She glanced up at Travis. 'Who's that?'

She pointed to a man in the group. The distance between him and the camera had resulted in a faint blurring of his features. Rebekah could tell he was white, his hair was black or a very dark brown, and he was one of the tallest of the men. He'd worn a grey suit, white shirt and black tie to the fundraiser. His eyes were just blotches, dark spots obscured by the lighting in the bar.

Travis leaned in. 'I'm not sure. There was no way to get a definitive idea of who was in the hotel that night because, although I had all the names from the fundraiser's RSVP list, the hotel bar is open to the public. Anyone here could have wandered in off the street.' He swivelled his head slightly, trying to get a better view of the man. 'Why? Do you think you might know him?'

Bowners used a finger to drag in the original surveillance shot from the bar – of what Travis believed was Louise, talking to little more than a nose, a mouth and a wide smile – and turned it so Rebekah could compare the two pictures, side by side. 'Take your time,' she said calmly.

But she wasn't calm, Rebekah could tell.

'I don't know if I . . .' Rebekah stopped. 'I don't think I know him.'

But then she looked at the man's face again.

Or do I?

She dragged the picture even closer.

She stared at his face some more.

And that was when it hit her like a train.

Before

After she got dressed, Rebekah came out of the bathroom to find him making the bed. He had his back to her, leaning over the mattress, dressed in a white vest and grey tracksuit pants. He didn't notice her to start with. For a moment, she stood in the doorway, uncertain what to do. She looked around at his place: it was nice, homely, photographs on the walls of old New York, the smell of coffee and bacon coming from the kitchen on their left, the living room, through a doorway ahead of them, flooded by early-morning sun. Behind the bed was a wall of red brick with an autographed soccer shirt, the name HENRY printed above a number 14, mounted on the wall in a frame.

'You like football?'

He turned, surprised to find Rebekah there, and then his gaze followed hers to the frame. 'Oh.' He smiled. 'Yeah, big fan. Thierry was my hero.'

She nodded, didn't know what else to say.

She thought again how good-looking he was. She was thirty-nine, and he was at least fifteen years older, his hair and stubble flecked grey, but he looked good on it. He was fit, his body strong. He took care of himself.

'Listen,' he said, 'I'm really sorry again about . . .' He faded out. *About all of this: last night, getting so drunk we don't remember anything, even each other's names.* 'Maybe we should have a do-over,' he added, smiling yet again, reaching out a hand to her, clearly hoping she would take it. 'Hello, I'm Daniel.'

She hesitated for a moment.

But then she put her hand into his.

'Hello,' she said. 'I'm Rebekah.'

They stared at each other, unable to come up with anything else to fill the gap. And then he laughed sheepishly, and she did too, and it seemed to clear the air.

'I feel I need to be honest with you,' he said, and dread welled in her. 'I *do* have someone else in my life, as I guess you do too?'

She grimaced. 'It's a bit more complicated than that.'

'Okay,' he said, and she appreciated that he didn't ask a follow-up. She didn't want to have to explain. 'I meant what I said earlier, though. I don't do stuff like this normally. It's not who I am. She and I . . . I don't know . . . I guess we're in a weird place at the moment, but that's not any kind of excuse. I didn't go out looking for this last night, I promise you. I wouldn't ever do that.'

For some reason, even though she knew barely anything about him but his name, she believed him. He seemed so sincere, so serious. She had the sudden compulsion to tell him about Gareth, about their split, because *in a weird place at the moment* was exactly the definition of their relationship too: they were split up, she was still hurting from his infidelity, but they'd reached an equilibrium where they didn't talk about getting back together, but didn't fight any more and weren't looking to move things on.

What was that, other than weird?

'I don't think I'm going to tell her about this,' Daniel admitted, his eyes creasing, as if the admission hurt him somehow.

She didn't know what to say to that because she didn't know which was better: admitting it or concealing it. She felt more comfortable with the second one, concealing it, burying it, but it would be a decision wreathed with aftershocks. She knew what type of person she was, so she knew already that every time she'd start to make some kind of peace with what had happened here – or as close to peace as she could get – a tremor would hit her. It was just how she was built. So she shook her head and said, 'No, I won't either. It's just too . . .' She couldn't think of anything to define her

situation other than the same word: *complicated*. It was so prosaic –
but it summed it up perfectly.

He smiled, trying to lift the moment, and a clumsy, inelegant
silence settled between them. They just looked at each other,
unsure what else to say.

'Well, I think I'd better be going, Daniel,' Rebekah said.

'You remember the movie *Beverly Hills Cop*?'

She frowned, thrown by the change of direction.

'Don't worry,' he said, holding up a hand, 'there's a point to this.
What I mean is, that film, it was *huge* when I was at high school in
the eighties. I was a teenager, and I thought I was so cool, and what
was even cooler was that, not only could my friends and I quote all
the best lines Eddie Murphy had, I actually shared the same surname as the character he played.'

She still didn't get it. So what?

He saw her confusion and shook his head in apology. 'Sorry.
What I was just trying to say, very inelegantly, was that my name's
Daniel Foley if, down the line, things get . . . less complicated.'

He was saying he liked her.

And he wanted to get to know her.

She looked at him, how handsome he was, how polite and awkward he could be, how self-deprecating and apologetic, and she felt
a momentary buzz.

There was something about him she liked too.

But then she shook the whole idea from her head. Her life was
already a mess. This would just make it worse. She needed things
to calm, not escalate.

'Okay,' she said.

'Okay,' he repeated, seemingly relieved she hadn't balked and
run for the door. He smiled again: it was a nice smile. 'Well, you
know where I live now.'

She nodded.

'And you know my name.'

'I do,' she said. 'Mr Daniel Foley.'

'Axel Foley,' he responded.

'What?'

'That was the name of Eddie Murphy's character in *Beverly Hills Cop*,' he said, 'so that's what everyone started calling me. It's what friends call me.'

Rebekah just nodded again.

'I'm not Daniel to most people,' he said. 'I'm Axel.'

The Back Seat

Six months ago

The parking garage was quiet.

That was one piece of good luck.

Hain exited the elevator and started looking for the Lexus. He found it quickly, its hood longer than the cars either side of it, the front end nosing out, like an animal breaking from cover. He checked around him again, making sure that no one else was on this level, then hurried down the angle of the ramp. As he walked, he started going over the back story he'd already invented for the man called Stewart Laurence Hain. His time as Nick Tillman was done. That ID was finished. It had been finished the second Axel called him and told him what had happened. Tillman, however careful he'd been, was a trail that could eventually lead back to this moment. Hain wasn't. Hain was brand new, an alias that was a complete dead end.

The front seat of the Lexus came into view.

Axel was on the driver's side, his hands on the wheel, shirt unbuttoned at the top and black tie removed. Their eyes met through the windshield.

Under Hain's gaze, Axel shrivelled.

Hain picked up the pace, his attention switching to the rest of the garage, searching for signs of people exiting the elevator, arriving, on phones, smoking in corners. He was still in the clear. When he got within sight of the Lexus, Axel buzzed down the window, but Hain didn't wait: he yanked the driver's side door open.

'Get out,' he hissed.

'Thanks for coming —'

'Get the fuck out.'

Axel did exactly as he was asked.

'Button up your shirt and put on your tie.'

As Axel followed his instructions, Hain took yet another look around the garage. 'Did anyone see you down here?'

Axel shook his head. 'No.'

'Are you sure?'

'Positive.'

Hain glanced inside the Lexus.

'What am I going to do?' Axel asked.

'Lower your voice.'

'What am I going to do?' he repeated, a whisper this time.

'You're not going to do anything.'

Axel frowned. 'What do you mean?'

Hain ripped his eyes away from the Lexus, then turned to Axel, his face burning with rage. He wanted to break this prick in half, choke him, beat him. Instead, he took a breath, and said, 'I mean, you're not going to do anything. You're going to go upstairs and act like nothing ever happened.'

They stared at each other.

Hain frowned. 'What? That's a stretch for you?'

'No, I just . . .'

'You just what?'

'I just don't know what to say to everyone.'

Hain gave Axel a long, withering look. 'Are you shitting me?'

'No, I —'

'You're the biggest fucking liar I ever met in my life. You lie to people all the time. It's what you do. It's who you are. So think of this as just another piece of ass and I'm sure you'll be able to come up with something credible.'

'Okay,' Axel muttered again, belittled.

'People need to believe everything is normal. You need to go up there and be Axel, or Daniel, or whatever the fuck you're calling yourself tonight.'

'I know.'

'So look normal.'

Axel straightened his clothes. His hair.

'If you're not convincing,' Hain said, 'you screw us both.'

Axel didn't respond.

Hain took a step closer. 'You understand?'

Axel nodded.

Hain grabbed hold of his neck. 'You don't look like you're listening to me.'
He was speaking through his teeth, spitting the words into Axel's face. 'I'm not
going down for this, you hear me?'

Axel tried to nod again but couldn't move his head.

'You hear me?'

'I hear you,' he wheezed.

Hain held him there for a moment, against the car, digging his nails into
Axel's throat. And then, finally, he released his grip and stepped away.

He looked inside the Lexus again.

Louise Mason's dead eyes stared back.

8
Freedom

69

In the late evening of Friday, 1 April, six months after the disappearance of Louise Mason, and twelve hours after Frank Travis took a ferry across to Crow Island and found out that Rebekah was still alive, a body was found in Fort Washington Park, beneath the George Washington Bridge. The victim – a white male, in his mid-fifties – had apparently committed suicide, scaling the barrier at the edge of the bridge, then jumping two hundred feet to his death.

The man's name was Daniel Foley.

Axel, to his friends.

He was unmarried, his parents had died when he was in his twenties, he had no siblings and appeared not to have been in a relationship with anyone at the time of his death. But Foley wasn't a recluse. In fact, the opposite. Within hours, detectives at the 33rd Precinct were able very quickly to paint a picture of who he was, not least via Foley's colleagues at Retrigram, the social-media giant, where he'd worked for two decades in publicity and had been a hugely popular member of staff. He was called 'kind', and 'generous', with a 'fantastic sense of humour', and despite fairly modest academic qualifications – a business degree from Staten Island College, which he'd completed in his mid-twenties after originally dropping out of high school – they said he was very often the smartest guy in the room. Almost universally, the people who'd known Daniel 'Axel' Foley, from school friends he'd kept in touch with, to the people at Retrigram, described feeling shocked at the news. One said, 'If I was asked to name a person *less* likely to commit suicide, I couldn't think of one. Axel was never anxious, never despondent; he didn't have low self-esteem, he was never tearful, didn't lack energy. He hadn't lost weight, he never talked about his sleep being disturbed ... I mean, all the things I know about depression, he didn't suffer from. I can't think of one reason why he'd jump.'

Yet he had.

So, the next day, the cops at the 33rd started pursuing the idea that Foley might have been pushed. If it was a murder, it might better explain why he'd done something so apparently out of character, so drastic.

But they couldn't find any evidence of anyone having shadowed Foley to the suicide spot.

Traffic cameras around the bridge showed him walking west on 178th Street, and taking the south walk on Haven Avenue, a spiral of concrete that corkscrewed around to the eight-lane upper level. From there, he went most of the way to the first suspension tower. In the minutes afterwards, no other pedestrians exited the same way as Foley had gone in, and none went west to New Jersey, so no one was on the bridge with him at the time. When detectives rolled on footage from the rest of the night, using three cameras at three separate points, all they found were new angles on the same thing: Daniel Foley leaping to his death.

It was one hundred per cent a suicide.

They just didn't understand why he'd done it.

But then, twenty-four hours on from Foley's death, late on 2 April, a cop from Suffolk County PD named Bowners changed the direction of the case when she met with detectives at the 33rd Precinct and told them she might have something – or, more specifically, some*one*.

Her name was Rebekah.

70

Later, Travis told Rebekah everything about Daniel Foley, about the search for answers in his suicide, but for a while that night – after she'd IDed Foley in the picture from the hotel – Rebekah had been left to her own thoughts.

Travis and Bowners had exited the general store, and she'd remained behind with Roxie, stroking her, confused, hurt and embarrassed by having to recount the night she'd slept with Foley.

The man responsible for Louise Mason going missing.

Maybe the man responsible for all of this.

In her time on the island, even as she'd pinned the name *Daniel* to the corridors of the hostel, she'd never seriously entertained the idea that all of this was to do with him, partly because other theories – and other suspects – seemed more compelling. Anonymous sex with a stranger seemed so low down the list of motives for wanting a person dead, it barely even registered, and it still didn't make total sense, even now. It had been a one-night stand. There was no mystery to it. Foley had lied to her about being in a relationship, but people did that all the time. It was just that the lie was normally about *not* being in a relationship.

On the drive back to New York, Travis attempted to help her make sense of things, but it was hard because he didn't yet have a full picture himself, and the closer they got to home, the more panicked Rebekah felt. She was desperately tired, she was physically and emotionally bruised, but mostly she was unexpectedly fearful about seeing her girls. She'd lost so much weight, had a big new scar on her face, and her hair was shorter than it had been at any point since they were born. What if they didn't recognize her when she walked through the door? What if they wanted to be with Gareth, not her?

By the time they exited the interstate in Brooklyn, she could hardly think straight. Roxie was moving around on the back seat, pressing her nose to the glass as the city whipped past, uncertain where they were or where they would end up. Beside Rebekah, Travis didn't say anything for a while, and then started trying to reassure her: 'It's going to be okay, kiddo, I promise.'

They pulled up at the brownstone.

There was a uniformed cop outside.

Rebekah looked at the living-room windows, saw the curtains twitch, and then Noella peered out. Their eyes met. The second Noe started waving excitedly, Rebekah welled up. Travis put a hand on her arm and then Noe was hurrying out of the front door. A second later, Gareth followed, Chloe in his arms, half asleep. And then, finally, hesitant and using her dad's leg for cover, Kyra appeared. Through the glass, Rebekah heard her say, 'Look, Daddy, there's a doggie in the car,' and she pointed to Roxie.

The cop moved aside as he saw what was about to happen, nodding at Rebekah as she got out. Rebekah wiped her eyes with the sleeve of the sweater that Bowners and Suffolk County PD had issued her, and then Noe broke from the group, sprinting towards her.

She launched into a hug. 'Never do that again,' she said, into the side of Rebekah's face, Rebekah hugging back hard. When she broke off and looked at the house again, Gareth and the girls had come all the way down the steps, Chloe now fully asleep on her father's shoulder.

Gareth smiled apologetically. 'Sorry. I tried to keep her up.'

He leaned in and hugged her and, as he did, Rebekah put her mouth against the top of Chloe's head, her nose, her cheek, breathing in her daughter. She kissed her – over and over again – and touched a hand gently to Chloe's face. Her daughter's skin felt so soft and Rebekah's fingers were so marked now, so bruised and damaged, that she worried she might hurt Chloe somehow. But she kept on sleeping soundly.

'Hello, Mommy.'

Rebekah looked down at Kyra. She'd been gently encouraged to come forward by Gareth, had maybe even been told what to say. Rebekah dropped to her knees on the sidewalk, so that she was on the same level as Ky. She'd grown so much in five months.

'Hello, sweetheart. Do you remember me?'

She nodded once.

'You haven't forgotten your mummy?'

'What's that?' Kyra pointed a tiny finger at the scar on the side of Rebekah's face. 'Were you in a fight?'

'No,' Rebekah said. 'I just had an accident.'

'Does it hurt?'

'Not any more.'

Her daughter's eyes went to the car.

'Is that your doggie?' she asked.

'No. I'm just looking after her.'

'What's her name?'

'Roxie.'

Kyra started to giggle. 'That's a funny name.'

'She's a funny dog.'

And then they looked at each other again, and Rebekah said to Kyra, 'You'll never know how much I missed you.'

And she brought her daughter into her arms and she didn't let go.

71

The reason for Daniel Foley's suicide became apparent once Rebekah had IDed him. Bowners, who was soon jointly working the case with detectives from New York, handed the two security-camera shots from the hotel to the NYPD lab in Queens. Using facial-recognition software, technicians were able to prove that the man Rebekah had identified, and the man who was talking to Louise in the bar, were the same person. To make sure, techs then used a photo of Daniel Foley, provided by his colleagues at Retrigram, to compare with the man in the hotel bar. It was a match.

Foley was the person talking to Louise.

Rebekah found out all of that from Travis, who in turn had been given the information by Bowners. He asked Rebekah to keep it between them, because he knew Bowners wouldn't approve, but it was clear Travis was struggling in the same way, shackled to unanswered questions. It was one of the reasons why, thirty-six hours after arriving back in Brooklyn – her second day at home – he returned to see her once again.

Roxie greeted him at the door, barking and pawing at him, and as he bent and played with her, Rebekah realized, for the first time, that she was going to keep the dog. There was no question now. Roxie belonged here. She'd take care of the paperwork once this was over.

Whenever that is.

Earlier, sitting at the windows watching the sun rise, she'd had the wistful idea that she just had to accept her freedom for it to be true. Now it seemed obvious she was kidding herself.

Until Hain was caught, she was confined to the house.

Rebekah set the girls up in the living room with a couple of episodes of *Dora the Explorer*, then she and Travis moved through to the kitchen.

'Is there any news on the email Gareth sent Stelzik?' she asked, keeping her voice down, even though Gareth was at work and she doubted either of the girls could hear. She just needed to know.

'I asked Bowners and she says one of their technicians traced it to an IP address in California.'

Rebekah frowned. 'California?'

'The IP address belongs to a —' he checked his notebook '— VPN. You know what that is? I didn't until last night. It's a Virtual Private Network. So, basically a wall that shields your real location and your IP address.'

'So we don't know if it was Gareth or not?'

'Do you think it's likely he would use a VPN?'

She thought about it: it was possible, but it suggested a level of caution and forethought that he'd failed to show when he'd dropped his phone in the car and left her access to his 'Willard Hodges' emails.

It wasn't Gareth, it was someone else.

She felt an intense flood of relief that she and the girls weren't unsafe in the house with Gareth, that she *did* know him, that her ex-husband *was* still the same man she'd left behind, for better or worse. She looked at Travis and, not for the first time, felt drawn to him: it was like, even after a short time together, they understood each other, without having to say a word.

Travis didn't think Gareth had sent the email either.

But there was still the question of why the message had been sent to Stelzik in the first place.

'If we're to assume Hain and Lima had access to *your* emails and phone activity,' Travis said, 'I think it's fair to assume they had access to Gareth's as well, including the email address he was using for his affair. My guess, though we'll have to wait on confirmation of this, is that they sent that email to muddy the waters. In a way, it's clever because it's the type of lead that looks big, that will have you wasting days and weeks trying to chase it down, and by the time you realize it's a dead end, you've given them the time they needed to patch up leaks elsewhere. It's a tactic Hain's employed before. You remember I told you about that anonymous call I got, telling me to look at your brother again?'

Rebekah said she did, but she was more drawn to something in Travis's face, a kind of sadness that had lodged there after he'd mentioned the anonymous caller. She lowered her head slightly. 'Are you okay, Frank?'

'Yeah,' he said, rubbing his chin. 'I just got a question I need to figure out, and I don't know if I really want the answer.'

'We can talk about it, if you like.'

'Thanks, kiddo,' he replied, and smiled at her. 'Maybe later.'

She nodded, not wanting to press him, but it was clear that it was to do with the anonymous call. Eventually they circled back to Bowners.

'She's running with the idea that Foley murdered Louise the night of the fundraiser,' he told her, after she'd made them both some fresh coffee, 'or at least shortly afterwards. It seems unlikely, given everything we know about him, that it was a deliberate, pre-meditated act. If he was that kind of killer, if it was in his make-up, I suspect you wouldn't have walked away from him alive the morning after you . . .' Travis trailed off. It was clear he knew how much it hurt Rebekah to recall what she'd done with Foley. 'Anyway, that type of guy, single, attractive, successful, it's very likely he had his fair share of women, maybe even believed he was irresistible to them. That would certainly explain Louise: she was going out with Johnny and she didn't sleep around, but she was friendly, person-able, and she was beautiful. Maybe Foley read the signals wrong, maybe he tried to force something that wasn't there, maybe she didn't like it, and then . . .'

Rebekah could fill in the rest.

But something didn't make sense. 'Thing is,' Rebekah said, 'he *did* try to kill me, or at least Lima did, presumably under the instruc-tions of Hain and Foley. Maybe Foley wasn't a killer – but he wanted me dead.'

Travis nodded.

'So why did I have to die? Because I *slept* with the guy?'

He flipped back in his notebook. 'We've found out that your friend Kirsty went to the same high school as Foley. They weren't there at the same time because she was fifteen years younger than him, but he was part of some alumni tutoring programme and spent time there working with students. She got to know him originally through that, and then I'm told Kirsty and her husband became big socialites up and down the east coast and it just happened that they started to move in the same circles as Foley . . .' He looked up at Rebekah.

She could see what he'd left unsaid.

That explains how you came to have sex with him.

'In a way,' Travis went on, 'Kirsty's kind of central to all of this, although unwittingly. She'd got to know Louise through the One Life, Second Chance foundation. Louise was a patron and Kirsty was on the board. She knew you through college and knew Foley through being at the same kinds of social functions down the years. And it was inevitable that she, Louise and Foley would all end up at the fundraiser together, as Retrigram is a big contributor to the foundation. The only person who wasn't there that night was Johnny.'

He paused and Rebekah imagined they were both playing the same film in their heads: Noella not calling Johnny from the hospital, Johnny not having to leave Louise at the fundraiser, and then Foley not being able to get Louise alone.

'Anyway,' Travis continued, 'rewind twelve days from the fundraiser to Saturday, September eleventh, and Kirsty comes back to New York for the weekend. You and your college pals go out and end up at the Zee Club. You said Kirsty suggested going there, and she confirmed as much to Bowners: she knows the owner of the club through some other charity thing. So that's why she and you were there, and the reason Foley was there was because the Zee also happens to be close to the Retrigram offices, so it's a regular hangout for their staff. Kirsty knows Foley, she introduces you both, then . . .' He faded out again.

It still didn't answer her original question, though. Why would Hain and Lima try to *murder* her just because she'd slept with Daniel Foley?

Travis was already talking again: 'Maybe Foley offered to give Louise a ride home, came on to her, things got out of hand, and . . .' He stopped. This was the culmination of a half-year search. These were the answers he'd always sought and yet a part of him didn't want to face them. 'That theory would fit the endgame: six months after he kills Louise, the same day he finds out you're still alive, the guilt, the potential repercussions, it all gets too much for Foley, so he heads to the George Washington Bridge and jumps.'

In the living room, Kyra shouted a number in Spanish.

'Yeah, but still, why did he try and have me killed, Frank?'

Travis glanced at his notebook, with a pained expression. 'Hain and Lima were watching you. They were reading your emails and listening to your calls. It looks like the whole surveillance thing was a result of a conversation that Hain must have had with Foley *after* Louise died, maybe asking Foley if there were any other women in his past who might cause him trouble.'

'And he said me?'

'Correct.'

'Why would I cause him trouble?'

She felt like she was stuck on repeat.

Travis let out an anguished sigh. 'That's what I was getting to,' he said. 'I don't think they were worried about Foley himself being compromised. They were worried about how Foley's actions – the murder of Louise, his sleeping around, then the night with you – compromised the next rung of the ladder.'

Rebekah frowned. 'The next rung of the ladder?'

Travis nodded.

'You mean the person *above* Foley?'

'Right,' he said. 'The person Hain *really* works for.'

A Message

Two days before getting the ferry out to Crow Island, Travis had to go back to Police Plaza for a meeting with Amy Houser about the cold cases she'd given him. He'd found it hard to concentrate on anything except Louise Mason and the Murphys since watching the surveillance video from Montauk harbour, but over the course of six days he'd tried to make some headway on Houser's cases. When he arrived, she was already waiting in the foyer.

'How you doing, Trav?'

'All good, Lieutenant Houser,' he said, although that wasn't the truth: he was feeling unnerved. He hadn't slept properly for almost a week, and could see the missed hours in his face.

'You look tired,' Houser said. 'You been up working these all night?'

'You know me, Ames. No half-measures.'

She took him to a meeting room where they went through the files, one by one. At the end, they decided that there were two with the potential for re-examination.

Afterwards, Houser led Travis back to the Cold Case Squad.

Captain Walker looked up as they entered. She was in a small office in the corner, the blinds up so she could see all the way across the floor. As soon as she spotted Travis, she got up from her desk and wandered over to him.

'Mr Travis,' she said.

He noted the use of 'Mr', not 'Detective', even though it was technically correct: he wouldn't have minded, but she made it sound like a putdown.

'Captain,' he replied.

Walker just stood there as Houser started going through the drawers of the filing cabinets, pulling out new folders for Travis to work on. Walker was making him uncomfortable, but either didn't know it or didn't care. When he glanced at her, he thought she looked stressed too: her hair, a striking red, had begun escaping from a bun; her skin was sallow.

'What part of England are you from?' Travis asked.

She frowned. It was possible she wasn't capable of polite conversation. More likely, she was wondering what she lost by telling him. She struck him as the type of person who didn't like to share details of her private life, which was part of the reason that Travis did it. For some reason, the 'Mr' had annoyed him, as well as her standing there and watching him, as if he were unwelcome and untrustworthy, and had to be monitored.

'I'm not,' she said eventually.

'Oh, I thought someone said you were English –'

'Well, whoever told you that was wrong.'

Houser slammed one of the cabinets closed and brought back a bunch more files.

Just as she put them on her desk, Walker said, 'Well, it was good to see you again, Mr Travis. I'll catch up with Amy later and see what you've brought us.' She framed that last part like an insult, headed back to her office, closed the door and dropped the blinds.

'I didn't know human beings could maintain a body temperature of absolute zero,' *Travis muttered to Houser, who burst out laughing. They both looked to the office again, just in case Walker was watching.*

'I'll admit,' *Houser said, 'she takes a while to warm up.'*

'So do glaciers.'

Houser tapped the files. 'I've got a couple more to add to this pile,' she said, 'but one of the detectives down on Major Crimes worked both of them back in the day, so I asked him to take a quick look at the paperwork for me yesterday – kind of a refresh-the-memory thing – to see if he recalled anything that didn't make it onto the page. It's a long shot, but you never know. If you wait here, I'll just go grab the cases.'

'Sure.'

Houser headed off to the elevators again.

As he waited for her, Travis brought the stack of files towards him and started leafing through the one on the top. It was a murder from March 1999: a cab driver, shot and killed inside his taxi at 5 a.m. as he waited under the elevated tracks on Brighton Beach Avenue. The more pages he turned, though, the more his thoughts began to drift and, pretty soon, all Travis could think about was the ferry in two days' time: what he'd seen on the security cameras, and what he was likely to find when he got to the island.

What if it was just more questions?

The phone on Houser's desk started ringing.

It was external.

He glanced at it, presuming that one of the other members of the squad would pick up. But when it still went unanswered, he looked out and saw that they were all on calls themselves.

He picked up. 'Cold Case Squad.'

'Is Houser around?'

A male voice.

'She's not at her desk at the moment. Can I take a message?'

'Who's this?'

'Uh, my name's Frank Travis.'

There was a long pause. Travis couldn't hear anything on the line at all: no hint of background noise, no people, no traffic, nothing.

Then the man spoke again: 'Travis?'

He frowned. His name had been said in a way that made it sound like the caller might know him. Travis tried to work out if he'd heard the man's voice before somewhere. 'Yeah, that's me,' he said. 'I'm Travis. Who's this?'

The line went dead.

It was only a split second later – as he took the phone away from his ear and stared at the handset – that a prickle of dread crawled across his scalp.

Travis did know him.

He had heard the voice.

It was the same man who'd called his line the previous December, in the last days of Travis's search for Louise Mason. It was the man who'd left the tip about taking a second look at Johnny Murphy. And as he realized that, Travis realized something else: the common factor that connected both of the calls.

The person who'd taken the message in December.

The person whose phone had rung now.

Amy Houser.

72

'There's someone else involved in this?'

Travis nodded. 'Someone with much more to lose.' He paused, a flutter in his face, like a shadow shifting. 'Foley's crime had the potential to expose this person, to compromise them – perhaps professionally – and so did the night *you* spent with Foley. We know why Foley killing Louise would be a problem for this person – a murder is a problem for anyone with something to lose – we just have to figure out why you were such a danger as well. We have to figure out if any other women Foley slept with were targeted in the same way as you. I mean, Foley wasn't married, he had no girl-friend that we know about, so it shouldn't have mattered who he shared a bed with. But it did. It mattered so much that Lima tried to kill you. So there's really three questions here. Why does it matter who Daniel Foley slept with? What makes those women dangerous to the person Hain works for? And *who* is the person he works for?'

Again, there was something in Travis's face, a kind of residual pain laced to the end of that last question, and this time it was so much like looking at her father, at the expression of grief he'd held in the weeks after Mike died, that Rebekah could read Travis like a book. She leaned across the table slightly, closer to him, and said, 'Frank, do you know who this person is?'

He looked up at her and a smile twitched at the corner of his lips. 'Cops I used to work with, they called me the "Sphinx" in interviews because I was so good at not showing emotion. Not any more, I guess.'

'So you *do* know who this person is?'

'I have a suspicion.'

'Who?'

His face creased into a grimace. 'Would you mind if I didn't talk about that for now? I know it's a deeply unsatisfying answer, but I need to make sure that I'm right before I start throwing accusations around.' He glanced through the door, into the living room, watching the girls. 'If I'm right about this, though ... well, it'll break my heart.'

Rebekah tried to work out who Travis might be talking about. Someone he knew? Someone he'd worked with?

Could it be a cop?

Eventually, he pulled his notebook towards him and, turning a couple of pages, slowly began to gather pace again. 'On Foley's Facebook page, someone on Bowners' team found a photograph of him, with some pals, at a restaurant. There's a guy in the background. They think it might be Hain.'

Travis reached into the breast pocket of his shirt.

It was a printout of a photo. Foley was in the foreground, along with five men and three women. There were even more faces behind them, including one obscured slightly by the darkness of the restaurant.

He'd been circled in red pen.

'It's not clear if he's there *with* the group,' Travis said, tapping a finger to the face of the man, 'or whether he just happened to be in the shot, but he doesn't seem to be keen on having his photograph taken either way. That would be exactly the type of behaviour you'd expect from a man who uses an alias, even when he thinks he's alone. Bowners has her team calling all of the people in the picture here to see if any of them can ID Hain.'

'That definitely looks like him,' Rebekah said quietly, remembering the man on the island, his face, the feel of his hands on her throat.

'I think so too,' said Travis.

The only difference was that both times she'd seen him in the flesh Hain had had a shaved head and no facial hair. In the picture with Foley, he had the beginnings of a beard and a thick mop of hair.

'I strongly suspect that Foley and Hain knew each other,' Travis said, 'otherwise this picture is the most outrageous coincidence in the history of policing. And if we're to assume that Hain is the type of guy you bring in to clear up a mess, it's likely he helped Foley make things go away after Louise was murdered. As for you and Johnny, I think it's a pretty safe bet now to suggest that you were the primary objective. They decided to target Johnny simply because you and he were together on the island that day, and maybe also because he'd been around Louise on the night she was killed, had spoken to her, texted her. He was a link to her. To put it crudely, it was a kind of two-for-one. If Johnny was going to be somewhere remote like Crow Island, and *especially* if you two were going to be there together, it was too good a chance to turn down. If you hadn't gone together . . .' He stopped.

Things might have turned out differently.

'You're saying I got Johnny killed.'

'That's not what I'm saying.'

'If I hadn't gone with him –'

'No,' Travis said, more forcefully than Rebekah was expecting. 'None of this is your fault. How could you possibly have known?' He eyed her, making sure she wasn't going to break on him, then, very slowly, picked up where he'd left off. 'Hain is the type of guy who'll like to plan. He wants things running like clockwork. What happened with Louise was the opposite. And when things get disordered like that, you start to feel the pressure. That's why he rushed into the Crow Island plan to kill you. It's why he made that anonymous call to me about Johnny. It's why I believe he sent that email from Gareth's account to Stelzik. With no pressure, you can see what desperate ideas those are. *With* pressure, even smart thinkers like Hain screw up. Whatever his reasons for not being there personally the day Lima tried to kill you, whatever his reasons for not doing it himself, as soon as Lima messed up, Hain was in panic mode.' His eyes went to the Facebook photo. 'Sadly, Lima had no known associates with the name "Hain". Maybe we'll have more luck with these people.'

From the next room, Kyra began singing 'I'm The Map' from

Dora, then tried to get a reluctant Roxie to dance with her. Rebekah watched Travis as he gazed at the girls. There was a distance to his expression that Rebekah had never seen before, as if he was recalling something from his past, something that had shaken loose on hearing Kyra. In that moment, Rebekah realized she'd never asked Travis if he had kids of his own, but it seemed impossible that he didn't. The more she looked at him, the more she recognized the expression flowering on his face: he was caught in a memory, a flicker from history, where his own kids were this age.

'Are you all right, Frank?'

He snapped out of the moment. 'I'm good, kiddo.' He seemed to understand what had sparked the question. 'It's just nice listening to them in there, that's all. Anyway, maybe I should be asking you that question.'

Rebekah shrugged. 'Johnny might still be here if I'd let him go to that island alone.'

'You can't think like that, Rebekah.'

'I know he's not alive,' she said quietly, and forced a smile, sad, painful. 'I *do* know that. I accepted it months ago . . .'

She blinked, didn't want to break down again.

'We'll find Johnny,' Travis said, pushing his coffee cup aside, reaching across the table so that his hands were almost touching hers. 'One way or another, I promise we'll bring your brother home.'

73

After the girls had gone to bed, Rebekah and Gareth ate together. He'd been living in the house for almost the entire time she was on the island, and now he didn't have any other place to go – other than a hotel. He hadn't offered to move out, and she hadn't pushed it. He'd just shifted his things into the spare room.

He had been good to her since she'd got back, thoughtful, attentive, which had made it much easier. She didn't know if that had resulted from him spending such a long time believing she was dead, or if the new job and new hours had given him a different perspective on home and family life – or if all of it was some sort of act, a performance that would eventually wear off. Rebekah hoped it wasn't the latter, and didn't want to think about it too hard for now even if it was, so she embraced every small moment as it arrived – small moments like eating linguine together.

She hadn't told him a lot of what had happened to her. In fact, she hadn't even mentioned Foley's name, let alone the night they'd spent together. She'd tried to confess when they were alone the previous evening – Gareth had seemed more considered and willing to listen – but the words had stuck in her throat. Afterwards, she'd felt like a coward.

But, then, once dinner was over and Gareth had washed the plates, he came through to the living room, to where Rebekah was sitting and reading, and said, 'There's something I need to talk to you about.'

He sat down opposite her, a look on his face she couldn't place.

Was he nervous? 'What's going on?' she asked, putting down the book.

'This is really difficult.'

She eyed him.

'You've got to understand, Bek, I thought you were dead. I thought you were never coming back.' He pushed his lips together. 'And before that, before you even *went* to the island, you and me, we were separated, and had been for months. And I know it was my fault, I know that, but I . . . I just . . . I . . .' He was staring at his feet. 'I don't know what your expectations are.'

'My expectations?'

'For the two of us.'

She frowned. 'You'd better spell it out, Gareth.'

But she knew what was coming. And then she realized that, when he'd heard from her out of the blue for the first time in five months, when she'd told him she was still alive, the hesitation she'd heard in his voice wasn't entirely down to the fact that he'd told the girls Rebekah was dead.

There was another reason.

'I've met someone,' he said.

Before they'd even had a chance to talk about it, Bowners arrived at the house.

Gareth – in a more familiar echo of the man Rebekah had known before the split – saw the opportunity to avoid a difficult conversation, and offered to give them space, near-sprinting out of the door. Bowners must have believed it was a selfless act because she turned to Rebekah and said, 'He really didn't need to leave on my account.' But Rebekah looked at her and said nothing, and it seemed obvious that Bowners saw the embers of unfinished business. 'I'd offer to do this in the morning,' she added, 'but I've got to drive back to Long Island tonight.'

'It's fine,' Rebekah said, forcing a smile. 'Being stuck in the house is starting to get to me, that's all.' It wasn't the real explanation for the way she looked, but it wasn't untrue. She hadn't left the house in almost two days. She didn't want to be away from the girls, but being trapped inside felt unnatural and oppressive. In a weird way, there were moments when it felt worse than being on the island, because at least then she'd had the freedom of the car.

'I know it's tough,' Bowners offered.

No, you don't, Rebekah thought cynically, then pushed aside the animosity. It wasn't Bowners' fault. Until Hain was caught, all she was doing was trying to protect them all. 'Any news on Hain?' she asked.

'Not at the moment.'

'Do you even know who he actually is yet?'

'No, not yet – but we're making progress.'

Her reassurances were starting to carry less weight: Rebekah had been back nearly forty-eight hours but didn't feel any safer. If anything, she felt less relaxed than ever. It didn't matter that she had cops outside her home, or that – thanks to blurry Facebook photos of Hain – the net might be closing.

Hain still hadn't been captured.

He hadn't even been IDed.

They went through to the kitchen, and while Rebekah filled the kettle, Bowners checked in with the patrol officer on the back porch. She'd already done the same with the one out front. There were six officers in total, working eight-hour shifts in pairs, and the next changeover was in fifteen minutes, at 10 p.m., when Rebekah's favourite, Henriks, a silver-haired officer in his fifties, arrived. He had the calm reassurance she'd needed on her return to the city. The officers had a key to the basement, which had access doors at the front and back of the house, so whenever they turned up, they'd use the doors to move from one side of the brownstone to the other.

'I won't take up much of your time,' Bowners said, and came back into the kitchen, closing the door. 'There's just a few things I need to run by you.'

Rebekah finished making them some tea.

Bowners continued: 'I saw Frank this afternoon. We got talking about the case, and then about a whole bunch of other stuff.'

'Okay.'

'He was telling me about this nightmare you get.'

Rebekah sat down, failing to keep the surprise out of her face. She'd told Frank about it on the drive back from Montauk, the sheer terror she felt every time it returned. She'd described everything, from the tan carpets and cream walls, to the way Roxie had begun to infect the dream more recently. She told him about the way the *7*, of the *127* on the apartment door, was always askew, and how she'd always think, *Seven is meant to be a lucky number.* And, finally, she'd told him about the inside of the apartment, the way music would start playing and her feet would sink into the carpet. She told Travis about how she'd be pinned to the spot, as someone behind her – a voice, neither male nor female – said to her, *I think you should stay, Rebekah.*

She shivered as she replayed it.

'Why are you asking me about a dream?'

Bowners opened a folder that she'd brought with her.

Inside were some photographs. She started to spread them across the table and it took a second for Rebekah to register what they were of – and then, as she did, it was like someone had grabbed her by the throat.

'Because I don't think it's a dream,' Bowners said.

Rebekah couldn't breathe.

She felt paralysed.

'I think it's a memory.'

74

Bowners spread out the pictures: the mezzanine level, where an office had been set up; the black and chrome kitchen; the living room with its widescreen view of the city; and then the bedroom – bed, nightstands, walk-in wardrobes and a shower room. The fine detail had never made it into her dream – *her nightmare* – but she knew it was the same place, that Bowners was right.

This was the apartment that had haunted her.

'Where is it?' Rebekah asked, her voice unsteady.

'It belongs to the social-media company, Retrigram,' Bowners said.

Retrigram. The company Daniel Foley had worked for.

Rebekah swallowed her nausea.

'It's a penthouse apartment they own on Columbus Circle, over-looking Central Park. They clear it for events. When it's not being utilized for that, staff are allowed to book it for one-night stays at a subsidized rate. Daniel Foley worked at the company for a long time. What you might *not* know is that, for a three-year period, until December last year, he owned an apartment on the eleventh floor of the same building – the next one down from this one. This was *127*. His was *118*.' She stopped again, waiting for Rebekah to put it all together.

She already had.

'The morning after you two had sex,' Bowners said, not sugar-coating it, like Frank Travis had, 'we believe you woke up in his *actual* apartment. But the night before, after you left the nightclub, he brought you back to *this* place.'

She pointed at the photos of *127*.

I think you should stay, Rebekah.

'Why would he do that?' Rebekah said. She glanced up from the pictures and, this time, caught Bowners looking at her differently.

'Why did he switch apartments midway through the evening?' Bowners responded, her neutrality replaced by something less poised. 'It's speculation at this point, but we think it might have had something to do with the Retrigram apartment having a private elevator. It meant he could get up to the top floor without anyone seeing you together.'

'Why would he care if we were seen together?'

Bowners held up a finger. 'I'm just getting to that.'

Rebekah's eyes returned to the pictures of Apartment 127. Her dream-memory didn't do it justice: the views were incredible, the décor immaculate, the walls of the living room and the bedroom decorated with big, Retrigram-themed oil paintings that looked like Jackson Pollocks.

'Shit,' she said quietly. 'I remember being drunk, but . . .'

How the hell don't I remember him moving me?

'I need to tell you something else,' Bowners said.

The tone of her voice was frightening.

'What is it?' Rebekah asked, but she wasn't even certain she wanted the answer now.

Bowners' eyes went to the pictures. 'It's about the night you spent with Foley.'

'What about it?'

'You said you had a hard time recalling any of it?'

'I was drunk,' Rebekah said, rattled, scared.

'But enough to experience a blackout like you had?'

She stared at Bowners.

It took a second for the implication to land – and then Rebekah felt like she was falling through the floor. 'No,' she muttered. 'No way. No. *No.*'

Oh, please, God, no.

She felt like she needed to puke.

'Do you normally lose time when you drink?'

No, never. Never in my life.

Except for the night I met Foley.

'You're saying that asshole *drugged* me?'

The entire room was dropping away.

'We can't prove it definitively now,' Bowners said, trying her best to sound comforting, 'but we've been speaking to some friends of Foley's, via a Facebook post he made. One said he'd been drunk once and started telling them he'd gotten hold of some "roaches".'

Fuck.

Rohypnol.

'I'm sure you know they're illegal in the States, but not down in Mexico, so it means they're coming across the border all the time . . .' Bowners faded. None of that mattered. 'I'm really sorry. After all you've b–'

'So he raped me?'

Silence.

'That's what you're telling me, right? That piece of shit roofied me and *raped* me.' The word was so abnormal, so malignant, it was hard even to form.

'We can't say for sure after this time –'

'But he did, didn't he?'

Bowners swallowed, but Rebekah could see the answer.

And now, finally, they had the reason.

Not just about why Foley had switched apartments midway through the night. He'd presumably done that because he didn't want her to recall what had happened in *127*. It was an insurance policy in case snatches of information came back to her. If she woke up in his actual bed, it would be in an apartment that bore no resemblance to the one she'd been attacked in, so any memories she had of the assault wouldn't align. It was why he'd felt so comfortable being so honest with her the next morning, even going so far as to give her his actual name. Did that mean a part of him *liked* her? Was that why he'd appeared to be so kind? Was it his messed-up way of apologizing to her? Or was it all just an act, a part of his routine, his MO? She didn't know, but it had worked: she'd thought

Apartment 127 was just a place conjured in her head, and she'd left his apartment liking him, despite herself.

But that was only part of the explanation.

Only part of the story.

Because now they had the reason why Rebekah was targeted, why Hain and whoever he worked for wanted her dead.

Daniel Foley didn't just sleep with women.

He raped them.

Out of Hand

The next morning, Travis was invited to a meeting at One Police Plaza at the request of Bowners. The meeting started at 11.30 a.m. and was still going two hours later. He sat in a conference room with people he barely knew as Bowners, on a video feed from Suffolk County Police HQ, described what she and Travis had talked about the day before: the dream.

As soon as they'd realized that Rebekah's dream was a memory, that Daniel Foley wasn't some harmless ladies' man but a rapist, potentially many times over, Travis had floated the idea to Bowners that maybe he should be the one to tell Rebekah. They had established a relationship, it felt to Travis like she trusted him, and it wasn't arrogant to suggest that it might be better coming from him. But Bowners had shut him down, perhaps understandably: he wasn't a cop any more. At best he was a consultant, at worst just a civilian. So Bowners had gone to the house last night, and on the way back to Long Island she'd called Travis and told him how it had gone: 'She's in shock, as you might expect. She's angry, confused.'

'I'll give her a call.'

'No,' Bowners had said. 'Hold off for now. It's important we don't overload her. I've spoken to someone on the CVAP team and she's going to call Rebekah tonight, then go to the house in the morning.'

The Crime Victim Assistance Program. It was the right thing to do, the correct procedure, and if Travis was still a cop, he would have done exactly the same thing. Even so, he still wanted desperately to talk to Rebekah. He couldn't make any of this better, but he wanted her to know he was around.

'One of the theories we're running with at the moment,' Bowners was saying, her voice bringing him back to the insipidity of the conference room, 'is that Daniel Foley either didn't give Louise enough of the Rohypnol the night he killed her – or she came around much quicker than he'd expected.'

Travis looked at the faces surrounding him.

Some were making notes, some just staring at the image of Bowners on the screen. He turned further in his chair and looked out at the floor. There was no one he knew out there either. Anyone he knew in this building was on the level below, although — as he thought of Amy Houser, of his suspicions about her — he realized that might not be true anymore.

'After that,' Bowners was saying, 'things got out of hand.'

Out of hand.

Three words so insufficient, so utterly inadequate in summing up what had happened to Louise Mason the night she was killed, they were as worthless as no words at all. And even if it had gotten out of hand at the fundraiser, it hadn't gotten out of hand the night Foley raped Rebekah. His actions weren't an accident. They were done lucidly, deliberately, and with pre-meditation.

Travis tuned out the rest of the meeting.

And then he started to think about Amy again. Was she involved in all of this? Did he know her at all? Could he trust her?

At 2 p.m., the meeting finished. Travis took the elevator down to the Cold Case Squad, and as he came out, he almost collided with Captain Walker.

'Mr Travis,' she said.

Mr again, *Travis thought.*

'Captain,' he responded.

'Are you here to see Amy?'

Travis glanced across the floor and saw Houser at her desk, hunched over a keyboard. 'I am,' he said, stepping past Walker.

'Look, uh, Frank, I apologize if I was a little short with you the other day.' Travis stopped as she ground to a halt again. It was obvious that apologies didn't come easily to her. 'When you asked about my accent.'

'Forget it.'

'It's been a stressful initiation.'

'Honestly,' he said. 'It doesn't matter.'

She nodded her thanks.

'New Zealand.'

Travis frowned. 'Pardon me?'

'I was born in New Zealand, not England, and moved here with my family when I was eight. Some words still slip through, I guess — although I can't hear them myself any more.'

They talked politely for a while longer, then Travis headed across the floor to Houser while Walker returned to her office.

'How you doing, Ames?'

Houser startled at the sound of his voice. 'Trav.' She snapped closed a file on her desk. 'Did we have a meeting today?'

'No. I was upstairs on that other thing.'

'Oh.' She nodded. 'Right. The woman on the island.'

'Rebekah.'

Houser nodded again. 'Rebekah. Right.'

They looked at each other for a moment.

'You okay?' Travis asked.

'I'm good,' she said, breaking into a smile. 'Sorry. You just caught me at a bad time. I had my head in a million different things.' She looked at the desk again, and Travis wondered if she was checking to see what she'd left out. His eyes followed hers, pinging between various pieces of paperwork. Nothing immediately registered with him — except, perhaps, for the file she'd closed.

She looked at her watch. 'You wanna take a walk?'

'A walk?' He frowned. 'Around the office?'

She smiled. 'No. I thought we could grab a coffee.'

He looked at her desk again.

At the file she'd closed.

'You're not too busy?'

She glanced at her watch once more, then stood, sliding the file under another and putting both into the top drawer of her desk.

'No,' she said. 'I can always make time for you.'

75

The CVAP advocate was called Cassandra and she sat with Rebekah for an hour as the kids played in the next room. Whenever one wandered through, the conversation would freeze and the two women would chat to the girls as if everything was perfectly normal. Then, after they returned to their toys, things would start up again, and Rebekah would have to go back to that night.

After Cassandra left, it felt like a part of Rebekah had been torn away. She watched the girls through the living-room door, the joy in them, the pristine innocence, and rubbed her eyes, expecting to find tears. But there were none. She hadn't cried since Bowners had told her the truth about that night with Daniel Foley. All she felt was hollow, as if a chasm had been carved inside her, a void she would never be able to fill.

Her eyes fell on a shelf next to the window.

At the end was a snowglobe.

She hauled herself out of the chair, and went to it, picking it up and looking through the glass to the runner inside. A few snowflakes roused. She thought of Johnny, of the day he'd brought it to her, could still see his face as he handed it over. She remembered how he'd told her that the streak of grey under the runner's feet, and the patches of green either side, were meant to represent Central Park. But the grey strip and the finite boundaries of the glass made Rebekah think of somewhere else instead.

The Loop.

Being trapped on Crow Island.

She shook the globe and set it back on the shelf, and as she watched the runner vanish in a tiny white tempest, she thought of her brother again.

I miss you so much, Johnny.
Please come home to me.

Frank Travis didn't turn up at the house that day.

Since her return home, the hours had been long and lonely, even though she had the girls. Noella had popped by two or three times, but both she and Gareth had to go to work and the cops actively discouraged visitation from anyone outside Rebekah's inner circle, or what was left of it, to lower the risk to her.

So she'd begun to look forward to the times when Travis came by, not only for the adult company but because she genuinely liked him. He had a calmness that reminded her of her dad and brought her closer to the memory of him. When Travis was around, it was easy to forget that her entire life had been turned inside out.

She tried calling him on his cellphone before lunch, but it just rang and went to voicemail. She left a message the second time, midway through the afternoon: 'I was just wondering if you were coming around today,' she said, then paused, unsure what else to say. In the short time she'd known him, it was unusual for him not to pick up. He'd told her to call him anytime.

After dinner, she tried again, and when her cell actually *did* ring, it was Gareth telling her he was going to be late.

'Okay,' she said simply.

'I've got this project I need to –'

'It's fine, Gareth.'

They hadn't talked since his dinner-table confession the night before, so he would assume it was about that, but it wasn't. She didn't necessarily blame him for moving on; she even thought a part of her had accepted it would happen before she ever left the island. But she didn't want to get into the practicalities of it now. It felt so utterly trivial. She hadn't spoken to Gareth yet about what Bowners had told her, or about Daniel Foley, and both those things weighed on her far more heavily than what was left of her marriage.

Noella phoned about thirty minutes later. 'Hey, hon,' she said. 'I'm so sorry I haven't called today. Work has been a total friggin' nightmare – not that that's an excuse. But tomorrow's my day off, so I'm coming round first thing in the morning, and I'm staying all day, and you and me are gonna talk, and we're eating all of this cake.'

Rebekah smiled. 'You got me a cake?'

'I *made* you a cake. It might taste like shit.' She was being self-deprecating: Noella was a legendarily good baker. 'Just put on a loose pair of sweatpants.'

At 10 p.m., she was dozing on the couch when her cellphone shattered the silence. She sat up, half asleep, and grabbed the phone off the table, trying to clear her head, hoping it might be Travis. But it was Henriks, the older cop who worked the night shift and stood guard outside her back door. He was letting her know that he and his partner Sanchez had arrived outside.

She got to her feet, wandered through to the kitchen, and opened the door to the yard. Henriks was standing outside, on the steps leading up to the porch, with his phone to his ear. When he saw her, he hung up, slipped his cell into a pouch on his belt, and said, 'Evening, young lady. How are you doing?'

'I'm good.' She forced a smile. 'How are you, Jimmy?'

He'd told her everyone called him 'Jimmy' because of his surname.

'All good,' he said. 'You look tired.'

'I am.'

'Well, why don't you go get some beauty sleep?'

She thanked Henriks and closed the door.

Heading upstairs, she looked through the balustrade to where the girls were sleeping. It felt good to be close to something normal, something perfect and uncorrupted. On the walls beside her there was a cascade of photographs, still including shots of her and Gareth, but many more of the girls. There was the one of her dad, Johnny, Mike and her in the diner, and then individual pictures of Rebekah's father, her brothers, her friends. At the top, on the left, was a shot from Rebekah's college days, a blurred, overexposed image of her and Kirsty. It had been taken on a night just like the one when she'd gone home with Daniel Foley.

For a second, as she thought of the man who'd raped her, all she could hear was her own ragged breathing – but then, slowly, another noise faded in.

A subtle low hum.

She'd never heard it in the house before.

76

Rebekah went downstairs and looked out of the living-room windows at the block. An NYPD car was pulled into the kerb, at the bottom of the steps. It was the same one that Henriks and Sanchez had brought the previous night: it had a dent in the front fender, on the driver's side. Sanchez normally stood guard out front. He wasn't as much fun as Henriks, younger, more stoic, but it was clear he was serious about his job. In the two shifts he'd done already, Rebekah hadn't seen or heard him take as much as a bathroom break.

But tonight Sanchez was nowhere to be seen.

As soon as she noticed that, she noticed something else: the door of the squad car was ajar. Why would they leave it open like that? Even in a low-crime neighbourhood, it was simply asking for trouble. Worse, it was careless, and neither Henriks nor Sanchez was careless.

Rebekah looked towards the kitchen, sliding her cellphone into the pocket of her pants. The noise she'd heard, the subtle hum, was getting louder.

What *was* it?

Roxie wandered into the living room, but Rebekah instantly grabbed her collar and dragged her out again, into the spare bedroom downstairs. 'Just stay there, okay, Rox?' she whispered, closing the door, looking across the living room again. Something was going on. She could feel it, instinctively.

'Jimmy?'

She walked to the entrance to the kitchen.

The back door was also ajar.

Through the gap, she couldn't see Henriks or Sanchez, only darkness. But on the floor, just inside the door, was the source of the noise she'd heard.

An NYPD smartphone.

It was facing up, the screen blinking, the messages coming direct from the 911 operator. Every time an alert landed, asking for officers in the area to respond to an emergency call, the phone would buzz against the floor of the kitchen, shifting a little. Rebekah looked from the phone to the porch.

'Jimmy?'

It was pitch black outside.

'Jimmy?'

She was six feet from the door, next to the light switch for the backyard – fingers already reaching for it – when something gave her pause.

'Jimmy?'

Outside, she could see a hint of grey in the dark now.

'Jimmy, is that you?'

A shape.

A person.

She reached forward and pushed the light switch – and that was when the shape moved. It grew bigger, instantly, forming out of the gloom like an apparition, a second before light erupted across the porch.

She'd been right: it *was* a person.

But it wasn't Henriks or Sanchez.

She backed up, hitting the edge of the counter, stumbling into the table, her legs weak, her body shaking. The table shifted, tilting one of the chairs over. A coffee cup she'd been drinking from earlier rattled and came to a rest.

And then a moan escaped from Rebekah's throat.

Slowly, Hain entered the kitchen.

77

Rebekah looked from Hain to the back door.

The light revealed more than she would ever have chosen to see. Henriks was lying on his front, his head visible in the gap between the door and its frame, his eyes open, an entry wound in his face. Next to him, slumped on the stairs of the porch, was Sanchez: Rebekah could see his eyes too, the blood that had pooled under him forming a ruby lake.

Rebekah thought of the squad car out front, its open door. Had Sanchez dropped everything to come through to the back? Had he heard a struggle? A gunshot?

None of it mattered any more.

They were both dead.

Hain started coming around the table, towards the door that led from the kitchen to the living room. He knew that if he blocked that, there was no way out for her. She could escape into the backyard, but she'd still have to go through the basement to get out onto the street, and he would easily cut her off through the front. Rebekah had told Bowners the night before that she was starting to feel trapped inside the house.

Now she was.

Four days' beard growth, thick enough and dark enough for it to have subtly altered the dimensions and appearance of his face, partly helped cover a plum-coloured bruise on Hain's left cheek. He had cuts all over too – a dark beanie was pulled down, trying to cover some of them – and his gait appeared to be angled left because he was carrying an injury to his right leg from the car crash. On that side, in his hand, was a pistol, a tube attached to the end of it. Rebekah didn't know a lot about guns, but she knew what the tube was.

A silencer.

It was why she hadn't heard any gunshots.

She felt the hairs on the back of her neck stand up – and then a harsh flutter at the base of her throat as her gaze switched to what was on his jacket.

A blue and gold badge. An NYPD detective shield.

'You're a *cop*?'

Hain just looked at her.

Except Hain wasn't even his real name: Bowners and her team had been looking in completely the wrong place for him. They'd been searching for felons, trawling databases for a man matching his description. Bowners said that Lima had done time in Rikers, and it stood to reason that Hain would come from somewhere similar. But he didn't. He wasn't a criminal – or, at least, not one who'd been caught. He was a man tasked with finding them.

The rest saturated her, like a flood.

It was why he always disappeared into the background when photos were about to be taken. It was why the only pictures of him were dark, or out of focus, or he was at the edges of them, impossible to identify. It was why he used an alias, even when he was on his own. Because as long as he remained that way, if anyone *did* come looking for him, as they had been for the last four days – trying to hunt him using the blurred photos he'd left in his wake – he had the perfect disguise to hide behind.

The blue of the uniform.

The gold of the badge.

Rebekah thought of her girls, asleep upstairs, oblivious to every day of Rebekah's last five months, then saw something else out of the corner of her eye. More movement on the porch. More grey in the shadows.

Her blood froze.

Another face formed out of the dark, like Hain's had a minute before. This time, a woman stopped in the doorway.

'Hello, Rebekah,' she said.

The Plan

They were already walking away from Police Plaza, towards the Starbucks on Pearl Street, when Amy Houser told Travis she'd forgotten her cellphone.

'I'll meet you there,' she said, and didn't wait for his response. Travis stopped, watching her hurry back towards the ugly brown building, and then his eyes went from Houser to the thirteen floors of windows. He couldn't see into any of them – but he wondered if someone inside was looking back.

'What have you got yourself into, Amy?' he said quietly.

A few minutes later, she made the call.

'He's arriving now,' she said.

'Okay,' Hain responded. 'You sure you got the guts to do this?'

There was no deference from him now. He still respected her, still owed her, but he was no longer a flunkey she could push around. Clearing up Axel's mess had made certain of that: she needed him more than he needed her.

'I can handle it,' she said.

Travis entered Starbucks and stood at the end of the queue. There were five people ahead of him and the place was packed. He looked up at the menu: Houser would want a flat white with almond milk, and as he thought of that, as he thought of how well he knew Amy, or thought he did, how much he'd always liked her, a spear of pain bloomed under his ribs.

He didn't want her to be involved in this.

He didn't want her to be dirty.

'Just get him to the parking garage,' Hain said.

The line drifted as he spoke, the wind crackling at his end, and she could hear traffic. He was on the move, heading towards her car, as planned. She went over it again: she was going to have to persuade Travis to go with her, get him to believe there was something she needed to show him in the trunk. She'd have to pretend it was to do with Louise Mason or Rebekah Murphy. Whether he would trust her was another thing entirely.

He was on high alert, she could tell.

'Are you there?' Hain said. 'Did you hear what I said?'

She'd almost forgotten about him.

'Of course I heard,' she said, trying to reassert some measure of control. 'I'll do my part. You make sure you do yours.'

She hung up and looked at Travis. He hadn't seen her when he came in. She was partially hidden on one of the stools, her back to him, watching his reflection in the window.

She walked over and joined the queue behind him.

He still didn't notice her.

She wondered what he was thinking about.

Maybe Louise. Maybe Rebekah.

Maybe Amy Houser.

Travis didn't know she was there until she said hello.

When he turned, she was already smiling at him. It was warm today, but while Travis felt a little flushed after the walk in the sunshine, she looked immaculate in a navy-blue pant-suit and white blouse. Her hair, a striking silver-blonde, was tied in a ponytail and it showed off the angles of her face.

He looked at that smile again.

People always said she didn't smile much.

But she always seemed to smile at Travis.

'I didn't see you there, Chief,' Travis said.

Chief of Detectives Katherine McKenzie smiled again. 'Oh, I think you can drop the "Chief" if we're in Starbucks, Frank.'

78

She came further in, looking around the kitchen.

She was tall, elegant, dressed in a black coat that fell all the way to mid-calf. Her silver-blonde hair was clipped away from her face, she wore a dusting of make-up, and her nails were painted blue. She used one to tap out a soft rhythm against the edge of the sink as she passed it. At the kitchen table, she stopped and pulled out a chair, then gestured to the seat next to her.

Rebekah didn't move.

'We've never met,' the woman said. 'I'm Katherine McKenzie.' As they looked at each other, Rebekah vaguely recognized her. But from where? 'Why don't you sit down?' McKenzie said, but again Rebekah didn't.

Instead, she thought, *Could I scream?*

Would the neighbours hear?

Were they even in?

'You've got a look on your face that tells me two things,' McKenzie continued. 'One, you can't quite place me. And, two, you're thinking about doing something stupid. So, look, here's the deal: sit down and, as long as you don't do that something stupid, we can discuss where Johnny is.'

Rebekah's eyes narrowed. Was she playing her?

'You know where my brother is?'

From his position on Rebekah's right, Hain flicked the switch for the outside lights, returning the yard to darkness. As he did, McKenzie sat down, unbuttoning her coat, revealing a black dress with blue trim. 'Truthfully? *I* don't know exactly where your brother is.' She nodded at Hain. 'But he does.'

'And what? He's just going to lead me there?'

Neither of them answered.

Hain wasn't going to lead her anywhere.

He'd come here to kill her.

Rebekah glanced furtively to either side of her, searching for anything she could use as a weapon. But even if she found something, what did she have in her home that could compete with a gun?

'The recognition thing,' McKenzie said. 'That'll be because you probably saw me in a newspaper or on the evening news, talking about police work.'

And that was when Rebekah put it together: McKenzie was a cop too – but much higher up the chain. She remembered seeing her photo. As if she'd second-guessed her, McKenzie said, 'I'm chief of detectives.'

They were all in on this.

Every level.

'Why are you doing this?' Rebekah asked.

Her voice betrayed her.

'This is a nice place,' McKenzie replied, looking around the kitchen as if the question hadn't even registered. 'Me and Axel – Daniel, I guess you knew him as – we shared an apartment back in our twenties that was about the size of this entire kitchen.'

Foley had been this woman's partner.

Another missing piece snapped into place.

'I remember the first thing Axel did was buy himself this big leather recliner,' McKenzie continued, forcing a smile that was flat and inexpressive. 'He could be a selfish prick like that, but I loved him and, back then, I either didn't notice, or I just wilfully ignored the warning signs.'

Her eyes came back to Rebekah.

The warning signs.

'Believe it or not,' she said, 'Axel had a comic's sense of timing.'

'No, he didn't. Your boyfriend was a rapist.'

'He wasn't my boyfriend, sweetheart,' McKenzie responded.

'You think I'd be doing all of this for a guy I was sleeping with? If it was as simple as that, I'd have just got him –' she waved a hand at Hain '– to pull the trigger on Axel the night Louise Mason died. There's no boyfriend, no *husband*, worth this.'

Rebekah frowned. 'Then who was he to you?'

'Let me tell you about some of the people I work with first. They think I'm a lesbian. They call me "The Dyke" behind my back. They do it for two reasons. One is that it's a defence mechanism among a certain category of male officer who can't accept that women aren't barefoot and pregnant at home. They think "lesbian" will hurt me, or degrade me in some way. I mean, that's the calibre of some of the morons I'm dealing with in that place.'

She looked around the kitchen again and her gaze stopped on the shelf next to the window. She was looking at Johnny's snow-globe. For a moment, as absurd as the idea was, it was like she knew how important it was to Rebekah.

'The other reason that people think I'm a lesbian,' she said, 'is because they know nothing about my private life. They see me hiring women and don't see me with men. The reason I hire women is because I trust them more. And the reason people don't know anything about my private life is down to Axel.'

She ripped her eyes away from the snowglobe.

McKenzie's shoulders rose as she sucked in a long, protracted breath. 'You were right about the rapist part. He was very definitely that. But it didn't stop him having this almost comical ability to ruin things. Take Louise Mason. I only got promoted to chief of detectives just under a year ago, so when she died, I'd had my feet under the desk for five months. Five months, and twenty years of trying to get there because I was unlucky enough to be born with a pair of tits. When Louise died, I'd *finally* started building the team around me that I wanted. I'd got rid of all the assholes, the misogynists, the racists, the pieces of shit eating away at the department, like a cancer, so you know what? I turned up at that fundraiser pretty pleased with how things were going. And do you know what Axel was doing at the same time as I was arriving at that party?' McKenzie traced a painted nail along a fine gouge in the kitchen table. 'He was smashing Louise Mason's skull to a pulp.'

Her words were like an earthquake.

It was the first time anyone had admitted the truth, the first time that someone who knew Daniel Foley had confirmed it.

McKenzie seemed to realize as much. 'You may as well know how we got to this point,' she said, the rest of her sentence hanging there between them, unstated but understood: *because when we leave here you'll be dead*. 'So, no,' she continued, 'Axel wasn't my boyfriend. You can always replace the man you're having sex with.'

She looked up from the table.

'But family . . .' She sighed. 'You and I both know that's different.'

Family

'You got family, Frank?'

They were still waiting in a queue for coffee. Travis looked out of the window, wondering where Amy Houser had got to, and then he turned his attention back to Katherine McKenzie. He smiled at her, thought again how attractive she was when she did the same, and said, 'Yeah. I've got two kids. A son and a daughter. Mark, he lives out in LA and does something I don't fully understand with video games. Gaby's in her final year at Midwestern.'

'Chicago?'

'Correct.'

'That's nice,' McKenzie said. 'You see them much?'

He shrugged. 'Not as much as I'd like.'

'Doesn't help that you're working your ass off at the NYPD, even when you're supposed to be retired. How's all that Rebekah Murphy stuff going?'

'Getting there, I think. It's pretty complicated.'

McKenzie nodded.

The queue still didn't move.

'What about you?' Travis said. 'Have you got kids?'

'No,' she said. 'I missed the boat on that.' Travis didn't know how to respond. 'Would have been nice,' she added, as if she thought she'd made him uncomfortable. 'I just never found the right man . . .'

Her eyes stayed on him, flashing briefly in the light from the window, and Travis felt a momentary buzz. It had been so long since he'd found any woman attractive, and they'd appeared to find him attractive in return, that he didn't know what to do. And then, for some reason, he thought about Naomi, all the things she'd said to him over the years, and that was when gravity started to pull at him: McKenzie was chief of detectives; she was

461

probably ten years younger than he was; she was good-looking and industrious. He was old and directionless.

Why would she ever be interested in someone like him?

McKenzie started talking about being married to the job, and maybe sometimes regretting it, and then Travis mentioned Naomi and how it was hard to strike a balance. Eventually, at the front of the queue, Travis offered to pay for McKenzie's drink, but she refused and said his black coffee was the least the NYPD owed him after all he'd done.

When they were waiting at the end of the counter, she smiled at him again, and said, 'You're easy to talk to, Frank, you know that?'

'Are you serious?'

She seemed surprised by the comeback. 'Of course I'm serious. Haven't you heard the rumours? "The Dyke" is physically incapable of opening up.'

Travis grimaced.

'Don't worry,' she said. 'The name doesn't bother me.'

'At all?'

'There are other things to worry about.' The traces of something drifted across her expression. Before Travis could work out what it was, she said, 'Anyway, I meant it. You're easy to talk to.'

'My ex-wife would've disagreed.'

'Well, she's wrong.'

She seemed to mean what she was saying, to enjoy his company, and as he thought of Amy Houser again, for the first time in days his initial thought wasn't about the call he'd picked up at Amy's desk, or his doubts about his friend. Instead it was about what Amy had said to him when they'd come out of the meeting with McKenzie: McKenzie liked Travis.

'Family can be hard sometimes.'

Travis tuned back in. 'I'm sorry?'

'I was just thinking,' McKenzie said. Her eyes were on the windows of the coffee shop, but she wasn't looking at the sidewalk, at the street, at the crosswalks and traffic lights, she was caught somewhere else. It was almost as if she'd let her guard down without knowing it. 'You talking about your ex, about being so far away from your children. Family is hard sometimes.'

Travis studied her. 'Do you have family close by?'

She rocked her head from side to side, like the answer wasn't an easy one. 'Sort of. I grew up in a shitty house in Staten Island. I loved my mom, I truly did, but she had her own problems – mental-health issues, I guess you'd call it these days – and my father was a waste of oxygen.' She blinked a couple of times, and it seemed to break the spell. 'Way to bring the mood down, Katherine. This is what I mean, Frank. You reel people in just by being so damn nice. You must have been a hell of an interviewer.'

'I had my moments,' he said.

'I had a half-brother,' she said finally, her face different this time, Travis unable to quite decipher it. 'That's where I was going with that. He was the product of one of my dad's many affairs – and when his mother died, he came to live with us. My dad refused to adopt him, we never fostered him. In terms of the system, he just kind of fell through the cracks. That wouldn't happen these days – maybe shouldn't have happened back in the seventies, but it did.'

'Are you two close?'

'We were,' she said. 'Very. He was two years older than me, and I'd always wanted a brother. But, I don't know, there was . . . something in him.'

Travis frowned. 'In him?'

'He could be weird. He got into some trouble at school. My dad was a major-league asshole and the two of them went off like fireworks at home. When your father tells you he never wanted you, over and over, that tends to screw you up. So my brother, he started acting out. It began in his teens. He did some stupid things: vandalism, petty theft . . .' She was eyeing Travis as if unsure whether to form into words whatever picture was in her head. 'He used to hurt things sometimes. People. Animals. I remember my father lost his shit one night when he found out next door's cat had crapped in our yard and, the next day, the cat's got a broken leg.'

They just stared at each other.

'He was just trying to please my father,' she said softly, but Travis saw an echo in her face, a hint of doubt perhaps, and he wondered if that was just an excuse. Maybe her brother hadn't hurt that cat to please a father who didn't want him.

Maybe he just liked to hurt things.

Just then, their coffees were put at the end of the counter, and – like a light being switched on – McKenzie broke into a smile. 'Shit, I don't know why I'm saying this.'

Except, for some reason, Travis wasn't sure that was true.

It was like she'd been holding her breath: she'd never been able to tell anyone *about her brother, yet had always wanted to; to her, he was a ghost that needed exorcizing. But now Travis was wondering why she'd chosen this moment to let the breath go. Why, of all people, did she tell him? Why would she let her guard down in front of a guy she barely knew? She'd built an entire career out of never giving an inch. Even if, as she'd said, Travis was easy to talk to, it still felt like something was amiss.*

She looked at the third cup of coffee waiting for them on the bar, the side marked with the name 'Amy', and said, 'You waiting here for Houser?'

'I'm supposed to be.'

McKenzie nodded. 'That's a shame. I wanted to show you something.'

He was thrown by the statement.

'It's in my car,' she said, and looked at her watch.

'Your car?'

'It might be pertinent to what you're working on.'

Travis frowned. 'What do you mean?'

'I'd rather not discuss it here,' she said, looking around.

Did she mean the cold cases that Houser had given him?

Or did she mean Louise Mason?

Or Rebekah, Travis thought, glancing out of the window.

Still no sign of Houser.

'It'll make sense when we get there,' McKenzie assured him.

Intrigued, Travis said, 'Sure, okay. Let's go take a look.'

79

'Axel was my brother,' McKenzie said quietly. 'Maybe not in the way that the law recognizes, but in every way that mattered. A lot of the time, growing up, he was *all* I had.' Her eyes had returned to the snowglobe. 'But Axel, he was . . .' She stopped. 'Uncontrollable.' Then she sniffed, almost shuddered, as if escaping a riptide, and Rebekah remembered something: the morning she woke up in Foley's apartment, he hadn't actually said he was married, he'd said, *I feel I need to be honest . . . I do have someone else in my life. I don't think I'm going to tell her.*

'He was in that hotel bar and he put something in Louise's drink. She looked like she was wasted. He told her he was going to drive her home – not that she was probably in any state to argue – but where he really planned to go was the same place he took you: that Retrigram apartment. The publicity team handled the booking system there – and guess *who* in the publicity team took it upon themselves to be the first point of contact? The role he had over there, it should have been an assistant's job.' She leaned in, elbows on the table. 'But Axel liked to know when that apartment was free.'

McKenzie almost smiled, but there was no joy in it. 'Over the years he's been with a lot of women, but I think, as he got older, they stopped flirting with him as much, and they definitely drew the line at sleeping with him, and that frustration would have built in him, angered him, made a weak man like Axel feel small and rejected. He was . . .' She seemed to be weighing up the right way to say it. 'He was addicted. Sex was maybe the most important thing of all for him. You see a lot of men like that: all they have to contribute to the discourse is their dick.' She closed her hands again, nails pressing into her palms. 'Difference was, Axel wasn't wired right, so when women stopped giving it to him willingly, he didn't just accept it – he got some pills and switched tactics. That way, no one ever said no to him. Younger, older, the type of girl – like you – who wouldn't drop her panties for a stranger, he took them back to that apartment. And the next morning, when they woke up, with no memory of what had happened, there he was, Mr Nice Guy, Mr You Can Trust Me, Mr Isn't It Crazy We Got So Drunk That We Can't Remember Anything. Of course, I never knew he was doing any of this shit until the night he killed Louise. That was when it all came out. That was when we found out it wasn't just one mistake. There were so many he couldn't even remember their names . . .'

Rebekah felt something pulse in her throat. She didn't know if it was anger, or fear, or nausea, or all of them. 'So – what? One day,' she said, her voice little more than a tremor, 'he just decides to become a serial rapist?'

'No,' McKenzie said. 'That side of my brother, that darkness, it existed in him for a long time before then. I saw flashes, on and off, for years. As a cop, the things I saw in him would have set off all sorts of alarms in my head. As a sister, I denied them and pretended not to notice.' Rebekah's mind spun back to something McKenzie had said earlier: *I wilfully ignored the warning signs.* 'Well, maybe that wasn't entirely true. I suppose a part of me always worried that he might screw up my career in some way. That was why I put up a barrier between us early on. He never knew the number of my actual cellphone, just of a burner. He didn't know it was a burner, but it insulated me. I didn't call him, I didn't email him, I tried to limit being seen with him in places I might get recognized. I let him come to my house, but only at night. I told myself that it was fine to be cautious, justified: I was being reasonable in wanting to protect my career. I told myself, "Axel's got issues, and someone could use them to hurt me." But that wasn't the reason I did it, I see that now. That sort of behaviour, it wasn't ordinary precautions. It was above and beyond. I knew what he was capable of. I'd *seen* it growing up – so a part of me was always waiting for it to happen again.'

And then Rebekah's attention switched: Hain had taken a step closer to McKenzie, still silent, but there was something in his face. Was it a message?

'I've wondered a lot in the time since,' she said, appearing not to notice, 'why he didn't just screw these girls in back alleys, or in places where they weren't going to remember his face, his name or where he lived. In a way, I suppose waking up in his apartment, it made women like you less panicky, less likely to talk about what had happened, or report it, because the "blackout drunk" story would make sense. But knowing Axel, knowing the way he was when he didn't have this addiction buzzing in his head, how placid, even tender, he could be sometimes, I think he probably *wanted* there to be more. I think with certain women, like you, after the deed was done – after the buzzing in his head had stopped – he just wanted to feel normal. I think he really did like you in that moment. I think he saw something in you. But he went way too far. That was the problem with Axel. That was why we had no choice but to come after you like we did. He didn't just tell you his *actual* name, he told you his nickname, its origins. He told you his *surname*.'

I think he really did like you, Rebekah.

She thought of her dream, her memory.

I think you should stay, Rebekah.

The whole thing was repellent, but Rebekah hardly had time to process it: Hain had taken another step forward – and, this time, she saw the message.

He was saying, *Stop.*

This isn't a confession.

Except for McKenzie maybe it was. Maybe it was a chance to give voice to all that she'd pushed down about her brother, all the hatred she'd felt for the way his choices had almost derailed her life and career. After all, where else would she be able to admit to what her brother had done – and what she herself had kept secret – other than in the closing moments of another woman's life?

'We need to get this done and go.'

Hain spoke for the first time.

Rebekah looked at him, his gun, and he looked back – but McKenzie was totally unmoved. 'You don't get to tell me that,' she said, almost whispering it.

'We haven't got the time for this shit.'

'I think,' McKenzie replied slowly, 'given your monumental screw-up is still breathing –' she gestured to Rebekah '– we've got all the time I say we do.'

Hain stayed where he was, silent.

'He was down in Miami,' McKenzie said, as if she knew what Rebekah was thinking: why hadn't Hain just taken care of her himself instead of letting Lima do it? 'He was part of a joint task force down there, busting some asshole from the Bronx who thought he was Tony Montana. With you, everything was so last-minute. We'd been listening to your calls, reading your texts, and then all of a sudden you decide to head out to Crow Island, and we've got our perfect opportunity to make you go away. Only Hain wasn't here. He was twelve hundred miles away.' She shrugged. 'So, reluctantly, he ended up sending this other guy, "Lima" – this former CI of his – and, well, I guess we know how *that* turned out.'

Lima hadn't just been a criminal: he'd been an informant.

Hain shook his head at her.

He didn't like any of this.

'A comic's sense of timing,' McKenzie said, her words echoing the ones she'd spoken earlier. There was a distance in her all of a sudden. 'I was literally speaking to the commissioner at the fund-raiser when Axel called me.'

They were back on the night Louise was killed.

'"Kathy, help me,"' McKenzie said, her eyes staring off into space, her voice altered, imitating her brother's. Even mimicked, the effect was chilling. '"You gotta help me. I've done something terrible."' She stopped. A beat, and then she looked up at Rebekah. 'He'd taken her down to his car, in the parking garage beneath the hotel, and she'd started to wake up. He screwed it up. Different set of pills, not as strong. Worse, she began fighting back, so he punched her – and, after that, he totally lost control.'

'Katherine,' Hain said, 'stop –'

'He kept punching her until her face was just paste.'

An awful, shattering silence.

Even Hain didn't speak, didn't move. And, in the quiet, the rest of what happened that night filled itself in: Foley called his sister, then she called Hain.

'"Hain",' McKenzie said, using his name but talking to Rebekah. 'He's bristling. He doesn't want you to know this, and I understand why. He's been trained to internalize everything, to deal with it in silence. I've seen him do it for a long time. I know what he can do. I know what he's *prepared* to do – and what he *has* done – for a little extra money. He's very good at fixing things. Me? I don't find it as easy. To me, "fixing things" – that just means digging up dirt on opponents, not killing or raping, not burying you way out to sea.'

Her face contorted.

'Although, I don't know . . .' She glanced over her shoulder, at the grey shapes on the back porch. A flicker in her face, as if she was finally becoming cognizant of what she'd done. 'I guess I knew what I was getting into. If you're ambitious, you have to be prepared to play dirty. And if you take one step into the shadows, like we did that first night when we made Louise vanish, you've got to be prepared to go the whole way. There's no retreat. The kind of decisions I made that night – that I've made tonight, coming here – you don't make them if your definition of "fixing things" only extends as far as spreading a little dirt.' She nodded to Hain again. 'He said I shouldn't come, but I felt I had to.'

Rebekah glanced at Hain. He was six feet from her, the gun against his leg, his gaze rooted to hers. She thought of the girls, and then of Gareth. What time would he be home? The longer this went on, the longer Rebekah stayed alive, but the longer it went on, the more Gareth was likely to be caught in the middle. Another innocent, cut down on Katherine McKenzie's road to power.

McKenzie rubbed a finger against her lips, as if everything she'd said tonight, all her words, had scalded her. 'I had it all planned out,' she said, 'always have. Chief of detectives was just another stepping stone. Next, I was going to be the NYPD's first ever female commissioner, and after that? I could run for mayor. I could probably kiss a few asses in DC and get the nomination for secretary of Homeland Security. I've always been prepared to do what I had to do to get where I wanted. I was prepared to take part in the weasely little games that get you the positions of power. I can be ruthless. But this? Louise. You. Your brother. All the other women Axel violated and walked away from, whom we don't even know about, who don't even know they've been *raped*: this isn't a game. When Hain called me and told me you were still alive, when he finally made it back to the city – on the run from the same organization he spends his days working for – and he told me we'd have to silence Frank Travis too –'

'Wait, what?'

'– because he knew way too much about this –'

'Wait a second, wait a second . . .'

They looked at each other.

'Are you saying Frank's dead as well?'

Rebekah's throat felt like it was closing.

Unmoved, McKenzie just looked at her, as if she pitied her naïvety. 'Of course he's dead,' she said. 'Did you really think I could leave him alive?'

Exorcism

'I'm really sorry about earlier, Frank,' Katherine McKenzie said, as they took the elevator down to the parking garage. 'I don't know why I told you that.'

He looked at her. 'You don't have to apologize.'

'I've never really told anyone about my brother.'

She met his gaze, and this time she was much harder to read: she was the woman he'd heard about, her expression blank as a wall.

'Well,' he said, 'I'm glad you felt I was worthy.'

She just nodded.

As the elevator doors opened onto the bottom floor of the garage, she pointed towards her car — a dark blue Mercedes — and said, 'I've got some files in the trunk. I really think it might help.'

'Okay,' he replied.

But something didn't feel right now.

He'd been so caught up with what was going on in the coffee shop, so fixated on the idea that McKenzie seemed to like him, in the excitement he felt, that he was certain now he'd overlooked something big.

His cellphone buzzed in his pants.

He grabbed it out of his pocket. It was Amy Houser asking him where he was. He glanced at the cardboard drinks tray he had in his spare hand, his and Amy's coffees in it, then at McKenzie, who was looking at him, then tried to clear his head.

He replied to Houser, telling her he'd be five minutes.

As they approached the Mercedes, McKenzie used her remote to pop the trunk. It sprang up, revealing an empty space with two big boxes.

'There they are,' McKenzie said.

Travis's cellphone buzzed again.

Houser for a second time.

I think Hain might be a cop.

Travis felt himself stumble.

'Is everything okay, Frank?'

He glanced at the text again, then stopped eight feet short of the Mercedes, his cellphone still in one hand, the drinks in the other, looking between McKenzie and the two cardboard boxes — and he knew in that second that he was right.

Something was wrong.

But, by then, it was already too late.

'Don't move,' a voice said behind him. He felt a gun press to the back of his skull. He'd never seen or heard an approach.

But he recognized the voice.

The man who'd called with the tip about Johnny.

The guy who'd dialled Houser's phone.

Travis looked at McKenzie again and, for a second, he thought he saw something glint in her eyes. Regret, maybe, or remorse. And then he realized why she'd told him about her brother, why she'd tried to exorcize that ghost.

Because it would never matter.

Travis would never be able to tell anyone.

'Now get in the fucking trunk,' Hain said.

80

'Frank knew way too much about Louise,' McKenzie said, 'about you, about all of these cases. It was a shame. I really did take a shine to him. He was smart, kind. In the short time I spent with him, it was easy to see why he was a great cop: he had a disarming quality. He was someone you could trust.' She stopped and in her face there was written a sadness that looked completely authentic. 'Talking to him today made me realize I had to come here tonight.'

For a moment Rebekah didn't understand, but then it clicked: McKenzie had confessed to Frank about her brother, and some part of her had liked it.

Now she was confessing the rest to Rebekah.

She felt a vibration in her chest, a swell of sorrow for Frank, and then McKenzie was talking again: 'I just sat there, and I listened to Hain tell me what needed to be done, and after I shot Frank . . .' She faded out, but those words remained. She was the one who had done it. She had killed him. Rebekah felt like she might be sick. 'After I shot him,' McKenzie said, picking up again, quieter now, 'it finally hit me. I thought, Look at what I've become.'

Hain stepped forward. 'Katherine.'

'I don't know what I'm doing any more.'

Rebekah wasn't sure if she was talking to herself or to Hain.

But, for the first time, Rebekah saw an opportunity. Hain had stepped past her, was occupied, had let her drift from his field of vision. She looked left, at a kitchen knife hanging off a magnetic strip on the wall. It was at least three steps away, and that was still too far, even with Hain distracted. On her right there was nothing, just a swathe of empty countertop. Except that wasn't quite true.

In the middle there was a granite chopping board.

'I've become everything I've ever fought,' McKenzie said softly. A tiny smear of mascara reached out from the edge of her face, like a black vein. 'I'm a killer.'

The gun moved in Hain's hand.

As they stared at each other, Rebekah took a step to her right, closer to the granite board.

'Katherine, listen to me,' Hain said, inching closer to the table. 'I know what's happening here. It's the same thing that happened with Travis earlier, and if you keep talking like this, the next time you spill your guts it'll be to someone who actually matters. People think you only confess once – but you don't. You keep *on* doing it – you've already done it twice in one day – because it makes you feel better for a while. It's like a drug.' He was at least an arm's length away from Rebekah now. 'But this needs to be the last time you ever open your mouth about this, you understand me? Because if you keep on doing it, next time, I promise you, it won't be worm food, like Frank Travis or this bitch – it'll be a cop, or a journalist.'

McKenzie said nothing.

'This needs to *stop*.'

He wasn't just talking about McKenzie confessing. He was talking about doing what they'd come here to do: severing the sinew that connected Rebekah, Louise and all the other victims of Daniel Foley. It was obvious that he was way beyond where Katherine McKenzie was. He'd seen death and he'd caused it.

And it had claimed all of him.

Finally, McKenzie muttered, 'You're right.'

'Okay, good.'

'We need to finish this,' she said softly.

'Okay,' he replied, glancing at Rebekah. 'Okay, goo–'

He never finished his sentence.

The gunshot cut the room in two – a sound so loud it was like the entire house moved – and by the time Rebekah reacted, Hain had already been thrown against the countertop. His head whipped back, blood flecking Rebekah's face — and then he collapsed like a ragdoll against the kitchen cabinets. When she looked down at him, her ears still ringing, his fingers were clutching a chest wound.

Horrified, shaken, Rebekah screamed, 'What the *fuck*?'

But McKenzie was in the same position at the table.

She'd hardly moved, her eyes glazed.

In her hand was a snub-nosed pistol.

'I think it's time to call the cops,' she said.

81

Rebekah was shaking, the adrenalin thundering in her blood.

'Call the cops,' McKenzie repeated.

As Rebekah stared at her, unsure if she was serious, Roxie started barking from the other room.

'*Call* them.'

She reached into her pants and pulled out her cellphone. *I don't get it*, she thought. *Why would McKenzie shoot him?* Except, of course, she did get it. McKenzie had needed to come here and confess – because that was the only way she could ever be free. Her secrets – the guilt, the remorse, the shame – were the same prison that the island had been to Rebekah.

'I need to help him,' Rebekah said, pointing to Hain.

McKenzie shook her head.

'He's going to die if we do nothing.'

'Just call the police,' she said again, and finally turned the gun on Rebekah. It looked bigger now, scarier. 'Call them before I change my mind.'

Rebekah called 911 and told them there had been a shooting in her house. She gave them her address but didn't mention McKenzie's name. The second she hung up, McKenzie moved the gun, the weapon becoming slack in her hand, and pointed it away from them. 'He told me it was better if he came alone.'

Her voice was bereft of emotion. She wasn't looking at Rebekah, or Hain. She wasn't looking at anything. She was looking into the future: the moment the police turned up, and her career and ambitions were over, and everything she'd worked for was gone.

Hain's chest was moving but he was starting to drift.

'His real name's Bobby,' she said. 'Robert. But whenever he was dealing with stuff like this, he'd always use an alias. He'd switch between them all the time.' She looked at Hain. 'In my early days as a captain, we were at the same precinct and I did him a favour, got him out of a tight spot that might have cost him his badge, and after that he started doing things for me, fixing things, digging things up. And the more he was around me, the more he'd see of Axel, the more the two of them hit it off. Not that it was hard. Axel hit it off with most people. He was a liar, and liars can be charming.' She smiled at the irony of that statement, because she was a liar, same as Foley was.

She leaned forward.

'Hain.' She smiled, because to her that was just a stage name. 'Yeah, he helped cover it *all* up. But there were some things we had no control over. We had no idea how many women Axel had assaulted because *he* could barely remember. Maybe it was ten, maybe it was fifteen. He didn't know. Some of the women he vaguely recalled, but we couldn't find them based on only knowing their first names. For most others, we didn't even *have* a name. To him, they were just shapes that passed through his life. So the whole time, it was a guillotine hanging over us, because if these women suddenly remembered Axel, we were exposed. At any moment, one of them might have a flash of recollection and – *boom* – that was the end. They'd dig into his life, and although I'd insulated myself from him, they'd find me there somewhere, despite my best efforts.'

In the distance, sirens started to fade in.

'But if Axel committed suicide . . .' She shrugged. 'I can tell you from experience, a rape, a *series* of rapes, we're going to work those hard. Cops, we'll follow that road until we get to the bastard who did it. But a suicide? No one's going to pursue that for any length of time. No one's following the data trail. If it looks cut and dried, we write up the report and then we tie a bow around it.'

And Rebekah understood the rest: if one of the women *did* suddenly have a flash of recollection – a name, perhaps, maybe a physical

477

description, or some vague memory of how Foley's apartment looked – it was going to be way harder to find the man responsible if he was buried under six feet of dirt.

'Hain persuaded Axel to go out to that bridge. He didn't push him but he made him take the leap. He said to Axel, if he didn't jump, he'd put in an anonymous call to the NYPD and tell them about Louise. He'd frame him for you and your brother. He'd tell the cops about the other two we took care of.' She paused, realizing that she'd never mentioned this part before. 'We *did* manage to find two of the women from the details he gave us. We got rid of them; hunted them down and made them vanish – like Louise, like we thought we had with you.'

The air chilled.

Now there were three other women, plus Johnny and Travis.

It wasn't a murder, it was a massacre.

'Of course,' McKenzie said, 'Axel had no idea there was zero chance of us ever putting in an anonymous call to the cops, because it would bring questions to our door that we didn't want to answer. But we laid out the choice for him: make the jump, or live out your days rotting in a prison cell. A man like Axel, who went around doing whatever the hell he liked, he'd never last in prison.'

More sirens, even closer.

McKenzie looked towards the living room, as if she expected to see cops in the house. If she'd had any doubts about her decision, it was too late now.

She heaved her shoulders and let out a long breath. The words had been coming fast, tumbling out of her, a desperate need to unload everything. But now she quietened. 'Secrets,' she said. 'They're like those buoys you see out in the ocean. You can hide them, you can drag them down to a hole in the deepest and darkest part of the water, but eventually . . .' A tormented smile traced her lips, a wraith drifting in and out of view. 'Eventually, they'll force their way up. In the end, secrets float. It's just a question of how long they take to get to the surface.'

And Rebekah had got to the surface.

She was the secret that came back.

'I needed to come here,' McKenzie said softly. 'Nothing I've wanted in my life was worth this. I haven't slept since the night Axel killed Louise. I'm not sure I slept properly for the entire time he was in my life. All I knew was that I couldn't do it again. I couldn't cover up another lie. When I found out you were still alive, I knew I had to look one of you in the face and admit to what I am.'

As sirens entered the street, McKenzie reached down, into the pocket of her coat. Rebekah heard something jangle, then McKenzie placed a set of car keys on the table. She glanced at Hain, a look in her face that was hard to interpret, before returning to Rebekah. Pushing the car keys towards her, McKenzie said, 'These are for you. It's parked at the Walgreens on Prospect.'

That was a couple of blocks from the house.

'Why are you giving me these?' Rebekah replied.

'Because Travis is in the trunk.'

Rebekah's stomach sank like a shipwreck.

'I had this photograph of you all for a while,' she said. 'You, and your brothers, and your father, the four of you on the front porch of that house you all lived in down on 81st Street. Hain dug it up from somewhere. I don't know where he got it, but I'm glad he did. I used to look at it a lot when I got home at night, just study it, your faces, and weird as it sounds, I felt jealous. I could see how tight you all were, how you'd forged something remarkable even after your mother abandoned you, and I never had that. I only had this.' She looked at Hain, at the gun, at the blood on the walls of the kitchen, and then pushed the car keys even closer to Rebekah. 'I'm sorry we took Johnny away. I can't give him back to you – but I can at least do this much.'

I can't give him back to you.

'Where's my brother?'

'I don't know,' McKenzie said. 'That's the truth. I don't know what happened that day. But Hain will.' Her eyes went to Hain again: he was hanging on, moaning gently. 'I do know something, though. Your brother . . .'

She stopped, almost winced, as if she'd been shot too.

'He's buried in a grave on that island.'

The words crashed against Rebekah.

She'd told herself that Johnny was dead, had known it on some level for five months. But hearing it was different. It felt like a part of her had been torn out.

She was home.

She was finally safe.

But, without Johnny, something of her would always stay lost.

9
The Scar

82

Three days later, the police found the skeletal remains of Louise Mason's body in salt marshes in Jamaica Bay. There were two other bodies alongside hers: a French exchange student called Mathilde Roux, twenty-two, whose parents in Paris had reported her missing seven days after Louise disappeared; and Carla Lee, thirty-three, who had worked in a bar in Tribeca and was reported missing by her husband three days before Rebekah went to Crow Island. When investigators spoke to family and friends, no one remembered either woman talking about a man matching Daniel Foley's description, let alone the idea that they might have been raped. Like Rebekah, it appeared the other women had no recall of the night they'd spent with Axel – but Hain had killed them anyway, just to be safe.

Four days after that, a search team returned to Crow Island to recover Johnny. Both days they were there it was overcast, unseasonably cold for early April, and when a task force arrived in Helena, it began to sleet.

With them on that day was a detective called Robert Markowitz, who hadn't buried Johnny himself but knew where Lorenzo 'Lima' Selestino had put him. To Katherine McKenzie, Markowitz had been 'Bobby'; to the Detective Squad at the 46th Precinct in the Bronx – where he'd worked – he was 'Mark'. Until that night in her kitchen, Rebekah had only known him as Hain.

He was still working at the 46th Precinct, in Homicide, until the end. The day he'd called Amy Houser's phone, and Travis had picked up, it was in his capacity as a detective: he genuinely had no idea that Travis would be there. He was calling Amy Houser's line to ask her about a cold case that might have had links to a murder he was working. The media speculated about how a corrupt cop like Hain could be missed, but particularly how he could disappear for three days after leaving the island. Yet it was easy enough: he didn't disappear. There were 36,000 officers in the NYPD and 19,000 civilian employees. The day after he'd made it back to the city, he'd taken a sick day to go to the ER and get patched up from the car crash. The day after that, he returned to work at the 46th. His colleagues commented on his injuries, which he said were due to a car accident, but no one suspected a thing. He just did what he always did.

He vanished in plain sight.

And so Hain led the way – in prison greens, handcuffed, bandaged, his weight supported by two officers, slightly woozy from all the painkillers he was on – back to the island's forest. Detective Bowners had assured Rebekah, before the search team left for Montauk, they would find Johnny and get Rebekah the closure she'd been longing for. And on the afternoon of the first day, she called to fulfil her promise.

'We've found him,' she said quietly.

Finally, Johnny was coming home.

Katherine McKenzie was primetime news for weeks. The media tore her to pieces, speculating on every aspect of her career, her personal life, the folly and arrogance of her future ambitions. Rebekah read and watched some of it, but much more she ignored. A lot of the time it was because she was fending off interview requests herself, TV appearances, magazine articles, emails from a publisher asking if she wanted to write a book about her experiences. It was the incessant nature of it, the repetition of the questions, the complete absence of empathy, just a sustained parade of faces trying to get her to break.

For weeks, news trucks camped at either end of her road, annoying neighbours, pressuring Rebekah, journalists from papers, websites and TV channels all across the country hounding anyone who strayed onto the block.

Throughout it all, as she left the house to walk Roxie, or took the girls to the park, she remained silent. If there was one thing she'd learned on the island, it was how to do that.

At night, once Gareth had moved out for a second time and in with his new girlfriend, she'd lie awake, or she'd go through to the girls' bedroom and just sit quietly in the corner, watching them, and she'd think about Katherine McKenzie. And even after everything had come out, every awful detail had run in every news outlet in every city across the country, Rebekah would still feel a weird sense of discord: she hated McKenzie for all she'd been involved in, for every lie, every secret she'd helped conceal, every death; she hated her for all the pain she'd caused the family of Louise Mason, her complicity in the murders of Mathilde Roux and Carla Lee, for how she'd allowed Johnny to be torn away; she hated her for the way that countless women were living victims of Daniel Foley, and although they might have felt that something wasn't right, that there was a shadow they couldn't shake, they'd never be certain of why.

And yet . . .

Despite all of that being true, Rebekah couldn't deny that McKenzie had had a conscience, a twine of good that had refused to snap, because if she hadn't, she wouldn't have sat at the kitchen table in Rebekah's house and made her confession. All the ambition in the world, all the dirty tricks she'd pulled, all the things she'd allowed to happen on her watch, or turned a blind eye to, couldn't permanently unbalance her sense of what was right. It had remained unimpaired, even if it had taken her too long to find its hiding place.

And, of course, there was Frank Travis.

They'd found him in the trunk of McKenzie's Mercedes.

He'd been bound and gagged with duct tape.

McKenzie told the police that she and Hain had planned the

day: in the afternoon, they were going to get rid of Travis; in the evening, at precisely the time that the changeover was happening outside Rebekah's house, and the patrol officers' guard would be down, they would take care of her too.

Except McKenzie had been lying to Hain.

She'd woken up that morning and decided she couldn't do it any more. Her confessions, the ghosts she was exorcizing, first with Travis in Starbucks, and later with Rebekah at the house, had been products of that. She was done hiding, done killing. So, she'd talked to Hain, told him that he had too much blood on his hands already and that she would take care of Travis, and although she said Hain was suspicious – 'because he was *always* suspicious' – he agreed. McKenzie was a cop, after all. She might have spent the latter part of her career behind a desk, but she'd walked the beat, she'd been a detective.

She'd drawn her weapon thousands of times.

She'd killed in the line of duty twice.

She and Hain had got Travis into the trunk of the Mercedes, and then she'd said she would call Hain once the deed was done, and Hain could bury the body in the same place he'd put Louise Mason, Mathilde Roux and Carla Lee.

She called him at around 7 p.m. that night and told him it was done, that the Mercedes was parked in a Walgreens a block from Rebekah's brownstone. That played well with Hain: he once told her that the worst place to leave a car with a body in it was in a deserted back alley. People would pay attention to it there. No one paid attention to it outside a Walgreens. It played even better when she showed him the trunk: Travis was on his belly, his face bloodied, duct tape over his mouth and around his wrists, which were bound behind him. The tableau was good enough for Hain: he said he would put Rebekah's body inside the car too, once they'd killed her, and drive both her and Travis to Jamaica Bay.

But it was all staged.

Travis's face was a mess because McKenzie had put a deliberate cut in it and spread the blood out. He was on his belly so it lessened the chances of Hain seeing him breathing. She'd selected a parking bay as far away from any lights as possible because she knew Hain wouldn't want the trunk open for long in a public place. And all of that was why Rebekah felt so conflicted.

Because Frank Travis was still alive.

Because he got to tell Rebekah all of this himself.

And because they had Katherine McKenzie to thank for it.

83

The memorial service for Louise Mason took place at St John Cemetery, close to her parents' home in Rego Park. Rebekah left the girls with Noella, and she and Frank Travis, sporting a fetching bandage that stretched from his forehead to the dome of his skull, went together. They sat at the back as Louise's uncle, her cousin and her father talked eloquently through tears about Louise's life, her art, her successes and, most importantly, the person she was. Afterwards, Rebekah went up to Louise's parents and introduced herself. The three of them hugged for a long time. Perhaps, in some other life, it might have been unusual, an act that might have made one or all of them uncomfortable. But in that moment none of them questioned it.

Two days later, Rebekah was burying Johnny.

Noella stood up and read a eulogy for him that was so funny and heartfelt, Rebekah spent the entire ten minutes lurching between laughter and sobs. Johnny had wanted to be cremated, not buried, so there was no rain to contend with this time, no storm clouds above the East River, as there had been when Rebekah had said her goodbyes to Mike and to her father.

They held the wake in a bookshop, after it had shut for the day, three blocks from the house on 81st Street where they'd all grown up. It was a place Johnny had always loved, perhaps even the place he was at his happiest. Rebekah chatted to friends of his she hadn't seen for years, distant relatives who'd come all the way from Boston for the funeral, and for a while it was easy to forget the ache in the pit of her stomach, the anger she was feeling, the sense of hurt and betrayal. But at the end of the night, when just she, Noella and the store manager were left, Rebekah turned to Noe and said, 'Why wasn't she here?'

Noe frowned. 'Who, honey?'

'My mother.'

Noe glanced at the store manager and he headed out back to give them space.

'Forget her,' Noe said, putting a hand to Rebekah's arm.

'Why wouldn't she come?'

'Because she never comes, Bek.'

'But why not?'

'Because she's not *like* you, honey. How you feel about your girls, what you were prepared to do to get back to them, that's not who she is. If that was who she was, she'd have shown her face when Mike died. Hell, she wouldn't have walked out on you in the first place.' Noe put her arm around Rebekah's shoulders. 'You've got enough to think about without worrying about her. She abandoned you all. You three were only kids. You and Mike were just *babies*.' The inference was clear: *what kind of a monster would do that?*

'She hasn't even sent a bloody card.'

'Perhaps she doesn't know,' Noe said.

Except the day after the funeral a card arrived. Rebekah opened it, Johnny's familiar refrain – 'It's better than nothing' – echoing in her head. Inside, her mother had written, *I was sorry to hear the news about John.* But no name. No *Mum.* No *Fiona.*

Rebekah looked at the envelope: it had British stamps on the front, air-mail stickers, but no return address.

Again, she thought of Johnny.

He'd always kept the cards when they arrived.

Rebekah tossed hers into the trash.

84

A couple of hours later, Frank Travis arrived at the house. Rebekah had prepared some sandwiches and, while the girls ran around the backyard, she and Travis sat on a couple of old wicker chairs, under the shade of the porch, Roxie lying at Rebekah's feet, chewing an old slipper.

'This brings back memories,' Travis said.

'Were your kids crazy like this?'

He smiled. Kyra was running around in circles, singing a song she'd heard on the Disney Channel, while Chloe was laughing so hard she eventually lost her balance and plopped onto her backside.

'How are they doing?' Travis asked.

Rebekah watched Kyra as she poured her and her sister an imaginary cup of tea. 'They're doing okay,' she said. 'But sometimes they look at me and it's like . . .' Her eyes went back to the girls. 'It's like they don't remember me.'

'Give it time, kiddo.'

She glanced at him. 'And then there's this thing with Gareth. I don't know what I expected to happen between us when I got home. I didn't expect us to get back together, but I guess I didn't expect him to move on so quickly.'

Travis was quiet for a moment, his hands steepled in front of him. 'This stuff can be hard, Rebekah.'

'I think it's time you started calling me Bek now, Frank.'

'Bek.' He smiled again, fiddling with the bandage on his head. 'When my wife left me, Jeez, I was spinning like a top for months. It was nuts, because I wasn't even happy with her. I didn't *like* her.

490

But anything that tilts you, even if it's something small – and I'm not saying this thing with the girls is small, not at all – it can really play with your head.' Travis took a bite of his sandwich. 'It's like Louise. I got her home – not in the way I wanted to, but I got her home – and I'm still lying awake at night. It still feels like I failed her.'

'You didn't fail her, Frank.'

Travis didn't say anything, just took another bite of his sandwich, and they fell into a comfortable silence, watching the girls. After a while, Travis turned to Rebekah and said, 'They're maybe a little confused right now but they'll come around. Kids are remarkable. They're so much more resilient than we give them credit for. When they're this age, they adapt and move on. There's no rancour or regret. Soon, it'll be like you were never away.'

Rebekah looked at Travis, and felt an immediate pull towards him: this was the sort of speech her father used to give to Johnny, Mike and her when they were growing up – gentle, incisive words that would draw them back from whatever edge they'd wandered out to. She found herself reaching over to grasp Travis's hand, and – although he seemed taken aback – he soon took hers in return, understanding.

'Thanks, Frank,' she said.

He held her hand for a moment longer and then she saw his expression change, and she knew they were about to get to the real reason for his visit. In truth, a part of her had been scared to ask. If this visit was about Johnny, she knew it would hurt. She knew it from the way Travis was looking at her.

He placed the half-eaten sandwich on his plate, finished his Coke and then moved his hand to the inside pocket of his sports coat. When it emerged, a flash drive was pinched between his thumb and finger. Travis put it down, pushing it towards her. On the side, it said, *FAO: Frank Travis.*

'What's this?' she asked.

'They figured out what happened to Johnny that day.'

Rebekah blinked.

'Bowners and her team, in their interviews with "Hain", they've managed to put together a rough idea of what happened when you and your brother got separated.' He grimaced, as if he was having a hard time forming his words. 'They know why Johnny's wallet was at the lighthouse.'

'Why?' Rebekah asked, almost fearful of the answer.

'It sounds like, when you were trying to escape from Lima, Johnny didn't realize you weren't behind him to start with, and then when he went back for you – when he was calling your name – he couldn't find either you or Lima because you'd already drawn Lima away from the track, in the direction of that gully.' In the beat between sentences, an image of that day flickered behind Rebekah's eyes. Her tumbling into the gully, hitting her head and blacking out. 'After that,' Travis went on, 'there's a knowledge gap, but the cops seem to think that when Johnny couldn't find you he tried to run back up to the main road, presumably to flag someone down. Shortly after, Lima finished with you, because he thought you were dead, and returned to the parking area with the keys for Stelzik's Chevy. He used it to catch Johnny.'

'So how did Johnny get all the way out to the lighthouse?'

Travis didn't respond initially. Instead, it looked like he was gathering his strength, steeling himself for the final assault. 'He didn't. Hain says Lima caught up with your brother before Johnny ever managed to reach the top of that trail out of Simmons Gully. I mean, the track was almost a mile long . . .'

Something hitched in Travis's voice.

'According to Bowners,' he continued quietly, coming forward in his chair, 'a stretch of the Loop was cut off temporarily when a truck spilled some logs across it.' Rebekah remembered the night she'd got to the top there, in the middle of the storm, before she'd headed into Helena, and had found wood and plastic fasteners across the road. 'That meant when Lima was done . . .'

Done.

Done burying her brother.

'Once he was done, he couldn't take the direct route back to Helena, along the southern flank, because it was blocked. He had to go the other way around and come past the lighthouse. That was how Johnny's wallet ended up there. Apparently, according to Hain, when Lima was driving away from the dig site – after he'd buried Johnny – he spotted the wallet near the top of the trail. Your brother dropped it when he died. Lima didn't want to leave it out in the open there because he thought it was too close to the body, so he stopped at the lighthouse and dumped it there.' Travis reached over and took her hand again. 'I'm sorry, Bek. This is just . . .' But there were no words.

His other hand went to the flash drive.

'With two cops dying at your house,' he said, 'with the recovery of, first, Louise's body, and then the other two women's, then Johnny's, and then me, and all the other terrible shit that's been going on since the island, somehow no one got this over to you. It got missed. I know that Bowners is going to call you to apologize later on. She says they meant to show you days ago.'

'What is it?'

'Lima missed something in Johnny's pockets.' Travis stopped, looking at Rebekah, and as she wiped her eyes, she nodded, letting him know she was ready to hear. 'Johnny hid it in the coat's actual lining.'

'Hid what?'

'You remember that day at the forest you got back to find the window on the Cherokee had been smashed? You covered it with plastic wrap for five months.' Rebekah nodded. 'You remember how the dashcam got taken from the Cherokee, and it never made sense why someone would steal it?'

Rebekah frowned.

Travis pushed the flash drive all the way over.

'This'll explain everything.'

85

A week later, Rebekah left the girls with Noella for the morning and went into the city. She felt scared at first, frenzied; she stood on the front porch of Noella's house, unable to move, unable to rip her eyes away from the girls. But, her heart beating hard, she dragged herself forward and rode the subway in, and gradually, as the minutes passed, she started to calm down.

In the time she'd been on the island, her medical licence had expired and because she had made no attempt within three months to seek another two-year extension, she'd had to call the Office of Professions to explain what had happened. They'd told her, because her case was unusual, and because they were having a hard time understanding, to come by the office on Broadway.

After she was done filling out forms, she walked a block to Bryant Park, the sun beating down out of a clear blue sky, and found a table in the shade at the back of the Public Library. She'd brought her laptop, as well as the flash drive Frank Travis had given her the week before, and – in the zipped pouch of her laptop bag – something else: the card her mother had sent.

She'd fished it out of the garbage.

She had no real idea why. She still felt as much confusion about and contempt for Fiona Camberwell as she had the day she'd dumped the card in the trash can, but eventually she'd gone back to the kitchen, rifled through the old food, the chip packets, the detritus of her family's life, and reclaimed it. It was stained and wrinkled, but it had survived.

She opened it again now, looking at the message.

I was sorry to hear the news about John.

'Excuse me, would I be able to use this chair?'

Rebekah looked up from the card.

A man in his late forties, tall, broad, good-looking with dark hair, was standing next to her. He had a bag over his shoulder and a coffee in his hands.

'Sure,' she said.

He smiled at her. 'Thank you.'

He dragged the chair away from her table and set it up at the next one along. Rebekah's mind wandered again, back to her mother, to the flash drive, to the idea of going back to work, her thoughts moving fast.

'Are you okay?' the man asked.

She realized she was still staring at him. 'Oh,' she said, 'I'm so sorry. I was miles away.'

The man smiled again. 'Well, that's a relief.' He looked down at himself, his shirt, his pants. 'I thought I might have food on my face.'

'Ha, no, you're okay.'

'You'd tell me if I had food on my face, right?'

'It depends how amusing it looked.'

The man smiled a third time. He had a lovely smile.

'You're English,' Rebekah said to him.

'I am,' he replied. 'You sound like you might be too.'

'Not for a long time. I moved here when I was eighteen.'

'But you still have some of the accent.'

'Yes,' she said, 'for some reason, it's always hung in there. I like it.' She paused, thinking of Johnny, of how he'd hated his mid-Atlantic accent. The memory made her sad, so she pushed it away. 'Are you here on vacation?'

'Sort of,' the man said. 'I'm meeting a friend for a couple of days. She lives out in LA, and this seemed like a good halfway point for both of us. What about you?' He checked the time. 'Are you having an early lunch?'

'No, not yet. Maybe soon.'

He didn't pry, even though he must have been curious.

'I've been on a sort of career break,' she said.

'Okay. And you're thinking about going back?'

'More through necessity than desire.'

It was only brief, but as they looked at each other it was like something passed between them, an understanding of how onerous necessity could be.

'What do you do?' the man asked.

'I'm a doctor. An orthopaedic surgeon.'

'Wow, you look way too young to be so qualified.'

She laughed. 'Not as young as I'd like.'

'I'm guessing you took a career break to have kids?'

This time, she paused before answering.

'Sorry,' he said. 'That was incredibly nosy.'

'No, it's fine. It was a pretty accurate guess, though.'

He nodded. 'Please don't be creeped out.'

'What about you?' Rebekah asked, studying him.

'I'm an investigator.'

'Like a private investigator?'

'Sort of. I find missing people.'

Rebekah looked from the man to her mother's card, creased, tarnished, its lack of an address, the lack of a kiss, a sign-off, any clue about who she was.

The missing person who brought me into this world.

She turned her attention back to the man. He was watching her closely now, but not in a way that troubled her or made her feel uncomfortable. It was more like the look Frank Travis had always given her: curious, humane.

She reached out a hand. 'I'm Rebekah Murphy.'

He took her hand in his.

'It's lovely to meet you, Rebekah. I'm David Raker.'

86

The flash drive contained a single video file.

Seven days had passed since Travis had handed it to her, and Rebekah had watched it hundreds of times. She knew every single inch of it, every word, every blur, every accidental tilt and stumble. After a while, viewing it was like watching a flower die and grow simultaneously. Much of it she could barely even look at, yet she did, because the rest, much more of it, she cherished.

That night, after meeting the missing persons' investigator and trading cellphone numbers, she collapsed into the couch – the sun bleeding out in the sky, the girls in bed – and opened her laptop. A video window was already up.

As night slowly began to creep into the room, for a long time all she did was stare at the freeze-framed image on the screen, thinking of something her father had said to her in the days and weeks before he died.

Even the dead can talk.

In the end, he'd been right.

She pressed Play.

An image of Johnny started to move. He was mostly out of shot to start with but Rebekah knew exactly where he was: on the track leading up from the parking area at Simmons Gully towards the Loop. He was halfway, breath in front of his face. This was minutes after Rebekah had fallen into the gully.

Minutes after Lima thought he'd killed her.

Johnny was frightened. He didn't know if he was doing the right thing in leaving Rebekah. He'd gone back, hadn't been able to find her, thought the next best thing was to try to get help. But now she could see he'd lost confidence.

Now he felt as if he'd abandoned his sister.

Even so, he kept going, running, the video jarring and disorienting. Then he slowed again, seemed to remember he was holding the dashcam, and stopped. Briefly, he started turning it, trying to find something on it. The image was upside down, on the side, facing one way and then another: Travis had told Rebekah that no one had been quite sure what Johnny was trying to do. But she knew. On the drive to Montauk, Johnny had asked about the dashcam, and she'd told him Gareth had installed it, and that he'd said the dashcam had an emergency response feature that sent out an SOS if you were in a car accident. That was what Johnny was looking for in these moments. That was why he'd smashed the window of the Cherokee to get at the dashcam. He'd thought there was a button on it he could press. He'd thought, in lieu of him having his cellphone, it might get them found.

But, very quickly, he stopped looking.

Because that wasn't how the SOS function worked.

There was no button to press.

He broke into a sprint again, the dashcam still recording the spaces behind him, the ground, a skewed angle on the trees. He was running with it in his left hand. At one point, his legs turned and he was looking behind him, and as his body swivelled, he slowed, and the noise died for a moment.

There was the sound of a car engine in the background.

Lima.

He was coming.

Johnny started running again, faster, the picture a blur of movement. It became almost impossible to see anything clearly – until, out of nowhere, the dashcam came up to Johnny's face, as if he'd suddenly thought of something. The angle wasn't perfect: the camera was on the back of the dashcam, so the screen was facing away from him. He had no real idea if he was in shot or not.

'I don't know if anyone will ever see this,' he said, and although Rebekah had heard him say the same words countless times, something twisted inside her as he spoke. 'Someone's trying to kill us.' His voice frayed. He was terrified – of leaving Rebekah, of what might have happened to her, of what was going to happen to him. 'My sister . . . I don't know where my sister is. She might be . . .'

Dead already.

He faded out, glanced behind him.

For a second, when his face came back to the camera, he was white, the fear so utterly paralysing it seemed to have collapsed him, altered his features somehow. But then he looked behind him again, down the track, the forest on all sides of him – bleak, rigid, wind crackling in the dashcam's speaker – and it was like he understood that this might be his last chance to say something.

'Bek,' he said simply, his eyes watering from the cold, from her name and what it meant to him. Wind ripped through the trees. Johnny looked away again, behind him, and now there was a clear speck at the bottom of the track.

It was Stelzik's Chevy.

When Johnny turned back, there was terror in his face again – terrible, consuming – and it cleaved Rebekah in two.

He knew he couldn't outrun a car or a gun.

'If anyone ever finds this, if my sister's still alive, tell her that I love her.' He looked behind him. He was crying properly now. The cold had nothing to do with it: as the Chevy closed on him, tears were running into the corners of his mouth. 'I never said it enough. Maybe I never said it at all . . .'

He blinked more tears away.

'I love you so much, Bek.'

'I love you too, Johnny,' Rebekah said quietly.

And, finally, the screen went black.

To start with, Rebekah could find no good in what she'd been through. Nothing positive. Nothing she could use. Mostly, she tried not to think about all that had happened to her, reducing it to a scar in her past.

Yet as time went on, as her memories became greyer, as her pain began to subside just a little, in the cord of that scar, she discovered one profound and undeniable truth.

I know who I am now.

I know what I do.

So, whenever the doubts came back in the months and years that followed, whenever her courage threatened to take flight, she would return to that truth. She would tell herself who she was and what she'd become.

And she would promise herself never to forget.

My name is Rebekah.

And I survive.

Author's Note

For the purposes of the story, I've carefully altered some of the working practices and organisational structure of the NYPD, the Suffolk County Police Department and the American medical system. I've also taken some very minor liberties when it comes to dashcams, VHF radios and the layout of both Jeep Cherokees and Dodge Rams. I hope all of these things have been done with enough subtlety and care for them to have passed unnoticed – at least, until now.

Acknowledgements

I absolutely love working on the David Raker series and, as I write these words, have already started the next one. But after finishing *No One Home*, my tenth Raker novel in ten years, I spoke to my editor and agent and told them that, before I started No.11, I wanted to try something different. Basically, I wanted to work on an idea I'd been kicking around for a while – part-survival story, part-mystery, about a woman being stranded miles from her children, with no way back. I thought it would be a challenge creatively, not least because I'd never written a standalone – and, of course, I hoped, once I was done, it would return me to Raker feeling refreshed and even more excited about making people disappear. (In the books, obviously, not in real life.)

And to their credit, both my editor Maxine Hitchcock and my agent Camilla Bolton didn't balk . . . or pretended not to. I owe Max such a huge debt of gratitude for trusting me and backing me, as well as for her brilliant, elegant and incisive editing which improved the book immeasurably. And I owe Camilla so much too: her belief that I could write this novel never wavered once and she helped me clear my head and reset so many times. Agent, friend, guinea pig appreciator – thank you.

Another extra large, capital letters THANK YOU goes to the fantastic team at Michael Joseph and Penguin, who include (but aren't limited to): Jon Kennedy, Lee Motley, David Ettridge, Jennifer Porter, Katie Williams, Vicky Photiou, Liz Smith, Olivia Thomas, Christina Ellicott, Deidre O'Connell, Rachel Myers, Natasha Lanigan, Louise Blakemore, James Keyte, Laura Marlow, and Hazel Orme. A special extra shout-out to Rebecca Hilsdon for all her work on the edits and Beatrix McIntyre for being so ace dealing with what can only be described as 'Proofmageddon'.

At Darley Anderson, I'm so indebted to Mary Darby, Kristina Egan and Georgia Fuller in Rights, Sheila David in Film and TV, and Rosanna Bellingham and Jade Kavanagh, who all do such a superb job for me, day in, day out.

For helping maintain my sanity over coffees, pub lunches, texts and Zoom, thank you to my great writing pals Chris Ewan, Claire Douglas and Gilly Macmillan.

Thank you, as always, to my beautiful, brilliant family: Mum and Dad, who I love so much; my sister Lucy, and the Ryder crew, Rich, Hannah and Sam; the Linscotts – Boxie, Di, Delme, Kim, Declan, Nathan and Josh; and my awesome extended family, including my uncles Barry and John, and #1 aunty, Jo.

To the two people who have signed up for a life sentence by having to live with me: first, my daughter, Erin, who I love more than anything in the world and who makes me so proud every single day; and then my wife Sharlé, who dug me out of so many holes on this book, who unravelled and rebuilt all my terrible timelines, and who patiently spent two weeks (and every evening) on my proofs reassuring me that everything would be fine. I couldn't have done this without her.

Finally, to you, my wonderful readers. Thank you for buying, borrowing, talking about and recommending my books, for the lovely emails and social media messages, and for taking my novels to your heart. Quite simply, without your support, none of this would be possible.

Reading Group Questions

Missing Pieces is set partially in America. Discuss the role of setting and place in this novel.

Isolation and survival are important themes in *Missing Pieces* – discuss how these themes affect the decisions Rebekah makes.

The missing pieces of Rebekah's story are slowly revealed to the reader (and Rebekah) over the course of the novel – and there are a couple of red herrings along the way! Which stood out to you as a reader and how do you think the writer uses these to add to the story?

Who is your favourite character and why?

Discuss the theme of family in *Missing Pieces*.

What does retribution mean to Rebekah? Is this her driving force at the beginning of the novel?

Tim Weaver is known for keeping readers guessing. Discuss the ways in which you feel you are manipulated as a reader.

Four stories. Four cases. One connection.

THE SHADOW
AT THE DOOR

by Tim Weaver

When Paul Conister heads upstairs he doesn't return.
His wife Maggie goes up to find all the windows are
locked from the inside and Paul's phone and wallet
are next to their bed. He hasn't left. And there's no
sign of him anywhere.

This case brings missing persons investigator David Raker
into contact with three other mysteries. A deadly discovery
by the night patrolmen in an Underground station. A cold
case with a witness that no longer exists. A tragic shooting
of a young man with a terrible secret.

Four stories. One connection.
Only Raker can uncover the truth.

Coming autumn 2021 – pre-order now

The eleventh David Raker novel arrives in 2022 . . .

THE BLACKBIRD

*Missing persons investigator David Raker
has never had a case like this one...*

No warning. No survivors. No answers.

Ten seconds before the accident, Cate and Aiden Gascoigne's
car is recorded on CCTV. Inside the vehicle, the couple are
laughing – happy, untroubled.

And then their car leaves the road and plunges into a
ninety-foot ravine.

The impact should kill them. And if the impact doesn't, the fire
will: seconds after it comes to rest, the Land Rover bursts into
flames. By the time emergency services arrive, it's an inferno.

But the fire crews and forensic teams who expect to find the
charred remains of a husband and wife find something else
instead. Something impossible.

The vehicle is empty.

Cate and Aiden have vanished.

PRE-ORDER NOW